and
the
walls
came
down

and the walls came down

DENISE DA COSTA

DUNDURN
PRESS

Publisher: Kwame Scott Fraser | Acquiring editor: Kathryn Lane | Editor: Shannon Whibbs
Cover designer: Laura Boyle
Cover image: Don Mount: Jonathan Castellino; texture: unsplash.com/Dan Cristian

Library and Archives Canada Cataloguing in Publication

Title: And the walls came down / Denise Da Costa.
Names: Da Costa, Denise (Author of And the walls came down), author.
Identifiers: Canadiana (print) 20220431019 | Canadiana (ebook) 2022043106X | ISBN
    9781459750364 (softcover) | ISBN 9781459750388 (EPUB) | ISBN 9781459750371 (PDF)
Classification: LCC PS8607.A175 A53 2023 | DDC C813/.6—dc23

We acknowledge the support of the Canada Council for the Arts and the Ontario Arts Council for our publishing program. We also acknowledge the financial support of the Government of Ontario, through the Ontario Book Publishing Tax Credit and Ontario Creates, and the Government of Canada.

Care has been taken to trace the ownership of copyright material used in this book. The author and the publisher welcome any information enabling them to rectify any references or credits in subsequent editions.

The publisher is not responsible for websites or their content unless they are owned by the publisher.

Printed and bound in Canada.

Dundurn Press
1382 Queen Street East
Toronto, Ontario, Canada M4L 1C9
dundurn.com, @dundurnpress ✆ f ⊙

For Maxine, Michelle, & Mother

Chapter 1

Going Back

August 2004

Summer heat ushered the foul scent of sewers and exhaust into the streetcar as it shuffled through Toronto traffic. Patrons poured out of the Eaton Centre and onto the sidewalks. Through their scissoring legs, I searched the faces of the drifters installed on the pavement. This was a habit my sister and I picked up after Mother left, convinced she suffered from amnesia and had taken up with a band of homeless persons. This was a town desperate for the taste of a true summer like the one in 1993, when my mother, Aretha Ellis, fled the suburbs to escape the shame of a dream deferred. It occurred to me that she had been running her whole life from one thing or another.

As the vehicle accelerated, I clutched Mother's old baking tin on my lap, but the force sent me swaying into the next seat, startling the passenger sitting there. I hadn't noticed him until then — a handsome, stony stranger who recovered in time to grasp my shoulder and steady me. I shrank from his touch.

Denise Da Costa

"Thanks." I studied him for familiarity, seeing only the sharpness of his protruding brow line and cheekbones — a skull forming in front of me. I thought of my grandmother whose funeral I'd recently attended and looked away.

Farther east, we passed Jilly's Gentleman's Club, followed by a series of studio spaces and a commercial loft under construction. Onward, after a kilometre of residential area, we stopped at a brown-bricked, tumbledown complex in Regent Park. The building next to it was recognizable only by its location. The signage no longer read "Community Centre" but, rather, "Community Clinic." Same difference, my sister would say.

From there, I could trace the path Mother made me walk home one night. I was fourteen and stupid for having let my delinquent older friend, Richa, convince me to attend a dance party at the centre. The elaborate plan was anchored to a lie that placed me at Nicole's house, working on a school project. If my mother were to call, Nicole was supposed to claim I was in the bathroom. Yet, shortly after my arrival at the event, Nicole made an entrance. I was furious.

"Listen," Richa said to me. "If you're gonna get in trouble, it might as well be for something good."

She tapped a passerby on the shoulder and whispered in his ear. He shot me a smile. I cringed.

Having acquiesced, I found myself dancing at the back of the gym with the boy when my mother came barrelling through the horde, orbs of light pirouetting across her face. My dancing partner made a hasty exit. I was not as swift. She smacked me hard across the cheek. Nearby partiers let out a shocked cry but quickly returned to minding their own business — Caribbean parents like mine were known to take on bystanders.

Mother grabbed me by the collar of the black crop top I had borrowed from Richa and led me out into the parking lot. Her car sat idling with my sister, Melissa, looking on wide-eyed from the passenger seat. I went to open the door.

2

"Oh no." Mother shook her head and pointed to the main road. "The same way you got here is the same way you're getting home."

At eleven o'clock, I walked home, more afraid of what awaited me there than anything I might encounter on my journey. I knew that street like the back of my hand: there were one hundred and fourteen cracks in the sidewalk, three driveways, two stoplights, and at least three streetworkers who steadily held the block. Melissa called them "stars" because we never saw them during the day.

In the years since I'd moved away, gentrification had uprooted mainstays and entire communities along Dundas Street but not east of the bridge. East of the bridge there were no banks. No grocery stores. No windowed shops for one to stop and stare at pretty things. If not for the Don River, streetcars would simply detour north onto River Street and avoid the area altogether. I stood, rang the buzzer, then made my way to the exit.

The streetcar stop resembled a giant cigarette piercing the cement and tilting toward the pothole in the hot asphalt — a trap for thin-legged prey. I paused to adjust to the earthy stench and the remains of my old neighbourhood, Don Mount Court. Portions of the complex had been knocked away, and the colour from the surrounding buildings receded as if they were already disappearing. The untrained eye might not have realized it was public housing; it wasn't a high-rise flanked by brown row houses or a grim set-up of identical step-ups placed like crosses in a graveyard. The towering fortress rose high above the demolition equipment as though freshly unearthed, cracks spreading like spores across its stucco coat.

I followed the construction barrier to the rear of the complex where the carnage of past lives remained, yards of abandoned furniture and skeletal strollers tangled into the overgrown shrubbery. Vines weaved along the chain-link fence probing for the sun, which was busy staring at its reflection in the window of Mother's old bedroom. I imagined the spectre of a well-dressed woman staring out at the widespread demolition and the emerging skyline beyond. She would've found it ironic since the city expropriated the land in the 1960s to build the complex.

I strolled across the deserted courtyard and climbed one flight of steps, where I could look out from the balcony. Unused and abandoned, Don Mount held a semblance of beauty I would miss. In the park, an empty pair of swings swayed rebelliously against their fate, chains clanging, struggling to break free. Trees whispered and shuddered their leaves, the whole area a living organism.

It knows.

The management office, carved into the space between the stairwell and a bachelor apartment, was where tenants paid the rent. Or made promises about when the rent would be paid. Where seniors met before setting off to the "Blue House," the community food bank. Where they complained about the neighbours, the mice. The violence. I knocked on the door before entering, as was the custom. At the far end of the room, Camille Blanchard sat behind a wooden desk, on its surface a coffee cup, a telephone, and a stack of documents. Camille tapped the pile with a pen, then spoke into the phone.

"Tell them you have my authority to enter the premises." She saw me. "Hang on."

"One minute," she mouthed, then swivelled away, bursting into a hearty laugh before saying goodbye.

The office felt cramped compared to my sparsely decorated home, but it felt like I was visiting an old friend. At least that's what I figured it would feel like if I had been visiting an old friend.

There was a loud creak when Camille eased her stout frame around the desk. She was dressed for tropical travel, as always, in a flowy cotton frock that matched her depressed blue eyes. Threads of silver streaked her fine blond hair, which was pulled back into a tight bun. Never having been petite, the extra weight she had gained suited her; less so, the leathery tan that aged her by ten years.

"Delia, it's so good to see you." She went to embrace me, then glanced down at the pan I held between us. "Is that for me?"

4

I noted her pungent scent. Was she nervous?

"Of course." I handed it to her, relieved to part with the debt. She set the container on the desk, carefully unwrapped the foil covering, and clasped her hands together.

"Sweet potato pudding. Delia, you didn't have to — I did this out of kindness."

She took a slice of the dessert, then paused, and held it out to me.

I shook my head. "It's all yours."

She slipped the slice into her mouth.

"I had no idea you still lived around here. Thought you may have gone back to the suburbs or maybe overseas. Are you still in school?"

"Uh. Yeah."

After long periods of solitude, it always took me some time to reacquaint myself with the art of conversation.

"You look great, by the way," I said.

She shrugged. "By great — you mean large. Comes with age. Though I bet your mother didn't gain a pound. How is she? Fill me in. All you mentioned in your message was the book. What about your sister? I was so busy I barely had time to check in on you before the move."

Hand her the pudding. Ask about the diary. No dilly-dallying — that was the plan. However, Camille had her own ideas, including fabricating the events that led up to our leaving Don Mount Court. It was hard to believe she had forgotten that I had stopped talking to her.

"Everyone is fine. So, did you find my book?"

"We're trying our best, but it's difficult to get to. Are you sure it's there?"

I nodded impatiently.

"How did that happen anyway?"

"It was an accident. Can I go in and help?"

"Absolutely not. Too much risk. If something happened to you ..."

She popped another slice of pudding into her mouth, tilted her head, and peered at me over the top of her glasses.

"What have you been doing with your life besides studying — a boyfriend, maybe?"

"No."

Mother's voice was close behind. *Don't tell her a thing.*

"You're still young. You'll find someone." She winked.

I felt a momentary sting.

"Has anyone else come back to visit?" I asked.

"Those kids? Hm."

A twinge in her voice hinted at a deep hurt. The kind you'd find if you could dissect a parent's heart and see feelings.

"Do you remember that summer when I bought everyone popsicles?" She perked up. "The line went all the way down the stairs. Mario's hands went numb handing them out."

My eyes lingered on the desk where Mario and I spent our days during the best summer of my life. A stirring in my chest.

"How is he?" I said.

She studied me like she was playing a game. Baiting me.

"Quite well. Too bad your mother didn't think he was good enough or —"

Camille paused for a reaction. I said nothing, so she couldn't tell she had offended me. I was supposed to be the one who beat the odds.

She continued carefully. "Though, I admired her style — at least that was consistent. She could be nice but at other times so standoffish, you know? She'd storm in demanding to speak to my superior. And the letters she wrote to head office. Folks always asked about her. They could tell you all weren't from around here — the way you carried yourselves."

I shifted my feet, gazing at the scuffed floor.

Where is the diary? Oh, God. Has she tricked me? What if she already found it? What if she read it?

"Wasn't your father around at one point? I only ever saw … what was his name, Nevon … Neville? He was gorgeous. God, your mother had good taste. I remember this coat —"

The phone rang. Camille glanced at the telephone display before answering it.

"All set? Good."

She replaced the receiver, then turned back around, looking me over as if I was being appraised for an auction.

"You can go now, but promise me you'll come back to say goodbye."

I nodded, then raced out, only stopping once arriving at the porch. I brushed the bottom of my shoes on the concrete step, took a deep breath, and opened the door.

I stepped inside.

My body tightened as if I'd stayed out past my curfew or picked up on one of Mother's foul moods. She had a way of charging the air with her anger.

"Hello?" I looked around. "It's Delia. I'm here for the —"

Then I saw it, sitting on the edge of the banister, trails drawn across its dusty brown cover where someone had attempted to clean it. Holding it, I felt lighter, like I was floating.

The diary was a gift from my eighth-grade homeroom teacher, Mrs. Anderson — a nice lady by my naive judgment. Inside the front cover she had written, "Still waters run deep." I didn't know what it meant but took it as a complex adult compliment. Someone in authority had given me permission to have a voice, and though the pages were discoloured and brittle where it had been burnt, against all Mother's attempts to keep it from me, here it was. Here I was.

Chapter 2

A Lesson in Class, Hadsworth

1992

The city of Hadsworth, Ontario, encompassed two hundred square kilometres of protected green space and tedious cookie-cutter brick developments. If you weren't young enough to have time on your side, it was the kind of place where you felt you were going in circles. Every intersection looked the same. Every month. Every year. And we were on the outskirts of the vortex drifting in with the pull. My parents referred to our time there as the "meantime plan." Only a forty-minute drive to Toronto, the suburb was a suitable place to raise children — safe, with high graduation and university acceptance rates. While living there provided my parents with an illusion of modern civility and normalcy, the conservative hub was a united front of "the evolved," though not particularly involved, citizens who claimed to share a vision.

We rented the basement of a split-bungalow on a corner lot, a short walk from the local middle school. I didn't have a lot of friends, but I got along well with our landlord's son, Alex, a pleasant, bucktoothed brunette with an adorable bowl cut and a quick sense of humour. We spent loads of time playing video games, but our relationship was one of convenience; all that stood between us was two panel doors and a set of stairs. When we first moved in, I'd just started the sixth grade and I begged Alex not to tell anyone that I lived in his basement. No one else we knew shared a house with someone. I was afraid they'd treat me differently. It ought to have been an easy secret to keep. Then one day as I was taking the garbage into the laneway, I bumped into Alex and his friend Joey. They were heading back from a neighbour's pool, dragging float mats that left a wide, wet trail behind them. Joey stopped in his tracks when he saw me. With his skinny pale legs sticking out of red swim trunks, he looked like a matchstick on fire.

I don't remember laughing but I must have, because for the next few days, I spent a considerable amount of recess time staving off rumours of a budding romance between me and Alex. Our peers held court, demanding we explain ourselves. Alex insisted he didn't like me "that way" and that my family rented from his mother. Things only got worse from there. A short-sighted bully named Sam, who only spoke to girls who wore bras, left the tetherball game he was playing to put in his two cents.

"My uncle lives in my nana's basement. My dad says he's a loser." He shared a high-five with some other kid.

I sat in class, mortified and too distracted to do school work. Notes flew over desks. People teased. Except Alex, whom I ignored for two weeks, and even after, I never truly trusted anyone. On most lunch breaks, I retreated to the far corner of the library writing away my fears, fantasizing about my future wealth, and plotting the ruin of my enemies.

In winter, a pervasive silence filled the grey streets of Hadsworth until snow blowers and ploughs emerged to scrape the soft white snow to the edges of its suburban palette. In spring, everything came alive: the buzz of lawn mowers, gritting of saws, and clatter of wood drowning out the voices of children playing. By Canada Day, with short-term renovations completed, neighbours issued generous invites to my father.

"Cliff, come by this weekend to see our new so-and-so. Bring the wife and kids." As though we were generic accessories.

This was progress. After we first moved in, our landlords were inundated with questions about the well-dressed Black couple (or "coloured," depending on who was asking). My sister and I listened to our parents debrief as we washed supper dishes, Mother's body stretched out on the couch, head resting in Father's lap. He'd stroke her arm as they traded stories in broken patois.

"Rita, di man was staring so long I had to get out of the car and say 'good morning.'"

Rolling bouts of laughter ensued. Then it would be Mother's turn.

"There I was, minding my own business when dis ol' woman walking a little ugly dog stopped to ask if I was di cleaning lady."

"What?" My father reacted in feigned disbelief.

They kept their voices low, since the door to the main floor was six feet away and Alex's mother hovered over our heads. I observed them, realizing that having each other allowed them to laugh at the hurtful things.

Eventually, people came to see my father as non-threatening and Mother as the mysterious, stylish woman who declined their wine, which further intrigued them. After summer festivities came the chill of fall, followed again by winter, when we bolted up in our houses again. All trace of life manifested in tire tracks and footsteps in the snow, ice scrapers and shovels left leaning against the double-car garages.

•

Typically, on a Saturday, as Seventh-day Adventists, we would have been at church, but I chose to stay home while my parents took Melissa to have two cavities filled. She was already crying about it at the breakfast table, and I was unwilling to bear a long car ride of her tears. I sat in the cold yellow kitchenette in my purple pyjamas, my hair unbraided, swinging my feet above the shiny white ceramic tile. While enjoying my own company, I was startled by a jostling coming from the connecting door. Before I could call out, I heard Alex's mother in the stairway.

"Wait 'till you see the tile. It's gorgeous."

"They're all down there ... all four of them?" a strange woman said.

"Yes, the girls share a room. I don't mind."

"That's awful. I couldn't raise my kids in a basement," said the other woman.

The key rattled in the lock.

"Well, I'm sending Alex to live down here as soon as he turns thirteen."

Their short-lived laughter broke as the basement door swung open, and they stood transfixed on the threshold. My raised eyebrows met their tight crocodile smiles.

"I ... I didn't know anyone was home. Sorry about that."

"I'll let them know you came by." I waved.

Before my parents had removed their shoes, I filled them in — sparing no details — from the landlord's hasty entrance to their quick retreat into the mustard hollow of the staircase. My parents grimaced at the door, and when I finished, Mother quietly removed her heels and dropped her purse onto the counter.

"She brought a stranger in here." She turned to my father.

"They didn't come in," I said. "I was here."

Her eyes were fixed on the door. My father changed the topic, and they seemingly forgot until that night, when their voices came through the walls of our bedroom.

"So, she can show off the tile but won't replace the stove," Mother said. "It's an invasion of privacy, Cliff."

"Can't tell people what to do in their own house."

"I'm going to give her a piece of my mind."

"Give her a chance to come to her own reckoning. Calm down."

"Don't tell me to calm down. I knew the minute I met her, we shouldn't take this place ... acting like she was doing us a favour."

"I wouldn't say that."

"Of course not, because that would make you the critic — and that is my job."

The next day, as Melissa and I did homework at the table, Mother emerged from her room in a plume of rose, wearing a fitted black dress and a serious look.

"I'll be right back." She went out.

Moments later, at the ring of the upstairs doorbell, Melissa ran to the basement door.

"I need to speak with you, Helen," we heard our mother say, followed by the familiar tap of her heels against the floor.

"Is there something wrong with the stove again? I've been so busy. I was thinking since Cliff is handy ... maybe he can take a look."

"How dare you enter my premises and parade your company around like it's a museum."

"Excuse me? I have a right to inspect every area of my house."

"With due notice, which I did not receive."

"It's a simple misunderstanding. No need for you to overreact."

"I'm not interested in your assessment of my reaction to your mistake. Don't let it happen again. Thank you."

The front door slammed shut. Melissa and I scurried back to our seats and soon after, Mother came in, seething.

"When your father gets here," she said, "I bet he'll try to smooth things over, and I'm not interested."

She snatched the keys from the rack and turned to us.

"I'll park my car on the street and get tickets if need be. Don't need her goddamn driveway."

Mother left.

"Yeesh, she's so cranky," Melissa said.

"I kinda get how she feels," I said, thinking of the kids at school who made me feel small in ways I found difficult to explain.

•

Father spent the next few days talking Mother out of moving us into a hotel. She seemed angrier than the day of the incident. She was tired of waiting to have "enough." Tired of living under other people's roofs. Her mother, and her mother before, owned land and houses and farms in Jamaica, and they never knew what it was like to beg.

Within a month, Dad had taken up a second job at a warehouse on the other side of town.

"Are we getting kicked out?" I asked him.

"Of course not. We've saved up some money to put toward a house, but we need more." He leaned in and whispered, "I need to get your mother out of here or she's gonna kill somebody."

We chuckled softly.

"But you'll never be here," I said.

"I'll always be here, Delia." He kissed my forehead.

•

As the months went on, Father worked hard at making extra money, and Mother lined the basement walls with barrels of newly purchased housewares. Though he objected, it wasn't until mould crept

13

in that Mother got a storage space. The night before we moved the barrels, I spotted a new electric mixer sticking out of an uncovered container. When I brought it out, a beige crocheted doily came with it. Mother sauntered over, humming "One Day at a Time."

"Delia, I crocheted that doily when I was about your age." She spread the yarn mat across her palm. "My grandmother — your great-gran — taught me how. This was the first one. Right here." She pointed to a section of the web. "She started it for me and took me to about here, then I finished the rest by myself."

There hadn't been mention of Great-Grandmother Annabelle in years. In Mother's stories, she was always the nurturing hero, and Grandma Liz, the absentee mother who had abandoned her children for the First World.

"When we buy our house, I'll frame this and hang it in the sitting room." She smiled to herself, then tilted my chin up to look at her, and said, "Don't tell anyone about the house. Not even Alex."

Having been entrusted with such an important secret, I felt that I, too, was an integral part of the plan. This wasn't just about the ability to acquire a compilation of bricks and mortar, windows, and doors — it was something *more*. This dream, this house, would make my parents, especially my mother, happy. A kind of happiness I had yet to witness. A permanent feeling that no one could take away. We were being moulded for a spot on the social hierarchy that placed us on an even keel with our neighbours. Alex and his mother would be shocked and impressed when we bought a house, I imagined. Then, like my father later explained, they'd have to find someone else to help pay their mortgage. Our success sounded like something that would upset them, and that began to make me feel good.

Our new life began to take shape in my mind. A red-shingle-roofed two-storey with large stately windows and an attic with its own exit to a Juliet balcony. A twelve-foot kitchen island surrounded by stainless-steel appliances. A separate dining room with a table that seated six, then eight, then ten — all the while the room around it expanded to fit the frame. Soon the house morphed into a five-bedroom Spanish bungalow. It then occurred to me that ownership would not be enough. Had my parents considered the kind of house it would take to shake the perception people had of us? I didn't want what people like Helen could have. I didn't want to be equal. I wanted to feel the way I believed everyone else felt — that I was better.

On weekends, I snatched the newspaper from the basement side door and removed the *TV Guide* and the New in Homes section. I reviewed the new developments while Melissa sketched designs. One morning I came upon an article about the recession — a dangerous foreign word that sounded like something was going backward — devolving. I asked my parents about it over breakfast. Mother provided a simple definition, then explained how it impacted her job by doubling her welfare caseloads. Soon the conversation veered off to her usual topic.

"It's the reason so many houses are on the market and why it's a good time to buy."

My father seemed to pick up something in her voice he didn't care for.

"Interest rates are too high," he said.

"What difference does it make? High rates, low rates — better than renting."

"Our savings aren't enough."

"Then maybe we should get something smaller."

He sat back in his chair. "Maybe we should stop shopping."

Mother gave Father an unblinking stare. "Girls, find your room."

We went in, switched on the radio, and selected a board game from the shelf. I wished I hadn't mentioned the recession. I could still hear them through the ill-fitted room door.

My father went on. "If we don't do this right, we'll be doing this again in a few years — and I won't. We could have simply avoided all this years ago by moving to the States. If you weren't so proud and competitive with your brothers, we'd be light years ahead by now."

"Ancient history, Cliff — and a revised one at that. I stayed because I was smart enough not to pick up and leave because a man said I should."

"I guess you had options then. I suppose you still do."

My parents planned on moving to the United States? When? Why would Mother turn him down?

"What happens after?" Melissa asked me.

"After what?"

"After we buy the house?"

"We move."

"Will Dad still work all the time?"

"I don't think so."

"I hope not."

"Me, too. Connect four."

•

The first snowstorm hit Hadsworth during the second week of February. Mother called to say she was stuck at the Community Services office after a last-minute request from her supervisor. After digging her car out of the snow, she discovered her car battery had died. I was to hold down the fort. I cooked and served heaping piles of elbow macaroni and grated cheddar into our bowls. We ate in front of the television because no one was around to stop us. I stifled a yawn and looked up at the clock to see it was past nine. The long hand pointed to the kitchen window, where the snow had piled up against the glass. I turned to meet Melissa's worried expression.

"They'll be home soon." I put my arms around her. "Dad went to get her, but he's far away and the traffic ... it slows things down. We should go to bed."

She broke into a half-cocked smile of disbelief but followed my lead.

•

I opened my eyes and grasped my chest to settle my racing heartbeat. Had I dreamt the loud sound and voices? The digital clock on the side table read 11:45 p.m., and I hadn't heard my parents arrive. We were woefully unprepared for intruders. The most threatening weapons were either secured in the kitchen drawers or dangling from the hangers in Mother's closet. A rustling came from the bushes outside the tiny window. I sat up on full alert. We had no closet to hide in and beneath the bed would be a tight fit. I rested my hand on Melissa's back and wondered if this was the appropriate time to pray.

The front door opened and immediately my parents' voices roared in, a combative duel of consonants and punctuations.

"Liar," my father said.

I felt no relief that we weren't being robbed.

"Why should I need to ask you — am I a child?" Mother was speaking in her singing voice.

"Have you ever bothered to ask me anything that you hadn't already made up your mind about?" My father shot back. "It's clear to me now why you never wanted to go."

"Cliff, I won't tolerate your constant accusations."

"You've mistaken this for a debate. I had a vision for this family that is in line with God's design, and you continue to try to wrestle it from me."

"Wait, Cliff — no!"

Angry voices burrowed through the corridor behind my bed.

I pinched myself. "Wake up."

In my dreams I could dig a cellar beneath me with just a thought and slip into it, taking an unending food supply. Sit out the apocalypse, the four angels, or the zombies. Whichever came first.

Instead, I lay listening to my future unravelling in the adjacent room, and eventually, the doorknob hit the wall, and wheels came skating across the plastic runner. Then came the sound of slippers scratching — no, dragging — against the tile.

"Please," Mother said in a tone I had never heard her use.

"No."

Father's answer was absolute, like when I'd asked to see *Candyman* with Alex. Mother made no rebuttal and moments later, the screen door opened, filling the room with chilled air before it banged shut. I shook violently beneath my plump quilt.

Maybe I have a fever. I'm experiencing a vivid hallucination.

In the morning, I found Mother on the sofa in the frigid open room. Her long azure nightgown swept the floor, its white lace hem crusted here and there with slush. As I walked over to her slowly, I stepped in the melted ice that trailed from the entryway. I wanted to ask if she was all right, but her blank expression gave me pause. Melissa came upon us like this, me standing an arm's length away waiting for Mother to tell me what to do, and Mother still sitting there.

"Mommy!" Melissa stumbled past me and grabbed our mother by the shoulders. "Mommy, what's wrong? You're so cold." Mother's eyes went to Melissa, then back to the floor.

"Delia, can you make me some tea, please?" Mother said in a small voice.

I brewed a pot of peppermint tea. I turned on the heater we weren't supposed to use because it was inconsiderate to the landlords. I cranked it up. I put on the television. Melissa fawned over Mother, spreading a large blanket across her legs and rubbing her back like they were dear old friends. I worried that my parents' commotion had been overheard and that we'd be put out. I wanted to get my mother a change of clothes but couldn't bring myself to go into the master bedroom.

After that night, something significant changed in all of us, but it seemed the most in my mother. Grandma Liz showed up a few days later. She and Mother had things to talk about, she said, and Mother hadn't spoken much since Dad left. I had chosen to ignore my deepest fears by believing that "it" — whatever it was — would be temporary. Father's return was inevitable.

On one occasion when I had an attack of doubts at school, I took reprieve in the washroom. I sat on the toilet and cried. Then at home I completed my chores and homework without being asked. Most nights, however, I stayed up alone, journalling and listening for the key in the lock.

Chapter 3

The Great Migration

May 1993

Dear Diary,

Mom didn't say, but I think we're moving. I just can't figure out where to. Her friend Neville dropped off boxes yesterday, and this morning I noticed pictures missing from the walls. Speaking of Neville, he sure has been making himself available lately. Mom says he's a "family friend." Whatever that means. She invited him for dinner and asked me to fix him a plate. I wish I'd told him to get it himself. Mom had better watch out. She taught me that boys don't do anything for free. Anyway, if moving means seeing less of that loser, I'm so down for it.

But what if she's taking us to Jamaica, like she keeps threatening? That happened to Riley, from church. One day he was bragging about going on vacation and next thing you know — poof — gone. What kind of an idiot is tricked into leaving the country anyway? Serves him right. I'd run away before I let that happen. Or maybe it's all a big surprise. Maybe my parents secretly made up and finally bought the house they were fighting over. I'd have my own room for my first year of high school. Ah! That would be so perfect. As if.

I am
Delia

Mother picked us up an hour after dismissal. She'd come straight from work, dressed in a starched white blouse, black pencil skirt, and heels. She wore her hair in a perfect French braid, a style I'd tried and failed to re-create because her hair was chemically straightened. By the time we arrived at the mall, the humidity caused my hair to shrink into tight curls. Mother pulled a brush and comb from the glove compartment and stood in the parking garage, fussing about my head.

"What are you doing at school that gets your hair like this?" She yanked at a knot. "The movie is about to start. For the love of God, Melissa, pass me the hat sitting on the rear speaker."

Melissa smirked as she passed me a baseball cap.

"Whose is this?" I said.

"None of your business. Put it on." Mother set the car alarm. "Let's go."

After the movie, Melissa and I sauntered behind Mother, giggling and repeating our favourite jokes.

"The movie was hilarious. Right, Mommy?" Melissa said.

"It was okay." Mother fiddled with a new mascara she bought. "Kids have a different sense of humour."

The movie was my choice, so I felt disappointed. I was hoping it would make her laugh, a sound we seldom heard anymore.

"I'm so hungry," Melissa said.

Mother stopped, forcing us to a halt. "For Christ's sake, do you need to tell everyone? I will take you to the food court."

We did a silent victory dance behind her back.

"How do you get her to do that?" I whispered.

"Do what?"

"You know what."

She shrugged with a wide grin.

Melissa and I opted for chicken burger combos while Mother ate teriyaki chicken. We rested at a four-seater table by the window. Mother placed her purse on the empty chair beside her, where Father would've been seated. I looked at her curiously, wondering if she missed him as much as I did or if she was more relieved to have somewhere sturdy to place her leather purse.

"Thanks for taking us out," I said.

"You're welcome. Enjoy it because the rest of the month will be busy. We're moving."

I straightened up.

"Why? Where?" Melissa said.

"That's not important. Stop slurping your drink. In fact, that's enough pop for you." She reached out and slid Melissa's root beer away from her.

My sister appeared shocked. Her small hand curved as if still holding the cup.

"Delia, are you listening?"

"Yes, Mommy," I answered, wondering if she had informed our father of this.

"You can't tell anyone. Not even your friend upstairs. He'll tell his nosy mother. Can you believe she had the nerve to ask where your father is? Why is that any of her business? She gets her rent on time." She continued her tirade for a bit, though it sounded like she was no longer speaking to us but to the person who should have been sitting beside her.

When she left for the washroom, my sister and I turned to each other.

"Is Dad coming?" Melissa asked.

"Probably," I said.

"Yeah, she must've told him. Hey, why can't we tell our friends?"

"You know how it is with her lately. Everything's a secret."

Melissa eyed her confiscated drink.

"Don't touch it." I glanced behind us. "Just in case, we should find Dad to make sure he knows."

Melissa furrowed her brows and appeared worried

"Finish eating," I said. "She's coming back."

•

As it turned out, all the rental trucks were booked for the end of June, so our moving date was bumped up. This change of plans spared me the embarrassment of showing up to my graduation ceremony without my father. His absence would reflect poorly on me, as if somehow it was my fault. Still, as moving day approached, I grew hopeful that he'd turn up. I sought out signs of his impending arrival, jotting them down in my diary for reference — my own little book of Revelation.

One rainy evening, days before the move, Melissa and I packed our clothes while Mother directed us from the kitchen. I watched as she glided between cupboards selecting seasonings for the beef stew, and I recognized her blue dress, one she hadn't worn in a while.

"You look beautiful," I said, stepping out into the hall.

"Thank you, sweetheart."

"Dad loves that dress," I added.

Mother jerked around and slammed her fists on the cutting board, making us jump.

"I don't care," she said, her voice shredding the air.

Melissa burst into tears. I held my breath, afraid to say anything else. Afraid to move. Too shocked to cry.

"Never mention that again."

The dress, or Dad?

She made her way toward me. I closed my eyes, bracing for a smack, and flinched as I felt her pass by.

"Hush," she said to my sister, then went to console to her.

For the rest of the day, I was careful not to open my mouth too wide when I spoke, for fear my father's name would come tumbling out. Later, I turned to the last page of my diary, where I'd compiled a list of things not to say when Mother was around. I fished my special gold-ink pen from the coiled book spine and wrote, "Dad."

Once, while out for a walk, my sister asked me out of the blue, "Did Dad leave because he's sick and had to go away to die alone?"

I looked at her. "Where did you come up with that?"

"I dunno. He's been gone since February. That's a long time."

I nodded in agreement.

"So, why'd he leave?"

"He's just too classy," I said. "He couldn't stand living in the basement anymore."

"Where'd he go?"

"Uh … he's probably got a new job where he travels a lot."

"So why doesn't he call?"

"He does. Just not when we're at home."

While I made up stories, I tried to find out what really happened. I reread my diary entries, searching for a moment when he said, "I'm leaving," like they did in the soaps. What I found was a transcript of a quarrel I must have found interesting.

"Every week I see new shopping bags and barrels — how much is this all costing us? We have no space for this."

"I'm putting them in storage," she said.

To which he replied, "I'm trying to put a roof over our heads, not towels and food processors."

"I beg your pardon?" she said. "Do I get paid with Monopoly money?"

He promptly apologized, and then she got angry.

"This isn't about the stupid barrels. You're upset because he brought me home when the car broke down. You were at work — as usual."

"To buy the house you want," he said.

"No, the house we need. What's more important, pride or money?"

"A man can have both."

"Oh, that must be nice."

As recorded in my entries, they went on like that for weeks, playing "mad-tag." I felt that aside from their arguments about money, my parents got along, and so my father, a principled man, would never skip out on his family. Some unrelated urgency must have caused his sudden exit. Based on Mother's avoidance of the topic and her frequent foul moods, I figured it wasn't a mutual decision.

At school, everyone went on talking about their perfect lives, planning for the end-of-year school trip and the graduation ceremony. I couldn't say anything about Dad, so I dedicated the last two pages of my diary to signatures and wrote a note at the top that read "Moving: June 1993." I expected sympathetic goodbye notes with sad faces and phone numbers. I was still trying to fit in — on my way out.

Alex caught me crying in the line after lunch, so I told him about my dad. He could relate. Well, kind of. His parents split five years before because his dad cheated. A few months later, Alex gained a stepmother.

"Like on the soaps, right?" I said.

He said, "Yeah, like that."

"My dad didn't cheat, though. This is different."

"Be prepared for shit to hit the fan, my friend," he said. "My mom was off work for months and had to see a shrink to get happy again."

"Whoa. Whoa. That's not what's happening to my family," I told him.

"Sounds like you don't know what's happening. I mean you don't even know where your dad is. You're moving all of a sudden and some strange guy is checking your mom out ... you should ask your mom if she needs help."

I asked him if he was bat-shit crazy. This was why Mother told us not to talk to people. As a kid, all your peers are idiot know-it-alls, and the adults are eager and too jaded to give objective advice.

Around Mother's birthday, I expected my father to call. It was always extra special since it was close to Mother's Day. The year before, he had made a big fuss and spent an hour in the bathroom with his noisy electric shaver. He refused to go to a barber, even when Mom begged him to.

"It's a waste of money," he said. "I'll end up with a fungus and go bald. Then you'll divorce me and marry some hunk with a head full of hair."

"You're ridiculous." Mother tried to sound upset but I saw her smiling.

He looked great that day, his hair cut squarely along the hairline to hide his widow's peak, his tailored blue shirt tucked into brown trousers, and his shoes pointed and shiny. The morning after, over breakfast, Mother raved about their night out.

"I had my shrimp tossed in garlic and butter, the way I like them."

Our father winked at her over the top of his teacup. We weren't supposed to eat shellfish or drink alcohol, but as a late adopter of the Seventh-day Adventist religion, Mother had a rebellious streak. Dad didn't seem to mind.

This time around, I spent Mother's birthday lingering around the phone while she dressed for a night on the town — with Neville. Always close by, conveniently available, Neville. Neville with the fancy car, rubber-soled shoes, and black Kangol hat. A strapping man with curly brown hair and pin-drop freckles who seldom laughed. What he did, mostly, was work. He could lift heavy furniture and fix things that always seemed to break down eventually anyway. I never saw him play a board game or watch sports. He never took us on rides or asked how our days went, like our dad did. He liked to dress up, go to parties, and hang out with other single men — maybe even women. That was the kind of man he was.

We made Mother birthday cards that earned us perfumed hugs and tangerine kisses on our cheeks. Later, when Neville brought a small bouquet of roses, Mother set them in a thin vase on the counter. I eyed it as I packed the kitchen supplies, restraining myself from knocking it to the floor. Then later, as we watched *Carrie* for the third time, my sister asked what I'd do with telekinetic powers.

"I'd fling Neville over the fence," I said.

She shook her head. She'd use her powers to be a good Christian. I tuned her out and listened for the phone call from my father that never came.

The next morning, Mother was up early making breakfast, looking tragic but beautiful with her tousled hair and smoky eyes. The sunlight coming through the small basement window reflected off her pearl satin nightdress, setting her aglow.

"Did you have fun, Mommy?"

"You know what?" She looked reflective. "I did. I also noticed you were very busy packing last night. That must have taken a long time. Thank you."

"You're welcome." I clasped my hands behind my back and took a deep breath. "After we've finished cleaning our room, can we please ride our bikes?"

"Sure. Be back in this house no later than eleven o'clock."

She pointed sternly at an empty spot where the clock had been. I had packed it the night before. She laughed. Then, as I turned to walk away, she said quietly, "Delia, did your father call last night?"

I was startled. "No."

"Hm. Okay, thanks." Her face fell, and she returned pensively to her pot, leaving me with a burden of misplaced emotions, her unwarranted gratitude and my father's questionable guilt.

•

When we moved to Toronto from the suburb of Hadsworth in the summer of 1993, it was beyond hot. Unbearable. Just after dawn on moving day, I woke up to find two outfits dangling from hangers in our otherwise empty closet, white long-sleeved shirts and jeans that Mother picked because she didn't want us to "catch a draft" and get sick. I grabbed my diary from beneath my pillow and got dressed. Mother came to usher us into the car.

"What about the mattress?" I asked.

"Leave it," she said. "We need the room in the van."

We made our way to the car, my sister and I resembling fraternal twins rather than siblings aged ten and thirteen. Melissa called shotgun, so I sat behind Mother. A U-Haul van drove out ahead of us just before Mother started the engine. I asked who was driving it. Mother told me to put my seat belt on and keep quiet. Melissa and I exchanged a look.

Could it be him?

I lowered my head. "Dear Lord, if it pleases you, let it be Dad."

"Delia, pray so we can all hear."

I looked up and met Mother's stare.

"Sure," I said, then mumbled a prayer about taking us safely to our destination.

As the car pulled away, I glanced back at the house. A light went on in an upstairs window. I wondered if that was Alex's bedroom. I hoped that he would miss me. Soon our tract housing subdivision tunnelled onto sparse main streets. It was a bittersweet departure into the unknown.

The station wagon was out of coolant and by the time we hit the main highway, the car felt like a greenhouse. The pen slipped from my sweaty fingers as I wrote in my diary, imagining my father stepping out of the van when we arrived at our destination. My flimsy frame swayed to the rhythm of traffic and speed bumps that made sketchpads out of my pages. The van ahead made a right turn at the lights, but we went straight through. Melissa leaned over to Mother.

"Our stuff went the other way."

"He's stopping at the storage to grab the barrels. We'll meet him there."

I sensed Melissa was fixing to ask our mother who "he" was. I shook my head at her. I didn't want to know.

. The car came to a stop at Bayview Avenue. I met Mother's eyes in the rear-view mirror   a brief look passed between us before I broke the stare. On Sabbaths, my father, a draftsman by trade, would drive us through the city boroughs after church. Once, he took us to the Bridle Path neighbourhood, where mansions sat on heavily treed lots.

"I wish we lived here," I had said. "They're so lucky."

"Lucky?" my father said, sounding offended. "Is that why you study in school, or why your mom and I work so hard?"

"No, Daddy."

He dangled his left arm outside the driver's side window and slowed the car.

"These families came from all over the world to make something of themselves. Like your mother and me. Some had a good head start, but there is no such thing as luck."

I sulked.

"Never want for what others have, Delia. Use your God-given talents, proper upbringing, and education to build a good life."

"Yes, Daddy. I will." I tried to sound grateful.

Melissa leaned over. "Thou shalt not covet, remember?"

I narrowed my eyes at her and turned back to the window. If I'd only brought my diary, I wouldn't have to hear anyone else's opinions about my thoughts.

The next time I asked to return to the Bridle Path, Father refused. My initial reaction had revealed a flaw in his parenting strategy. Success should have inspired me to work harder. I failed the test.

Mother accelerated past Bayview Avenue, heading deeper into unfamiliar territory. Melissa sat up front with her teddy bear, Toby. Today, she was the head scout, responsible for spotting desirable areas. Houses only. No apartments. Melissa motioned with a raised thumb. Just ahead, a subdivision of two-storey detached homes on emerald lots. A flutter went off in my chest, but we went on — the streets sinking and swelling. Rows of trees gave way to an endless stretch of grey, out of which stoplights and tenements sprang, ' blocking out the rising sun. I kept my diary open, scribbling a few sentences as they came to me and trying not to hope.

Chapter 4

The Parable of the Lost Town

June 1993

Dear Diary,

I'm so nervous. Lord, if Dad is driving that truck, I'll be the happiest girl in the world. I promise to get all As and keep my room clean. I just can't figure out why he'd choose the city. It's a different world — all the stores, old churches, and glass buildings, the people sleeping on the street. How did they end up here? What if that happened to Dad? What if Mom kicked him out and he has nowhere to turn?

Anyway, now we're slowing down in front of a massive white building. Where are we? Oh no. I hope this is not it. Well, it is.

I am
Delia

We breached the crest of the bridge as the sun started its run. The car stalled, bringing us to a halt. I inched away from the window, fearing something would leap out of the fog. Mother toggled with the gears until the engine whinnied back to life, then steered the rattling vehicle into the apartment lot and parked. We sat dazed, staring up at the complex. The sprawl erased evidence of any structure that preceded its existence, save for a muddy dribble of a ditch carved alongside the laneway and a small plot of land vomited from the murky Don River.

Melissa clutched Toby to her chest. "Why are we stopping here?"

Mother raised a hand. "Keep quiet, child."

The property started on Dundas Street and extended south along the Don River and the winding Don Valley Parkway. Along its perimeter was a stretch of backyards where the occasional plant managed to secure root and flourish. Save for this, the landscape was a canvas of cement and plaster, leaving the residents to provide colour against its pale walls.

Mother opened the driver's side door and set her legs out carefully, smoothing the wrinkles in her jean skirt. Not many people would don such a get-up for this occasion, but not many people were like my mother. She went to the trunk and opened it.

Melissa groaned. "Where are we, Delia?"

"I don't know, but if this was Dad's idea, he has some explaining to do."

I glanced back in the direction from where we had come. The bridge seemed a long distance away, much of it hidden by the smog that hung over the ravine. Across the river, other buildings rose and fell in quadrate clusters toward the urban core. We were not downtown but on the outskirts of it, shoved off in the drain gate.

No corner lot or in-ground pool for you, Delia.

Mother rapped on the window and chased us out of the car. She wrestled a pail from the side of the trunk and handed it to Melissa.

"Grab the other bag and close the trunk," she said to me. "Then meet me at unit seventy-six. I'll open the door."

She carried on, seeming confident with her purse swinging by her side. Over by the backyards, she paced for a bit, then stopped and stood, arms akimbo.

"This place sucks," Melissa said.

"Be quiet, Mom's coming back, and she's pissed."

Mother approached, looking troubled.

"What's wrong?" I tried to conceal my sarcasm.

"For Christ's sake, where are the unit numbers? We'll need to go to the front."

"I can wait here for the truck," I said.

"Come on. No time for talking." She walked away.

I rolled my eyes.

"One day she's gonna see you do that," Melissa said.

"I wish she would."

We followed Mother, skylarking along the way. Melissa struck me playfully with her pail, and we jostled until we came to the entrance of a tunnelway. Inside, the exposed brick had been tagged with black spray paint, the ground littered with broken bottles, wrappers, and remnants of cigarettes, creating a collage on the pavement. It opened to a large courtyard with a basketball court. A few residents wandered about, watching with a hint of a heedful observation, as though counting a flock of returning sheep. We met Mother at unit seventy-six. She led us in and closed the door behind us.

The apartment was painted in bland beige from ceiling to laminated floor. Its front and rear entries opposed each other, connected by the lone central hall with a closet and an entrance to the basement. In seconds, one could run through one door and out the other. Very handy for a getaway. I eyed the breakfast nook and tiny kitchen. At the back of the unit was a living room with large windows overlooking the lot. That was the end. Front to back in ten giant steps.

"That's barely a backyard," Melissa whined.

"At least we have one now."

In terrible times, it never helps to state the obvious. I was all about silver linings now.

Mother came up behind us.

"Oh — looking for something to do? Change your clothes and start cleaning."

It was just like her to ruin every potentially exciting moment. I glared at her back.

One day I'll be grown, and I'll be gone, and you won't be able to boss me around.

We darted down the hallway and up the steps to check out the second floor. The windows in the two smaller rooms overlooked the court; the master bedroom faced the city.

"Dibs." I ogled the next largest option.

"We'll see what Dad says." Melissa skipped off before I could answer.

While I scoured the fridge, Melissa slowly unpacked, taking frequent breaks. I, too, found it difficult to focus; every sound from outside sent me scrambling to the window. The house had become unusually quiet, and I realized Melissa had deserted her post. I found her upstairs, where she and Toby had taken up residence on the mattress in what was to be my room. She sat up when she saw me.

I stood over her. "Slacker."

"I'm tired and hungry. I can't work under these conditions."

Mother called up the steps. "The truck is here. I'm going out to help. When I get back this kitchen better be spotless."

As soon as she went out, I ran into the master bedroom, with its large, grubby windows. Melissa was on my heels. Outside, Mother stood by the fence, talking to two men who were hauling a dresser out of the cargo section of the truck. One was not my father; the other's face was blocked by an intrusive oak tree.

"Is it him?"

"Wait." I rubbed the pane with my sleeve.

"Lemme see." Melissa pushed me.

"Back off."

Finally, the man stepped out into the open.

"No." I let my head fall heavily against the window.

Melissa folded her arms. "It's not fair."

I glared down at Neville, who, at Mother's orders, was unloading another piece of furniture. He had to be the reason for the move to this awful place. How did he convince her to make such a poor decision?

I forced my eyes open to keep the tears at bay and quietly scolded myself for breaking my own rules. I'd written it on my list: "Don't get your hopes up, Delia. Hope is not a strategy."

We went downstairs to watch the furniture being moved in. Mother had a penchant for large fragile things that were heavy and difficult to clean. A clamour erupted and I rushed outside to discover Neville and friend standing over Mother's toppled dresser — the one made of mirrors. Two other men and a teenage boy came to their aid just before my mother joined them, and they all hunched over the evidence. I took notice of the boy. Our eyes met; his soft brown irises were rimmed with coal lashes. He brought a fractured drawer over to me, but Mother asked him to set it down on the front step instead.

Shortly after, back inside, Mother wondered aloud whether she should have offered the boy a reward. I supported her eagerly, saying, "I'll find him." My voice sounded high.

She shot me a look and I had my answer.

I watched on as they filled the first and second floors, then the basement. The smallest bedroom became repurposed as temporary storage, which meant Melissa and I would be sharing again. Lastly, Neville brought in the glass dining table and set it down.

"It'll take a miracle to make this place presentable." Mother wiped her forehead.

Neville chuckled. "Knowing you, it'll be a palace in no time. You just have to make the best of things."

Somehow they managed to make everything fit, but what we had gained in space amplified the loss of our father, whose presence would have meant so much more.

Melissa and I observed our new neighbours as we unpacked. We saw more women than men and more small children than we could keep track of. Later that afternoon, I spotted who I'd been waiting for; the boy with the brown eyes exited from a unit on the other side. He stopped to chat to an old couple before joining the basketball game in progress.

"I forgot my diary in the car. Wanna come with?" I said to Melissa.

"I'm too tired. We've been doing this the whole day," she groaned and threw herself onto the mattress.

I left her there.

On the way out, I passed Mother berating Neville about the damaged furniture. I grabbed the car keys from the table before they could see. Near the court I knelt, pretending to brush dirt from my shoe while sneaking glances at the boy. He breezed past his opposing teammates before sinking a layup into the net-less rim. Two girls cheered from the other side. I wondered who they were. He looked over and caught me staring, so I hurried off to Mother's car and hopped into the back seat.

•

Night's first clouds hovered over the city's factories. I'd lost track of time while writing. Something had shifted in the complex; an unsettling mood had descended with the dusk, and distant murmurs and music came from the upper suites. People congregated in corners and yards. I left the car and scrambled across the poorly lit lot into the dark entryway, daydreaming that the boy was on the other end, basketball in hand.

I was waiting for you. That's what he'd say.

"Hey! Watch your step."

I jumped back and let out a scream.

A figure rose unsteadily to his feet from the crook of the alcove, a man using the wall as a brace. He stretched over me, arms dangling — a brown bottle in one hand.

"What you doing out here, huh? Where's your motha?"

He stepped forward. I turned to run. A hefty hand enwrapped my forearm. I yelled and struggled to get away, dropping my diary in the process.

It was Neville. "Shh."

His eyes followed the man, who was staggering out of the tunnelway.

"Did he do anything to you? Why were you just standing there?"

"Ouch. No, I'm fine." I pulled out of his grip to get the diary.

"You and that stupid book. Why can't you write inside? You could've gotten into trouble." He shook his head. "I warned your mother that you kids are too sheltered to handle yourselves here."

Footsteps drew near; someone was in a real hurry. Neville had me by the arm again, and this time I did not pull away.

"I don't mean to say there aren't nice people here, but ..." He struggled as if we spoke different languages. I waited for the next word of advice, but his pager went off. He checked it, then clipped it onto his waist.

A waft of stale urine was stirred up by the wind.

"Do you have the keys?"

I nodded and handed them over.

"Tell your mom that I'll be back."

Once I walked away, he went off whistling.

I prayed my mother was too distracted to notice my absence and was relieved to hear her fiddling around in the basement when I came in. I found Melissa where I'd left her.

"Took you long enough." She offered me a share of the spiced-bun-and-cheese sandwich.

"Oh, I'm sorry I couldn't make it back for dinner in time. I only almost died."

"What?"

"It's so dangerous. These guys were hanging out by the truck like they wanted to steal it. I think they were drug dealers."

Melissa reached for Toby, her eyes growing large.

"I waited in the car until they left. I was basically trapped for like an hour. Then in the tunnel, this drunk pervert tried to attack me. I barely got away."

Melissa clapped.

"Delia, I don't know why you don't have any friends. You tell the best stories."

I ignored her backhanded compliment. I was proud of my ability.

On the way to bed, Mother checked in. Her figurine-like silhouette stood in the entryway. We paused our activity and waited. I assumed she was thinking about my father. Like I was.

"This is temporary," she said. "We're here but we are not of here. Do you understand?"

We nodded.

"It's been a long day, so time for bed," she continued. "By the way, Delia, I saw you earlier getting all dreamy-eyed."

"What did I do?"

"Don't play stupid. I know how girls get at your age. Don't let me catch you looking in the direction of that boy. You have plenty of time to grow up, and then you'll have your share of bills, boys, and buns in the oven."

As Mother turned away, she tripped over the edge of a lifted laminate tile. I was mimicking her when she wheeled around and pointed right at me. I sobered up.

"Keep your eyes straight ahead around here. You hear me?"

"Yes, Mommy," we chanted in unison.

While my sister slept, I thought of ways to discreetly locate and contact my father. My thoughts shifted as I scanned the quiet court, my gaze landing on where the boy in the jersey lived. The lights were off. I wondered if he was awake and thinking about the shy girl with the pigtails who just moved in.

Chapter 5

A Certain Affliction

July 1993

Dear Diary,

So, it's official. We're poor. According to Mother, we're here to save money. Whatever. No wonder Dad left. He wouldn't be caught dead living in public housing. It's disgusting — not that we've seen much more than the parking lot, which is where that cute guy was today.

He was staring at me! I wanted to smile back, but Mom asked what I was looking at and gave me the death stare. She can't keep me locked up in here forever. I'm determined to meet him. Maybe it'll turn out that we go to the same school. He'll introduce me to his friends. Maybe this summer won't be a complete bust after all. As if.

I am
Delia

•

Days after the move, we brought the empty moving boxes into the basement, where we flattened then stacked them by the barrels, lined up like tin cans against the wall. We counted them. Fifteen. Right then, I promised myself to be the kind of woman who only bought what was needed. That way if I wanted to leave somewhere or someone I could pick up and be gone — like Father. I wouldn't need a man to help me either.

"I don't care if I'm alone," I told Melissa. "I'm never gonna live like this. I'll keep it light as ever."

"Never say never." She fumbled with a latch. "What's in all these barrels anyway?"

"House stuff."

"Does she keep a list?"

I shook my head. "She memorizes everything."

"Like you?"

"I guess," I said, feeling proud as if Mother had selectively passed on the gift to me.

I began listing the contents I knew of, my sister looking impressed — then skeptical as I went on.

"Did you hear that?" Melissa interrupted. "A squeaking sound from over there."

She pointed at the makeshift laundry.

"Nice try."

"I'm not kidding, and I'm not sticking around to find out what it is." She rushed upstairs.

I turned to leave when I spotted something white under the steps — my father's draft table. It and four large containers marked C.E. were tucked away in a corner. I ran my hands over the surface and rubbed the grit between my fingers. Standing there, among what little had been deemed his, I wondered how he was managing without it — the table he loved. How could he live without my stories, Mother's stewed oxtail with lima beans, or Melissa's affection?

Maybe he had met a terrible end, as Melissa had feared. An image of my father veering into traffic floated into mind. Mother, too distraught to tell us and tormented by his memory, left the basement suite back in Hadsworth for a tenement. She wasn't thinking straight. It explained why she had "jumped out of the frying pan and into the fire," as Grandma Liz would've said. I inhaled heavily, the back of my eyes burning. It felt too real. I shook the thought away. Instead, I pictured him sitting on a wooden garden chair on Grandma Maureen's porch — the only part of the house I remembered — in his left hand, a glass of sorrel drink with three ice cubes. He missed us, but he was happy.

That evening, Mother and Neville returned from their errands with more furniture, a tiny beat-up dresser and a twin bed. When Neville moved the dresser into the smallest room, he came out and gave me a thumbs-up sign.

I gave Mother a quizzical look.

"A room is a room." She offered me her empty palms, having nothing left to give.

She averted her gaze to the space above my head, then went to see him out, leaving me to consider my new bedroom and the reflection of a frowning child in the mirror.

Though my room was the size of a large walk-in closet, it put me out of Mother's direct view. She was unable to see me at the edge of the bed, waiting for the boy to turn up. He gave me something to look forward to at the loneliest time of my day.

Nightfall in Don Mount brought sirens, incessant barking, and claw-shaped shadows reaching across my sheets. Outside, the coliseum of archways stretched across the poorly lit court. In each corner, loiterers hid in the crevices, dots of ember expanding and dilating around their lips as they smoked. To calm myself, I conjured memories of my parents' laughter. I had never been afraid before, but that part of me that felt safe seemed unreachable. Across the hall, I heard the scratching of Mother's slippers, and I fell asleep to the sound of her pacing.

•

A scratching sound travelled like the rapping of fingernails, low along the floorboards. I opened my eyes, letting them adjust to the dark. The sound came again, from the direction of the dresser. I imagined a giant hairy insect with raptorial legs. Off I ran to Melissa's room, where she lay at the bed's edge, Toby's rear end sticking out from under her shoulder. Her silk headscarf had fallen to the floor, and her curls fell like licorice cotton candy across the moonlit white sheets. I whispered into her ear and shook her gently. She muttered something nonsensical. I had become accustomed to us sharing a space and missed her when she slept.

On summer nights past, about this time my father would've arrived from his second job. At the click of the lock, I'd make my way quietly to reheat the meal Mother had left for him in the oven. I'd take a cold bottle of malt from the fridge, open it, and put it on the table. With a cup of Horlicks in front of me, we'd sit at the table and talk.

"So, Delia, what was the best part of your day? What was the worst?" Or, "What about your mommy, what did she do today? Were you helpful? And Melissa?"

He'd offer me only two forks of his dinner because eating late wasn't good for my metabolism. Then I'd tell him everything he wanted to know as quietly as I could and tap him on his wrinkled knuckles when he drifted off.

One night he got talking about the houses in the neighbourhood where he worked.

"They're old wartime houses, mostly. Low-roofed, tiny. Like cottages, with yards that go on for days."

"Is that where we're going to buy our house?"

"No," he said, like he'd just decided. "I wouldn't raise my kids there. At night, you get to see a place for what it really is. When all the children and hardworking folk are asleep — the others come out."

What others? I wondered but never asked.

He'd finish his meal, pat his stomach, and say, "Thanks, love, for the company and the stories. Good night."

"Good night, Daddy," I said aloud to no one.

The room went still. My sister had stopped snoring. I rolled her over and put my ear to her chest, listening for the steady slow beat that had lulled me to sleep over the years — a fitful habit I picked up from watching my mother when I still carried a lunchbox to school and my sister still slept in a crib. Stirring, Melissa inhaled a long, shuddering breath and twisted toward the wall. It reminded me of games we used to play. *Play dead. Hold your breath. Moosha-moosha-moosha — freeze.* The scratching started up again, this time the sound coming from the direction of her closet. I snuck in beside her and fell asleep.

•

Mother's Monday morning bedlam woke me. I stretched and stepped off the bed and onto the Christopher Pike novel I had been reading the night before. I picked it up and disturbed a tiny insect that had taken refuge beneath it. It scampered away and disappeared under the bookshelf. I rubbed my eyes. Had I seen a baby beetle? There came a knock at the door, then Mother entered as I was saying "Come in."

"Delia, the knock is only a formality. You have no business keeping the door closed anyway. Now, have you seen the box with my black heels?"

"No. You're going back to work already?"

She went to the closet, and there followed a series of *thwacks* as she flipped open the lids of the boxes inside.

"Yes. The welfare policy change is causing absolute chaos. I'll need to put in some extra hours. I really hate moving," she said from behind the closet door. "What time is it?"

I glanced at the clock on my dresser.

"Six thirty. You're early."

"Not anymore. Not with this traffic." She turned her back to me. "Fasten this, please."

I hooked the open clasp of her skirt.

"Thanks." She moved into the hall. "Check the notepad on the table." She called back instructions all the way down the steps and out the door.

The main floor smelled of nutmeg and sweet milk. I opened the window by the table before taking up the notepad to read the list of reminders. We were to expect the cable company: "Ask for ID." I fantasized that the cable technician would show up wearing a red cap, head lowered, as he stood at the door. When he provided proof of his identity, the company card would read "Cliff Ellis."

Under "Emergency" she had written the numbers for the main switchboard of the Family Benefits office and Neville's pager. I let out a howl.

She can't be serious. I picked up the pen and scratched out the note and wrote, "Call Grandma" — just before my sister could see.

"What did she say?" Melissa read over my shoulder. "Aw, man, I knew she'd make us do math. What is the point of summer break? She should've been a headmaster."

"Prison guard," I corrected. "Imagine what it'd be like if we had a normal mother?"

Melissa took her finger and drew an imaginary bubble over my head like they did in the comics. I pretended to toss my ideals into the bubble: our aunt Marie, whose modern "Canadian" lifestyle involved spending weekends at the cottage. She'd host birthday parties and let us wear bikinis and eat cold baloney with mustard for breakfast. We stood back, looked at our ideas, and smiled.

After completing our academic exercises, Melissa folded laundry while I cleaned the bathroom. I tied a T-shirt over my face before pouring a stream of bleach into the toilet. I shoved the toilet brush into the bowl, looking away as I scrubbed.

"Delia, I thought I felt something crawling on me last night," Melissa said.

"No, you didn't. It's just the tiny hairs on your body."

I thought of telling her about the scratching, then changed my mind; she'd be in my bed every night, and Mother would blame me for putting thoughts in my little sister's head. All those Stephen King books and vampire movies. Our house would become censored, like China.

"After the phone gets hooked up today, we'll call Grandma to find out where Dad is."

"Good idea, Delia. Then when Dad comes back, at least we can ride our bikes."

"I want to do more than ride a bike. All my friends get to travel, even Alex is at the cottage."

"Weren't you guys supposed to go to Wonderland? Guess that's not happening, eh?"

Melissa really knew how to rub it in. Our former friends lived starkly different lives. They were either being whisked away from mosaic Toronto or being shipped between one parent's house and the other. It was a complication I was beginning to hope for. *Hope is not a strategy.* I stepped into the hallway and took in a deep breath.

"I can't spend my entire summer in this hellhole."

Voices poured in from outside. I rushed to the window and pressed my face against the warm pane, listening to the heavy bass and the thud of rubber thumping against the pavement.

"It's him!"

"Who, Dad?" Melissa joined me.

"No, silly. The guy."

He shot a three-pointer from what looked like half court. I opened the window wider to let his boasting roll in.

"He's really good," I said.

"And cute." Melissa grinned.

We watched as the boy and his teammates dominated their opponents, leading to a triumphant end. Melissa and I cheered loudly. That was when he looked up. I stepped back.

"He saw me."

Melissa went to say something outside the window.

"No." I yanked her backward.

She studied me. "You like him, don't you? I knew it."

A strong rap at the back door sidetracked us.

"Don't answer it," Melissa said. "What if it's a burglar?"

I sucked my teeth. "Who's gonna steal from us — we're poor."

"Touché."

It was her new favourite word, ever since Carlton said it on an episode of *The Fresh Prince of Bel-Air*.

•

As soon as the cable technician left, my sister planted herself in front of the television and flicked through the channels. I called our grandma Liz.

"Hi, Grandma," I said when she picked up.

"Hey, sweetheart. I was waiting for your mother to call and give me the new number. I knew you'd fill me in. How are you?"

"Bored."

"I don't believe that. Your mother's whole purpose in life is to keep you occupied."

I brought her up to speed on our lacklustre summer.

"You girls should be outside playing — not learning how to be a housewife," she said.

"Mom thinks it's too dangerous."

"It's Toronto, not South Africa. Ridiculous."

"Huh?"

"Never mind. She's being overprotective. I'll talk to her."

"Thanks, Grandma. And one more thing, have you heard from Dad?"

A pause.

"Please don't tell Mom I asked."

My grandmother sighed deeply. "Your mother gets very irritated when I get involved. Tell you what, I'll make a few phone calls and see if I can connect with him. We talked briefly, but he moves around."

"You did? How? Is he okay? Where is he? Can you give him this number?"

"Calm down. He's fine and will answer all your questions at the appointed time. I will give him the number if your mother is okay with it. That I must ask, Delia — out of respect for her."

"You're the best. I love you."

"I love you both. Kiss Melissa for me, and you two stay out of trouble."

"We will."

I hung up and winked at my sister. "Grandma's on it. I think she'll come through."

After finishing dinner, I switched on the TV and sat on the couch. Melissa hung back in the kitchen mixing passionfruit juice. A shriek jolted me out of my seat, followed by Melissa's frantic footsteps coming down the hall. She clutched my arms and stepped on my feet like she intended to climb me.

"A mouse!" She sobbed. "It — it touched me."

"Stop being dramatic — wait here."

Clenching my hands, I stomped heavily toward the site, hoping to scare it off. I was relieved to find our newest house guest was nowhere to be seen.

"I'll tell Mom when she gets home," I said. "She'll know what to do."

When Mother arrived, she was barely through the door when we rushed to meet her. She collapsed into the sofa and we removed her shoes.

"I smell dinner," she said. "I'm starved."

Melissa picked at her fingernails.

"Wait," I mouthed, then to Mother I said, "I'll get your dinner ready."

We all sat down to eat. From across the table, I noted the traces of fatigue on Mother's face.

"Can't you take more time off?" I asked.

"Um," she said as if considering it. "No."

"How come?" Melissa piped in.

"Irma and Carol are on vacation and I'm their backfill."

"What about when they get back?" I asked.

"I've been a bit late what with the traffic into work, and the supervisor already has it in for me. She wants to give my job to one of her friends."

"She can't do that," I said. "That's not fair."

"Tell me about it. If anything, we need more staff. This welfare reform is killing me. I have thirty-five cases and no time to investigate fraud."

Melissa glanced up from her plate. "Fraud?"

"Sometimes," Mother said, "people don't follow the rules. That's what the reform is about. Like my client ... let's call her 'Ava.' Someone called in to report that Ava, who has four children, is living with a man, which is a breach of policy. So, she could lose her subsidized housing and be fined for overpayment."

"You're not allowed to have a boyfriend if you're on welfare?" Melissa asked.

"Of course — he just can't live with you," I said. "It's considered another source of income. You should report it ... if he's living with you. Right?" I looked over at Mother.

She nodded, but I couldn't tell whether she agreed with the rule. Then she said, "I'd rather move back to Jamaica before I beg these people for help. I couldn't live like that. A woman leaves one controlling man for another — the government."

I thought about poor Ava and her boyfriend. Why was he living with her anyway? Why couldn't she live with him? Maybe he didn't have the space for four kids. Maybe she wanted to have somewhere of her own. Safety. I made a mental note to cross social worker off my list of possible careers. If I couldn't make the rules, then what was the point?

"Enough of all that." Mother took a long drink of water, then waved the unasked questions away with a hand. "This fish is delicious. Good job, Delia."

I beamed.

"So, what did you two do all day?"

"Nothing," I said quickly.

Melissa stepped on my foot.

"Not now," I whispered.

It wasn't often that we had a whole day of peace. My sister stayed quiet. Thank God.

•

Melissa's scream was loud enough to wake the neighbours. I figured she had seen the mouse again. I dragged myself out of the bed and went into the hallway where Mother had come out, eyes squinting.

"Lord, have mercy. Chil', are you trying to give me a heart attack?"

A few critters scattered into the hallway. I backed away and grasped at my door.

"They're everywhere!" I said.

Mother removed her slippers and began to swat at the intrusion of cockroaches. Melissa danced around on her toes, wailing.

"Delia, what are you waiting for? Kill them!" She slapped away. I looked on, frozen in terror.

•

The morning after, Mother met me at the foot of the steps, holding a notepad and pen.

"Here." She handed me the items. "Write a letter to the head office. Tell them you demand an exterminator."

I gave her a strange look before I could stop myself.

"Go on," she said. "This is important. I learned how to write business letters in the sixth grade. This school system is really behind. Write properly — not all loopy like a little girl. Use a different word so they'll take you seriously. Writing well is how you get people to listen to you. They can't see what you look like. Use that to your advantage."

Leave it to my mother to turn a tragedy into a learning opportunity.

"Delia, don't forget to tell them about the mice," Melissa said, her eyes growing full.

Mother looked at me in horror. I exhaled loudly and filled her in.

After Melissa's discovery, roaches showed up everywhere: the closets, the shower, and the kitchen. Mother had us repackage our non-perishables into mason jars. To my chagrin, she even invited Neville to help. I worried that he would stay the night, like the week before.

Sure enough, at dinner, I sat across from Neville. He tilted his chair on its rear legs. We were not allowed to do that — it ruined the furniture. Father never tipped his chair back. He was a man of class. Mother came to the table with her meal. Strands of her hair floated around her face.

"Did you pack my lunch?" he said.

So, he is staying. Great.

She shot him a look. "This is the first I'm sitting down since I got home. Delia, can you please pack Neville's lunch?"

I clenched my teeth. "Yes, Mommy."

"Can you put more meat than rice?" Neville said. "Oh, and a malt. It's hot in the warehouse."

The sardines went mushy in my mouth. I excused myself from the table.

He turned to Mother. "Did you see the police blockade down the street?"

"There's always something happening out there, but we don't bring it into this house. Work is stressful enough. You know, a girl came in today, only a year older than Delia, and pregnant with twins. Twins."

I turned off the tap so I could listen.

"Her mother put her out. Now she'll be removed as a dependent, which means her mother will be over-housed and she'll have to move, too. A woman's life is cursed."

"Woman's life? What about these boys causing trouble around here? Those young boys." He pointed at me with his fork. "Stay away from them."

I waited for Mother to interject, remind him I already had a father, thank you very much, and that I was a street-smart young lady who knew how to handle herself. But she only stabbed a piece of yam with her fork. What could she say? Our father had shown his cards.

Neville went on about how often the police stopped him that week and how awful young people were. His empty plate sat near the centre of the table where he had pushed it. When I picked it up, I noticed the way Mother had stopped eating to listen to his monologue, her chair pulled up close to his. Her morning's eyeshadow had melted away; she batted her eyes slowly, with the pleased look of a cat that didn't mind being stroked. I told myself it was all an act — a survival tactic. Mother was pretending to be someone else. She needed him to think he was worthy so that he would stick around and help her to forget my father. I went upstairs.

While journalling, I recalled one of my parents' conversations. It happened one evening a year back. We were all in the den having tea.

"A trip to Cuba," my father said. "That's where we should take the kids. I've always wanted to see where my grandfather was from."

"A new house and a vacation." Mother laughed. "You win the lottery, Cliff?"

"We'll be broke, but happy." He winked at us. "Right, girls?"

We nodded.

"Cuba." Mother tapped her wedding rings against her teacup and stared into space. She kissed him on the cheek. "Why not?"

I craved the feeling of excitement when they discussed the future they envisioned and the look she wore when they were together — stripped from her now: the veil of my father's love.

Chapter 6

The Don

September 1993

The Toronto skyline was burnt into the rusting dusk. Wisps of exhaust rose slowly from its ruins; aside from that nothing moved. It was the Friday before the Labour Day weekend, and Mother was out "closing the mall," her last-minute shopping for our school supplies, weeks behind schedule.

Melissa and I kneeled on the sofa by the open window, letting in the dewy air that smelled of damp cement and decaying okra plants from Mother's make-do garden. I'd hollowed out two pen shafts and filled them with talc. We held them up, pretending to smoke as we perused a flyer.

"Free community barbecue in the second court," Melissa read. "All are welcome."

"Hmm," I said. "Mom has errands to run, then she's going out with knucklehead."

"She won't let us go."

"I'm asking anyway."

"You just want to see that boy."

I shrugged. "You may not care about having friends, but in high school I won't spend my lunches hiding out in the library."

"What if there's another drive-by shooting? Barbecues are like target practice here."

"Don't be a drama queen. That happened across the bridge."

She eased down off the couch. "You're nuts. I'm not coming with you."

I blew the last of the talc out of my makeshift cigarette and acted like it didn't bother me one bit.

The next morning, I crossed the hall, then paused at the master bedroom door to rehearse my question. I raised my fist to knock. The door opened to reveal a topless Neville looking over his shoulder at Mother. Along his jawline, a fresh crop of stubble had grown.

"I have to get there early," Mother said from inside. "She overbooks on Saturdays."

He turned and met my cool expression.

"Good morning," he said, like he was prompting me to be polite.

"Morning." I brushed past him.

The bed was made and on the satin sheet Mother had arranged a purse and a sequined minidress the colour of her wedding ring. She stood gazing into the closet, finger on lips. Beneath her eyes, her complexion darkened as if something had settled into it.

"Mm. I never know what to wear to these parties Neville brings me to. Young people dress differently."

I shuffled my feet, drumming up some courage.

She turned to face me. "Sorry — did you want something?"

Yes, tell Neville to get lost. Oh yeah, and can I go outside and meet people my own age?

"Um, there's a community barbecue event —"

"Community," she said. "That's code for charity. There's food in the fridge."

"But —"

She raised her brows and cupped an ear. That meant I'd be pushing my luck to press further. I turned and left before she could throw something at me.

After they left, I joined Melissa at the table. I skimmed the film from her porridge, which she had let grow cold, then I set the bowl on the placemat.

"You didn't ask, did you? Knew it," she said.

"For your information, I asked, and she basically said it was up to me, so I'm going to check it out. Since you're scared and all — you can stay here alone."

Melissa spooned porridge into her mouth and pondered. "What time does it start?"

I smiled. "In a half hour."

The sky was clear besides a single smudge of white cloud, as if God had placed a thumb there to rub something out, then changed his mind. We sprinted like we'd been sprung from traps, legs pumping down the path that snaked its way through Don Mount. Beneath our feet, the building's crumbling exterior littered the pavement in shavings of plaster resembling communion wafers. I pretended they were petals of white roses placed along the pathway by the commoners welcoming us. The path led through an overpass with an enclosed lobby with an elevator and a door to a laundromat — both labelled M.T.H.A. to remind us we were on government property.

Finally, we arrived breathless into the southern courtyard. I drew deep into my lungs the scent of torched red meat. Neighbours around us were dragging plastic chairs into other yards to join others in drinking and chatting while speakers blared. We came to the centre of things — a sand-filled playground, where a sizable boy rammed through the lineup for the yellow tube slide. He disappeared into it, then seconds later, sailed out the bottom and landed on his belly. He bawled. A young woman rushed to his side, snatched him by the arm, and scolded him.

Melissa smirked. "For once we won't be the only ones who get yelled at and spanked."

"Amen to that." I searched the perimeter for our decoy destination and found it. "There it is. This way."

With the corner store in sight, I set off toward it, expecting Melissa to follow. Quickly, I realized she wasn't with me; I glanced over my shoulder. She had stopped — petrified like she was auditioning for the part of Lot's wife in a church play. I followed her gaze to a brutish pit bull sitting on its hind legs, its owner one of a group of chatty teenage girls; our worst fears manifested.

I went and took her by the hand. "Walk slowly."

She squeezed my fingers tightly.

We veered away from them: the thin, fresh-faced girl with an obliterating stare and a midriff the length of one of my arms, the identical twins with the strawberry blond braids and matching gold necklaces with scripted pendants, and the dog's owner, who was lighting a cigarette. She brought it to her mouth, keeping her eyes locked on me. Below her high ponytail, the hair was shaved close — something my mother forbade. She tugged the leash she held.

"Constantine, sit," she said.

Constantine sat on its hind legs.

I became conscious of my knee-length shorts and childish hair clips. An itch arose where the folded rib of my socks dug into my ankles, so I knelt to scratch it. At my sudden movement, the dog rose to its feet, and before I could stop her, Melissa picked up a stone and tossed it. Constantine growled and lunged. We ran.

The barking followed us to the Jug 'O' Milk convenience store at the end of the walk. We climbed the short steps and rushed inside the converted brownstone.

"I told you not to —" I started.

"Hello there."

Offside the entrance, the petite middle-aged owner observed from her glass-enclosed stall. Leaning on the counter was a curvy blond woman wearing a salmon-coloured blouse and blue jeans. She stopped scrutinizing her nails to inspect us.

"Good day," I managed.

They nodded in acknowledgement. I led Melissa deeper into the shop, feeling their stares at our backs. Before long, the storekeeper left her seat to trail us through the understocked aisles. I spotted her in the convex mirror and turned around.

"Yes, can I help you?" I said.

She pursed her mouth, gathering the dark hairs above her lip. "You have money?"

"Of course. We're just trying to find something we like."

"Whose are these, Camille? That new lady?"

The lady at the counter nodded.

"Oh." The shopkeeper drew back.

I recognized the name. Camille Blanchard was the building manager — one of the government spies Mother had warned us about. *Don't accept anything. Don't tell her anything.* Public housing staff were an extension of the system. They'd call the Children's Aid Society or the welfare office to report on the people they didn't like.

"Let's go," I said to Melissa.

"No." She yanked her hand out of mine. "She'll sic the dog on us."

"Is there a problem?" Camille straightened up.

Melissa nodded desperately. I should've left her at home.

"It's not a big deal ..." I told the strangers about our mishap.

Camille frowned. "She is not allowed to have that animal here. That girl thinks she's some kind of royalty. I'll take care of it. Treat yourself to a chocolate bar. Welcome to Don Mount." She stepped past us and out into the street.

The shopkeeper pointed to the candy display. "Well, go ahead. She's the boss."

I declined, however, Melissa, seldom swayed by Mother's grudges, took a chocolate bar and avoided my stare.

Distracted, we strolled outside into an awaiting entourage. The girl stood feet apart, leash in hand. The dog alongside, tongue lolling out of its mouth. Camille was nowhere to be seen.

"What do you want?" I asked, trying to sound tough.

She handed the leash to someone and approached.

"Why'd you tell Camille lies about my dog?"

"I didn't. It was chasing us."

"'Cause you and your lil' bitch sister were teasing him."

Melissa gasped.

"Nobody was teasing your dumb dog," I said, my voice trembling.

"Liar." She reached forward with both hands and shoved me.

I stumbled backward. "Don't!" Tears sprung to my eyes.

A small crowd had gathered. I balled my hands into fists and tried to remember what my uncle had taught me about where to place my thumb so it wouldn't break.

"Hey, Richa, cut it out."

The speaker emerged. It was the boy I'd been watching ever since moving day. He wore a chef's hat and an apron over his shorts and held a greasy metal spatula in his left hand.

Richa rolled her eyes. "Mind your own business."

"This is technically my business. You're scaring away my customers. Come on."

"You're doing that yourself in that wack outfit."

He folded his arms.

She pointed at me. "You're lucky he's here."

To my surprise, she smiled at him before turning to leave with her posse in tow. I turned my back and brushed away a stray tear. When she was a short distance away, Camille appeared.

"Thank you for handling that," she said. "I'd be out of a job otherwise. Perhaps you need new friends." She turned to me and winked. "These two young ladies moved in not so long ago."

He glanced over at us. "I know."

Then he walked away without a word, leaving me standing there. As if he had never seen me before. Like we had never locked eyes. My cheeks and ears growing hot, I was ready to head home when Camille said, "Have a burger before your mother gets back."

"How do you know she's not home?" Melissa said.

Camille raised her thin fair brows and surveyed the complex. "I'm in charge of all of this. It's my job to know."

Perhaps Mother wasn't being completely paranoid after all.

"All right, burgers!" Melissa struck the air with the chocolate bar package.

I groaned under my breath and followed.

On the perimeter of the basketball court, a low cement wall provided a sturdy seat from which we watched the boy working at the grill.

Melissa sighed. "Delia, I'm so glad he came to save you."

I spun around. "You're kidding right? Miss Blanchard sent him. If he hadn't shown up … that girl would've lost teeth. All he did was come over and make googly eyes at her."

"Maybe she's his girlfriend."

"I dunno. Who cares?"

I wondered if my sister had been reading my Sweet Valley High books, which were as off limits as my diary. Just then he started in our direction. We clammed up.

"Here," he said.

He shoved two paper plates in our direction, each with a hamburger. He then rustled two tins of Coca-Cola out of the cooler, which he rinsed thoroughly before offering them.

"We're not allowed," Melissa said.

I took one from him and pulled the tab.

"Thanks." I avoided eye contact — trying not to imagine us being friends.

He asked us if we needed anything else, then removed his hat, and untied his apron.

"Camille," he called back. "Gotta check on Johnson."

A cry went up, followed by barking. Across the way, a flash of crimson fur and fleeing pigeons.

"Would you mind walking them home?" Camille said to him.

"Sure."

Great, now he's really going to think I'm a kid. Though I wasn't angry with Camille. I believed she meant well and found it hard to stay mad at her.

I decided to get a head start, unsure I wanted to talk to him, but he caught up to me easily.

"Slow down."

"We're fine. I'm not afraid of her."

"Richa only picked on you 'cause you're new ... and small."

"Well, I'm sorry I don't look like I'm twenty-five," I blurted out.

He laughed, which made me consider that despite his picture-perfect smile, he was probably a jerk. I wondered if he owned any clothing besides athletic wear.

"So, what's your name?"

"Delia," Melissa said before I could answer. "I'm Melissa. What's your name?"

"Mario." He offered his hand to her.

Melissa shook it and giggled.

"Where'd you guys live before?"

"Far from here," I said. "Hadsworth."

He made a face. "Oh. That's really far."

"Feels like it. I'm not used to living in the ghetto."

He stopped abruptly. "Do you even know what that word means?"

"It means ... poor or like ... lower class."

He stared. "Not exactly. You should really look it up. Don't they have dictionaries in Hadsworth? We have some here —"

"We won't be here long. We're buying a house soon."

"For real?"

"Yeah, my dad's travelling for work right now but when he gets back —"

"Oh yeah, travelling, eh. I saw him yesterday."

"What?" I stopped, feet away from our place.

"You saw our dad?" Melissa said.

"The guy with the freckles and the blue uniform — the one always giving me dirty looks."

"That's our mom's friend," Melissa said, kicking at something.

Mario studied me as if waiting for me to clarify.

"What she said. Anyway, my sister has to go now." I handed her the keys and shooed her away. "I'll be in soon."

Mario waved at her as she slowly backed away.

"Like I was saying, this is temporary." I deepened my voice a little. "My mother works for the government and my dad's, like, almost an architect and we're —"

"Better than us?" His eyes met mine.

"That's not what I was going to say."

"I think it was."

I felt ice cubes form in my throat as I watched his mouth tighten. We stood facing each other, shuffling our feet. Finally, he spoke.

"I gotta go."

"Wait. I didn't mean it … what I said."

"Yeah, you did." He shrugged. "But a word of advice, drop the attitude. The kids at Park Public are rough. You've already made one enemy there."

I considered him. "Is that where you go?"

"No way. I go to St. Albert's. Park Public is a feeder for the Don."

I blinked.

"The Don Jail?" he said, as if I was an idiot. "Haven't you at least checked out your new 'hood? It's literally right there." He jutted his hairless chin northward.

Play it cool, Delia.

"Yeah, so what? It won't be my problem for long," I said.

"Sure. You're not the only one with plans to get out of here, but you'll have to wait your turn. Anyway, see you around, kiddo."

Kiddo?

I hated him, I decided. Yet, I watched him go, hoping he'd turn around and wave so I could ignore him. He jogged over to his unit, opened the door, and disappeared into the interior. I marched into the house and went straight to my room. I snatched my diary from the shelf and wrote about the arrogant boy from across the way. I filled two entire pages.

When Mother returned that afternoon, I went to see her new hairdo. She looked out from behind the coat closet; a mass of shiny black curls covered her head like ocean swells.

"Hi, Delia."

I stared back, open-mouthed.

"Velma was with another client," she explained. "I got stuck with the apprentice."

She rapped the curls with her knuckles, then shook her head at the ceiling as if God hadn't held up his end of some bargain.

It was easy to see where my sister got her dramatic antics. I caught myself giggling.

"It isn't funny." She tried to stay stern but then broke down laughing, too.

I wished she would never stop.

"Did you lose something?" I said.

"My keys."

Just then, Melissa entered, dangling a mass of keys the size of her fist.

"You left them in the car door."

"Oh dear. That's the second time this week." She bit her lip, then seemed to put her thoughts behind her.

"What did the two of you do all day?"

I turned away, unsure if the cold compress had lessened the reddening of my eyes. Mother tended to notice when something was amiss.

"We went to the corner store," Melissa blurted out, "and Delia got beat up by this girl. It's dangerous here, Mom. We have to move."

She had the nerve to look at me. "Right, Delia?"

"What? Which girl?" Mother kept her eyes on my sister.

"It was just a shove!"

Mother ignored me. "Wait — isn't today that charity event, feed-the-poor-kids or whatever?" She moved to the door and cracked it open, letting in a faint hickory odour and pulsing bass.

As she snatched her purse from the chair, she gave me a sharp glance. The sight of her toned biceps as she swung the door shut behind her sent my stomach into knots.

I turned to Melissa. "I'll never trust you again."

"Secrets hurt, Delia." She shook her head like I was supposed know better. "I hope she does find that girl and tells her parents. That'll teach her."

"I don't think that girl has parents." I bolted up the steps.

Melissa called after me. "You're not in trouble. She said you could go … right Delia?"

The phone rang.

Please, God, let it be Dad.

I pulled myself up onto Mother's high bed, narrowly missing her carefully arranged ensemble: jewel-encrusted earrings and a gold necklace placed above the collar of her dress.

"Hello?" I sighed at the voice. "Hi, Neville."

"I called before, and no one was there. I hope you stayed home like your mother said to."

I didn't answer.

"Please put her on the phone." He sounded annoyed.

"She stepped out."

"Tell her to call me. Something's wrong with my car."

"Okay, I will. Bye."

The new development was a good distraction. Perhaps upon hearing the news, Mother would forget about my misstep and channel her fury in another direction.

I skipped across the hall and flung myself onto Melissa's bed.

"It was Neville. Something happened to his stupid car. Wants Mom to call him." I rolled onto my stomach. "I bet he wants to cancel their date."

"You always think he's up to something. He's gonna take her. He promised."

"Wanna bet two bucks?"

"Deal."

"Why don't you like him, Delia? He's nice and he helps us out."

"He's good looking and that's not the same as nice."

I played lookout while Melissa, who was supposed to be helping, attempted the splits in the new pants Mother bought. She was determined to become the next Surya Bonaly — Melissa didn't know how to skate yet. One step at a time.

"Stop that madness or you'll rip your pants, and then you'll really get it," I said.

Mother came into view.

"She's back."

We scrambled for our books and pretended to read on the bed. The front door opened and closed quietly, followed by two thuds as shoes hit the floor. My palms began to sweat as I heard her climb the steps and come down the hall. The knob turned and the door pushed open. Mother stepped in. Her curls had loosened some — she had to be happy about that — but her face glistened with sweat, and on her neck a pronounced vein throbbed.

What had she done?

"I know how to deal with bullies." She stepped toward us. "The next time someone puts their hands on you, come straight to me."

"Yes, Mommy," we chorused.

"As for Mistress Blanchard — I paid her for the burgers and the Coca-Cola you drank." Her voice sharpened.

"Mommy, she was nice," Melissa said.

"Nice? People are always nice when they want something Melissa. Don't be simple. You wouldn't understand how these people think — what they can do."

"And you." She turned to me. "I left you in charge. When I say to stay inside —" She reached down and pulled me up by the collar until I was on my toes. "That's what I expect."

The fire alarm went off. She frowned deeper and released me.

"Go check the pot."

I dabbed my eyes with the back of my hands and left for the kitchen, where our dinner singed in our great-grandmother's old cast iron pot. Melissa joined me and fanned the lingering smoke out the front door while I inspected the food. The goat, which Mother had selected from her favourite Kensington Market butcher, had been meticulously seasoned two days earlier. I reached into the pot and pricked a piece with a fork. It fell away from the bone, tender, but tasted like salted ash. Beneath it, the charred meat had congealed and ruined the rest of the stew. The dish couldn't be saved. *To add insult to injury*, my mother would say — because she had left her "good-good" food on the stove to defend my honour.

"What are you gonna tell her?" Melissa's forehead was rippled with worry lines.

Mother's voice rang out. "Just be honest. You found something better to do — and that's fine, Neville. You're the one who keeps insisting I get out more and enjoy my life."

"She has bigger problems now. And you owe me two bucks," I tried to sound cheery, like I was over it.

Melissa conceded defeat with grace. She nodded and stretched her arm out for a proper shake. I knew she was relieved that I was talking again.

"I'm sorry, Delia," she said. "I didn't know we weren't allowed — and now she's going to be super peeved."

"It wouldn't have mattered." I hugged her, then I remembered something. "So today hasn't been super great, but we still got out and saw people. And we can turn things around."

"Sounds like something Dad would say, but I don't think that'll work with her."

I forced a smile. "I can fix this. Watch me."

•

Not long after, I sought out Mother to inform her of our dinner plans. She was napping, the glistening heap of clothing and jewellery surrounding her like a fallen halo. I put everything away quietly and left.

We concocted a meal from the week's leftovers: steamed basmati rice, corn and peas in butter, and two grouper steaks. I put out the china, silver cutlery, and crystal glasses Mother kept high in the cabinet. I went to wake her.

Midway down the steps she spotted the table. Putting a hand to her chest she said, "If I'd known I would've dressed in my good clothes."

Dinner was a success.

Mother washed the dishes after, and when we had settled into the living room, she said, "On my way home, I passed a lovely park. It's such a nice day. We should go."

"Yes," we both said.

Mother wore her sensible flats and a sun hat. She led us through the back gate, past our neighbours who were enjoying the last bit of summer. We arrived at Riverdale Park in time to catch the petting zoo, where we took turns feeding the sheep. Afterward, Mother and I sat on the hill watching three diamond kites resist the direction of their flyers. Melissa scoured the area for a better spot.

"I wanted to see the sun set." Melissa collapsed onto the grass, looking defeated.

"It's okay, honey. We'll just have to enjoy it from here." Mother brushed my cheek with her hand and set her sights on the heavens. "Look — the colour still comes across the sky ... not as vibrant but we still get a little beauty of our own. I've been thinking of buying a house in the country on a large property where we can look out at the sunset every evening at dinner. Just like my house back home ..."

I raised my eyebrows and nodded as she spoke, imagining this childhood home — where she had lived that secret life before I was born.

She smiled at us like God admiring his good work on the first Sabbath.

Chapter 7

Regent

September 1993

Dear Diary,

High school is the worst. I can't tell the kids and the teachers apart because everyone looks grown up. I sure do miss having Melissa around to talk to. I'll never tell her that, though.

When I got home, Mom copied my timetable into her notebook and started lecturing me. She's such a drag. Then came Neville with his unsolicited advice about staying out of trouble. He's in for a rude awakening when Dad comes back. Grandma is hot on his trail, so it won't be long. Until then we're like those families on the commercials — a bunch of stand-ins. It seems to be good enough for Mother. It must be

fantastic to be an adult and be able to replace anything you lose.

I am
Delia

My trip to school had been an eventless journey of solitude for the
first week. One morning I lay in bed paralyzed by thoughts of an
impending run-in with Mario or Richa. I'd managed to avoid them
both thus far. Mother rapped loudly at my door.

"Delia, are you up? I didn't hear the shower and your alarm
keeps going off."

"Yes, Mommy." I got up and rustled about until she'd left.

Melissa stopped in.

"Why aren't you dressed?"

"I'm trying to avoid an early death."

"Richa?"

I nodded.

"If you can deal with Mom, Richa will be a breeze. Plus, she
won't have her dog."

"Good point. Thanks, Mel."

Sometimes my sister knew exactly what I needed. Mother, too
busy now to help out on mornings, reluctantly straightened my
hair. I was thrilled. I swept it up into a ponytail and pulled out
some strands to fashion bangs. Donning a neon pink track suit
and matching headband, I made faces in the mirror, picturing
myself as better looking than I really was. With that image in
mind, I went downstairs, grabbed an apple, and went out the door
feeling great.

Beyond the trees, I spotted a small group of people waiting for
the streetcar, which was turning onto Dundas Street. I jaywalked

across the road to join the line. A boy in a navy-blue-and-grey St. Albert's uniform made his way toward me.

"Hey," he said.

I froze. "Uh ... hey, Mario. What's up?"

"Your mom is crazy — that's what. I will never cross that woman."

I wanted to disappear. Mother never divulged the details of the incident.

"They're calling her 'Tyson,'" he continued. "My granddad even heard about it. Oh, and he's really sorry about scaring you. Especially now, knowing who your mother is."

"Your grandfather?"

"Yeah, you've met him," he whispered. "Tall, skinny, kinda looks like me ... has a bit of an alcohol problem."

I studied his face for a resemblance while trying to conceal my shock. "Don't worry, I didn't tell her about him."

"Is she always like that?"

"You mean, angry? Only since we moved here."

"Johnson wasn't always the way he is now either. He's sick."

I nodded but he must have read the confusion on my face.

"Alcoholism is an illness."

"Right — of course."

He let me board the streetcar ahead of him and followed me to my seat. I kept waiting for him to take off with one of the other students from his school, but he stood by me where I sat, with his sports bag strung diagonally across his body. I mulled over his connection to the man in the walkway, wondering what his life was like. Mario, with the long skinny arms gripping the metal bar. Grandson of a drunk. Advocate of the people. Sports jock by day.

"Your dad get back yet?" Mario asked.

"No, but soon." I was surprised he remembered. "We've been in touch."

Without thinking about it, I tried to flash my hair, but my ponytail went where my head did. He didn't seem to notice anyway.

When it came my time to get off the streetcar, I offered him my seat.

"It's okay," he said, "My school is next."

I waited at the stop until the passengers cleared off. Through the glass doors, I saw him standing at the top of steps, preparing to disembark. It was only a moment, but he caught my stare and waved. I went to class in a daze, forgetting about Mother. And Richa.

•

Later, during our afternoon debrief, Melissa ate from a bag of white cheese popcorn she had snuck from the kitchen.

"So, what's your new school like?" I asked her.

"The building's old but the kids are nice. The boys are stupid. That's the same."

I laughed.

"What about high school?"

"Great. I managed to dodge Richa and ... I spoke to Mario and he doesn't hate me."

"No way! Good job." Melissa let out a shriek and clapped.

"Oh, do stop. You're too kind." I took a bow and noticed a shadow beneath the door.

I pointed to it. Melissa went quiet. Shortly after, it shifted.

"Do you think she heard us talking about you-know-who?"

Melissa shrugged. "So what?"

"Nothing. Enjoy being ten."

"Almost eleven."

Not long after, I heard Mother saunter into the hallway.

"I won't have it under my roof," she was saying. "I know ... I know ... she needs a father figure. I keep telling you I don't know where he is. Stop asking me."

By the tone of her voice, I could tell she was talking to Grandma Liz. My grandmother was supposed to be looking out for my best interests. She was supposed to be finding out where my father was. Instead, she was talking to my mother about me. I went to my room and slammed the door. When I came to my senses, I prayed Mother hadn't heard me.

Later, she stopped in to say good night but made no mention of my outburst. I remained vigilant, waiting for a spontaneous flogging until, finally, I heard the click of the light switch and darkness fell over the house. I finished a diary entry and looked out at Mario's unit. In one of the bedrooms upstairs, the light was on. A figure appeared and stood at the window briefly. I drew back. Was it him? The person went away.

•

Mario and I ended up on the same streetcar most mornings; our schedules synced, whether by choice or routine — it was hard to say. As if sensing something in the air, Mother stopped by my room more frequently before heading out. One morning, she caught me altering my hairstyle for the third time.

"I hope you're putting equal interest in your studies as you are in your hair."

"Yes, Mommy."

"And your attendance record better be spotless." She stood watching me. "I'm not leaving until you're out of this house."

I gave her a look of frustration.

"You have something to say?"

."No, Mommy, I just don't want you to be late."

She came over and yanked my hair back and twisted it into a single tight braid.

"There." She picked up my schoolbag and handed it to me. "That's all you need for school."

As I went past her, she eyed me suspiciously, but I noticed she remained in my room.

Mario was excited that he had made the school's basketball team. Competition was stiff, he said, and he beat out guys twice his height.

"Good for you," I said, only partly listening.

"What's up with you this morning?" He was staring at my hair.

I fiddled with the braid. "I was in a rush. I don't care what anyone thinks."

He wrinkled the sides of his mouth. "Not your hair. You're too quiet."

Then after a brief silence, he leaned in toward me.

"So, are you gonna tell me later — or what?"

"It's my mom," I said. "She's acting weird."

"This sounds very shocking."

"Oh, shut up. It's different. Ever since my dad left — I dunno, I just can't figure her out."

Before he could say anything, I continued. "He's gone. He's not on a trip. I don't know where he is. That's why we're stuck here."

Nearby passengers turned around. I sank into my seat.

Mario cleared his throat. "Oh. Well, I'm sorry, I guess — if he was any good to begin with."

"He was. He was perfect."

"Bullshit."

"You don't know him. My dad didn't cheat or lie or gamble. That's not our story."

He raised his hands. "I'm sorry your storybook life took a turn. Don't get mad at me —"

"I'm not."

"So, your folks aren't perfect. They're regular people."

Regular. I did not like the sound of it, or of him talking about my family like he understood them.

As I readied myself for my exit, I turned to him.

"If you ever get to know me, you'll realize that I am not *regular.*"

After I'd gone down the steps, I stopped, mortified by what I said. I looked back and sure enough, he was laughing.

During science class, the teacher's words filtered in and out, the conversation with Mario replaying in my mind. I asked for a break and set off to freshen up. When I turned the corner, Richa was waiting by the girl's washroom entrance. A bully at home. A bully at school. My threshold was breached.

She stretched an arm across the doorway. "Aren't you gonna say hi?"

I slapped it away and pushed the door open, locking myself in the first stall. She followed and waited outside.

"I know you've been avoiding me." She tapped her Doc Martens against the tile.

"Why would I do that?"

"Because your mom isn't around to stick up for you."

It was a shame that Mother, who was so good at hitting, had never taught us how. I left the stall and brushed past her on my way to the sink.

"I heard you and Mario are friends now," she said.

"Yeah. So?" My hands were shaking.

"He seems to think you're cool." She adjusted her gold necklace in the mirror.

"You don't have to be my friend — I'm not desperate."

The hall monitor entered and asked us to leave. I glared at Richa openly. It would be a mistake to let the faculty think we were friends. Richa must have caught on. She walked closer to me, elbowing me playfully. I walked faster to put some distance between us.

"Bet your mom doesn't know you're not such a goody two-shoes after all," she called from behind. "That's why I like you."

She turned down the cafeteria hall as I looked after her in surprise.

•

I left my last class ten minutes early to avoid running into Richa on the way home. I wasn't going to make it easy for her to mend fences or whatever she was trying to do. What did Mario say to her about me? Friends? Like he had to vet me first? Like he needed to convince her to like me. Like she was some kind of ghetto monarch. I was so deep in thought, I strolled past Mario on the sidewalk.

"Early dismissal?" he said.

"What?" I turned back and stopped. "Oh, hi. No ... actually I'm getting a head start on your stalker girlfriend or whatever she is."

Mario's expression changed. He rotated the basketball he was holding.

"So, you're one of those people who thinks a guy and a girl can't just be friends?"

"No, obviously. It's the way you two ... never mind. You talked to her about me."

"Richa wanted to talk to you. I said you wouldn't mind. Figured you needed a friend." He smiled like I was supposed to be grateful.

I readied my tongue to tell him off, but then he said, "Plus, I think you'll be a good influence." He bounced the ball against the sidewalk. "Not to mention you're the only girl I've ever known her to be afraid of."

I let him see me look surprised. It was probably the nicest thing a friend had ever said to me. I'd only known him for a short while but I believed him. I trusted him.

We caught the next streetcar, and during our ride we stuck to topics like homework and sports. I steered away from our earlier conversation, afraid he'd ask why I lied about my father. From there, I'd be forced to reconsider other statements I'd made, like Don Mount being a temporary home, or our inevitable move to a house, my not caring if Richa liked me, or that one day I'd wake up and my mother would be happy again. I still believed these things to be true.

Chapter 8

The Fraternal Twins

October 1993

Don Mount was only one of several social housing developments near the downtown core of Toronto. Its grandiose structure boasted a Cappadocia-like perimeter and arched gateways only accessible by one parking lot and adjoining laneways. Not far off, across the bridge, was its sibling, the behemoth Regent Park, sprawled across sixty-nine acres of prime real estate. Though bonded through blood, genetics, and history, Don Mount resembled nothing of its dark, labyrinth-like sibling. However, their shared qualities included their demographic — a mixture of new settlers and citizens, a modern-day Babel spanning two generations. The two joined hands at the bridge, trying to hold back their mother, the River. She was ever moving, slipping through their fingers, enforcing the boundary between their gluttonous father, The Don Jail, and the sole innocent hiding in their shadow, Park Public Secondary School.

There were only a handful of seats remaining in the detention room, one of them in front of Richa. I sat there. She slid a note over my shoulder when Mrs. Cole was distracted.

Thanks for not ratting me out.

No problem. The principal's a jerk anyway.

He's why Mario switched schools after first semester last year.

I read the note twice. He'd never mentioned that they went to school together. Then again, he seldom spoke of himself at all. He probably thought I'd judge him, what with me thinking I'm better than everyone. This would prove that I wasn't.

It had started innocently. A swarm of students poured out the cafeteria doors and into the field, where I happened to be. It was during gym class, and the teacher assigned one section of the group to stretch while the other ran laps. Having done my part, I went for a short walk and became an unwilling spectator of a fight between Richa and an older girl. Perhaps I should've sought out a teacher but I found myself entertained by Richa's agility and prowess. I may have been cheering — yelling, "Go Richa! Get 'er!" — when the hall monitor caught me and dragged me to the office because "bystanders were also a part of the problem." I pled involuntary stupidity and got detention without parent notification.

Halfway through the detention class, most students had left, and Mrs. Cole resigned herself to reading her *Cosmopolitan*. Behind me, the sound of crumpling paper and a book hitting the desk.

I turned around. "What are you doing?"

"Finishing my history essay. It was due last week." Richa picked up her pencil as it rolled away and bit on it.

I scanned her first paragraph. "Want me to proofread that for you?"

She gathered the sheets and handed them to me. "Yes."

She smiled broadly, for the first time seeming more like fifteen years old. I liked her handsome face: her untamed eyebrows, high cheekbones, and beakish nose. It felt good not to be afraid of her anymore, and our truce would make Mario happy. I was making corrections when a note sailed over my shoulder and landed on my desk.

Wanna walk home with me?

I glanced over my shoulder and nodded.

We cut through the football field to get to the main road, but when we came to an unpaved path leading through a complex of townhouses, Richa turned right.

"Hey," I said. "I don't walk that way."

"It's a shortcut. You don't want to get in trouble, right?"

"Yeah."

Only once, I promised myself. Mother would never know.

I pulled the strap of my backpack so that it was snug against me and stuck close to Richa. She said hello to a group of older men who knew her by name.

"You know a lot of people around here," I said, considering the faded bricked homes.

"My grandma lived here for a long time, then she transferred to Don Mount, and my mom stayed and had me and my brothers and sisters here."

The gravel crunched beneath our feet as we walked.

"I don't live with my mom," she said like she was expecting a different reaction from me.

"I figured," I said, feeling bad. Whatever it was that separated her from her family probably had a lot to do with how rough she was. Even the guys at school didn't mess with her, and I suspected it didn't help that she dated a reputed drug dealer.

"My mom's got like five other kids. They're cute, too." She shared her pink gummy smile. "We were terrorists. She couldn't handle all of us and I can't blame her. Grandma let me move in with her after middle school. I was there all the time anyway."

I thought it was wild that a kid could decide to move. All on their own.

"Did you like it ... here?"

She shrugged. "What's not to like? It's paradise."

"No, seriously."

"I know a lotta shit happens around here. People get jacked and shot, but it's so much more than that. It's community. You got family everywhere no matter if you're related. That's what my grandma says, and she's worked for rich people in their houses. She used to be a nanny back in the day. So she likes it here. Although she's always worried about me hooking up with some dude —"

"Let me guess — because you'll get pregnant and drop out of school."

"How'd you know?"

"That's, like, my mom's biggest fear. I'd be better off robbing a bank. Or liking girls."

Richa gripped her stomach and howled.

"Yep, eternal virginity would win me a one-way ticket to heaven."

"You're funny, Delia."

We took a narrow path that ran behind two commercial buildings. Two of the workers stood out back smoking. Their eyes followed Richa as we went by.

"Can I ask you something?" I said. "What did my mom say to you?"

"What didn't she say? I'm not gonna amount to nothing with my attitude and to leave you alone or she's gonna beat me. Blah blah blah. She came to my grandma's house and got me in a whole heap of trouble."

"Yikes. Sorry."

"She's gonna be mad, huh — about you and me being friends."

"Uh ... maybe, but she can't control everything I do."

"Damn straight. You gotta get out more."

The farther into Regent Park we went, the more crowded it became. People poured out of the yellow building lobbies; one man hawked his wares out of a shopping cart. Groups of men stood around drinking and smoking by the fast food shop on the ground level of one building. Music hummed. It was exciting — which was not at all how I imagined I'd feel about it.

When I got home, Mother met me at the door.

"Where were you?"

"Getting extra help with science."

"Mm-hm." She sucked her teeth.

I said nothing else. Less is more when telling a lie.

"How was your day?" I tried to sound cheerful, resting my bag on the chair and taking out my homework.

"Horrible." She shook her head.

I began to fret that the principal had called. I studied her expression, calculating how quickly I could get to the front door if she came after me. Yet, her expression sank. I sat, bracing for news about my father.

"I called in sick today." She set dinner on the table. "Forgot my purse this morning and came back. Your grandmother called and carried on. By the time I was ready to leave, the place was swarming with police." She looked at me wide-eyed. "Right outside the gate with big guns."

Melissa joined us, Toby clutched to her chest. "A boy in my class was picked up by Children's Aid because they took his parents away."

"How do you even know that?" I said.

Melissa shrugged. "People talk."

"Why didn't you tell your boss what happened?"

"And let them know where I live? I would rather die."

This is what Grandma Liz must have meant when she said, "Pride can kill you."

"Eat up. I'd like to catch the news," Mother said.

It's easy to pretend something isn't happening until it happens to you. We finished and gathered in the living room to watch Citytv.

"More on today's drug raid near the Regent Park area ..." said the female commentator.

"That's us!" Melissa said.

Mother put down the skirt she was hemming and sat erect. "Turn it up."

I scrambled for the remote and increased the volume.

The reporter stoically rambled off more details as they showed a clip of a man and woman being cuffed and put into a squad car. I didn't recognize them but felt concerned that they may have been related to the little boy Melissa mentioned.

The camera panned over to a group of residents close by for commentary; the large garbage bins in our parking lot swept across the television.

"Why'd they say Regent Park?" I said.

"It's close enough." Mother hadn't taken her eyes off the screen.

"And how did you feel about this happening in your neighbourhood?" the commentator shoved a mic at a passerby.

"Somebody needs to do something," the person said.

Mother scowled. "Ask someone a stupid question, you get a stupid answer."

There were a few more lines about it before they moved on to a story about a clever raccoon.

I was distracted and missed seeing Neville come into the yard. *Great.*

"Did you hear?" Mother asked him before he closed the door.

"It's all over the radio. Heard they took in ten people."

"This is nonstop. Everyday it's something else. I think a year is too long to be here."

"Now you're worried. What about when they broke into my car?"

His exasperated expression was familiar. I'd seen it on my father's face.

"Sell the house," she said. "With my savings, we could buy something."

We?

"Where's my brother supposed to live?"

Mother went over to him and rested her hand on his back.

"If we get something with a finished basement, he could live there."

He turned around to face her. "You sure are changing your tune. Anyway, it's not just mine alone."

"Your mother is not coming back from Trinidad. She'd be happy for the cash. Jude, too."

Melissa had switched the channel and was lying on her stomach in front of the TV. I noticed Neville staring intently at her, like she was somehow responsible for his decision.

"So?" Mother said.

"It's been two weeks and you still haven't answered me."

"This is about safety."

"Don't change the topic."

"All right. When I see you acting the part, you'll get your answer."

The mood of the room grew cool. I reached for the remote control and switched off the television.

"Hey!" Melissa looked back.

"Upstairs," I mouthed.

As we climbed the steps, I considered my mother's pleading, Neville's mysterious question, and the pensive look he'd given my sister. Back in her bedroom Melissa complained about Mother giving Neville a hard time.

"You're always sticking up for him like he's family," I said. "He should go have his own kids and leave us alone."

"He's too cool to be a dad." She played with her curls.

I squinted at her. "Has he said anything … or done anything to you?"

She scrunched up her freckled nose. "Ew, no."

I searched for signs she was lying — beads of sweat at her temples, picking at her nails. Our parents had warned us about men. She only widened her eyes at me and asked, "Did he do something to you, Delia? Is that why you hate him? I'll go down and tell Mom right now. I'll throw those ketchup chips he keeps buying me in his face."

"No," I laughed. "But I still don't trust him. Neville definitely wants Dad out of the picture."

Though I felt better about Melissa's safety, Mother's desperation was out of my control.

As the night rolled on, I waited for her to show Neville out, but their talk had spawned new activity. They went out and after returning, a loud hammering came from the area beneath me. Perhaps she was asking him to put up pictures. A strange thing to be doing at that hour. The door opened and closed. Finally, I thought, he left.

When I came downstairs the next morning, everyone else was already about their day, including, to my dismay, Neville. In front of him was a large bowl of cornmeal porridge with a side of fried dumplings — Dad's favourite breakfast. I met Neville's gaze when he looked up from his dish. He mustered a charismatic smile — the kind he must have reserved for the women he crossed.

"So, I've been meaning to ask, what's this about you getting beat up?" he said, as I sat down.

I said nothing, so Melissa filled him in.

"This sure ain't Hadsworth," he said.

He kept talking, but I was busy trying to sort out how he managed to worm his way into staying overnight. There was no proof of them having gone out partying, no dancing shoes tossed by the door, no lipstick stain, or running mascara. Just Neville, elbows planted on the table, looking triumphant and all-important, like an exclamation mark. All Saturday, he meandered around in his undershirt showing off his muscles and shoulder tattoo of a lion's head. As soon as he stepped out with Mother to run errands, I called Grandma Liz. The answering machine picked up.

"Grandma, it's Delia. I don't want you to worry but I really need you …"

I spent the rest of the day upstairs, away from Mother and Neville, their voices rolling up through the vents. I called Grandma Liz until I got her — ensuring she was appropriately alarmed. When we were done talking, I shelved my diary next to my collection of Roald Dahl books, then prayed for God to send my father home and Neville into exile, like he did Cain.

Chapter 9

March of the Matriarchs

October 1993

Dear Diary,

Mom came into my room late last night. If she'd showed up sooner, she would've caught me talking to Mario at the window, and then I'd be spending Thanksgiving weekend in the emergency room. When I got back, there'd be bolts on my window like those on the front and back doors.

I'll be fourteen soon, and I refuse to let her completely ruin my mediocre social life. Mario reminded me of that when he stopped by to ask what I was doing for my birthday next month. I think he was stalling, making up things to say. I do the same thing when I don't want to come home. I must have sounded like a fool going on about it. Johnson was probably drinking. Why didn't I ask? Oh no. Am I self-absorbed? I hope not.

I am
Delia

Melissa and I lay on the sheets we'd spread in front of the TV, eating sour cream and onion chips out of a bowl. A massive cookbook lay offside, the page open to a biscuit recipe I wanted to make for Thanksgiving dinner. Midway through *Aliens*, an orange cab pulled up outside our gate. The passenger door swung open and out came an older woman wearing trendy shades and a short fur coat.

"Grandma!" We ran out to greet her.

"Surprise!" She displayed all her very own teeth, including the one with the gold cap.

"You're always right on time." I smiled.

She squeezed me on the shoulder and winked at me, then slipped the heavy coat off her shoulders, and hung it over a chair.

Immediately, she went about examining each room, and I tagged along, watching her expression morphing from bewilderment to disgust as she went.

"When is your mother coming home?"

"Later."

She sighed heavily and pursed her lips. "I knew that child was hiding something. 'Everything is fine,' she said. Everything is not fine. Now tell me something, Delia, what on earth is in those barrels?"

"It's stuff for ... the house." It felt silly to say it aloud.

"What house? Lord Almighty. She and I are going to have a very long chat."

After a quick change, she came down in dark tights and an orange off-shoulder blouse. Broom in hand, Grandma pointed at Melissa.

"You! Put down that remote and find something to do."

"Grandma, how long are you staying?" Melissa said.

"Eh-eh. Trying to get rid of me already?"

"No."

"I'm staying for two weeks. Then I'm going to Jamaica to evict the tenants."

"I didn't know people lived there." I sprawled onto the couch. "Will you move back?"

She shook her head. "After nearly thirty years, it's a strange place to me. Plus, I'd be too far away from the family."

"You should sell it," I said.

"Absolutely not. A woman should never sell her sole property. It's security. Let's say your uncle and his wife split, I'll be out on the street right after him." She pulled the latex gloves off her hands.

"Are they having problems?" I said.

Wealthy people without children. What did they argue about?

"No, no. They're fine. I hope your mother will change her mind and let you visit so you can get to know them." Grandma hugged us both. "You know, your mother and her brothers were close once — almost like you two.

"Like most firstborns, Aretha was the apple of her father's eye. Then she had to share the attention with the twins. They doted on her, but being boys they could never behave themselves. Your mother had these porcelain dolls — gifts from her father. I never liked them because they never had any brown-skinned ones. Anyway, not long after he passed on, one of the twins broke your mother's favourite doll." Grandma paused to chuckle. "From then, she hid everything. I remember, I kept a picture of your grandfather in my purse. Then as I was packing to come to Canada, I couldn't find it. Then I was taking the bedsheets to the wash and guess what fell out of her pillowcase? The picture! I gave it back to her. You ever seen it?"

"I haven't," I admitted.

Grandma inspected the photographs on the credenza, taking the frames apart to get a closer look.

"How old was Mom when Grandpa died?" I said. Mother rarely mentioned him.

"She was small-small, around eight or so. This photograph, with her in the black outfit" — she held it up — "that was the day of the funeral."

I was stunned. Mother had never mentioned that either.

Grandma shivered. "Why would anybody want to remember something like that?"

"She must've been so sad," I said.

Grandma contemplated. "She struggled. See, I'm from a time when life was hard. When people died, we accepted it, else we'd be lost in a pain so deep that even the belief in heaven could not heal."

My hands felt clammy, and I found myself clasping them together tightly. I wanted to change the topic. *My father is alive*, I told myself.

"I'm sorry you lost your husband, Grandma," I said.

Grandma ran her tongue across her gold tooth.

"For a little while, Brent used to ask, 'Where's Daddy?' Then after, he started to say, 'Daddy gone.'"

"It must have been hard for you, too," I said.

Then she got up and went to pour herself a glass of sherry.

Melissa and I stole glances while she moved about, rings clinking against the crystal flute. We waited for her to continue.

"So, what have the two of you been up to?" she said.

"Trying to find Dad, of course." I had been wanting to talk about him as soon as I spotted her at the gate.

"Please tell me you haven't been obsessing over big-people business this whole time."

"But Grandma —"

"Delia, enjoy your childhood. Stop worrying. I have it under control. Now tell me about your life. Your friends."

I swallowed my frustration and allowed Melissa to ramble about the teams she planned on joining. Grandma Liz listened attentively, sipping her drink, stamping violet lipstick along the edge of the glass. I made a brief mention of Richa and Mario. By the time we were finished talking, it had long slipped my mind that she had changed the topic.

Later, Mother came in, stumbling onto the trail of suitcases before she noticed us.

"Mama?"

"Yes, dear. It's me in the flesh."

As they embraced, Mother studied me suspiciously and ran her hands through her mother's short curls. I shrugged innocently.

"Why did you cut it?"

"It suits me. That is what my daughter-in-law says. Was she lying?"

"I don't know. Does she lie? Never met the woman once."

Grandma laughed.

"You didn't tell me you were coming. I would've cleaned up and gone to the store."

"What kind of surprise would that be?"

"You're too much. Let me fix us some tea." Mother went off.

My grandmother squeezed my hand, her rings cold against my skin. "I hope you don't mind me stealing your room. It'll only be for a little while."

"No problem," I said. "Just don't read my diary if you find it."

"But how else will I get a little drama without my satellite TV?"

Well past nightfall, the melodic voices of our matriarchs continued, their laughter and stories filling the recesses of our home. Surrounded by my grandfather's walnut credenza and my great-grandmother's quilt, they breathed life into the ghosts of those long gone. At one point, I thought I heard four female voices in the ruckus as I drifted off to sleep.

•

I pushed through the crowd of students by the cafeteria doors and headed to where Mario stood at the edge of the racetrack. He was speaking to a girl I'd seen around. She was writing on his arm. I took a deep breath and composed myself before approaching.

"What took you so long?" he said.

"Our class was kept back because of one moron."

Mario turned back to the girl and kept talking. He ran his hands over his head as he smiled at her. I tapped my foot and glanced at my watch. When I couldn't stand it anymore, I took off.

"Hey, wait up." He chased after me.

"Stay with your friend," I said.

"What difference is ten minutes gonna make?" He pulled his sleeve over the ink.

"Have you forgotten who my mother is?"

He gave me a strange look, then asked if I was mad at him. I denied it but felt exposed. There are benefits to not letting anyone get too close, otherwise they'll know how you feel even if you don't say. Maybe that's why Mother kept few friends.

We got to the townhouse complex Richa had taken me through. Near the entrance two men stood smoking; a strong, pungent scent of marijuana arose.

"Let's cut through there," I said.

"Nah." Mario glared at them, then put his head straight, and kept walking. "I'd rather get home alive. That's Richa's boyfriend."

I picked up something in his tone. Jealousy? It was hard for me to tell how they felt about each other. I didn't ask.

"Fine, but if I'm late, my mother will literally kill me. And it'll be your fault because you don't like some guy."

"You're clueless, you know that?"

"I'm not stupid," I said. "You don't like him, because maybe back in the day you and Richa were a thing."

My cheeks grew hot.

"Richa and I were never a thing. The guy is an ass clown, and I'm pretty sure he's going to screw up her life. Which brings me to you. Would you please not joke about your mother killing you. She's abusive and it bothers me. I don't want to be disrespectful, but —"

"No, she isn't! She's strict — like other good parents."

He stopped talking.

I was angry with him, I realized — for keeping me in the dark about his love life. He obviously had one and I didn't want him to.

Our arms brushed as we walked slowly, but soon we came to the stoplight by Don Mount Court. We stood watching the cars whiz by, animating the fallen sunset leaves. I found myself leading him across the street to the grove of trees past the convenience store. We tiptoed to the bench, avoiding the earthworms that had burrowed their way out of the rain-soaked soil to slither across the pavement.

Mario removed his jacket and placed it on the damp bench so I could sit.

"Thought you were in a hurry," he said.

"Are you?"

"Not really."

He turned away and played with his hands. "So, are you going to tell me why you're upset or are you just going to be a kid about it? I don't play games, Delia. I'm too old for that."

"First of all, you're fifteen. You treat me like a kid. I see the way you talk to other people like … Richa. Plus, I tell you everything and you never talk about yourself … your girlfriends or why you live with Johnson."

"If you want to know something, just ask."

"Why should I have to? It's just a normal thing to share."

"I don't like talking about things that make me upset." He pressed the tips of his fingers together, thinking.

I waited. Eventually he spoke.

"Johnson raised me and my sister but not by choice. One day after school he picked us up and brought us to his place as usual. That day our parents just never came home."

He was quiet for a little while, then said, "First, no one told us the real reason why. My sister found out from the older folks. She didn't really tell me at first. Then, like, weeks later my dad called."

"Uh-huh." I nodded, urging him on.

He pointed behind us at the grey stone building that stood on a slight elevation, partially concealed by its tall perimeter fence and towering evergreens.

"Don Jail? No way." I looked at him.

A single nod.

"Is he still there? What happened? What about your mom ... sorry ... sorry."

I was relieved to see him nod again.

"It's okay," he said, sounding years older than he was. "My parents were busted taking drugs across the border."

His eyes searched my face for perceived judgment.

I shook my head, trying to reconcile the news.

"After Mom was released, she moved back to Guyana."

"Why'd your mom leave? It's kind of a dad thing — taking off."

"Like yours?" He considered me.

"Well, kinda ... yeah."

"So what, are you worried?"

"I just have a really bad feeling."

Anything could have happened to him: a plane crash, a car accident. Or maybe ... maybe he would meet someone, like Alex's father had. What if he found someone else to love? Anything was possible.

"So, you're staying then."

"No way," I said without thinking. "Eventually, I'll find him. I'll go."

I decided on it right then. It felt strange to commit myself to a plan of my own. Something big. My grandmother and her mother owned land, houses, and yards. I heard how my great-grandmother had laid the first level of foundation for her own shelter. I wasn't going to be some gullible woman abandoned by her husband or dragged off to jail, away from my children because of some get-rich-quick scheme. Mario didn't hear me. He'd already decided who I was. He couldn't see me shifting form right before his eyes.

I was about to say more when I heard the faint squeal of brakes. A car pulled up by the curb. The tinted windows rolled down. Mother reached over and pushed the passenger door open.

"Get in."

I don't know what made Mario reach out and squeeze my hand, but he did briefly, then walked me all the way to the car. I wanted to smack him.

"Uh, good afternoon, ma'am," he said with a wave.

Mother gripped the steering wheel at ten and two as if she were taking a driving test. When she didn't look his way, Mario said, "All right. Later, Delia."

I'd barely made it into the passenger seat when Mother pulled off, and though the ride home was short, she cursed me the entire way there. I didn't dare move until the hem of her tapered long coat went through the car door and my legs stilled from the wobbling.

Inside, Grandma stood on a chair switching out the drapes.

"Well, this is a strange scene." She hooked more pins into the rod. "What has her so riled up? You're not that late."

She stepped off the couch and stood, arms akimbo, studying her work. Mother appeared, thumbing the belt on her waist. I ran a finger over the perfect line of dried scabs on my wrist. The belt had been thin and light — not like the one she was wearing now. My breath quickened.

Grandma is here. I'll be fine.

"Those are the curtains you made, Mommy. They look nice." I tried to steady my voice.

She just kept looking at me.

"Upstairs," she said.

My grandmother stepped down from the chair. "Aretha, aren't we taking the girls out?"

"What for?"

"Early birthday celebration for Delia before I leave."

"Oh, she's already been celebrating with that boy — on the *street*."

"He's just a friend," I said.

Mother, now halfway down the corridor, changed direction and headed toward me. She took me by the shoulders and shook my five-foot frame.

"You think you're a woman, but I'm going to fix you."

"Aretha, are you mad? Aretha!"

"I'm talking to her and she's talking to you. Who does she think she is?"

Grandma's hands covered Mother's — prying her fingers off me. "Delia, go."

I ran away from them and up to my room like those kids on TV, except I left my door open. No need to incite more anger.

"I hate her," I sobbed.

My sister rushed in. "Shh, she'll hear you."

"I don't care." I buried my face in the pillow.

She switched on the radio and went to the door to listen.

"Hey, come here." Melissa beckoned me over.

"You're bending the rules," Mother was saying.

"Your rules can't be bent, they only break."

"So, I should let her run wild and end up with the first boy who tells her she's pretty?"

"She's smarter than that, Aretha. Girls will choose from the choices they have. Who do you expect her to befriend around here?

Why don't you rent in another neighbourhood? Use the money you saved for the house."

"Rent? Again? You've been living the good life too long. Let me enlighten you. The rent here costs three hundred dollars less than the basement. If I rent where I'd like to live — I'd blow through my savings, and I wouldn't even have the security I have here. Not to mention the embarrassing questions I must contend with when I apply in those areas. Where's my husband? What country am I from? You think I haven't tried?"

"But if you just make up with Cliff —"

"Don't put that on me. Why does everyone deserve their own roof but me? Because I will not march to Cliff's orders? I must get everything approved by him. Where I live. Who I can talk to. How to raise my kids. I know you've been calling him behind my back and telling him my business."

"I did no such thing."

"You're encouraging him. You'd like it if he carried me off to Timbuktu — the middle of nowhere. You want me to tolerate things you wouldn't stand for."

"What kind of nonsense … he's their father and still your husband."

Muttering.

"Jesus Christ," my grandmother said.

Melissa and I exchanged a look of shock. Grandma never took the Lord's name in vain.

"Good thing she's leaving tomorrow," Melissa whispered.

"No." I shook my head. "That's the worst part."

•

The next day, I followed my grandmother around the house, trying to convince her to delay the trip. Even with Mother in earshot, I made my case, hoping to hurt her feelings. Eventually, Mother left to attend to Melissa's hair. Grandma patted my knee and gazed off into the distance.

"Don't worry. She's just fishing," she whispered.

"I know," I said. "Sorry she got mad at you."

A wave of a hand.

There was a brief silence between us.

"I guess nothing gets by you anymore. Not that much ever did."

"What's wrong? Did something happen to Dad? Please, just tell me."

"You'll hear from him shortly. Keep that between us."

"Really?" I could barely contain my joy. "I won't mention it, I promise."

Grandma didn't smile. "Keep an eye on your mother and let me know if she gets … quiet."

I nodded, knowing what she meant. It happened before, in Hadsworth.

"Let me ask you something. How often is Neville here?"

"Too often for my liking."

She chuckled. "I can't stand him either, but not to worry. It's temporary."

How long is temporary?

"And how is he — with you and your sister?"

I tried to come up with something incriminating. "Well, he's no father figure."

"What about Melissa? It seems she's taken to him."

"That's because he spoils her."

"Does he? Well, isn't life unpredictable. Don't worry, he's harmless."

"You don't even know him."

"Delia — don't ever tell your elders what they know and don't know," she said firmly.

She went for her purse where she had stashed her passport and pulled out four green bills. "Happy birthday. Buy something other than books for once. Have some fun."

"I will, Grandma. I love you."

Later, my sister questioned me about my conversation with Grandma as we ate cheese sandwiches and sipped on tea. I told her I didn't know anything.

"It's like Dad just vanished into thin air," she said. "Like those people on *Unsolved Mysteries*."

"I'm pretty sure he wasn't kidnapped by aliens."

"Says you."

"Maybe we should report him missing."

"No."

"Why not?"

"Because that's for people who want to be found."

All the way up the steps we traded jabs until we got to the hallway and branched off into our rooms.

I was grateful, though sad, as I sat crossed-legged on the rug helping my grandmother pack. She folded a skirt and pressed it firmly into the suitcase.

"How long is the flight?"

"Four hours. I'll get there late today, but tomorrow I'll be up with the roosters."

Mother came up behind me. "Delia, can you excuse us, please?"

I left quickly and closed the door, then lingered in the hall. They hadn't spoken much since the argument.

"Did you think about what I said?"

"You have work, Aretha."

"I can take time off. We're overstaffed." She spoke with an air of desperation. "I'll invest the money I have left into that house. I've found a lawyer. We can put my name on the title, like Papa wanted."

"A man in a grave has no wants. He had no right to parcel off something that didn't belong to him alone."

"Oh, so to spite him, you'd have me and your grandchildren live in poverty."

"Children don't care about home ownership. They need security and happiness. In the short time I've been here, I've watched you twist yourself in knots trying to be seen as a certain someone, striving for your ought-to-be self. Men have made you rigid and brittle. That's why I haven't picked up another since your father. One was quite enough for me."

"I thought you came to help me."

"Help — not enable." She sounded like she was talking to a child. "Make other plans."

I repeated all my grandmother's words, wanting to absorb her quick wit and sharp tongue. Mother was stumped now and said nothing. There was only the sound of a zip being pulled around a suitcase. All Mother's lies about work had amounted to nothing. I had already informed Grandma of her hectic schedule.

Before leaving, my grandmother stopped in. She stood by my bed and called my name.

"I'm heading out now, sweetheart."

I kept my eyes closed. "Bye, Grandma."

She sat and whispered into my ear. "Do me a favour. Don't get in between your mother and father. I know you mean well, but honey, he's not here to bear the brunt of the fallout, and an absent party makes for a poor foe."

I thought on it. "Okay."

She stood, sending the mattress springing back into shape. I listened to her footsteps put distance between us. They went out of the room and trailed down the stairway on the other side of the wall.

At bedtime, Mother appeared with a clean comforter for my bed. She covered me with the thick blanket.

"Your grandma seemed to have a lot to say."

"Not really. Mostly about my birthday."

"Mostly?" She raised a brow. "What do you want this year?"

To see my father.

"Nothing."

"You're not like your sister," she said. "You never ask for anything."

"I'd like a Walkman, but Dad said they're too expensive."

"When did you speak to your father?" she sounded alarmed.

"It was last year," I said quickly. "He promised he'd get me one when I turned fourteen."

"Anything else?"

"Um, to visit Aunt Marie," I added. "That wouldn't cost anything."

She frowned. "You haven't asked for her in a long while. Why now?"

I opened my mouth, but no words came out.

Mother scoffed. "This was your grandmother's idea."

"No."

"Delia, my mother missed out on a lot of my childhood when she immigrated to Canada. So now, she meddles. You can't make up for lost time. Remember that."

I saw her glance in the mirror at her own reflection.

"I can manage my own kids. I'm in control. So, no, you won't be seeing your aunt Marie."

"Can I call?"

She studied me. "Are you having trouble understanding the word *no* or do I have to get loud and mean?"

"Sorry."

She left me, switching off the light and leaving the door open on her way out.

Chapter 10

The Seekers

November 1993

Dear Diary,

Now that Grandma's gone, Neville's been dropping by again. He even stayed over twice last week, which meant I had to see his stupid face in the morning. Yesterday, he went grocery shopping and bought a huge bag of Melissa's favourite — ketchup chips, which I hate. What's gotten into him? He's not the only one acting strange — Grandma's been calling a lot. When she does, Mom goes off to her room to speak in private. She always thinks people are listening in on her calls. What does she have to hide? Besides Dad, of course.

A couple of missed calls came in from private or unknown numbers who never left a message. I really think it's him calling. He's never missed my birthday before, and I can't believe he ever would. I can't help but wonder if he's safe. Grandma warned me not to worry but I can't always trust what adults say. I missed all signs of trouble before this, and I won't be caught off guard.

I am
Delia

My mother, who considered privacy something ceremonious and fragile, rarely spoke about her personal life around us. After our move to Don Mount, I found myself suddenly on the outside, behind her locked bedroom door.

I believed that only a few people knew anything about my mother's life: Neville, Pearl from church, some extended family members whom she kept at a polite distance, and our grandma Liz. When she called, I was surprised when she immediately asked for Mother, who was so excited by the call that she abandoned all decorum.

"Hi, Mom.... No. When?" There was a long pause. "I'm not calling Marie's house. She and I ... we don't 'take tea.' He'll have to call me." She raised her voice. "Why should I beg? It won't matter. He's going to hold this over my head for years. You know how he is.... Stay out of it."

I considered telling Melissa, who was sitting under a blaring hairdryer, but the risk of misleading her and the ensuing disappointment stopped me. Earlier that day, I stopped her from asking Neville where our dad was — she figured they were friends. It prompted me to try to recall any interactions between the two men. According to my diary entries, Neville's resurgence in Hadsworth started with Mother's falling out with the landlord and Neville's subsequent appearances coincided with my father's absence, which was around the time of the infamous argument. I could still remember that morning, the sharp cold of tile on the bottoms of my feet and my mother's expression, which I now recognized as a look of regret.

•

It was only late fall, but the streetcar was packed with winterproofed students; bulky coats took up the capacity of twenty riders. At each stop, another sea of people boarded, forcing us to breach our personal space. Mario was so close to me I could feel the heat emitting from his chest through the opening in his coat.

"You're so quiet," he said. "What's up?"

I repeated the conversation I'd overheard between Mother and Grandma Liz.

"She's hiding something else." I shook my head. "I want to know. My dad will tell me."

He looked at me. "Will he?"

"What are you trying to say?" I asked.

"What happens when you don't get the answers you want? Like, where he's been and why he didn't come to see you."

Mario had questions. Doubts. As I batted away his rebuttals, I felt more certain that my father had a legitimate reason for leaving. Defending him staved off the unknowns as I argued him into existence, restoring him with a blend of real and imagined characteristics that further reinforced him as a good man. I became deeply involved in the debate.

"He can't just show up and not explain himself."

Could he?

"What if he's like a stranger now? Think about all you've gone through since he's been gone and what he's been up to. Seeing someone isn't the same as knowing someone, you know? People leave and then they just show up. And it's like, who are they at that point? Then what?"

Mario's eyes had never been closer to mine, but he was elsewhere — somewhere I hadn't yet been. I wanted him to come back, to say something to remove the doubt his words had raised. Even so, I kept telling myself that my father was not like the others. He would show up and prove everyone wrong. Then for a split second, I was afraid.

"He'll call on my birthday for sure." I shuffled toward the exit doors.

"Sure," he said. "See you later."

I went out, feeling defeated.

Before I could get far, Mario stuck his head out of a window. "Hey! What are you doing for lunch tomorrow?"

"Nothing."

"I'll come get you."

"Okay." I wanted to scream.

I felt giddy. My preoccupation with my parents decreased as I anticipated my lunch date, and I began to wonder how else I wanted to spend my birthday. It was mine to celebrate, after all. I was learning how to look forward to events — the ones I had control over. Even those unlikely to come to pass.

By afternoon, my fear returned. As soon as Mother went into the basement, I snuck her phone book from her purse. I found my aunt Marie's number and memorized it. On my first call attempt, the automated voice mail picked up. On the fourth try, I started to leave a message. The line clicked, then went dead.

I pressed the phone hook twice. Nothing. I huffed and made for the kitchen. Maybe the phone jack had disconnected.

Mother stood by the plug, the grey telephone cord hanging from her fist.

"So, I guess you want me to be mean."

I stood still while she screamed at me.

Don't cry. Don't give her the satisfaction.

She snatched me by the collar and gave me a shake. I tried to have one of those out-of-body experiences my English teacher told the class about, where she and her brother floated about their neighbourhood into the night. Not that it would block Mother out.

"Looking for your father, weren't you?" I let my tears fall but made no sound.

She shook me again. "What did you tell them about me?"

I met her piercing stare. Her grip slackened.

"Always sneaking around, but I'm a step ahead of you and your father. Cut from the same cloth the two of you," she said. "Remember, he's not the boss anymore. He gave that up. Nothing in this house happens without my say-so. Now, get out of my face."

I went to bed without apologizing or doing any homework. I sat at the end of my mattress, with the lights out, seething. She had been lying to us, pretending not to know where our father was. Our father, who, I realized, was, in fact, our business — even more than he was hers.

•

The next morning, Melissa came into my room singing the birthday song. I covered my head with a pillow, exhausted from having stayed up late journalling my discontent and plotting my exit plan. I couldn't disappoint my sister.

This a new day, Delia. Get it together.

"And there's gifts!" Melissa handed me a box as I sat up. "From me. Happy fourteenth birthday, geezer."

I unwrapped the present, a set of rose-scented bath beads.

I hugged her. "You're the best."

"There's more." She went to the dresser and brought back a larger box and a card.

Inside the card were two red fifty-dollar bills attached by a paperclip. It was signed, "To my sweetest Delia, never change. Love, Mom." I threw the card on the bed. The second gift was a Walkman.

"I can't believe it!" I rummaged through the discarded wrapping for a note and found none. My heart sank.

Melissa studied me. "He'll probably call later," she said after a while.

"Yeah, I bet," I said.

We were both looking in the mirror. "I'm gonna wear something nice today. Mario's taking me to lunch."

She clasped her hands in front of her chest and danced around. "Can I pick your outfit?"

"Fine, as long as it's not pink."

Melissa was already tossing things out of my closet.

•

I was surprised to see Mario in the front lobby of school, instead of outside. He stood by the doors, looking serious. My heartbeat raced as I neared him. I tried to think of something clever to say.

"Hi," I managed.

"Happy birthday." He leaned over and wrapped his arms around me, then pulled back.

I froze. "You, too. I mean ... thanks."

We laughed nervously.

He looked me over. "I almost didn't recognize you with your hair out."

Then he reached out, almost touching it. I drew a deep breath, and he pulled his hand back.

"Yeah, you look different, but really nice. I mean you always look nice, but you know."

I thanked him again and as we went out the doors, I hooked my arm around his elbow and held it there. He took me to a wing and burger restaurant at the corner of Parliament Street and Queen Street. I went for my purse after placing my order, but he stopped me.

"I got it," he said, taking out his wallet.

I stood back to give him some space. I'd watched Mother do the same over the years. I never asked why. I realized that Mario didn't ask why either. It was some strange unspoken understanding. So many interactions were built on this learning.

"No, we'll be staying here," Mario said to someone behind the counter.

I felt like I was supposed to do something. I went to find us a booth.

As we ate, Mario's eyes darted around.

"Relax," I said. "She's at work."

"What about the last time?" He held my wrist and pushed my sleeve up.

I pulled it down. "She's laid off me."

Mostly.

"Johnson says at this age, if your mother hits you, it's a fight." He kept his hand on mine.

"Holy smokes," I said. "Don't be such a downer."

"Can't help it. You don't see the danger, but I'm telling you. It's gonna wear you down."

I rolled my eyes.

"Hey. If you decide to run away, you'll tell me first. Right?"

I snickered. "Run away? That only happens on TV or, like, in houses where the kids are abused."

Or in homes with alcoholics.

"Promise." He was serious.

"Okay," I said.

He raised his paper cup of soda. "Happy fourteenth."

I knocked my empty cup against his.

For dinner, Mother made my favourite meal of oxtail with rice and peas, and afterward, she and Melissa sang "Happy Birthday" over an ice cream cake, like they did every year. Without my father's voice, we were all soprano, no harmony, but I was in good spirits from my fake date with my not-boyfriend.

"Neville's working overtime, so he'll be late," Mother said as she cleared our saucers.

Fine by me.

She even let us stay up late to watch television, even though it was past our nine o'clock bedtime. I kept my eye on the parking lot while filling Melissa in on lunch.

"Mario's so funny," I said. "But sometimes a bit too serious, which is annoying."

"You're always serious."

"Shut up."

"Did he ask you out?"

"No. We're just friends."

"But you like each other. Maybe he's shy. You should ask him out."

"No way."

"Tricia says that these days if you want a good man you have to pick him yourself."

I made a face. "Tricia is twelve, and her only concern should be BEDMAS and how to cartwheel."

Melissa rolled her eyes.

I checked the phone log. Nothing. I returned to the living room and went to the window.

"Looking for Dad?" my sister said.

"No." I turned back to the TV.

•

That weekend Melissa and I were watching a depressing show about criminals on the loose. Maybe it was all the talk about running away, but I suddenly felt grateful for health, strength, and shelter.

And a mother who didn't sell me to her boyfriends or run a crack house. God be thanked for that — but the whole episode just made me more desperate to find my father. My life wasn't the worst, but something was definitely wrong.

I searched through the phone records and discovered that the last call recorded was two days before. How could that be? I leaned against the freezer and studied the phone. The wires were secure, but someone had muted the ringer.

I showed Melissa.

"Look," I said softly. "She's been clearing the calls."

Melissa peered at the screen. "Why would she do that?"

"So he can't call us."

"You're so paranoid."

"Oh yeah? Watch." I went to the phone and dialed *69.

After the second ring, someone picked up.

"Hello?"

"Dad?"

Melissa's face lit up.

"Delia? Happy belated birthday, love — you finally got my message? Do you like the Walkman?"

"I love it. Thank you. What message?"

Melissa reached for the phone. "Can I talk?"

I pushed her hand away.

"I've left plenty, and I gave my number to your mother a while ago. Didn't she pass it on?"

"No."

He went quiet.

"Dad, hi. It's Melissa." She snatched the handset. "Where were you this whole time? Delia and I —"

Mother had come down to see about the fuss we were making.

"It's Dad." Melissa offered up the handset.

Mother gently took the phone and brought it up to her mouth. "Cliff ..."

We left her to explain herself. From outside the bedroom came the sound of rubber slamming rhythmically against the ground. I went to the window and opened it.

"Pssst!"

Mario looked up and saw me. After a peek at our kitchen window, he jogged over with his basketball in hand. He lifted his toque. "What's up?"

"I spoke to my dad."

"Cool. Fill me in tomorrow so your mom doesn't come out and kick my ass."

"Okay. Tomorrow morning," I said.

I watched him practise free throws for a few minutes. I smiled to myself, then remembered not to get attached. Eventually, everyone leaves. I went to take account of my belongings and consider what to pack first.

Before turning in for the night, Mother stopped by my room, where Melissa and I were putting away all the clothing we'd outgrown.

"I've arranged a time for you to see your father," she said.

We cheered.

She looked sad, as if our seeing him was some sort of loss. I piped down.

"You're coming, too, right?" I asked.

"We'll see." She came over and licked her thumb to groom my eyebrows.

I hated when she did it but didn't protest.

"Back to your room, Melissa. Lights out."

"G'night, Mommy. G'night, Delia." She skipped away.

When we were alone, Mother said, "Don't mention this to Neville."

I nodded. Finally, we were on the same page. "Of course. That would be foolish."

She gave me a strange look. I waited for her to berate me for trying to sound "grown," but instead, after a brief pause, she leaned down and kissed me on the cheek.

"No reading tonight. Go straight to bed." She stopped at the door. "I love you, Delia."

"Love you, too, Mommy."

While the others slept, I sat up scribbling notes in my diary. I hadn't thought past my father's arrival. What would it truly mean? I pressed the pen to my lips, surveying the second-hand dresser, the tiny bed without a headboard, and the dirty windows. It was only the first semester. It wasn't too late to change schools — to move.

•

Before my father turned up, Mother had been pressing Neville to be more present. I thought it strange that she would ask this of him, a man who, to my knowledge, had no children. He accepted the challenge with a certain reluctance but was only able to offer what was opportune and within the short span of his wheelhouse. A night on the town. Well-maintained appliances. A warm bed. I resented my mother for her lowered expectations. Over time, however, I noticed her dissipating tolerance of him after the phone call with Dad.

Melissa and I lay on the floor with our ears over the vent, listening to their latest quarrel.

"Where the hell were you?" Mother said.

"I ran into a buddy from work. Emmie, you remember him?"

"No. I remember you promised to get my winter tires."

"Well, Emmie told me Johnny is at Marie's house, so I went to see him."

"You went to Marie's house?"

"Mm-hm. And guess who I saw? Cliff."

I grabbed Melissa's hand.

"Is that so?" Mother's voice got quiet.

"You don't seem very surprised."

"What did he say?"

"Nothing. What are you expecting — a love letter?"

Something crashed to the floor, followed by heavy footsteps stomping up the stairs. Melissa and I scrambled for the bed.

"You didn't go there to see Johnny — do you take me for a fool?"

"I should be asking you that. I know you've been talking."

"What did you say to him, Neville?"

"Nothing to tell. He's so proud anyway, he played like he didn't even know me."

"Next time, meet Johnny at a bar."

"I ain't afraid of Cliff. Never been."

"Don't make me cut you off for good."

"You're going to free me? You promise?" A wicked laugh.

"Sometimes you disgust me. Just take the car to the mechanic and leave the house key on the table. Good night."

Someone descended the stairs and went out the back door.

Melissa looked confused. "So, Dad and Neville aren't buddies anymore?"

"What makes you think they ever were? I mean, clearly Neville likes Mom."

"Like … a girlfriend?"

"Oh, Melissa. You're so precious." I patted the top of her head the way I did whenever she said something simple.

A few days later, a phone call came in, and as usual I rushed to answer it, hoping it would be Dad.

"Hello?"

"What took you so long? I'm looking for Neville — is he there?" Mother asked.

"No. What happened?"

"I'm stranded. I need a lift."

"Should I try him again for you?"

"You know what? No, I'll find my own way," she fired back, finally sounding like a woman who didn't need anything from anyone.

Neville turned up eventually, bursting through the door like a knight who'd shown up too late to save the princess.

"Where's your mom?" he said. "She's been paging me."

"Yeah. She's been trying to get a hold of you but said not to bother."

He sat in a huff and rubbed his reddened eyes. "I have been working overtime, and I haven't eaten. Can you make me a plate?"

I gave him a side-eye.

"Please?"

I couldn't believe his gall. He'd left my mother stranded, and now he wanted to be fed. This is why we didn't have pets. You can't just get rid of them when you're tired of them. I went to the stove and opened the lid of the cast iron pot of salt beef and stewed peas. Although Neville was from the islands, he had an intolerance to pepper. So, I cut a wedge of Scotch bonnet and slipped it into his share where it would be disguised among the finely chopped sweet peppers. I scooped a spoon of rice onto the plate and set it on the table in front of him.

"Thanks."

"Mm-hm."

I rejoined Melissa and lay back with my hands behind my head. From the living room, I heard the chair legs skate across the tile. A succession of quick steps to the sink and then the sound of gushing water. I laughed into the cushion as I heard him rummaging through the fridge.

"What's he doing?" Melissa said.

"Getting what he deserves."

She gave me a strange look and turned back to watching *Living Single*.

We were gathering ourselves to head up to bed when the gate slammed shut and a silver sedan pulled off. I watched Mother come up the walk. She strode in, appearing dry, though it had been snowing for hours.

"So, you're alive," Neville said. "Where's the car?"

"At the garage."

"I'll call Mike in the morning."

"It's not with your mechanic. Good night, girls."

She walked straight through the hall, past the kitchen, and up to her room without asking about dinner. Melissa and I looked over at a visibly irritated Neville. I wondered who gave Mother a ride.

Neville kept to himself until Saturday. We came down to make breakfast and found him polishing a pair of black size-eleven loafers at the table. He stood when he saw Mother.

"I made you something. Sit." He pulled out a chair.

She did as he said, squinting at him as he went to the stove.

"I was thinking it's been a long time since I've been to church," he said.

After an immense clamour he emerged, hands holding bowls.

"Oh, Lord," I whispered, elbowing my sister. "He's finally trying to poison her."

We choked down our laughter and watched Mother cautiously mix her porridge. Neville stood nearby, wringing his hands. It was an embarrassing thing to watch.

"I found Mama's Bible —"

"Not today," Mother said. "There's no room. I'm taking Pearl and the girls."

"Oh."

It was strange to hear disappointment in his voice. Melissa and I hid our discomfort by stuffing our purses with sweets and Jamaican gizzada pastries for the long Sabbath service. Neville sheepishly followed us to the back door.

"Let me warm up the car."

Mother adjusted the cheetah-print scarf around her neck, with the keys tightly clutched in her fist.

"That's all right, I got it." She stepped out into the backyard. "Come on, girls."

I felt a pang of guilt. "See you."

"Bye," he said.

We drove to church, ending a long hiatus. I quietly considered Neville's unusual behaviour while Melissa and I passed notes in the back seat.

Me: *Did you have any of the porridge?*

Melissa: *No way. I poured it down the drain and had dry Cheerios.*

Me: *It was lumpy. I'm starved.*

Melissa: *Sucks to be you.*

Mother drove past Pearl's street.

"Excuse me, Mommy," I said, "I think you passed Pearl's house."

"Pearl?" She met my gaze in the rear view mirror. "We aren't getting Pearl anymore." Her eyes went back to the road.

•

The church was a century-old building situated in a densely packed, residential midtown neighbourhood hidden between the stretch of boutique stores facing the main street. Every Saturday, worshippers' cars lined the treed boulevard for two blocks. We scored a spot close to the door and made our way through the well-dressed parishioners gathered in the foyer. A small group of them were laughing and patting someone on the back.

"Good to see you, brother."

"Yes, yes. Happy Sabbath."

"Welcome back."

One woman spotted us. "There they are," she said.

The man turned. It was our father standing at the sanctuary doors, waiting to greet us.

Chapter 11

The Perils of the Pious

November 1993

Dear Diary,

This is unreal. It's only been two weeks, but Dad's return has improved life by, like, 80 percent. If it feels anything like this when Jesus comes back — I'm in.

Grandma says I should wait a few weeks before I ask Dad any questions. Mario disagrees, but I'm with Grandma on this one. Gotta find the right timing. Funny enough, he's got all the questions. He met with my teachers this week. Thank God my detention didn't come up, or I'd hear it. He also keeps fishing around about why we didn't call him back. I'm trying not to interfere, but if he finds out that Mom screened his calls, he'll be upset with her, and things are shaky enough with Neville lurking. I wish that guy would catch a clue. I think I'll throw him one. One last time.

I am
Delia

Something outside the kitchen window had Mother's attention. Something other than the ice pelting down like marbles, forming a thin sheet of frost. Using a dishrag, she rubbed at an oil stain on her blouse, then she raised a hand to her face.

"I think we should put off church this week."

"No!" Melissa said. "Please, Mommy, can we go?"

"We'll take the bus, so you won't have to drive us," I said.

There was something bigger than salvation at stake.

"Okay, stop harassing me. We'll go, but if the car slides into a ditch, it'll be the two of you digging it out."

Our victory holler drowned her out. She went into the kitchen and returned with our supper.

"You shouldn't be eating this late. I'm sorry."

We shifted our books aside.

"It's okay. Melissa and I had a snack earlier. We're staying up until we finish our homework."

"So we can spend more time with Dad," Melissa explained.

Mother headed for the steps.

"Aren't you going to eat?" I asked.

"If you must know, I'm going to call your father and let him know you girls changed my mind, just as he predicted."

We waited until she was out of earshot.

"Phew. Good thing you got to him first," Melissa said.

"I told you'd she'd try to back out. Let's hurry. I want to clean up, so she won't have to."

Melissa nodded with little enthusiasm.

We ate, then finished our homework, and while Melissa crammed the leftovers into the fridge, I made Mother a plate and called her to the table.

"Thanks, honey," she said. "I almost forgot to eat."

She tightened the belt of her silk robe and took a bite of yam before sitting down.

"I tell you one thing — next week I'm taking my lunch. If that supervisor thinks she can work me to death she has another think coming."

As she was taking us through her day, there was a knock at the door.

"Delia, would you mind? It should be Neville."

I shot her a questioning look. I felt I'd earned the right.

"Well?"

Seriously?

I tried to hide my annoyance as I answered the door.

"Good evening," he said, then stepped in.

"Hi."

He walked past, leaving me to play doorman. He removed his wallet and keys and set them on the table, I observed with curiosity. He went to kiss Mother on the cheek. She shifted out of the way.

"Good night."

Melissa gave him a pitying look. "How was work, Neville?"

"Not bad, thanks for asking."

I shook my head, thinking how easily my sister could be taken in and that I'd have to protect her forever. Run away? Mario must be crazy. I'm the only one holding things together.

Neville made his way over to the microwave and opened the door. "Where's my food?"

"In the fridge," Mother said. "Help yourself."

I hid my glee as he searched clumsily through the pots. Melissa pointed him to the cupboard with the plates. He murmured as he searched the fridge a second time.

"No juice?"

No one answered.

He poured himself a glass of water and went to sit. Mother excused herself.

"Where are you going?" he said.

"I'm finished." She deposited her dishes into the sink and went upstairs.

"Can't wait to see Dad," I said to Melissa so Neville could hear.

He paused before putting the next fork of food in his mouth.

•

The next morning, as I scoured the linen closet for the iron, Mother's room door opened and she stepped out, cosmetic bag in hand.

"Church again?" Neville called from the bedroom.

"If you have a problem with that, Neville, take it up with God." Mother set down her belongings and came over. "Need help?"

"Yes, please."

I wanted to yell at her — what she was thinking, having Neville sleep in her bed while our father was back in the picture?

"Neville, please bring the ironing board to Delia. It's by the window." She disappeared into the bathroom. Soon the shower switched on.

I dragged my feet to the master bedroom door, which was slightly ajar. Neville was easing himself out of the bed. He flung the satin sheets off, and for a moment, I glimpsed his partly naked body before he reached for a towel to cover himself. I stared at my father's younger, more strapping opponent. Did he know what he was up against? As Neville approached, I turned away, afraid he would catch me staring.

I held the ironing board like a shield. "Thanks."

"You're welcome." He lingered. "You all seem eager to go to church today. Special occasion?"

"Guest speaker," I said, with a smug smile.

"Let me guess — Pastor Ellis?"

A chorus of "How Great Thou Art" erupted from the shower. Neville scrutinized the bathroom door.

"Church is full of hypocrites, Delia. Be careful."

I dressed in silence, thinking over what Neville had said; then my thoughts turned to Mario as I imagined how he looked without a shirt. I stopped myself. It was Sabbath. People didn't think about things like that on God's sacred day.

•

Mother gripped the steering wheel, navigating the weary Chevy as it skidded along the sparse streets. When we came to a stoplight, she rubbed her drooping eyes and yawned.

"Only two more years, then I'll be the one taking you and Dad around," I said.

"I can't wait to hand over the wheel."

It was nice to be able to talk about him without her getting angry. Maybe now I could start crossing things off that long list. Things were turning around. I'd get around to Neville soon enough.

"The light's green," Melissa said.

Mother hit the gas pedal.

Our parents' first meeting had lacked the affection I expected, although it was getting harder to remember how they were — before. Maybe this time they'd hug properly and kiss. I tried not to overthink Mother's lack of enthusiasm. Yet when recalling how Mother's face would light up at the sight of Dad, the image of

Neville getting out of bed looking like some kind of pharaoh kept getting in the way.

As soon as the engine died, we bolted from the car into the church. We removed our coats beneath the stained-glass window in the dark foyer. The organ moaned.

Melissa poked me. I looked up to see Father was making his way toward us in a coal-grey suit. We rushed to his side.

"Daddy!"

"Shh keep it down." He put an arm around each of us.

"I got an A on my English essay," I said.

Melissa jumped in. "And I got perfect on my art assignment."

"Really? That's great. I can't wait to hear all about it later."

By "it" do you mean my school project, or the last eight months of my life?

We met Mother at the door.

"Good morning, Aretha." Father helped remove her coat. "You look lovely."

"Thank you." She turned to us. "Get to class. You can see your father later."

"Aw, can't we stay down here. Sabbath school is so boring."

"Melissa, don't start with me."

"Listen to your mother," Dad said. "It's only an hour, and I'm not going anywhere."

I stowed away his promise in reserve, then hugged my parents before heading up to the balcony. From the staircase landing, I paused to watch as they stood an arm's length from each other, talking. Soon, a couple made a beeline for them. A church elder shook my father's hand eagerly, while his wife pulled Mother into an embrace, a stark contrast to the isolation I felt after my parents separated. I figured it was why Mother had stopped attending. When I'd asked if we were going to church, she'd say, "I'm not going back there." I brushed the thought away. It didn't matter now.

Melissa waited for me outside the classroom door.

"You missed it," I said. "They were totally connecting."

Her eyebrows went up. "Good thing we came today. Right?"

After Sabbath school class, we sat in the balcony and browsed through the lengthy service agenda. The announcements were next, followed by the children's story, two prayers, and a fifteen-minute song service. On the second page, I stumbled on the sermon topic, "The Seventh Commandment." I racked my memory.

"Melissa, hand me that Bible."

I took it and flipped just past the first chapter to Exodus. Adultery. I leaned over and scanned the congregation, spotting my parents on a hard, unforgiving church pew in the back row. As if he sensed me, Father looked up and nodded. I waved back. Mother gazed down at her lap, likely reading the agenda and plotting her escape.

Pastor McClelland made his way to the pulpit. At six foot five, his stature added to his self-proclaimed authority as a man of "unquestionable faith." His smile, pressed on like a sticker, emphasized row upon row of teeth and a wide glistening chin. My father called him "shark mouth" — in jest. When he took the microphone from its stand, it became lost in his giant grip. He prayed, then began.

"Thou shalt not commit adultery —"

"Bo-o-oring," Melissa whispered. "I'm outta here. You coming?"

"No."

She shrugged and left for the basement to join the group of other uninterested youth, as I once would have.

The pastor pointed at the crowd as he preached. I followed his accusing index finger to the target. He made a wide arc — everyone. Before, I had found it easier to rationalize my married mother having a "friend." Being in church after having seen Neville in Mother's bed felt wrong. Worse yet, if my father knew about Neville, the sermon would remind him and paint Mother in an unpleasant light. My heart raced as Pastor McClelland roared, sweat streaming down the side of his face onto his long black tunic.

I wondered if there was a sermon suitable for rebuttal, one about a father who left his children and his wife alone to go God-knows-where for God-knows-what-reason.

Melissa returned in time for his segue into Revelation. This was his favourite part, I imagined by his enthusiasm, where he got to remind us that after Christ's return, sinners like my mother would burn in the lake of fire while the non-cheaters ascended to heaven for a thousand years.

"God sees all!" Pastor bellowed.

At this point, Mother placed her laced-gloved hands on the back of the bench in front of her and pulled herself up out of her seat. Father followed.

We met them in the foyer, where Father was handing Mother her hat.

"I told you we wouldn't have to get them," he said, sounding unbothered.

I felt better. "Where are we going now?"

"Boss?" He turned to Mother.

"I was thinking of heading home," she said, shoving things around in her purse.

"Aw, can't we go see Aunt Marie?" I asked. Melissa and I looked at Mother, hopeful.

"Aretha, it's a great idea. She'd love to see the girls."

"It would be an intrusion."

"Not at all." He smiled but his voice was flat.

"But my car ..."

"I'll bring you back before dark. Wait here. I'll get the car warm."

"But ..." Mother said.

Father was out the door with a decisive stride, his dark wool coat fading into the snowdrift before the tall wooden doors swung shut. Mother's expression deflated; her shoulders hunched. We locked eyes, and she looked away. What was her problem? Had the sermon "stuck a thorn in her craw," as Grandma Liz would say? Did she feel judged? By whom, the pastor? God? Certainly, not my father, who was in a great mood and had offered to spend the afternoon with all of us. He was being so nice. Why was she trying to sabotage our happiness and her own?

We waited a few minutes before going out. Father was still chipping the ice from the window of a silver Chrysler.

"Sometimes being early is not an advantage," he shouted.

I smacked my sister.

"That's it," I said. "That's the car that dropped Mom home."

"Dad came to our house?" she said. "Why didn't he come in?"

"Neville, duh."

"Oh — right."

From the back seat of the car, I watched their well-rehearsed routine: Mother fastened her seat belt, then reached for Father's coat and his Bible, which she put along with hers into the pocket of the passenger door. She folded the coat across her lap, then brushed the small crystals of ice from it onto the floor. He nodded at her, then accelerated. This was a good sign. They'd worked things out — and had done so quietly for our benefit. How often had they met without us?

Mother pulled down the visor to reapply her lipstick in the mirror. In our religion, women weren't supposed to wear cosmetics or jewellery. Mother wore both. She never kept Sabbath, nor did she quote scripture in casual conversation.

"Should we pick something up for lunch?" she said.

"Marie's expecting us. I only asked to be polite."

I smiled and relaxed into my seat. He was taking charge without letting my mother realize it. Brilliant.

The snow thickened as we drove farther west, until it was coming down in sheets. Melissa stretched out across the seat with her head in my lap. I stayed awake but kept my eyes closed, enjoying my parents' voices.

"Get a new car," my father was saying. "We've already poured thousands into it."

"Nev—"

My heart leapt as soon as Mother let out the first syllable of Neville's name.

She cleared her throat. "Cliff, I've already been using my savings."

The car hung a left and slowed to a halt, its indicator ticking away impatiently. I peeked through squinted eyes. I saw my father look away. He was upset. I could feel it right through me.

Please say something. Anybody — say something.

"It's Sabbath. Let's talk about something else. The day has been perfect so far — aside from this weather and shark mouth's sermon." He let out a breathy laugh that sounded different from the one before.

"It's not funny." Mother rested her hand on his.

He didn't pull away. "As your mother would say, if we don't laugh then we'll cry."

"Cliff," she said, softly, as if his name meant one hundred words in a language only the two of them knew. Like he was far away, and she was calling him back.

While Mother's carelessness disappointed me, my father continued to show how patient he could be. I assumed he had forgiven her. After all, it was he who had left. She should have been relieved. Yet the way she wrung her gloved hands in her lap reminded me of the moths trapped in the light fixture in my room.

Two large oak trees stood at the foot of the driveway, their leaves plucked away by autumn's greedy fingers. The previous August, when Father had visited our aunt on his birthday, Melissa and I lay on the damp cold ground beneath them, admiring their majestic branches.

"It must be beautiful in the summer." Mother sounded awestruck.

The car pulled up in front of the white double doors, and Father gave the horn a quick press to confirm our arrival. As soon as he opened the driver's side door, we rushed out, only to be stalled by a last-minute chat with Mother, then his inability to sort out the correct key.

Looking at his enormous key set, I wondered where all those keys led. The door cracked open from inside and our aunt peeked out.

"Welcome, family."

Aunt Marie was a thin, statuesque woman with bright eyes and dark skin like my father. They both resembled my grandmother Maureen. Marie was single and childless, which made her the best aunt because she spoiled us rotten. As soon as she we were within reach, she pulled us into the smooth fabric of her dress, smelling of food, baby powder, and hairspray. Then she moved on to her brother. To my mother, she extended a formal hand.

"Aretha, it's been a long time," she said. "You must be freezing. I'll turn on the fireplace."

Melissa and I lingered in the foyer, admiring the curved wooden staircase that led from the upper rooms to the basement. The scent of Murphy's oil soap emanated from the mahogany floor.

Mother poked me in the shoulder. "Don't just stand there."

I went to the kitchen and returned to the dining room with a dish of green beans. I set it down on the farthest side of the long table and sat between Mother and Melissa.

"Cliff, the girls have grown beautifully." Marie marvelled as if my mother hadn't taken any part in the process.

Someone descended the stairway. "I hope they haven't grown too much."

"Uncle Johnny!" Melissa and I jumped up and went to hug him.

Johnny popped up every few years, told a few good stories, then disappeared to a place my parents called "away." Our father spoke of him between deep sighs of concern. Mother responded in monosyllabic sounds, huffing or scoffing.

"Who are you? I don't have any nieces this old. I'm a young man."
We laughed.

He leaned back and considered me. "Child, you look exactly like your father."

"Everyone says that," I said.

He moved to Melissa. "So pretty."

"Isn't that something?" He posed the question to the rest of the table. "You never know how a child will grow."

He walked over and rested his hands on my mother's shoulders with a mischievous grin.

"Aretha. Long time no see. It's good to have the family together again, eh?"

My mother poured herself a glass of sparkling water. "It sure is. Surprised to see you."

"You telling me you didn't know I was here?"

"It's Saturday." Mother wouldn't look at him. "Thought you'd be at the track."

"Let's say grace," Father said before Uncle could respond.

A chorus of "Amens" allowed us to finally plunge into the feast of vegetarian dishes: veggie loaf, Swiss steaks, curried soy chunks, and brown rice. Melissa and I were shameless. Ignoring our mother's warning glances, we piled our plates high.

"That's enough," Mother cautioned.

"Let them eat. Soy is good for the brain and there's plenty," our father said.

Mother shrunk into her chair.

"So, do you live all alone, Auntie?" Melissa said. "This is a pretty big house for one person. Our house is so small and there's so many of us."

I slapped her leg under the table and didn't dare look at either of my parents.

"Well, I'm not exactly alone." Marie glanced over at her brother. "Your father has been good company."

In a glance, a thousand words passed between them, but my aunt's smile never wavered.

"What about me?" Johnny turned to Marie.

"Once in a blue moon your uncle will drop by — when he wants something."

Johnny adjusted the two thick gold necklaces that poked out of his open-collared shirt.

"I'm the youngest," he said. "You're supposed to take care of me."

"We've been doing that for a mighty long time," my father added.

Mother ate with her head down. I saw her wipe her hands against her legs, like I did when my palms were sweating. My father's laughter came in short nervous bouts. Glancing around the table, I felt uneasy. Aunt Marie drilled us about school. I wondered if she had picked up something in my expression. I forced a smile and answered as my father and his siblings nodded from across the table. Mother listened on. None of it was news to her. When we ran out of things to say, it went terribly quiet. Mother was running her tongue over her front teeth.

"May we be excused?" I said to her.

"Sure, but before you go off, clear the table."

Aunt Marie nodded. After, Melissa and I snuck into the sitting room across the hall while our father joined Johnny in the basement, leaving Mother and Aunt Marie alone.

"This is a beautiful home, Marie."

"Thank you. The upkeep is starting to feel like a chore. I'm thinking of buying a condo."

My mother responded in surprise and soon they began an upbeat banter about the trials of working in the public sector. Everyone was getting along. They must have been hungry.

The sitting room was painted in a moonlight grey, and the crown moulding design from the dining room was carried throughout this room. In it were an antique wingback chair, a chaise longue, and a wooden chest filled with family albums. We plunged into them.

"You have such a big mouth," I told my sister.

"I didn't say anything about Neville."

I shook my head at her and tried to remember what it was like to be young and clueless.

The chatter in the other room had reduced.

"There's cousin Emma and Patsy and May ..." I said loudly, naming the people in the pictures. My sister would be too young to remember them.

The voices picked up again. We silently flipped through the albums, marvelling at how we'd grown taller while all the adults grew wider. A faint clinking came from the basement steps. Johnny emerged, glass in hand, ice swirling inside the liquid. Father made for the dining room. He saw us.

"Johnny, come on," I heard my father say.

"Nah — I've had enough serious talk for the day." He sauntered over. Dribbles of liquid tipped out of his glass as he sat near the edge of the rug.

"Now you guys have the right idea. This is fun. This is what family should be doing when they get together." He picked up an open album and pointed at a picture of our parents at their wedding. "Girls, do you know how your parents met?"

"No."

My father popped his head in.

"Johnny, stop pestering the children."

"Cliff, take a seat. I think you need to be reminded yourself. You're getting old, and your memory is not too good."

Father reluctantly took a seat on the chair in front of us.

"Your mom was about nineteen and your dad was maybe thirty," he started.

"Twenty-seven," said Father.

"Yeah, yeah — the point is the two of us took the bus to visit Marie one summer."

"Oh yeah," I said. "You guys lived in Philadelphia and Marie lived here."

"Right," my father said. "We visited Toronto one summer to attend Caribana and ran into your mother and her brothers there."

"Yeah, but how'd you meet. Did you talk to her first?" Melissa asked.

"Heh! Girls, your mother was there all primped up, and it was a big group of them. It was —"

"Johnny —"

"Cliff, let me tell the story, man." Johnny set his glass down beside me.

I winced at the strong sharp scent.

"Anyway, they were easygoing people, a couple of guys and some girls, and we were talking to them. Then I bet your father ten dollars to talk to your mother because he was just staring her down, and it looked bad. Then to my surprise, he walked right up to her and told her she was stunning and that he would come back and make her his wife one day. Just like that."

My father, who seemed to remember this fondly, laughed heartily, clutching his midsection.

"Uncle Johnny, did you pay Dad the money?" Melissa said.

This sent my father's laughter into overdrive until Aunt Marie called us for dessert.

Melissa hurried off with Father, but I stayed back with Uncle Johnny as he went through the photographs. There was one of a great-uncle and others with displaced family members taken in places we'd lived before Hadsworth. Johnny's speech slowed as he reached the bottom of his glass. He snickered at some picture that amused him, his bony shoulders bouncing as he did. When he picked up a large black album, a smaller red one toppled out of it. I picked it up.

On the front cover was a black and white picture of my father's mother, Maureen Ellis, in her nurse's uniform. I flipped through it, passing a few blank pages until I came upon a series of sepia photographs, one of which was a family portrait. I recognized my father right away, standing next to Aunt Marie, in a pair of dark trousers and a light shirt, his skinny neck and long serious face capped with short, jet-black hair. Marie wore a high-collared dress, an emerging beauty with a deer-like aura about her. Then there was Johnny, leaning against my seated grandmother.

His features had changed with age, but he still had the same narrow eyes separated by the high bridge of his nose. He did not resemble his siblings — not due to rogue DNA but because his genes were derived from a more diverse pool. Story had it that Johnny was adopted by my grandmother when she married his biological father: the stocky, pale gentleman standing directly behind her in the photograph. Young Johnny didn't seem to care that Maureen wasn't his real mother. Now he sat grinning into his refilled drink and ruminating on days long gone.

On the last page of the album, there was a Polaroid taken of a group of young people. I began to pick out faces: Dad, Johnny ...

"Hey, Uncle Johnny." I tapped him on the shoulder. "When was this?"

"Caribana, 1977." He pointed excitedly. "That's your daddy and me ... and Brent and Bryan ..." He looked to see if I was listening.

I nodded.

"And that's —"

"Is that ..." I slipped the picture out and held it up to the light.

There, with his arm around my mother's shoulders, was a sturdy, attractive fellow.

"Neville," I whispered, looking up at my uncle for confirmation.

He nodded, taking the photo. "That's my boy. We go way back."

My sister came in with ice cream smeared across her mouth.

"I was gonna bring you some, but you can't eat in here," she said to me. "So get your own. Come on, Uncle Johnny."

He stood to leave.

I grabbed his hand. "Wait, I have questions."

Johnny stared back with glassy eyes and pressed an index finger to his lips. Mother was watching from the front bay window. She began straightening chairs and setting cushions back in place.

"The snow seems to have let up," she said, "and it's getting late."

"Mommy, can we stay?" Melissa said. "Daddy?"

"Melissa!" Mother said. "We don't invite ourselves into other people's homes."

Father interjected. "Aretha, I live here, remember?"

"We have four bedrooms," Aunt Marie said.

"My car — it'll get towed," Mother addressed my father.

"You should be so lucky," he said.

"I want to leave."

I could tell she was struggling to contain her anger. She gripped the nearest chair so hard, I thought she was about to upend it and send it sailing across the room in the direction of someone — whether it was Melissa, my father, or my aunt, I could not tell. For once, it wasn't me.

Aunt Marie turned and left the room looking cross.

I wondered if Mother's outburst could work in our favour. If my father could see what we were dealing with.

"It's not fair." Melissa sniffled.

Uncle Johnny observed from the table, holding his spoon like one would a cigarette. His expression was like he'd expected it all. I wondered how come I hadn't noticed it before — the way my father's family treated my mother. What did they think of her?

In the end, Mother won. My aunt came to the door and discreetly passed me a folded sheet of paper.

"Call if you need anything," she mouthed, then said, "Aretha, thank you for bringing the children. Cliff assures me that I'll be seeing more of them."

"Thanks for lunch, Marie. Lovely home. Truly." Mother offered an icy stare from the steps.

Uncle Johnny joined us in the foyer. We exchanged an uncomfortable glance.

"Next time," he promised.

As the door closed, Aunt Marie approached him, her eyes filled with words.

On the way back to the church, I rubbed my sister's back and hoped that by staying awake, I would dissuade my parents from arguing.

"The house is gorgeous." My mother broke the silence finally.

"Yes."

"It must be expensive with interest rates being as high as they are."

"She makes a good living as a nurse."

"It was nice of her to have us. By the way, is she dating anyone yet?"

"She's happy. That's what matters."

"I find it peculiar for someone to have all that space to themselves."

"People want different things for different reasons. Marie does what makes sense at the time to achieve the best possible outcome, then she decides to be happy with her decisions."

Neither of them said anything more. At the church, Dad cleared Mother's windshield while Mother kicked the snow from the tires before getting in to start the car. They operated like a team even though they were upset with each other.

Just a little bump in the road, Delia.

I could picture Mario's expression when I told him. Okay — a few bumps to iron out.

The car was colder than it had been earlier in the day when the sun had been beaming through the glass. Mother turned the radio dial to a jazz station as we drove down St. Clair Avenue. The last of the store patrons walked below the brightly lit storefronts, mere shadows in their glare. At one point, Mother reached a hand into the back seat, blindly searching as if to check if we were still there. Or if we were really there, I couldn't tell. She found Melissa's knees and patted them, and when she searched for mine, I extended my hand to reach hers. She squeezed it, then returned to the steering wheel. Light from a passing vehicle sent a beam across the right side of my mother's face where a tear had left a blazing trail down her cheek.

Chapter 12

Awakening

December 1993

Dear Diary,

Neville and Mom had this huge blow-up, and this time he was angry. Something about Uncle Johnny having 100 percent proof of something and I don't think they were talking about rum. Ha! Whatever it was — thank you, Uncle Johnny! I was worried when I realized Neville's known my parents forever, but it looks like we've finally gotten rid of him. Things are looking up. Dad hasn't mentioned moving in, but it's only a matter of time.

I'm doing my part, too, keeping the house clean without being told and doing my homework. And since Mario and Richa will be away all winter break, I'll be stuck inside. Mother'll be happy about that.

Speaking of which, Richa's been pressuring me to make a move on Mario. Meanwhile, she's still with that loser she keeps complaining about. I told her to dump him, and she got all upset, like "he buys me whatever I want." Does love make you a complete idiot?

If I can't find a guy like Dad, or maybe Mario, I'm signing up for the bachelorette life like Aunt Marie. She's got a terrific house, an awesome career, a nice car, and all that with no husband or kids. Hell, she's spending her Christmas in Mexico. Can you beat that?

I am
Delia

In the early breaths of winter, Don Mount was a grey granite fortress, and by December we interned ourselves within its walls while snow rained down on us like ash. We listened to the radio, cranking up the volume when any song by Maestro Fresh Wes came on. Occasionally, our father would send up a warning call about us listening to foolishness. Oddly enough — Mother didn't seem to care. She carried on in her cryptic manner, leaving Neville's sudden and prolonged absence unaddressed. At least she was consistent.

•

It was still weeks before Christmas, and our mother was out shopping for her favourite holiday. Outside my window, under the grove of trees, two squirrels skittered about, the sole pedestrians in the court. It had been that way all week, the cold, rutted streets and barren sidewalks. Melissa and I grabbed opposite ends of a bedsheet and started folding.

"That's the second time this week," Melissa said. "I bet she's with Dad."

"Probably, but don't get your hopes up about him moving in," I said. "His job is only guaranteed for a few months. He can't move if he doesn't know where he'll be working next."

Melissa sat, chin in hand. "Being grown-up sounds super hard. I feel sorry for you."

"Don't bother. I won't be living like this. I won't make their mistakes."

After we'd finished the laundry, I called Mario. He picked up on the fourth ring.

"Finally, what took you so long?" I said.

Johnson's boisterous and incoherent yelling erupted in the background. It explained Mario's lacklustre greeting.

"Sorry," he said. "What's up?"

"I haven't seen you all week. Wanna come with us to the store? She's not here."

"Uh, okay. Give me a few minutes and I'll come to you."

Mario seemed distracted — barely greeting us at the door. I took the hint and hung back. Melissa threw her arms around him. That got his attention.

"How's your dancing coming along for the school talent show?" he asked her.

"It's okay. Except this girl Tessa, who thinks she's all that — she's all like, 'Oh Miss, I know how to do that, I take jazz and ballet'— I can't stand her."

He playfully grabbed Melissa's hands and invited her to do the cha-cha-cha. She obliged, the two of them stomping across the frozen grass as they went into the streetlamp light and out of the shadows.

Back at our door, Mario handed Melissa the grocery bag with the milk I'd bought. He glanced back at his place.

"Is it a good idea for you to go home right now?" I asked.

"I'll put on my earphones and lock my door. Get some homework done. At least try. Tia took off to her friend's place. Said she couldn't take it."

"Without you? I'd never do that to Melissa. She's coming back, right?"

"Am I Black?" He waited for my laugh before he went on. "My sister isn't like me. When I go, it'll be for good."

"Did you have dinner?"

"Not yet. There's nothing but beer in the fridge, but I can't buy anything. I'm saving up."

I looked at his shoes and wondered if that was what he was willing to starve for. I let the thought roll around in my head briefly, but someone — a better version of myself — gave me something else to say.

"Wait here."

Inside, I filled one of our lunch containers with stewed chicken and rice. When Melissa gave me an odd look, I explained. We both met Mario at the door with a grocery store bag of food.

Mario peeked into the bag. "No way. She'll kill you."

"Not a chance," I assured him. "She's a social worker."

"You wouldn't think."

I stepped out and shoved the bag at him. "Don't let your pride kill you."

He wrapped his arms around me tightly and kissed me on the forehead.

•

Nearly a month after Dad's reappearance, Mother called us down, I thought to delegate more housework. We found her eyeing a mound of dry ingredients in a stainless-steel bowl. She poured water from a measuring cup into the centre of the mound, then began kneading the dough.

"Tomorrow, your father's coming for dinner."

There was a lingering bitterness in her voice, as if the dinner had been a consolation prize. Neither Melissa nor I made any attempt to mask our delight.

"What time?" I said.

"In the afternoon."

Her phony lack of enthusiasm did not fool me. She was as anxious as we were to fill the empty seat at the table. I rushed upstairs before she could say anything else to dampen the mood.

I sprayed furniture polish onto a dust rag and rubbed a shine into the top of the scratched wooden dresser. Did Dad like the scent of lemon?

"Do you remember the rules?" I asked Melissa.

"Yes. Don't ask Dad questions."

"What else?"

"Talk about the good times we used to have."

"And?"

"Don't mention Neville."

"Perfect."

The dinner was an opportunity to remind our parents of the family we had once been and the legacy they dreamed of fulfilling, and that we, too, were stakeholders in this plan. I inspected Melissa's room and spotted a raggedy Toby propped up on her pillow.

I grimaced. "He's in rough shape."

"Dad's gonna be disappointed."

"Don't worry. I'll stitch him up."

Mother's clothing spanned the entire length of her closet, causing the rod upon which it hung to sag in the middle. I reached into the sea of fabric and beyond it, felt the plastic handle of the Singer sewing machine cover. I pulled the container out and snagged Neville's sole navy-blue suit. It slipped off the wire hanger and hit the ground with a thud. How could she be so careless to have his clothes on display with our father around? It could not be seen. I set the machine on the floor and snatched up the suit. When I did, a plain black box tumbled out of one of the pockets. I reached for it and flipped the top open. A hundred sparks went off in my chest at the sight of a thin, gold band with a single mounted diamond. It explained the question Neville had posed and Mother's refusal.

"Are you okay, Delia?" Melissa shouted from across the hall.

"Yeah. I'll be right there." I shoved the box into the pocket and tucked the suit behind the overcrowded shoe rack.

Our voices were indiscernible chatter beneath the chug of the machine. Melissa stood over me — hands on hips as I worked.

"What if Mom and Dad figured things out and are officially getting back together and that's why he's coming to dinner?" Melissa suggested.

"If that were to happen, it would mean we're leaving. He won't live here."

After coming across the ring, I knew my father would never hang clothes in that closet. Never sleep in Mother's bed. He only came upstairs to use the washroom — and never ventured any place else. Nothing about that reality brought me the joy it once did.

"He'll take us somewhere nice. I'm pretty sure he'd send us to private school," Melissa said.

Melissa pushed the hair from my face and cupped my chin in her hand.

"You're gonna be super sad without Mario, but don't worry, I'm sure we won't move until summer."

"Oh — I wasn't even thinking about that." I avoided eye contact. "Here's Toby. It's a bit of a shabby job, but it's the best I can do."

Now that she had mentioned him, Mario was all I could think about. A growing anxiety began to build at the reality of leaving him.

Buck up, Delia. Dad's back and it is all going the way you wanted.

The sweet scent of brandy-soaked fruit filled the kitchen, reminding me of Hadsworth, where Mother used to bake on weekends.

For Dad's dinner, I wore a white blouse and long green skirt. Melissa picked a polka-dot baby-doll dress, with a matching headband to hold back her thick hair.

"Do I look ... parentable?" She batted her eyes, trying to look innocent.

"Of course, dahling. What father wouldn't want to raise you?"

I watched the clock all afternoon until he arrived — fifteen minutes before the scheduled time. Melissa ran to meet him at the back door. I fiddled with the hem of my blouse until he had recovered from her stifling embrace, then went to greet him.

"Hi, Daddy."

"Hey, honey, you look great."

Mother sauntered in, her flowy coral dress sweeping the floor. We moved so he could properly receive her.

"Cliff ... nice to see you. Thanks for coming." She kissed him lightly on the cheek.

He stepped back to look at her. "Wow. Is it new?"

"New to me!" she said.

He smiled, aware of her thrift-shopping hobby.

"I recognize this shirt," she said, inspecting his collar. "I can tell you ironed it because you missed the important parts."

"Getting the correct seam line is the least of my worries."

After a moment, Mother clapped her hands in excitement. "Let's eat. Someone likes their food piping hot."

"Your mother knows me well," he said to me.

How well do you know her?

I chose the seat next to Melissa to force our parents to sit together, then watched my father's eyes follow Mother back and forth from the kitchen. When he pulled out a chair for her, I found my sister's hand and squeezed. We bowed our heads for grace. He said a prayer, then thanked Mother for her hospitality. She nodded. At dinner, I asked politely for the potato salad and allowed Father to take the first share of the meat before passing it on to the rest of the table.

"Aretha, you've outdone yourself."

"The girls helped a lot." She acknowledged us from under long, dark lashes.

I stared at her often as I ate. It was no wonder she had two men vying for her attention.

"So, girls, about school ... I have some concerns about the curriculum."

"Such as?" Mother rested her cutlery gently on a slant in the middle of her plate.

"It isn't challenging enough from what I can tell."

"I agree. I'm glad you're looking into this. I can't afford to take any more time off."

"Bah, you won't be there long."

Mother tilted her head. "Pardon?"

"Friends of mine recommended a school with an exceptional reputation."

I wondered who these friends were.

"What school is this? And what does that have to do with my job?"

He reached for his glass of sorrel and took a sip. "It's in Georgia."

"No. My answer hasn't changed since you tried to convince me to move years ago."

"And if you hadn't refused me, we'd be further ahead."

Mario. I had finally met a boy I liked, who also happened to think I was great. I saw us driving away from Don Mount and Mario shrinking as we gained distance. I saw his copper skin blend into the elm trunks. His waving arms into branches. I saw him fade into the streets as the road carried us away. My vision blurred.

Melissa stepped on my toes.

I sat up straight. "Dad, is Georgia where Grandma Maureen lives? How's she doing?"

I was happy when he changed the topic to his mother's failing health. Mother played along, though I could tell by the pained look on her face that she wanted to return to the subject. She pulled at the edge of her sleeve and rocked in her seat.

As dinner progressed, I began to experience waves of panic whenever one of them would speak.

"Are you okay, Delia?" Mother said. "You've barely eaten."

"Yes. I'm eating slowly, that's all."

A group of young boys walked by the window cursing and laughing noisily. Father turned to Mother to show he had heard. He turned to us.

"Do you like it here?"

"It's okay," I started.

"No," Melissa said.

I looked down at my plate.

"It's not so bad," I heard myself say. "The people are really nice."

"Yeah," Melissa said. "Like Richa, who picked on you, and now you guys are besties."

Father folded his hands. "In life, friends will come and go. Can't let them hold you back."

"Yes, Daddy."

I disagreed with him, and the words felt strange coming out of my mouth.

Mother insisted on clearing the table alone, so we offered our father a tour. On the upper level, we came to my room. I opened the door and was met with the overpowering odour of furniture polish.

"Is this your room, Delia?"

"Yes, Daddy."

"Hm."

I quickly pointed out mother's bedroom, then diverted to the basement, bringing him to see where his draft table was stored.

His eyes darted about the poorly lit room, fixing on the surplus of barrels against the wall. He wandered among them, his back to us, stopping to test the lids. The ones he found open, he sealed shut with the metal lever.

"It's too dark down here," he said, after a while.

"I bought a set of hundred-watt bulbs," I said.

He looked surprised. "Well, okay then. After dessert, I'll show you how to change it."

"Mom already showed me."

"Oh."

"I wanna learn," Melissa said from the steps, where she felt safe from the mice.

"And you should," he said, "but dessert first. Looks like you're eager."

Just then, Mother called us up. Our father sent us ahead, hanging back to switch off the light so that he would be the last one left in the dark.

Dessert was sweet potato pudding. We ate, then retreated to the living room, where Melissa and I sat on the loveseat opposite our parents, our excitement diminishing as the time for his departure drew near. We listened in as they talked like old friends catching up after running into each other at a train station.

"The current welfare system isn't sustainable," Mother argued.

"It could be a good time to get back into nursing."

I observed them; my father, his posture rigid, sat with his feet apart and firmly placed on the ground. Mother spoke faster than she usually did and kept asking if he was all right.

"Rita, relax."

"I can't help it," she said, with a girlish giggle.

I closed my eyes and replayed it in my head. Held on to it. I knew this docile version of Mother would vanish as soon as our father went out the door.

"Melissa, how did your volcano project turn out?" he asked.

She started to tell the story, then got to a certain part, and began to snicker.

"What's so funny?" he said.

I jumped in. "Uh — it's just that … a mouse got stuck on one of the glued parts."

Melissa burst out laughing. Neville was the one who had lost a sock to her project.

"We had a few mice before and every now and then." Mother glared at me.

My father turned to the window. "Well, I'm not surprised. There is practically no space between your backyard and the garbage. I understand why you'd want to move — believe me."

He nodded at her to convey an understanding of her circumstance, but even though he was surrounded by the contents of his previous home, he was like a stranger judging her. When he glanced at his watch, Melissa went over to sit between them. I studied his face.

"It's freezing outside. You should stay," I said.

"I wish I could, but I'm on the morning shift this week." He stood up.

Mother's smile flattened into a horizontal line across her face. She excused herself and went to the kitchen.

While I retrieved his coat, he inspected the insides of his shoes, flipping them over and tapping the soles to check for insects.

My sister wrapped her arms around him. "Stay."

I pretended not to see her. "It's clear. I checked the pockets."

"Thanks, love."

"Do you think we can spend next weekend with you?" I asked.

"Absolutely."

Mother returned with leftovers packed in a large bag. She observed Melissa.

"Enough," she said.

Melissa released him and fell back to stand beside me. Father straightened his clothes.

"I'll pick the girls up on Friday."

"We'll see."

"Friday," he said.

Mother followed him silently out the door. We grabbed our shoes and coats, then hurried out behind them, stopping at the gate beneath the young cedar, its branches casting veinlike shadows around us. They hugged, then Dad turned around and waved before getting into the car. Mother dawdled by the driver's window. Melissa wiped her face with her sleeve. I should have said something. Asked why he'd left us in Hadsworth. I would have come away with something. I put my arm around my sister.

"I'll show you how to change a light bulb. Come on, let's go inside. It's freezing."

From the living room window, I stopped to watch the sedan ease out into the night.

Chapter 13

A Parable of Hope

December 1993

It was the last week before the winter break, and Richa and I followed each other to our respective lockers to grab our things to leave. She briefly mentioned that her boyfriend, Naveed, was in court and without blinking then moved on to her favourite topic: my non-existent love life. She was dressed in a new track suit and a pair of Fila sneakers she couldn't afford.

Richa snapped her fingers, jogging some memory.

"By the way, that tenth grader — the one who just transferred from St. Albert's."

"Yeah."

"I heard he asked about you."

I put a hand on Richa's shoulder. "From who?"

"The twins. Apparently, dude showed up in the caf at lunch asking for Delia and wanted someone to point you out."

"Is there some other girl with my name?"

"Nope. Someone is talking about you over at that school." She paused to consider me. "Why didn't you tell me you and Mario hooked up?"

"What? We didn't. He wouldn't say that."

"You know how guys talk." She eyeballed me like it was my fault. "They probably asked who he's checking out. I told him not having a girl makes him look like a punk."

"I don't even like him like that."

I'm going to murder Mario. Then Mom will win. She'll have been right about boys — about everyone.

Richa laughed. "Why are you lying?"

"Richa, we're not going out. Plus, I'm not his type. You've seen the girls he talks to."

"He's not into those girls. Mario acts like he's a player, but he's just a nerd who happens to be a wicked athlete. Delia, he's pretending to be cool. He's not like those other guys."

"Other guys like Naveed?" I tilted my head at her.

"Nuh-uh. Nobody is like my Naveed."

"Whatever."

Richa snickered. She found my dislike of Naveed hilarious — almost like she agreed with me. It made me furious.

"The fact is, Mario had to say *something.*"

"No, he didn't, and for the record, I'm not like girls around here. I don't let guys disrespect me. I'm going to give him a piece of my mind."

"Aw, there you go. You're so petty." She pulled out her pack of cigarettes, then looked over her shoulder at me. "Who's that?"

A car idled at the edge of the school parking lot.

Crap.

"My dad."

He stood, hands crossed, outside the passenger door.

I jogged past Richa toward him.

"Hey, Daddy. I didn't know you were picking me up today."

"I can tell. I heard you before I saw you."

We both got into the car.

"Who's your friend?"

"Richa."

"I see," he said. "How did you do on your math test?"

"Fine. I got a seventy-five."

"I see. You seem upset," he said.

"Yeah. I'm terrible at graphing integers."

"Sounds like you would benefit from socializing less and studying more."

"I studied for hours. I'm just not good at it." I drew a sad face on the foggy window, then erased it with my sleeve.

"Since when?"

My father's displeasure was understated but unbearable. *Why is everyone giving me a hard time? When will it be my turn to hold them accountable? When is a good time to ask questions you are not supposed to?* Mario had plenty to answer for as well. My only solace was the unreliable source of the story: Richa's close girlfriends.

At home, Dad reviewed our homework, then served dinner just as Mother arrived.

"There's an accident on the Gardiner Expressway. Take Lakeshore," she said to him as he left.

She joined us. "He made soup! Precisely what I felt for."

Afterward, we played cards and watched the news.

"See? Your homework is done, and you still have free time. This is why it's good to be home early and to have an adult present." Mother's eyes met mine.

"It's nice having him here," Melissa said. "Will he be coming to stay?"

"Oh," Mother said, "I couldn't tell you, my dear. He's a man with options. You can't ever predict what someone with options will do."

We left our mother watching an old black and white TV show and retreated upstairs. Melissa settled in with a book while I called Richa to complain about Mario some more. I sat in the hallway, the phone cord wrapped around my fingers, listing all the reasons I didn't like him. After the call, I found a contemplative Melissa in her room, book tossed to the side.

"You're still mad at Mario? He said you're his girlfriend, which means he likes you."

"No, it doesn't. There's more — and no, I'm not going to tell you. And stop eavesdropping."

"It's not rocket science, Delia. Obviously, you're worried about your reputation. Tricia says girls like you never end up happy."

"Tell Tricia to keep my name out of her mouth."

Everyone was full of unsolicited advice.

I caught the early streetcar to school to put distance between Mario and me. I tried to read a book to take my mind off things, but I kept losing track of my spot. Things didn't get any better. At school Nicole cornered me in gym class to ask about it, and at lunch, the twins advocated on Mario's behalf while Richa stood by, tapping her feet, giving me the "I told you" stare.

The school day ended with an assembly. I was the first out the door, hoping to get a head start on the crowd. I had everything settled. I would cut him off, return the mixtapes he made me, and pay him back for all the food he'd paid for while we hung out. Then I turned the corner nearest to my locker, and there he was.

"Excuse me, you're blocking my way," I said.

"Hold up, let me explain." He stepped aside.

I opened my locker door so hard the mirror fell off.

"It's not what you think. Me and the guys" — he lowered his voice — "we were shooting the shit. Just talking guy stuff. Then this one idiot …"

He picked up the mirror and rambled on until the dismissal bell went off and the hallway erupted. As I was locking up, a girl wearing a miniskirt and thigh-high stockings stepped in between us. I wondered if she knew it was two degrees outside.

"Hey, I came to your last game. Do you remember me?" she asked him.

She swung her ponytail over a shoulder and addressed me. "Oh, were you two talking?"

I looked her in the eye. "Move."

She made way for me. Hanging out with Richa had its benefits.

"Sorry, I have to go," I heard Mario say before joining me as I went out the side door.

Sometimes I wished he wasn't so damn polite.

It wasn't Dad's day, so we walked back without fear that he or Mother would run into us.

"I'm sorry, Delia, I know you're pissed, but it just slipped out. They asked which girl I was with, and Kwame from second court said your name. I just didn't deny it."

"Did you tell them that I'm sleeping with you?"

He looked genuinely shocked. "No. Who told you that? Richa?"

"You left it up to their interpretation, and now people think I'm easy. Some guy came to my school looking for me like I was having a sale."

He broke into laughter. "That's not what happened. He just wanted to vet you. See if you were up to par. They do that."

"That's not fucking funny. It's demeaning."

"I know, I know." He groaned. "I'm sorry. I told him not to. It just got out of hand. They're good guys. I promise."

"Are they? Well, that doesn't help me because now they think I'm taken."

"Is that a problem?"

I noted his change of tone.

"What if I was interested?" I shrugged my shoulders.

"Wait." He stepped in front of me and placed a hand high on my chest. "What are you saying right now? Interested in what?"

"In one of your teammates?"

"No, you don't want what they're interested in. If you think about it" — he was talking faster and faster — "I did you a favour. The whole point was to make sure that nobody would mess with you."

"Great. No wonder I'm the only single girl in our grade."

I tried to walk around him, but he stepped to the side to block me, narrowly missing my boots.

"I don't think you should hang out with Richa anymore."

"Richa is not the problem. Last I heard, you were checking out that girl on the track team and also — you're not my man."

He threw his head back like I'd slapped him.

Richa had let it slip that a girl had taken an interest and that Mario hadn't exactly discouraged her. His eyes were darting around, like he was mulling things over.

"Richa!" he said. "Why do I tell her anything?"

It was a stupid question and he knew it. Aside from me, who else would he tell? Sounding remorseful, Mario asked to carry my heavy knapsack. I let him. I wasn't as angry anymore but didn't want to let on. He still hadn't asked me out or even admitted to being interested. Maybe everyone was wrong. Maybe we were just friends. We walked the rest of the way home in silence, neither of us straying too far away from the other.

•

For days, I had been successful at avoiding Mario. Realizing that I had strong feelings for him that he didn't reciprocate made me uncomfortable. I thought if we saw each other less, the feeling would go away, but one morning there he was, dusting off a seat for me on the 505 streetcar. He must have gotten on at the previous stop.

"Hey," he said.

"Hey."

"Still mad at me?"

Still talking to that girl?

I'd rehearsed my response with my sister, who kept insisting we patch things up. I had to be mature, apparently.

"I don't hold grudges. Anyway, you've been a good *friend*. I'm not gonna freak out the first time you make a mistake."

He gave no obvious reaction to my insult.

"I didn't tell them you did anything."

"Yeah, but still, you could've said something."

"True. My fault. So, what about that guy. You gonna talk to him?"

I gave him a look.

"Got it." He leaned back in his seat and looked around to see if anyone had heard.

I changed the topic to the new developments at home and was taken aback by his empathy toward my mother. He soon revealed his true thoughts.

"I keep thinking how much of a hard time I give my mom. I just don't understand why she didn't stay with us or take us." He raised his shoulders. "And I feel bad because my dad is here, and I don't really give him much grief."

"My grandma says it's easier to take things out on the people who are around," I said.

"True."

The transit operator called out the next stop.

"This is me." I stood up.

He studied me and smiled. "You look good."

I snapped my fingers at him. "I know."

Then I went out the doors.

Chapter 14

Blindsided

January 1994

Dear Diary,

Dad came by on Christmas morning but only stayed long enough for brunch and to watch us unwrap our gift — a computer. I love that thing so much. Don't worry, diary, I won't trade you in for WordPerfect. Dad bought Mom a new Bible and hymn book set engraved with her initials. I don't think she liked it. I guess one out of two isn't so bad.

I got Richa a journal. She wasn't thrilled but I bet one day she'll use it. Everyone needs somewhere to write their feelings out. It sure makes me feel better. I've even started a list of things I want to do this summer. Richa thinks she can score us tickets to the TLC concert. We were hoping the Nirvana tour would stop in Toronto, but it's only going to Vancouver. I can't wait to get older so I can go wherever I want and live my own life.

I am
Delia

We stepped into the hazy void of the new year, entranced by its enticing optimism. My father's impromptu school pickups made it difficult to see Mario. So on his sixteenth birthday, I told my father that I had an early dismissal and asked him not to pick me up. Now that I was older, my relationship with my father had become more difficult. It was not something I'd considered. I found myself afraid to make him cross and desperate to stay innocent in his eyes. A part of me believed this would keep him close. So I seldom asked questions and pretended to agree with him. The more I lied, the easier it became.

•

I met Mario at his place. He didn't invite me in, which usually meant Johnson was on a binge.

"I'm surprised you showed up," he said. "Are you sure your father isn't around?"

"That's rich, coming from you. You're always working or practising."

"Yet I still make time to see you."

"Stop picking a fight. How's your birthday so far?"

"Uneventful. Do you know that today skin will freeze within ten minutes of being exposed? Why couldn't my mother have chosen another month to have me in? Right — because I was an accident."

"So was I," I said. "My parents got married because my mother got pregnant."

"Oh, you're one of those kids," he said, patting me on the back as if he felt sorry for me.

I shrugged him off. "They were in love. Although I think it was my dad's idea to get married. He's a little older and more traditional."

"No wonder he's so churchy." He pointed at his own chest. "I was the proud product of two people who would rather take money from the collection plate than put any in."

I chuckled. "What were they like together? Do you remember?"

He smiled a little. "They're still together."

"What?"

"They're apart physically. That's all."

"How is that even possible?"

He looked annoyed. "Two people just have to decide. Simple."

It's his birthday, I reminded myself. *Be kind.*

By the Jug 'O' Milk convenience store, we stopped so Mario could help the shop owner pour salt over the store steps and sidewalk.

"So did they call?" I asked when he rejoined me.

"Mom called this morning but as for my dad, who knows? It's still early. Johnson stayed up until midnight so he could be the first one to say 'happy birthday.' Then he brought me a beer."

"No way."

"Yeah. He's hilarious, but I'm getting worried. He's having trouble keeping up with his meds on the evenings when I'm at work."

"That sucks."

"Yeah, well, anyway, yesterday I found five birthday cards in my locker."

I hated it when he changed the topic from something serious, but I went along with it.

"From girls, obviously. Your many fans. Anyone I know?" I tried unsuccessfully to tone down my sarcasm.

He stopped walking. "Are you mad?"

"Why would I be?" I stopped as well. "It's not like I'm your girlfriend, remember?"

There. I said it. I had tossed the ball onto the court for play.

"Well, of course not — you couldn't be."

"Why not?" I blurted out.

"Because," he said, smugly, "I don't have a girlfriend. I'm sixteen now. It's time to sow my oats."

I groaned into my purple scarf. It was my own fault. Boys were less mature than girls, and Mario was no exception. He was so deceiving with his rational responses, his muscles, and his swagger. He walked faster, forcing me to quicken my short steps. I wanted to hug him and push him into the fire hydrant all at the same time.

By the time we got to the main road, the snow had melted right through the lace holes of my shoes, dampening my socks. Sneakers looked more fashionable than boots, but they got you nowhere in the winter. The storefront of his favourite food joint had a glass bay window littered with the newspaper clippings of its glory days, a compilation of reviews yellowed from age. Inside, hardened grease clotted the ceiling and ventilation fans with a thick mustard sludge. Behind the counter the owners, an elderly Chinese couple, were going about their business at the fryer.

"Hey," they said to us.

We waved. The wife thanked the customer who was dropping a coin into the tip jar.

It was Camille.

"The birthday boy is here." She made a minor fuss with the owners.

I settled in a seat looking out at the street and removed my shoes. I placed my feet against the heater and blew into my cold hands. Camille sauntered over. She slipped into the booth; her massive jacket draped over the table.

"Are you guys on a date? Don't worry, I won't tell your mother, but you'd be smart to stay away from Richa." She leaned toward me. "Glad you're making better choices.

"So where does your mom work?" Camille asked. "I mentioned her to a friend who works at the welfare office downtown, but she didn't recognize the name."

"She works for another region, outside of Toronto," I said.

"That's why she comes in so late," she said. "It's tough being a single parent."

Mario set down the tray. "Thanks for paying, Camille."

"Oh, I can pay for my own," I said.

"Not a problem. I already took care of it." She stood and offered Mario the inner seat but didn't sit down again.

"Thanks," I said.

The bell on the counter rang.

"My order's up." She grabbed her coffee.

"Finally," I said when she left. "She's nice but so nosy."

"You sound like Johnson. She's just lonely."

"Well, maybe she should move to the Bahamas to be with her husband."

"She has a son from her first marriage. She shares custody."

"Good grief," I started then stopped myself. Around Mario I always felt judgmental in my opinions. "How is the new job going?"

"It's easy. Cash registers aren't rocket science. When are you coming by?"

"I don't know. With Dad around, I can't go anywhere."

"But he's been back for half a second," he said, flustered. "How's that going, by the way — the return of the magician who made himself disappear for months?"

"Why are you being so nasty?"

"I'm sorry, but this guy, I mean, I've seen him — I get it. He seems like the perfect dad — yet he still hasn't apologized or, I dunno, explained why he didn't call. Now he shows up and you're supposed to drop your friends?"

"He didn't say I couldn't hang out with my friends."

"Did you tell him about my parents? Is that why he won't let you talk to me?"

"No. I don't want him to think I have a boyfriend. Mom tells him lies about me and gets me in trouble."

"That's nuts. Delia, you're like the perfect daughter. Johnson can't stop saying how intelligent and well-mannered you are. Delia this and Delia that. You're always doing chores, taking care of your sister. You cook all the time and you get good grades."

I wanted to record him so I could listen to it on repeat.

"Is he coming today? Do you need to rush back to meet him at school and pretend you had class?"

"No."

"Good. Let's go to the mall."

"Why?"

"To shop. Are you really a girl? Sometimes I wonder about you."

We took route 505 to the Eaton Centre. I watched him shop for shoes that looked exactly like the ones he already had on, and a new jersey. Boy shopping was about as interesting as buying pads at the pharmacy. Our expedition improved when we decided to see a movie. I insisted on paying.

On the way home, I fell into talking about my father's desire to take us away from "Dump Mount Court," trying to convince Mario that my dad was great.

"I'll believe it when it happens."

"Okay, I'll shut up about it."

Maybe he was a little envious. I'd be, too, if my parents left me with an unfit guardian, but instead of going out on his own, which he was now old enough to do, he was choosing to stay. If I didn't dread the idea of him leaving me, I'd tell him, *Mario, sometimes it's in one's best interest to cut ties.*

We came to the park, where a slight young boy wearing only a windbreaker busied himself making snowballs. Mario called to him. He looked up, wiped his runny nose with his sleeve, and made his way over.

"Hey, buddy, where's your mom?" The kid pointed up at the second floor.

"Well, you can't be outside like this. Come on." Mario took his hand.

I waited inside the staircase, where it was warmer. Mario returned alone.

"I like that you guys look out for each other," I said.

"You guys? Seriously, you're still saying that? Oh, right, Daddy's going to save you from the ghetto and take you back to the suburbs."

A brisk gust of air swept in from the open street. I pulled my coat tighter. "I'm not as excited to leave as you might think. What about you? In a few years you'll be off to become a big sports star."

"You'd be happy that I was gone?"

What is happening?

"No! I meant —"

When he smiled, I knew that he understood.

"Or we could both stay," he said.

"What?"

"Me and you. We could stay here and run this place. Our parents can kick rocks."

This was new. I shoved my hands into my pockets and listened.

He pointed at the court. "First, I'd put up a new rim with a net. A fresh floor. Paint. Then put some rafters up. No Blue House. We'd plant gardens. All the kids would have the best of everything."

He nudged me.

"Well, I guess that would make you a Don. You'd be … the Don of Don Mount."

He licked his lips and nodded at me. "I like that. What about you? What would you do?"

"I'd rent the entire upper floor and renovate it. Make a massive penthouse."

Mario looked serious. "Can't do that. It's government property."

We burst into laughter. We were close to my place and saw that the kitchen light was on.

"Your mother might be there."

I shrugged. "She gets angry no matter what I do, so I might as well do what I want."

"What if she tells your dad?"

"If he wants to control my whereabouts, then I guess he'll have to live here."

"Well," he said, "I'll be available tomorrow for your therapy session."

"Stop it."

He was right. I'd taken leave of all my senses and rather than going home, I circled the yard and walked Mario back to his unit. It was quiet.

"Thanks for hanging out with me and paying for the movie. I feel like a chump."

We stepped toward each other, then inched back a little. I looked around. Our neighbours were making their way home, heads down. When I turned to face Mario again, he was closer, leaning in. I stood on my toes and stretched my hands around his neck.

"Happy birthday," I said.

As I pulled away, he caught my elbow and brushed his lips across the side of my face, edging down to my mouth and pressing in with a touch as light as the wings of a hummingbird.

He smiled shyly before going in and closing the door.

I lingered outside until the warmth of him left me — for the first time noticing the snow drifts climbing the corners of the complex. I could feel tingling in the tips of my fingers. My lips and neck burned all the way up to my earlobes.

"Hey!"

I looked up. He was at his bedroom window. "Go home."

As I approached my door, I took one last look up just as the setting sun licked the tips of Don Mount Court's walls, its last glow bittersweet.

When I got in, Melissa was eating dinner. The fork fell out of her hand when she saw me. She was barely able to get the words out of her stuffed mouth.

"You're in so much trouble."

"Why?"

"Um … because it's almost five thirty."

"Delia Ellis, get up here!"

Mother sat cross-legged on the edge of the bed, phone to her ear.

"You deal with her." She threw the receiver down and brushed past me.

"Hello?"

"Delia, where were you?" my father asked. "You said today was an early dismissal. Your mother says you didn't have school at all."

"We're on an exam schedule; it's different every day. I was right around the corner."

"Which corner? With who? Child, if I wasn't at work, I'd be on my way there. This isn't like you. Were you with that boy your mother keeps talking about — Mario?"

"We hung out. That's all." I tried to sound confident.

"Let this be the last time …"

He lectured me for a few minutes more before asking to speak with my mother. I paused outside the door.

"Grounded? Rubbish! I need to cut her down a size ... easy for you to say, I'm doing this alone ... well, I'm not the journalist Jojo Chintoh — I can't be everywhere all the time."

Their quibble didn't worry me. They needed to remember how to parent as a unit, and circumstances like this would continue to highlight the problem. If it required my getting in trouble every now and then, it would be worth it.

Dreamlike, I drifted off into my sister's room on an emotional high. I decided to let her beg for the details, then reveal very little. She was still eleven, and the gap between us was widening quickly. To tell her that Mario kissed me seemed innocent enough.

"No way," she said, when I told her.

"Yup. He definitely likes me more than a friend."

"Well, I guess I can tell you about Curtis." She bit her bottom lip.

"Who's Curtis?"

"My boyfriend."

"Your what?"

"Yup. And yesterday he kissed me on the lips. Just a peck." She threw herself onto the bed and kicked her feet. "He's so cute!"

I should have known my sister would one-up my moment. I made her promise to point out Curtis the next time I walked her to school.

In my diary, I documented every part of my day, including a reminder to threaten Curtis, then turned off the light, and went to see if Mario was still awake. Mother had taped a plastic sheet across the window to keep the cold out. I gently peeled back one corner of the barrier, cringing at the mould growing on the sill. Across the way, Mario's silhouette moved about. I watched for a while, mesmerized, then lay in bed. I had forgotten to eat dinner and hadn't studied for my English exam. I had angered my father for the first time since I had eaten my sister's baby food, and my parents were still not living in the same house. I let myself imagine that things would stay exactly this way. I placed my hands behind my head, untroubled, thinking of Mario and how wonderful our time spent together had been. I didn't know it then, but through sheer defiance, I was able to experience something wonderful. Houses are nice but I wanted *this*.

I was drifting off to sleep when the door swung open, smashing into the wall. I jumped up. Mother appeared at my bedside. She reached down and grabbed me by the scruff of the neck. I fought her off, backing away until I hit the wall.

"Listen to me," she screamed. "The only reason I'm not going to cut your ass tonight is because of your father. The next time you're late from school, just keep walking right past this house." She straightened her robe, turned, and left.

The force of the door shutting behind her sent my diary toppling from the shelf. I left it there until I had stopped shaking, then lay awake for most of the night, the last one left in the dark.

Chapter 15

The Waning Moon

February 1994

Dear Diary,

The honeymoon is over. Instead of moving in together, Mom and Dad are just splitting the work (us). I'm losing my mind trying to keep track of my stuff. Having two homes is not as glamorous as Alex made it seem. I feel home*less*. All I have is two different people bossing me around. I got a big fat zero on my lab report because I forgot it at Aunt Marie's. Then I thought I packed my diary only to find it on the bookshelf when I got home. I'd have a heart attack if either of them got a hold of it. I need to get it together. I asked for this, right? I wanted him to come back.

I am
Delia

The middle school gym was transformed for the winter talent show; the rafters were set back against the wall and chairs put out on the wooden floors. Mother and I sat in the third row from the front of the mobile stage just as the MCs, a pair of giggling sixth graders, addressed the crowd. The student performers lined up outside the doors awaiting their call onto the stage.

Mother leaned over to me. "As soon as Melissa's finished, we're leaving."

She was miffed. I couldn't tell if her mood was due to my father choosing work over Melissa's performance or the bills set out on the table. My sister's set was near the end of the event, despite Mother's protest to the supervising teacher to make it the first. The audience applauded as a group of three dancers took the stage. Early in the routine, someone bumped my shoulder. I looked up.

"Daddy!"

"Gotcha!" He kissed me on the forehead.

I moved seats so he could sit between us. Mother slapped him playfully on the back.

"What?" He laughed. "I wouldn't have missed this for the world."

But you have missed things. You've missed a lot.

I closed my eyes and swallowed, pushing the thought to the back of my mind. I leaned on his arm, his dark green sweater stiff, scratchy, and reeking of detergent. I told him he needed to use fabric softener, and it cracked him up. Melissa nearly lost her footing when she spotted us during her dance number, but for the remainder of the act she twirled and sashayed across the stage with a newfound burst of energy, executing her final act with a near perfect splits.

We stayed for the whole performance without Mother trying to leave and after the final act, my father turned to me.

"I could go for something salty with lots of grease."

"Queen Wings," I said. "It's so good, and cheap."

We met Melissa at the door. She was all smiles.

Mother turned her attention to me. "So how did you hear about this place?"

"Friends from school told me about it." I sensed her making a note to revisit the topic later.

•

After we ate, my father studied me as he wiped his lips with a napkin.

"This reminds me of a place your mother and I used to go to when we were young called the Steak Shop. It's near St. Clair and Bathurst."

Mother shifted closer to him. "It's still there, you know?"

"Really? We'll have to go sometime."

"Yes, I can't wait," said Melissa.

A lone female customer seated in the booth across from us got up and came over.

"You have a beautiful family," she said to my father.

He rested a hand over one of Mother's. "Yes, we do. Thank you."

Back at the station wagon, Melissa and I waited in the back seat, witnessing their lengthy goodbye. They stood inches away from each other — the distance between them shattered in the cramped diner bench. They kissed for such a long time I had to look away.

"I told you it would happen this year," Melissa said.

With a small pit of doubt and fear lodged in my gut, I returned her high-five and joined in her jubilant dance.

•

Routine is important. Without it, chaos ensues. It was the first thing my parents established once they rekindled their makeshift fire. In Dad's absence, our family was like a puzzle with a few missing pieces; now we were shattered glass. Neither of my parents wanted to give up the freedoms they gained in their time apart. Our lives became scheduled and monitored. The new normal, the business of family. Gone — the magic.

The dollar store shelves were filled with pink and red heart-shaped items, which prompted me to ask my father what he had planned for Valentine's Day.

"Nothing, we're working," he said. "Why?"

"I think Mom would appreciate a night out."

Dad gave it some thought. "Don't worry," he said. "I'll come up with something."

I contemplated whether my father was ever a romantic. He incorrectly assumed his efforts thus far had made up for his absence. I had to do something.

We helped Mother select an outfit for her date — an easy task given her extensive wardrobe.

"It's not like him to celebrate Valentine's Day," she mused as we ransacked her closet.

I had taken note of her cool reaction to the dinner proposal, the way she'd pursed her lips and said, "Okay," with a side-eye in my direction.

"Do you like this?" I pulled out a red, fitted cowl neck sweater.

She shrugged. "You're in charge."

Heavy violet drapes hung against the wall behind her, concealing the awful whitewash paint she dubbed "Metro-housing crème." There came two light knocks at the door, my father's signature. Melissa answered wearing one of Mother's church hats.

"Not yet. She's not ready."

"Hurry up, Rita. We're not going to the Shangri-La. It's just a steakhouse."

"All right, all right." Mother slid lazily off the mattress. "When did the two of you get so bossy?"

I shrugged and folded my arms.

She threw her hands up. "So — are you going to watch while I get dressed?"

Melissa and I filed out and lingered in the hall. We heard the spray of her perfume atomizer and the jingle of her bangles. She stepped out.

We marvelled. Father appeared with a single blue long-stem rose. She gave him a look — almost like she was asking permission, before taking it. Engulfed in the vanilla and rose notes of her perfume, they left for their date. We ogled them from the master bedroom window, swathed in the heavy drapes resting against our backs like capes. On my way out of the room, I stopped to absorb the space: the open closet door, the overturned jewellery box on the dresser, among its spilt contents my father's stainless-steel watch with the broken band and Mother's gold bracelet. I sifted through the pile with a finger. Their wedding rings were missing. It was clutter of the best kind — a domestic disarray I had longed for. I could hear light notes of music in my head. I pictured them dancing. *Will there be music at the steakhouse?* I should have asked.

"Isn't this great?" Melissa asked me, without wanting a response. She was rummaging through a makeup bag of Avon nail polish. "We all have a valentine."

It was clear that she was trying to get to me. I bit my tongue.

"You never know."

I rolled my eyes, but the scene had already begun to play out in my head. A chivalrous Mario, in uniform, greeting me at the door with roses, but he frowns and pulls away. The flowers are for someone else. The fantasy collapsed, leaving only a sinking feeling that materialized into a stomach ache.

"It's a made-up holiday," I said.

"Yeah, okay, whatever. You're starting to sound like Mom."

Though she was too young to articulate it, my sister wanted to say that my dismissive approach to my desires — happiness, belonging, joy — was to contest any feeling of hope. Hope had usurped failure to become my greatest fear. In the years ahead, my sister's passing comment would become my internal mantra and a disquieting judgment.

Around ten o'clock, someone came in. Dinner didn't turn into a full night out. I listened as one set of footsteps climbed the stairway. A deep sigh followed. From my bed, I could see in the mirror that Mother had stopped in the hallway. A night cloud shifted, and in the moonlight, I saw her hands reach up to remove her earrings, then necklace, and, finally, to wrestle the rings from her left hand. She held the hand away from her, spread her bare fingers, and considered them before moving on into her bedroom.

I rolled onto my back and stared at the blank ceiling. How terrible was it really, just us three? There was a distinct link between Mother's misery and the men in her life. Maybe she wanted to be loved but not owned, to give of herself and not surrender all of herself. I could relate.

•

I set my alarm a half hour early to give me time to get dressed before catching the streetcar with Mario. Melissa stood at the table shaking the last of the Honey Nut Corn Flakes from the cereal box.

"Is that cereal? That's not a meal," Mother called down.

"How does she know?" Melissa mouthed in disbelief.

I shrugged.

"I'm late for volleyball practice," Melissa explained.

Mother leaned over the edge of the staircase. "When you faint at school — don't call me. By the way, Delia, have you seen my keys?"

"No." I stirred some instant oatmeal in a bowl of boiled water.

"Help me find them and I'll give you a ride to school."

In frustration, I dropped my spoon. It let out a loud clang as it hit the bowl. Mother stopped her climb upstairs abruptly and came stomping down.

"Did your hand slip? Was the spoon too heavy?" she said.

I didn't respond. She wasn't looking for an answer. She shot me a disgusted glance before heading up.

"Well, have a great Valentine's Day," Melissa whispered as she eased out the door.

"Wait," I said, rushing to her. "Tell Mario I'll be late."

She nodded and hurried off.

Having lost my appetite, I ate only a few spoonfuls of my meal before tossing the rest down the kitchen sink drain, then went on another scavenger hunt for the keys. I searched the usual places: the front seat of the car, the locks, her purse, and the pockets of her coat. It took twenty minutes before I finally found them tucked behind the seat in the couch, after which I hurried to the second floor.

"Mom, here they are."

She was in my bedroom, the mattress lifted and the bare box spring in plain view.

"Oh." She let it fall. "Thank you."

I held my breath. Just the week before, I'd hid my diary there.

Mother smoothed the sheets on the bed before taking the keys from my outstretched hand.

"Ready to go?" she said.

I eyed the space behind her, wondering what else she was looking for besides keys.

"Delia?"

"Uh, yeah. It's okay. You should go straight to work. You're late and I have gym anyway."

She glanced at her watch and shook her head, rattled. "That's probably best. The last time I went in late, someone had gone through my files. It's my supervisor. She installed cameras in the smoke alarms, too. I'm going to report her to the union ..."

She looked at me — or through me, rather, carrying on the conversation alone.

I was eager to be away from her. The last thing I wanted was to be trapped in a small space with her, unable to escape. What would we talk about? What could I ask her? Nothing. I imagined as an adult, when I looked back at my childhood, memories of my mother would be a series of old stories and delegations. I put on my headphones, hit the play button on my Walkman, and headed out without saying goodbye. Music filled my insides — all the songs I loved. I was playing a mixtape that Mario had made for me.

The freezing rain turned the entire courtyard into a trap. I alternated between a light hop and short slides along the ice on the way to the crosswalk where Mario stood waiting on the other side.

I walked up to him, trying not to look excited. "I told Melissa to tell you not to wait."

He shifted from one foot to the other. "I know."

I couldn't tell whether he was angry or cold.

"I got you something." He reached into the front pocket of his sports bag. "I know you don't like real chocolate, but I knew you'd like this."

I thought back to Melissa's unrelenting enthusiasm. That bugger.

"I love white chocolate." I hugged him. "But I have to warn you — I didn't get you anything for Valentine's Day."

"Valentine's Day? What are you're talking about?"

His eyes diverted from my displeased expression, and he quickly sought out his wallet for his fare.

"You're a jackass," I whispered at his back, letting the screech of the streetcar drone out my voice.

•

After school, I walked home with Richa.

"What are you waiting for?"

"There's no point in dating. What are we going to do any differently?"

She inhaled her cigarette and looked at me in a way that made me feel childish. "Listen, you are trippin'. Girls are literally falling over him. They go to all his games and they're hot."

I gave her a dirty look.

"If you don't believe me, go and see. At least know what you're up against."

"Whatever. I'm not a stalker. Plus, I can't afford to be late again. My mother will kill me."

"You're still getting in trouble for that? Your mom is scary as hell, but you need to stand up for yourself."

"I'm fourteen."

"So, she can't really hit you. Tell her you'll call the Children's Aid Society."

"Tried that. She handed me the phone then told me to call the ambulance, too."

Richa howled. "Well, when I was your age, my grandmother tried to rule me, but I wasn't having it. Soon you'll be in the tenth grade. Boys aren't gonna holler at you if you're hanging out with your sister."

Richa often implied that my relationship with Melissa was a hindrance to my social life.

"You should come to the all-ages party at the community centre this Friday. It's freaky Friday, baby." She laughed obnoxiously and began to dance.

I dodged the cigarette she was recklessly waving around. There were times when I questioned our friendship. This was one of them.

"Yeah, I'll be there," I said sarcastically.

Richa hacked and coughed through her laughter. I found it impossible not to join her.

"You sure you don't wanna come to Regent with me?" she said.

"I have homework."

And your boyfriend is an idiot.

We parted ways at the intersection before the bridge. I continued straight toward home, thinking more seriously about attending the party, while Richa cut through a townhouse complex leading south.

At home, Melissa was sitting in front of the computer. I threw my knapsack and coat on the couch behind her.

"You trickster. Who knew you could keep a secret?" I tickled her.

"I'm a vault."

I narrowed my eyes at her.

"He may have paid me to keep quiet."

"That makes more sense."

She went into her backpack and pulled out a plastic-wrapped bundle of red candies.

"Look, Curtis sent me a candy-gram."

"That's nice. Hey, what are you working on?"

"Touch typing. Mom said I have to do this for one hour every day."

"Bummer."

"It's not so bad. Miss Phillips had me type up the trip forms. She said I'd make an excellent secretary."

"Better not tell Dad that."

Mother called while I was cooking. I balanced the phone between my ear and shoulder as I broke up the corned beef in the pan.

"Hello."

"Delia, I'm waiting for the maintenance supervisor to change this lock so no one can break into my office anymore. I'm staying to watch him, so I'll be late."

"Okay."

"Oh, he's here." The click of the receiver.

I thought the call was strange. There was something panicked in her voice, and Mother feared nothing besides disposable cutlery and bad credit. *She'll figure it out,* I told myself. I was done worrying about her.

I tried to imagine what a party would be like without a birthday cake and balloons. *Electric Circus* was all I could envision. Occasionally we stumbled upon the live dance show while flipping the channels late at night. I began to plot the details of my escape. Kids on television made it look easy. Wait until Mother falls sleep. Tie a sheet to something sturdy (like my archaic dresser). Toss sheet outside window. No. Too dangerous. Sneak down the steps and out the door — the front door. Not the one below Mother's bedroom. If caught upon my return, Mother would call Father and he'd show up with his packed bags, ready to move in.

When Mother came home, she checked in on us, then called her friend Pearl. It was late, but she was energetic. She spoke rapidly and loudly as if she wanted us to hear.

"I told the maintenance supervisor I'll sue. I could tell by the look on his face that I was right — he gave her the key. They're all in on it."

I found it concerning that my mother, who was such a good employee, was having trouble with her manager. My father was right. Mother needed to change careers. This job had her acting all funny. No job was worth that.

•

We were all sniffling. The cold my sister had picked up spread throughout the entire household. Mother had good intentions when she aimed to fix us with a proper meal, but at dinner she fanned herself with one hand after tasting her chicken soup.

"I'm sorry," she said. "I got to the pressure cooker too late. The peppers burst."

"It's delicious," Father said, between mouthfuls. "Not as good as mine."

I searched through my soup for the slimy discs of sliced okra swimming about in the spicy broth.

"So, I have good news."

We all set our spoons down.

Father smiled. "I spoke to Carl. It's a go. He wants me there in a few weeks."

Mother turned to him. "Isn't he in Philadelphia?"

"Georgia, actually. About forty minutes out from Mom."

She pushed her bowl away.

"It's a senior-level position and better yet, it's not a desk job." He stood up. "Can I take your dish?"

Mother stared into mid-air with a look of shock, but still she handed him the dish.

"Is this a sure thing?"

"Absolutely." He turned to us. "Ready to go?"

"No," I said. "We have to wait until summer."

Father looked at me quizzically. "Delia, I meant to go to your aunt's."

"Oh."

I handed him my dish without making eye contact, then went to pack my travel bag.

"I can barely hear anything because of the stupid tap," Melissa said from the doorway.

"Let me try." I moved her out of the way and stood in her place.

"Good news," my father was saying. "You'd have your house."

"You mean *your* house."

Someone turned off the tap.

"If I have no job," she said, "how am I supposed to contribute?"

"Aretha, we talked about this at dinner. Why are you acting like it's a surprise? When the girls are settled in school, you'll go back to work."

"After I get a green card, which takes forever."

"What or who are you really holding on to here?"

"My life."

"In marriage, there's no 'my.' That's what got you in this mess."

"Girls, your father is ready to go," she called.

Downstairs, I found him busying himself with his coat and shoes, the loudness of his activity signalling his anger. Great. It would be another weekend of him seething and Aunt Marie trying to cheer him up. Mother stood nearby, arms folded like a stubborn four-year-old. Melissa and I navigated their silence and made our way out. Father got into the driver's seat and slammed the door behind him.

"See you on Sunday," Mother called to us from the door.

Her voice was firm, not sad like I expected. Almost as if she had been waiting since their dinner date for him to bring this up so she could shoot him down.

My father alternated between the two left lanes, speeding occasionally in his attempt to reach the Caribbean grocery store before it closed. Between periods of tense tight-lipped road rage, he conversed with us.

"All that talking — and now I'm going to miss it."

"Can't we go tomorrow?" I asked.

"I like my fish fresh and since tomorrow is Sabbath, I'd have to wait until Sunday."

When did he become so boring?

Melissa piped up. "Dad, are we really moving away?"

He glanced at her in the rear-view mirror.

"It's up to your mother, but if it were my choice, then yes."

"But then Mom would have to quit her job and leave her friends," she posed.

"She'll get a new job," I said, looking at my father.

"If you get a job closer, you can live with us," Melissa continued. "Married people are supposed to live together, and the father is the head of the household. That's what the pastor said."

"Did he now?" my father said.

I could feel the shift in emotions. Melissa's eyebrows furrowed. I sensed her curiosity brewing.

"Daddy, how come you won't stay with us? Not even overnight. Neville slept over."

Any other reaction would cause more of a spectacle, so I switched on the radio, hoping to distract him from the horrible thing my sister said. I couldn't even look at her. Our father pulled into a plaza, put the car in park, and removed his seat belt to look back at Melissa.

"Melissa, you're old enough to know when you've overstepped."

"Yes, Daddy."

"Let's stop with these questions then." He turned around. "And another thing. Don't mention that man's name when I'm around. He's a friggin' pest. Been lingering around for years like that little boy you have around you, Delia. I know the type. Don't fall for it."

He started the car and didn't stop driving until we got to the house.

At Aunt Marie's, Melissa left her bag unopened by the door and went upstairs to the guest room. At the sight of her tear-stained face, I wanted to hit her.

"Hey," I said to her. "You're not going to ruin my entire week-end. Get your bag and put your clothes away."

She did what I asked, tossing her clothing into the drawers unfolded.

"I don't like it when he talks to me like that," she said.

"You're lucky that's all he did. Hey!" I grabbed her arm. "Listen to me. We are going downstairs and you're going to apologize."

"Sure. Right after he says sorry for taking off."

"Keep it down. You'll get him more upset."

"Who cares if he's upset? Aren't we all?" Melissa shook her head dramatically.

She was rattling off everything I'd been thinking about. Saying all I wanted to say but had become too afraid to. *When did that happen, Delia? When did you become so afraid?*

That evening my father said little. I filled the space with corny jokes and pleasant memories. It was exhausting. Like squeezing the last bit of toothpaste out of the tube. As we played Scrabble, I dropped several hints for Melissa to apologize; all were met with refusal. When it was time for bed, she went for the door while I hugged Father good night.

"Melissa, were you about to turn in without saying a proper good night?" he asked.

She looked away.

"And now you're ignoring me?"

His warning tone sent her inching back into the den where he sat. I'd been a bystander to her punishment before, but it had always been Mother. With our father, I didn't know what to expect. I stood back and observed him — this strange man.

"This whole afternoon you've been unruly and rather than apologize, you run off."

"Well, you —"

"Don't interrupt. Your comment was both inappropriate and hurtful. I raised you better. I'm deeply disappointed. Deeply."

"I'm sorry." Tears sprung from my sister's eyes.

He stood, towering over us. My chest tightened.

"I know why you're acting up," he said. "But I'm always going to be your father and deserve respect. No matter where I am."

My sister's arms dangled limply at her sides. I looked at him, waiting for more.

Where were you? Where are you going?

He said nothing else. When my sister appeared comforted, she went upstairs sniffling. I stayed behind. My father gave me a questioning look.

"Dad, can I ask you something?"

"Not now, Delia. Let me cool off."

I turned away and went to my room.

The guest bedroom was designed for a young girl, with rose curtains swept to each side of the window and secured with a ribbon. Against the shiny white headboard, two decorative pillows were propped up, bringing the pillow count to six. When we visited, we pretended to be wealthy heiresses living in a hotel. That night, it felt like any other room. It might as well have been a room somewhere in Georgia or Philadelphia. Timbuktu.

"Maybe she'll try," I said. "I mean why would she stay? She doesn't like her job. She hates Don Mount."

"She hates everything." Melissa threw her hands up. "And he hates her."

"Mel, that's not true."

"Delia, Mom's not going," she continued. "We're not going. That's true."

Melissa turned away and the light came through the window just then, falling on her face in such a way she looked like someone else — her future self. Pretty but serious.

"I'll talk to him," I told her.

"He's going to leave," she said calmly.

My heart was racing.

"It'll be fine."

"Really?" She turned to me. "Then why are you so scared?"

•

I spent the car ride home writing. Plotting. The idea of leaving Toronto and starting over was starting to feel like a chore. If we went and Mother was unhappy, she'd isolate us. They'd fight all the time, and worst of all, they'd be doing it for us. For me. There were other paths, like in the choose-your-own adventure books I borrowed from the library. I scratched the first plan out and started again.

In a year, I'd be old enough to get a part-time job to save for school, then after thirteenth grade, I'd go away. Somewhere near Dad, maybe. Then Mom could find a new job and Melissa could finish high school. Somewhere new that we got to pick — that I got to pick.

I got home, went to my room, and began my routine: unpacking the clothes into my second-hand drawers, putting the dirty ones in the broken plastic hamper. Then I sat on my single mattress with the uncomfortable springs and looked out at the court, wondering what I had missed while I was gone.

Chapter 16

A Dream Deferred

March 1994

Father was on his way to get us, but we had fallen out of our habit of preparing ahead of time for his arrival. We'd be gone until Sunday, then back home for the spring break. Richa and I had plans and I was looking forward already to returning.

"Melissa, did you move my deodorant?"

"You probably left it at Aunt Marie's." Melissa threw me her deodorant bar.

"Thanks," I said. "Don't forget your science textbook."

Mother hovered like a fashionable phantom, arms folded against her new robe. At one point she let out a huff, removed her slippers, and smacked a roach that was sneaking by.

"They're never going away. They're just a permanent annoyance," she said as if resigned to her fate.

The car horn blared.

We hugged her and went off to pack our bags in the trunk. I

was surprised when Mother rushed out. She came to the driver's side window.

"You think he's gonna win, Cliff?" she said.

Our father smiled. "If it's God's grace. Can you imagine, Mandela — a president?"

"They might declare that day a holiday back home."

"Mom has the whole nursing home glued to the television screen."

"Glad to hear she's still going."

A nod from Father.

"Well" — she patted the door — "I can't have these people seeing me outside like this. See you girls on Sunday."

Back into the house she went, taking long strides over the wet ground in her robe and flats.

●

As soon as the car pulled into the driveway, our aunt came outside to meet us, gym bag in hand. My mood immediately lifted at the sight of her.

Aunt Marie took us to the museum, bought me lip gloss, and by Sunday night, we were watching *Uncle Buck* and wondering how to delay our escape for one more day.

"I don't wanna go home," Melissa said to me.

"Me neither. I could use another day."

Richa and I weren't set to meet until midweek.

"Can you barf?"

I looked at her. "How exactly would that help?"

By some miracle, our parents came to some arrangement and we stayed. On Monday morning, my aunt called me to the phone. I assumed it was my father checking in from work. I thanked her and took the handset.

"Hello, Delia." Mother's voice sent shivers up my arms.

"Hi, Mommy."

"You've been gone three days. Weren't you going to call? That's rude."

"Uh …"

"Or maybe you're busy calling your boyfriend. That's why you like to go there, isn't it? So you two can make your plans, go to the movies, skip school … carry on behind my back. We really should move."

I held the phone away from me and let her voice blare through the receiver. Aunt Marie stood aside, bearing witness. Mother was saying my name. I put the phone to my ear.

"Yes, Mommy?"

"Wait, you don't want to talk to me? Now that you have your daddy, you don't need me anymore. That's all right. Give your sister the phone."

I called Melissa down, my voice trembling. I avoided my aunt's stare.

After a short one-sided conversation, Melissa handed the phone to me with a confused look.

"When you get home," Mother said to me. "I will deal with you."

She hung up. I wiped the tears from my face and replaced the receiver. Aunt Marie pulled me toward her.

"What did your mother say?"

I didn't answer.

"Why don't you and Melissa watch a movie downstairs. Something funny. I'll bring down some popcorn. Your mother always had a quick temper. Glad neither of you inherited that."

"Mom sounded super mad. What did you do now?" Melissa said.

I told her I didn't want to talk about it. Mother knew things she shouldn't have. Things meant just for me. I just couldn't figure how exactly she was eavesdropping when I'd been so careful. For a moment I considered Melissa and whether she'd be telling on me. *No,* I decided. *Never.* Mother just hated me. For the first time I really wanted to run away.

When Father arrived, my aunt caught him in the foyer for a debrief. Their voices travelled up the stairs and we could hear them from our room.

"... terrified, Cliff. She was shaking like a leaf."

"Aretha's always been strict," my father reasoned.

"She's too rough. I saw welts across her arm."

"Delia's been coming home late and hanging out, skipping school ..."

"That doesn't sound like her. I thought you met with her teachers?"

"I did and she's doing well academically, but I've seen where they live and who their friends are. Aretha tries to pretty it up, but she's desperate. If I appease her by moving there, she'll get comfortable and next thing you know I'll be giving up my career to settle for her delusions. Again. I have to step back."

"And let the girls suffer? Let me help."

"You're the last person she wants involved. I lost all my control when I left, and you encouraged me."

"I don't regret it. I was right about them."

"It's bloody embarrassing. I believed her and everybody knew."

"Cliff, you have to convince her to go with you. That man is never going to leave. As far as he's concerned, she's his."

They trailed off into a different discussion, one about Uncle Johnny's lack of discretion.

It was wrong of Mother to be with Neville, but it broke my heart that my father had given up and my aunt had encouraged him. Now Neville would be free to come back for my mother, "his girl." It was partly my fault Mother was angry. I left my dirty socks on the floor. I lied. I spent time with a boy I liked and went to places I shouldn't have — adding to her troubles. That was all on me.

When our father finally came upstairs, Melissa and I were sitting quietly on the neatly made bed with our packed bags at our feet. The door was ajar, but he knocked, and then came in.

"Put your things away." He came over and sat between us.

Has something happened to Mother?

"I have some news."

I braced myself.

"It's all settled. I've signed my job offer."

"Oh, that's great. You'll be travelling back and forth." I looked at him. "Right?"

An appreciative nod.

Melissa diverted her gaze to the closet door.

"So," he continued. "I'd like to spend a few more days with you."

"Makes sense," I said, trying to sound mature. "Did you tell Mom?"

"No, I'd better do that now."

He used the phone in Aunt Marie's room.

"They can do laundry when they get back," I heard Father say.

Melissa went to open her knapsack. I grabbed her hand and told her to wait.

Father spoke louder. "Aretha, I'll bring my kids back when I damn well please ... or what?"

As they argued, his voice grew angrier, his fury rising. I imagined Mother, phone in hand, spewing her condemnations. Shaking the walls with her convictions. *How dare you?* she asked in my head. *After what you did.* When it was finally over, I exhaled loudly.

"Finally," Melissa said. "I guess he won."

Hours after his victory, Father settled in the den, the flutter of newsprint the only sign that he was still awake. The doorbell rang. I expected to hear Uncle Johnny stumbling in. However, when Father answered the door, I heard another voice.

"It's Mom!"

"What?" Melissa said. "I don't care what she says, I'm staying."

I held my breath and waited for Mother to barge in and drag us out by our hair and heels. We would never see our part-time father, meddling aunt, or pink curtains again.

After a short stormy exchange, my father said, "I'm keeping them for the rest of spring break."

The argument was settled by the closure of the heavy front door.

•

On the last day of spring break, our father took us home. At each stoplight, I fought the urge to open the car door and tumble into the road. We approached River Street. My heart raced.

Please let her be gone.

Upon our arrival, she opened the door before I could insert the key into the lock. I had run out of wishes.

"Welcome home," she said.

She then immediately turned her focus to the cornrow hairstyles Aunt Marie had spent hours on.

I mumbled a brief "hi," then sat on the couch to remove my shoes. My father came in behind me.

"I thought Marie was out of town," she said to him.

"Change of plans."

"I told you I didn't want her babysitting them. I sent them to spend time with you."

She sucked her teeth and stomped off. He followed her and they picked up their quarrel in the kitchen. I went to unpack and find a new hiding place for my diary.

Before he left, Father called to us. Melissa yelled back and said she loved him. I didn't reply. He called my name.

"She's sleeping," Melissa said.

A few minutes later, there came a knock at my door. I shoved my diary into the crevice between my bed and the wall.

"Come in," I said.

My father appeared. It was strange to see him upstairs. "I knew you were awake."

I sat up.

"Delia, what's the matter? You've barely said a word these past few days and now this?" I didn't want to talk to my father. Instead, I took interest in my bookshelf. I landed on *The Friends* by Rosa Guy. I'd read that next.

He adjusted his collar and cleared his throat as if preparing to recite a speech. "Hey," he said. "Look at me when I'm talking to you."

I raised my eyes.

"I understand you're probably upset by my leaving, but your mother and I have talked this through, and this is an opportunity for all of us. It's not goodbye. I'll go first ... get settled, and then we'll see. Your only job is to get good grades and behave. That's it. Be yourself wherever you are, under whatever circumstances life presents. Even if you hate it here."

"I don't."

"Excuse me?"

I adjusted my tone. Pulled back. "She's changed ... ever since you went away."

My father sighed as if we'd had the conversation before.

"Delia," he said, "your mother is under a tremendous amount of stress. This country will take forty cents from every dollar you make. It's very difficult to progress."

"Is that why you left, before?"

"Before?" He lowered his gaze. "That had to be done to keep the peace."

"Your not being here made things worse."

"I'm willing to fall on my sword for not … being in touch earlier. That's all I'm going to say about it. Just focus on —"

"You're not here. You don't see how she is."

"Delia, I can't be here. It won't work." His patience was wearing thin and slipping off him like grease on wet skin. He was tired of my questions. I had just one more.

"Then how will it work when we come to Georgia?" I said.

My father rubbed his clay-toned hands together, his eyes searching. In them, I saw the sun rising over dense forests, cottonmouth snakes, and peaches. He was already gone.

•

The next day I waited at Richa's locker for fifteen minutes before one of her friends told me she'd been sent home for mouthing off to a teacher. I was hoping she'd help me with something. I returned to my locker and put my diary on the top shelf before securing the padlock. I left the school through the back doors. As I crossed over the field, Mario came down the sidewalk. I caught up with him and tapped him on the shoulder. He removed his headphones, exposing his elfin ears. His reception was cold.

"Well, look who's back," he said. "If I hadn't seen your mom's friend in the parking lot, I would've thought you moved away and didn't bother to tell me."

"I was gone because my father was showing my mother who's boss."

I told him that I'd asked my father the questions, but he didn't answer. He seemed to soften up then.

"And finally — his true colours."

"Don't rub it in. Wait … when did you see Neville the nuisance?"

"Few days ago."

I took a deep breath.

"It's her life to screw up. I'm not gonna let her do the same to mine."

"Wow. Every time you come back from your dad's place, you're a different person."

"Ugh. You sound like my mother. She complains about having to deprogram us, as if we're living the life. Dad makes us recite Bible verses. We can't even go anywhere by ourselves. I'm tired of them both."

"Speaking about being tired, I have work and a physics exam, so I'm skipping practice."

"Oh no. What did Coach say?"

"He gave me a hard time as usual. If he kicks me off the team, I'll change schools. And worst-case scenario, if I have to drop basketball …"

I gave him a skeptical look. "No. You need to keep your grades up and stay on the team. Can't Tia help out?"

He clenched his jaw. "Tia's trying to convince Johnson to move into assisted living."

"What did he say?"

He snickered. "He said, 'Ain't that where I am now?' Then he asked me to assist him with a beer."

"That guy."

More chuckling. "I wish you could've met him back in the day."

"Me, too. Why does he drink so much?"

Mario shrugged. "Habit. Stress from my dad being in jail, who knows? About the time you moved in, he started pulling all-nighters with his buddies in Regent Park. Last week was so bad, I called my mom. It must've freaked her out because she wants me to visit her for the summer."

He paused, waiting for my reaction. I wanted to say I was happy for him but couldn't get the words out. I just kept thinking of how in just a week of my being away, so much had changed.

What would happen if we lived in different towns? Different countries?

Don't get attached, Delia.

We stood on the sidewalk outside of Don Mount. I didn't want to go home.

"I should check on Richa," I said.

"Sure you want to take the risk?"

"I only got yelled at once this week, so I've got, like, two more offences before she brings down the hammer."

"Good luck." He started to walk away and then turned around. "Hey, Delia."

"Yeah."

Mario took a few steps toward me, then shook his head. "Never mind."

I could only watch as he left with his unspoken words — basketball clutched to his side.

•

It was sunset when I left Richa's. She had tried to convince me to leave earlier, but I stalled. Finally, she threw me out, saying she didn't want my mother turning up. I got home and found the door unlocked, which was unusual. I went in, the setting sun sending a blinding red glow through the large windows. Melissa's silhouette stood out in the light. I snuck up behind her.

She spun around, surprised. And something else.

"What's wrong?" I said.

"Dad picked me up, and we came to get you, but you weren't at school, so we came home to wait."

I had asked my father to pick me up from school this week, my poor attempt at a last-ditch effort to settle the friction between my parents. He hadn't agreed so I assumed ...

"And?"

She jutted her index finger at the glass. I squinted and saw on the other side of our fence a woman in slippers and a white housecoat — her hair clinging to the sides of her face. This was our mother — waving her arms around in public, yelling at my father. I almost overlooked their captive audience of one, a satisfied Neville observing from our backyard, where he stood inside the gate. I wanted to choke him.

"Everyone's going to hear them." I slammed my fist on the screen door latch.

"I want him gone!" Father pointed Neville's way.

"Stop it!" I screamed.

My father looked over and saw me, and the image of him — his expression conveyed the formation of some ill-fated idea bred of pure madness.

"Delia, take Melissa upstairs and pack your things."

Melissa grabbed my hand but neither of us moved. Father came to the gate, flung it open, and burst into the yard with Mother steps behind. Then Neville said something out of earshot that made Mother step in between them.

"She's not yours. You hear me?" my father screamed at Neville. "I put in the work. She bears my name."

Neville unfolded his arms and tugged at his leather sleeves. He postured over my father.

My father edged Mother out of the way and lunged.

"Don't!" I found myself out in the yard, arms apart — the referee among them.

The startled three looked at each other, shame settling onto their faces. Mother tightened the belt around her robe. Father shifted his gait and straightened his jacket.

"I am not this man," he announced. "This is not who I am. Delia, I'm sorry. Go get your things."

Mother planted her hand straight across my chest and held it there.

"Stay, Delia. Please."

My father was looking at her, and whatever she conveyed made him slip outside our fence and make a beeline for his car.

I pulled away from her and went to the gate.

"Dad!"

He crossed the lot toward the silver car parked askew, a flash of khaki trousers and grey wool. I turned to Mother. Our eyes met, a gurgle of grief escaped me.

"Come," she said.

She led us through the back door, held open by Melissa — our stilted steps like that of a funeral procession.

Nosy neighbours returned to their duties. They would talk. Camille would hear about it, I knew. She'd no longer think we were special.

I came to the end of the hallway, and realizing my mother had gone to her room, none of us followed. Instead, Melissa and I were left with Neville.

He pulled out a chair for me to sit. "Come, have something to eat. Let your mother rest."

I was too tired to fight him and hadn't eaten a full meal since breakfast. He served us reheated corned beef with rolls and poured three glasses of mauby-bark drink. Late into the meal, he lifted my untouched glass and held it toward me.

"The first sip," he said, "is the most bitter. After a few, you'll see how good it is."

I did as I was told and was surprised at how much better it tasted as I drank on.

After he left, I swept and mopped the floors, then straightened up the living room until the bottom of my feet hurt. Housework makes for good therapy.

I found my sister in bed. I nudged her to move over. She removed her headphones and Method Man's gruff voice emitted from the speakers.

"Mom was crying a lot. That's why I put these on."

"I'm sorry. I totally forgot I'd asked Dad to come by." I changed out of my clothes.

"It's not your fault. Why did he tell us to get our stuff? Did he really think we'd go?"

"I guess. I'd never do that. She needs us."

My sister picked up the headphones and prepared to fix them over her head.

"Adults don't need kids," she said. "They have us so they can feel needed."

I stared at my younger sister in awe.

"Touché."

•

The day of our father's departure, the forecast called for thunderstorms, but the sky was cloudless when his car pulled up outside our gate. I went to the driver's side window to talk to him. He was teary. We'd spoken once since the incident. He had been apologetic. It was not him, he claimed — it was circumstances. "See, that's why I have to stay away." I nodded, still numb from the scene. The memory of it and the anxiety, impervious to explanation. To apology. I needed to find a way to forget.

"I'm off to seek my fortune," he said, referring to my favourite childhood story.

"I'll miss you, Daddy."

He adjusted the mirror. "I'll call as soon as I land. Keep in touch with your aunt. She's worried about you."

"Okay. I'll go see her sometime," I lied. "And maybe I can visit you."

This was my compromise.

"Of course. That's the plan," he said.

My sister appeared looking visibly upset in an old *Care Bears* shirt Dad had given her. We were a sorry tribute. He opened the car door and got out to hug us both.

"Please remember to buy fabric softener and starch," I said.

He laughed. "And you keep the pepper away from your mother. I left my soup recipe in the top cupboard for her."

I snickered.

He glanced over at the empty doorway.

"Well, that's it."

"Love you," we said in concert.

"I love you both." He studied us.

He lingered on me a bit longer than Melissa; I broke away.

We waved and I started up the walk. My sister remained at the gate, her stare fixed upon where the car had been. I went back, wanting to ease her sense of loss. I could only stand with her, waiting to spot the silver roof as it crossed the bridge, and when it did, feeling empty after realizing that the past few months we had only been playing witness to our father's brief encore.

Chapter 17

Uninvited Guests

June 1994

Dear Diary,

Today I cut through the parking lot hoping to see the silver Chrysler and felt really let down to see Neville's car instead. It's been nine weeks and I still feel awful. Why does this feel worse than it did the first time? Mom's been sad, too — I've heard her crying, but she never lets us see, which is fine by me. I prefer to avoid her when she's in a mood.

At least she's staying off my back. Richa and I applied to the Jimmie Simpson rec centre to become camp counsellors, but we're only old enough to volunteer. Richa thinks it's pretty wack, so she's not signing on, but I don't care. I need to get out of this house and meet some new friends and some cute guys, too.

Mario and I are still "friends" — that's how he's been referring to me and I think he likes a girl from school. I don't own him. I'm just keeping everything straight. No gifts. No dates. I'm independent. In fact, I don't need him or Dad.

I am
Delia

Mother sat at the table, phone pressed to her ear, tapping the cord rhythmically against the table. I had been avoiding her for most of the day, so I'd taken my time to appear when she called. Earlier, I'd asked her permission to volunteer at the community centre, and as she was firming up a hard rejection, I quickly suggested summer school. She laughed me out of the room. Said she wasn't born yesterday and saw what I was up to. So when I finally dragged myself to the table, where she was sitting with the phone to her ear, legs crossed and swinging angrily, I tried to fix my expression and not give away my displeasure. I waited patiently, guessing it was my father on the other end of the line. He preferred to call on Sunday evenings, which set the tone for her mood during the week. Mostly, their conversations were cordial, but something had changed. Every so often she uttered, "Mm-hm."

She'd pinned her hair into a perfectly centred bun. I had watched from the hallway as she combed it that morning, looking into her silver hand mirror with the full-length glass behind. Then she could admire every angle of her many selves. Rita. Mother. Aretha. In every direction. She noticed me, then turned away. I wondered if she'd been crying again.

"I'll think about it," she said. "Here's Delia. She's been waiting." She handed the phone over, then left me.

"Hello?"

"Hey, sweetheart." His forced cheerfulness had become familiar after their talks. "Ready for your exams?"

"Yes, I've been studying all week. Where are you this time?"

"Stamford. Then I'm off to Houston."

This would not be the call where he would finally invite us to wherever he was. It explained Mother's sadness, that he had not kept his word — again.

"Before I go, put your sister on the phone and don't say she's in the shower or sleeping."

"It's just a coincidence. I'll make sure you get her next time."

"Okay." He sounded unconvinced. "Tell her ... tell her I love her."

"I will."

After we hung up, Melissa found me in the kitchen. She lifted a leg and wiggled her sparkly red toes.

"She's gone out," she said, before I could speak.

"Better take it off before she gets back. Anyway, he asked for you."

"I heard."

"Next time, I won't lie to him."

"He's the liar. He promised he would always be here. I wish he wasn't our father."

I bit down on my tongue firmly. To keep the peace — as Father would say. Except I learned that it could be done by staying and facing up to the uncomfortable. Even if that meant not saying much.

"He's better than Neville. I wish Mom would realize that."

"I've heard about this," Melissa said with confidence. "When the guy stops chasing the girl, then she has to chase him."

I glowered. "Pathetic."

Just outside, Mario shouted at a teammate between sounds of rubber slamming against the pavement. I tried to ignore it.

"She's so old school," I said. "She thinks there's only one way to be — like she has to do things a certain way or pretend to be a certain way. I'm not gonna care what people think. I'm going to be honest about what I want."

"Sure." Melissa peeked out the window. "Sure, you will."

"You'll see," I said.

At a break in the game, I slid the window open. "Hey, Mario."

He looked up, squinting.

"Come to the door," I said.

Melissa met him at the door and threw her arms around him, then quickly let go.

"Ugh, you're sweaty."

"I know, I'm sorry. Hey, Delia. Long time no see."

I stepped back to let him in. After a slight hesitation he followed.

"So," I said. "What's up? Everything good? Ready for your summer trip to see your mom?"

He shuffled his feet and looked about. "Can't wait to get out of here."

I frowned.

"Just kidding. Anyway." He smiled and scratched the back of his neck. "So, uh, we're playing capture the flag later. You guys should come."

"Okay," I said.

"Really?" He sounded skeptical.

"I live here, don't I? I'm one of them … one of you."

A high two-toned whistle signalled the resumption of the game.

He shook his head at me. "Nah. You're … just Delia. Nobody is like you." His eyes turned to the court. "Apparently."

Out the door he went without another word, leaving me wondering what he meant. My sister emerged from her hiding place behind the door with a determined stride.

"I bet Curtis is going," she said. "Delia, you better make it happen."

I promised.

I was fourteen and my mother would respect me if I was honest and confident. That was Richa's advice, though she was less polite about it. My confidence, however, faded the moment I heard the sound of Mother unlatching the gate. Until then I had forgotten about dinner. Cheerless, she dropped a few grocery bags on the carpet and tossed her leather purse on the couch before closing the door.

"What a long day. You should've seen the line at Honest Ed's." A few steps down the hallway, she stopped. "Dinner?"

I played with my hands. "I forgot to take the chicken out of the freezer."

She frowned. "I wrote it down. What the hell were you doing that you couldn't remember to do one simple thing?"

"Mommy, it was just a mistake," Melissa said. "There's some sardines left."

Wrong move.

"Wait, let me get this straight." She stood, arms akimbo, and put on her "pretend nice" voice. "Your bellies are full, and you want me to thank you for the air-cakes and wind-pies?"

Melissa and I stayed quiet. We never answered the trick questions. Mother's hand gestures became more animated. Soon, I feared, one of her hands would find us. I was waiting for her to strike when the front door opened. Mother looked down the hallway and smiled.

"Hello," she said.

My heart jumped. Footsteps approached.

It was Neville, carrying Chinese takeout. Melissa leapt from the couch and went to him, throwing her arms around his waist. A strange look passed between him and Mother. Then my little sister gazed up at the man who wasn't my father and said, "I'm so glad you're here."

As soon as we found ourselves alone, I turned to my sister.

"So, what, now he's your new daddy?"

"Don't say that." She started to cry.

"Stop — she'll hear you." I moved to wipe her tears away.

She batted away my hand. "I can't help it."

Behind her, the twilight sky was a dying fire. Soon the street-lamp flickered on; as we watched, shadows crawled across the lot. Excited talk. Laughter. A small crowd. I put my hands on the window-pane. Mario strutted onto the court, heading for a small group. He was waving one blue and one red handkerchief. After a while, he looked up at the window, saw me, and raised his arms in question. I shrugged. He nodded in understanding then turned back to *his* friends. I felt a new bitterness. I didn't believe in purgatory but figured the feeling was similar.

Mother strolled in without knocking. She clipped an earring on to her right lobe and stopped to gaze at her reflection in the mirror.

"I'm heading out," she said. "Empty the garbage. The roaches don't take a break."

Neville's car was barely out of view when Melissa and I tore out the door.

Everyone was gathered by the playground.

Mario came over. "What did you do, drug her?"

"Shut up." I hit him playfully, then in my Valley girl voice I said, "Now, like — show me how to play this inner-city game."

The group was made up of mostly older teenagers — some I'd never seen. A girl wearing baggy jeans and a jersey handed out glow sticks and flashlights.

"The parks are the jails. Lisa's on guard duty for first court, Mario and Harminder are captains," she said. "Captains, pick your teams."

Mario pointed at me first. "I choose you."

Melissa elbowed me. I couldn't help but smile.

Our team lost, but I didn't care. By the end of that night, running beneath the stars had become my new favourite thing. In the open sky, I saw all that was boundless and timeless; where God lived. And oh, how the darkness made light so beautiful. I stared up into it from the grass where Mario and I fell, exhausted.

Hearing his breath, I reached over to grab his hand and felt the heat of it.

For me, first love came in the form of cold, slick leaves, like tendrils against my skin, and the feeling of his hand against mine. At one point, I sensed he had turned to look at me in the dark. I let him watch as I counted my possibilities, charted my course in the heavens.

Richa's face appeared over me, blocking out the constellations.

"What are you two losers doing? We're getting Slurpees." She reached into her fanny pack and pulled out a twenty-dollar bill.

I listened for a voice, one telling me to go home. A warning. I waited for the fear of Mother's assault. Nothing.

We met up with another group of kids at an isolated playground with a geometric climbing dome and a two-person swing set. We got talking about whether Ewing or Fila sneakers were nicer, our summer plans, and somehow ended up singing "Free Nelson Mandela" even though he was already the president of South Africa. We didn't know how else to celebrate.

One of the guys turned to me. "I've never seen you."

"I've lived here for a whole year."

"She's like Rapunzel," said Richa.

I laughed along. The boy left from where he was and came over to sit on the swing beside mine. Out of the corner of my eye, I saw Mario shift in his position to face us.

"So," the boy said, "you got a man?"

I kept my eyes straight ahead.

Richa piped up. "Do you know who her mother is? Tyson."

The boy leapt from the swing and stood at a distance. They all broke out in laughter besides Mario, who was deadpan the whole time.

On our walk back, Mario seemed distracted, like he was trying to be present but something was pulling him back. Just short of the entrance that led to our courtyard he stopped, then fished a folded piece of paper from his pocket and handed it to me. I opened it and read it.

"I'll have to buy a long-distance card," I said. "Isn't your mom going to freak out if I call?"

"No."

"How do you know?"

"I don't know, Delia, but I can't call you, so, like — just call me." He cleared his throat. "So, Tim seemed to like you. I can't tell you who to like ... but he's a player. He goes after younger girls because he thinks they're easy. Not that you are." He scratched the back of his neck. "Because," he continued, "you are ... cute and really nice. Older guys will try to take advantage of that, so watch out. Don't let me have to beat anyone up when I get back."

My cheeks grew warm.

"I'm not interested in him. Anyway, I thought you were upset about something else — like seeing your mom. Are you nervous?"

"I'm a bit nervous about flying." He exhaled loudly. "I'm gonna miss playing ball."

We got to the door, and he hesitated. I wondered if he would kiss me again. I wanted him to. I wanted him to change his mind. Refuse to go on this journey. Stay.

He didn't.

Chapter 18

A Paradox of Hope

Summer 1994

Before long, the Chrysler's tire tracks were trampled over and 1994 roared on, swallowing up the fantasies about my father and mother reconciling. And the detached house with a yard, the barrels — empty — the new kitchen appliances on the marble kitchen island, the dog that Melissa wanted. It all dried up. My sister suffocated her sorrow with coconut cakes and Jamaican cheddar cheese that came from Ireland. Mother remodelled, switching out the linen to warmer colours. During the process, she hauled my father's remaining belongings out onto the back patio. She caught me watching.

"I'm donating them," she said.

"What about the drafting table?" I asked. "Can we keep that?"

"No. I'm tired of living in a graveyard," she said.

By the next week, it was gone. And just like that, Melissa and I became the last remnants of our father in the house.

Accepting that my parents weren't ever getting back together was a process. I had gradually stopped talking about moving since

Richa told me to shut up about it. One day I was going on one of my many "when I move" rants when she politely asked me for the exact date. I didn't have one, and said she was probably right that it was never going to happen.

Once I said it aloud, Richa looked at me, eyes wide, and said, "Fuckin' eh."

That was it and neither of us mentioned it again. The next thing she did was invite me to her mother's apartment, in Regent Park, and by the look on her face she wasn't taking no for an answer. On our way home from Richa's place, Melissa and I strategized.

"How are you gonna pull this off?" Melissa bit into a sour gummy and scrunched up her face.

I'd been thinking about it ever since Richa asked.

"Church. We'll ask to go to church."

"But we don't go anymore."

"She doesn't but why can't we?" I sipped from my can of pop. "If we take the bus and stay for evening service, it's an all-day affair."

"Ugh. Take the bus in our church clothes? Gross," Melissa said. "Anyway, what makes you think she'll let us?"

"Well, first of all, who doesn't let their kids go to church? Second, I'll make sure she knows Mario's gone away for the summer. I'll talk to Richa about it on the phone. You know she's always listening. I just need to tell her something she wants to hear."

Mother had stopped going to church as soon as our father left, but she never thought that Melissa and I would make the hour-plus trip voluntarily. It didn't take much convincing for her to let us go. She even bought us a strip of bus tickets and new stockings and slips to make sure we looked "decent."

That first Saturday, we set out with Mother's blessing. She seemed proud that we were taking an interest in church, and though I felt guilty about lying, I told myself it was necessary. It was the only way Melissa and I would ever see life beyond Dundas Street and Queen Street.

We waved goodbye to our mother, who was preoccupied re-organizing the kitchen cupboards. She decided that she didn't like mismatched cups and plates and was planning to donate all the ones with words. We got on the 505 streetcar heading west and took in all the transit riders to ensure no one we knew was onboard, then once the transit passed River Street, we rang the bell for the next stop.

Richa met us in the lobby of one of the buildings. She was wearing a sports bra and baggy jeans with a pair of sunglasses sitting on top of her head. Our eyes met and she smiled widely.

"'Sup." She came over and inspected us. "You guys look real fancy." And then she shook her head. "But please tell me you brought some gear, because this isn't gonna work."

Melissa zipped open her midsize purse that she claimed held clothes for the casual evening service. She raised an eyebrow at Richa.

"We have gear," I said.

"Okay, then, follow me."

Richa's family lived in north Regent, but she asked us to meet her at the high-rise where Naveed lived so we could walk over together. I wondered if she had slept there overnight and why she'd choose to be there when her grandmother and her mother lived a short distance away.

Melissa walked so close to me that the handle of her purse got caught in my lace sleeve.

"What is up with you?" I whispered.

She grabbed my arm and side-eyed an overdressed pudgy gentleman lurking against a chain-link fence.

"He's watching us."

"No, he's not. Stop." I brushed her off and walked faster.

•

The entry door was open, and Richa walked in without announcing herself. She waited until we'd filed in behind her, then shut the door.

"Keep your shoes on," she said.

Melissa and I exchanged doubtful looks but obeyed. We followed her into the living room, which was at the front of the house. It was sparsely furnished and simply themed: black, shiny furniture with holes. Along the arms of the faux leather sofa were circular, small burn marks. Richa led us to that sofa.

"Sit here. Don't move. I'll get her, then she can meet you, then we'll go."

We did as she said without a word, perching on the very edge of the seat just enough that we wouldn't slip onto the smelly carpet. I scanned the room; a one-seater with the middle torn out sat adjacent to us, small white tufts of cotton stuffing poking out of it. On the seat of our sofa, I noted tiny puncture marks in sets of four and shallow scars that stretched all the way to the ground. The culprit sat nearby, yawning, its patchy tail flicking lightly.

"Look!" I tapped Melissa on the leg.

"Oh, hi, kitty."

We could hear Richa's voice upstairs, but it was faint as if behind a closed door. I tiptoed over to the orange tabby and bent down to pet it. Out of nowhere, I felt a tug and saw a small pair of hands pulling at my sleeve. They belonged to a slight, inquisitive child wearing glasses that made her eyes look huge. I surmised she was Richa's youngest sister, whom she called her "tiny twin."

"You wanna play?" the little girl asked.

"No. I can't," I said politely.

She didn't bother with Melissa and ran straight upstairs, wailing.

"Them two," she said to someone.

Melissa stood, alarmed. "Let's get out of here. This place is weird."

"Wait." I shook my head. "I'm not leaving without Richa."

Someone answered the child and then we heard the procession of feet descending the stairs out of view.

"Richa, I told you not to bring your sticky-fingered friends here."

The girl turned up again. She pointed her little fingers at us.

"Look, Mama," she said to someone behind her.

A wiry lady, still in her nightdress, came from around the corner and scooped the little girl into her arms. Her brown hair was formed into beautiful dreadlocks, and she had a green clover tattooed on her outer wrist.

"They're not thieves." Richa came down the hall behind the woman. "This is Delia, my best friend. I told you I was bringing her over. And that's her sister, Melissa. Guys, this is my mom, Alice."

Melissa waved. By then she'd already made her way to the door.

The woman took me in. "I guess you look all right. All fussed up, too. My, my. I should ask what you two are doing hanging out with this one?" She motioned at Richa.

I snickered.

"They won't play, Mama." The little girl kicked so hard her mother put her on the floor. She sprawled out on her belly in protest.

"Briana, get up." Richa bent down and smacked her lightly on the leg. "Ma, are you going to tell her to stop?"

"No hitting, Richa. She carries on like this when the boys are out."

"Well, take her to the park or something."

"That's a great idea. Take her with you."

"What? No! That's why I hate coming here."

Alice held Richa's hand. "Your aura is green."

Richa gave a half shrug. Alice scrutinized me next.

"I can't see your aura." She raised a finger to my face. "I'll fetch my sage stick. Don't move."

As soon as Alice was out of sight, Richa spoke quietly to her sister.

"Briana, find your slippers and put them on. When Mom comes back, she'll take you to the park."

Then she turned to me. "Why are you still standing there? Let's bounce."

We all gathered at the door.

"Serves us right," Melissa mumbled. "I knew this was going to be a disaster."

"I thought we were going to change here," I said, feeling sorry for Briana, who had begun to sob.

Richa shook her head. "We'll go to Nicole's place. She's an only child, and her mother isn't annoying."

At Nicole's apartment, we ate grilled cheese sandwiches with ketchup — the best I'd ever tasted — then watched movies with some kids we met at the park. Everywhere we went with Richa and Nicole, people treated us like family, inviting us into their homes, offering us food, and asking about our lives like they cared. We returned to Regent many times, always with Richa, and often wound up in apartments with people whose names we weren't sure of. It felt so good to be out of the house. Soon, we stopped watching the clock. We stayed later. Then once, we got all the way home before realizing we'd forgotten to change into our church clothes. We slowed things down after that. When you've been up on your luck too long, you're bound to go down. That's what Grandma Liz said, and that woman never told a lie.

•

Though he lived elsewhere, Neville stayed close, holding Mother up like a fragile prop. The departure of my father and the preceding events left her splintered. I resented her for it — her betrayal and the way she used the sharp shards of herself to prick us. Neville let her be. I expected an offhand comment or two from him about my father, but he said nothing. He had foreseen his triumph long ago and had been picking his teeth at the finish line, waiting for the rest of us to catch up after stumbling through the obstacle course.

•

Not a single pot of soup was cooked in that house that summer. Or any time after that. Mario had just returned; it was the start of tenth grade and everything that came with it: great expectations and empty promises about all the areas I would improve. There was a knock at the door, and I opened it to a waiting courier. They handed me an envelope, then rushed off to their next stop. The letter was addressed to Aretha Ellis, the sender — my father. I held it up to the light and flipped it around a few times but couldn't make out the wording.

Melissa snatched it from me. "Divorce papers, I bet."

It was my first thought when the man showed up at the door, but he didn't say, "You've been served," like they did on TV, and so I convinced myself the letter was something else. Anything else. I shook my head.

"That's not how it works," I said. "They'd have to be separated first. He'd have told me."

"Yeah, okay. I better get dressed before Neville gets here." Melissa was through with this conversation.

"I still can't believe she's throwing him a party. Why do adults need birthday parties?"

"I know, eh?" Melissa said. "She must really want him back."

"I guess. You better hurry up — Neville's about to leave."

Around this time, my mother's actions — and often, her where-abouts — were unknown to me. Gone was her predictable schedule and mannerisms to which I'd become accustomed. The party, another rare gesture, puzzled me.

As soon as she came through the door, I handed her the couriered letter. She opened it eagerly, then sat on the couch, purse still strapped around her arm.

"I'll check on the food," I said. "I already finished the potato salad, the coleslaw, and the lasagna. I'm making the rice, now."

"Okay." Her eyes trailed over the words in the document.

I left her alone and, not long after, watched her climb the steps, still reading. Once she was upstairs, the phone lit up. I knew she had to be speaking to Dad and was tempted to listen in, but couldn't afford getting caught and making them both angry. Instead, I sat at the table fretting. Perhaps he had sent a cheque hidden between the folded pages. People don't send long love letters by courier, do they?

I stayed by the phone until she came storming down to the main floor, pushing aside the chair I was sitting on to make her way to the stove.

"Don't you smell that?"

"No." I looked on, helpless.

"Christ, Delia. How did you let this burn while you're sitting right here?"

She heaved the pot of rice into the sink and turned the tap on full blast. Steam shot to the ceiling.

This pot burns everything, but the other pot has somehow disappeared — the pot you claim your supervisor broke into our house and stole.

She sized me up. "What good are you? I should send you to your father."

"I wish you would," I blurted.

Her fist pulled back quickly, and I recoiled from it, bringing a hand to my mouth to feel the thin line of blood. Mother, her face pained with regret, went into nurse mode. Off to the freezer she went. She returned with a chip of ice.

"Hold this," she said.

I pressed the ice to my lips and waited for the numbness to set in. She watched me, wringing her hands. Was she worried I would tell, or return fire? Perhaps I should have defended myself, but then what? Her regret was brief; the party took precedence, and she started on a fresh batch of rice. When I was certain she didn't want anything else from me, I went to my room.

The screen door opened multiple times as Neville carried in what sounded like hundreds of shopping bags. I could hear Melissa singing off-key as she came up the steps. We met at the top of the stairs. Her song got caught in her throat.

"What happened to your face?" she said.

I recounted the event.

"Geez, were you trying to get punched?" She leaned in for a closer look. "Maybe Cliff told on you ... remember you complained about her."

"I'm sure it was that letter."

Melissa's expression made me question it. Dad, being a thousand miles away, was the poor foe Grandma had alluded to.

"What are you going to do? The party's tomorrow."

I stared in the mirror. "I think I'll parade myself around just like this, so everyone can see."

"Did it hurt?"

"Only a little. I mean she didn't apply force. I wouldn't have teeth left if she did, right?"

"Yeah, 'cause she's really strong. She didn't really want to hurt you."

"Exactly."

We thought quietly to ourselves for a bit. Then she took something from the back pocket of her shorts. "Got you a Skor bar."

"Thanks," I said, and took it. Although, I suspected she had bought it for herself.

Mother hummed an old reggae tune as she went about the house in the best of spirits, her grudge match behind her. I brooded alongside, helping with the final preparations on the spruced-up first floor. She had found the time to sew curtains, hand towels, and matching cushion coverings. Neville had applied a fresh coat of beige paint to the living room walls and new mats were laid across the linoleum. My swollen lip, now an unremarkable bulge, was another aesthetic victory.

My parents had rarely hosted anything, and I was unaccustomed to the heightened level of anxiety. Melissa and I worked right up until the party of strangers poured into our tumbledown unit, until the table was covered with foil-wrapped dishes and liquor bottles. Guests helped themselves to drinks and danced toward the living room into a blare of ska, old school reggae, and calypso. Mother expected us to remain in our rooms, but we dilly-dallied, making ourselves look helpful as we picked over the food, tasting only what we recognized. I indulged in a moist slice of rum-infused cake from my spot on the steps.

"Who are these people?" Melissa said a tad too loudly.

"Neville's folk," I whispered. "I bet they don't even know Mom."

If they were unsure of what their relationship was, Mother made it evident by the way she draped herself over Neville and the awful gold crushed-velvet suit he sported.

As night fell, empty glasses appeared around the room. Neville went by like an aura in his tacky shimmering suit, accompanied by Mother, whose loose crepe gown, the colour of Himalayan salt, spun in and out of his grasp. They went by again and again, forehead to forehead, swaying, her laughter getting louder at each turn.

Occasionally my father and mother would dance on a whim — to anything really, from the wispy scratch of sounds on wax to the baritone thunderstorms that rolled in with spring. I wondered what it would be like to dance with Mario, to rest against his chest, and close my eyes, and leave the world without ever dying.

At some point the crowd moved into the backyard, where they could dance and smoke outdoors. I left the table and went to collect the empty glasses, stopping just short of the hallway. The basement door opened, and I saw the skirt of a dress, the lightest hue of teal, snaking around a pair of brown legs. I stepped back, then peeked around the wall. The woman wore her hair in long braids

that roped down her back. What was she doing in the basement?
I parted my lips to ask, then she turned to the basement steps and
beckoned with her hand to someone. A human-size spool of gold
came through the door. Neville. He leaned down and whispered in
her ear, then touched her briefly and gently on the small of her back.
She nodded and moved aside. Neville strode past her unsteadily,
and made his way to the back door. When he opened it, the sound
of the crooning crowd rolled in; my mother called his name, and he
disappeared into the throng. The lady turned around and saw me.
She froze. I studied her wordlessly, then went upstairs. Melissa was
in the master bedroom trying on makeup.

"Clean up," I told her. "Today is not the day to piss her off."

Then I returned to the party without mentioning what I had
seen.

The music stopped. They were being called to the table for cake.
Mother had let her hair out, her curls frizzed by the heat and sweat.
Compliments followed her down the hall to the table, where she
led a chorus of "Happy Birthday" in Neville's honour. I watched
her hand atop his, guiding the large knife into the cake I'd made.

"We should do this more often," some moron suggested.

A refrain of agreements followed, and glasses raised in unison,
signalling a call for toasts.

"When are you all getting married?" Neville's brother, Jude,
called out.

"When you finish school and move," Neville said.

Scattered chuckles and plates of rum cake were passed around
the room. The heavy beats started up again, and the crowd
moved toward them, leaving behind their debris. I surveyed the
room and spotted a bottle of Bailey's Irish Cream. Curious, I
went over and poured myself a drink.

●

Later, I checked on Melissa, then slipped into my sandals, and went out, away from it all — the strangers and our mother, who was caught up in Neville's orbit, the two of them a small hurricane in a room. My stomach churned.

Mario answered his door, still pulling on a shirt. I stared unapologetically, wondering where the boy I knew had gone. He'd only been away for a summer, and everything about him seemed different, the shape of his face, the sparse hair above his lip, and his skin, dark and clear like he was baptized in molasses.

He came onto the patio. "Hey, short stuff."

"Hi. Can you come out for a bit? Don't worry, she won't be looking for me."

"Cool." He nodded in the direction of the music. "Is that your house?"

"Yep. My mother, believe it or not," I said.

"Wow." He scratched his chin. "Things are really going sideways, eh?"

"You have no idea."

After he'd slipped his shoes on, we headed for the parkette on Dundas Street.

"So, how was your summer?" My tongue felt heavy.

"Not as good as yours, I heard."

Richa and her big mouth.

We sat and stretched our feet out toward the empty street. In the distance, the pop-pop-pop sound of fireworks. Or something else. Mario pressed his hands into the bench and looked down the street as if on guard.

"Well, I guess you already know, so no need to fill you in," I said. "How'd the rest of your visit go? We only spoke that one time."

He relaxed a little.

"My mom turned out to be different from what I expected. She's super spiritual. A vegan. She does yoga every morning. Tia looks more like her than I do, but she's really into sports, which is supposedly where I get it from. One thing, though — she was always late."

He jumped from one story to the next and I listened, marvelling at his summer spent farming and fishing. He barely played basketball, he said. There was just so much more to do. I asked about his other relatives.

"My other grandparents and cousins are kinda simple. They're from the country."

"Simple. Sounds a little judgmental," I said.

Am I slurring?

He moved the hair out my face. "Been hanging around you too much, that's why."

I laughed, the lukewarm air carrying my voice into the night. I felt warm and drowsy. I inched closer to him on the bench. Our eyes met.

I leaned in to kiss him. "Ouch." I winced and pulled back.

He squinted at me. "What happened to you?"

"My parents might be getting a divorce," I said.

He shifted away from me. "Finally."

"How can you say that?"

"Who'd want to be married to her? Look what she did to you."

I touched my lip. "She's not hitting him. Just because she's not a perfect parent, it doesn't mean she's a bad wife. You wouldn't understand."

"Why, because my parents didn't go to a church, take pictures in a park, and spend money so other people could complain about the food at the wedding? I'm glad they didn't bother. And that doesn't give her the right to do that to your face."

I sat back and let the numbness take over. If he wasn't going to kiss me, then there was nothing to do but float away. Feeling nothing was a step up from feeling awful.

A few minutes passed.

"Delia!" he barked. "I'm talking to you. Are you sleeping?"

"What?" I blinked at him.

He narrowed his eyes. "You're drunk."

"No, I'm not," I said too loudly. "You think you're an expert on everything."

"Get up. I'm taking you home. I leave for two months, and everything goes to hell. Johnson's back on the bottle. Richa's taking joy rides to Detroit. Tia's living in Miami with some guy. I'm never leaving again."

He lectured me all the way to the front door and folded his arms as he watched me go in.

I snuck upstairs unnoticed. Melissa stood at the window, talking to someone outside. She noticed me when I came in.

"She's here, Mario," she said. "No, she's not drunk — just mesmerized by your buffness."

I went over and waved. He looked relieved, like someone who was happy to be home. I knew then that my father was wrong. Healthy friendships are essential. I only wish I'd written that down.

The sound of shuffling feet below me, a sign of departing guests. I should've been seeing them out, but I was on strike. I lay in bed. I reached up and spread my fingers apart, letting the light pierce through the spaces. The ceiling became a moving memory, the waning moon making its way across the night sky, Mario reaching for me. Neville emerging from the basement. Mother's sharp knuckles against my face. Liquid metal spreading in my mouth. The sight of Mother's polyester dress gleaming like spun candy.

Chapter 19

Motherhood

June 1995

Dear Diary,

I cannot wait for the tenth grade to be over. This year was absolute trash. If I hadn't aced my first math midterm, I'd be doing a makeup credit for sure. Mom's too busy concerning herself with Neville's mysterious whereabouts to be of any help. When I have kids, I'll hire a tutor. Especially if I end up raising them alone. Actually, my kids are going to private school. I don't care if I have to work two jobs.

Kids cost a lot. Mom has been complaining to Grandma about bills and the car (which, by the way, is in the shop again). I never thought I'd see her taking the bus. That's why I need my own cash, so I don't have to keep asking for money. Mario says he can get me a job with Camille. The government has a program and I'm eligible because I live here. Finally it comes in handy for something (besides endless entertainment and the best friends EVER). Canada's Wonderland ... here I come!

I am
Delia

I dragged myself out of bed at six thirty, listless after a restless sleep. Well into the night, I kept rehearsing my conversation with Camille and the subsequent one to be had with Mother. By morning I was frazzled. I decided to tell Mother about the job, which would demonstrate my maturity. I'd then present my argument, that my earning an income was mutually beneficial since an allowance would no longer be required.

Yet I rose to a house devoid of the familiar morning commotion: the hum of the exhaust fan, the static from the radio, and Mother's singing. Nothing. I sat up in bed, rubbed my eyes, and shoved my feet in my slippers.

"Mommy?"

I'd missed her again. I could never tell what time she started work anymore. On occasion, she'd wake up and set to cleaning before work. Twice, I'd arrived from school to find her busy at the stove, still in her work clothes. She offered no explanation, and I knew better than to ask.

"Why are you up so early?" Melissa came downstairs with a comforter draped around her entire body.

"Why are you dragging your sheet across the dirty floor?" I shook my head. "Anyway, Mom already left for work."

"Thank God." Melissa collapsed onto her knees.

Mother had promised my sister a "beating" after finding dirty socks in her drawer. A call from Mother's friend Pearl deferred the punishment until morning.

"Lucky," I said. "I guess you can go back to bed."

"Don't need to tell me twice."

I was in the kitchen when Melissa threw herself heavily onto the mattress, sending a *whump* above my head. While relieved, I felt uneasy about Mother's convenient absence. It seemed too good to be true. With all my extra time, I made omelettes for Melissa and me, then wrote my own late slip for school. A grocery list with a note and a fifty-dollar bill was affixed to the fridge with a pineapple magnet. "Get groceries. Take a cab home," the note read. I snatched it from the door, put it in my pocket, then went to see Camille.

That evening, I wrestled the grocery bags out of the cab and carried them into the yard, feeling the plastic handles cut into my palms, I contemplated a life where we were being raised by our father. He and Mother had always shared household duties, but their roles were not interchangeable. Dad dealt with the car maintenance, and though he was capable, it was our mother who prepared most of our meals. The arrangement seemed fair, though I wasn't sure how they came to it. I only knew that as a single parent, even with our help, she shouldered much of the burden. There was much we couldn't do. Would our father have done as good of a job? Was this why Mario's mother left, because raising two children alone was too difficult? Maybe she wasn't as brave as my mother. Or maybe our mother didn't know she had a choice. Being a woman and a mother suddenly seemed terribly complex. Like being two people. Except — you weren't. I think my father had tried to tell me this once.

My mother had enrolled in night college classes, and we'd spent those evenings alone with our father. One day, as Melissa and I played with our Cabbage Patch dolls on the living room mat, I stopped to ask how much longer dinner would take.

"Fifteen minutes and it'll be done." He dried his hands and came over. "Are these your students, Professor?"

"No, Daddy." I laughed. "They're my children."

"What?" He counted them. "Six kids? Where's their father?"

"At work. He's a doctor and I stay home."

He looked serious. "Hm. Not sure I like that idea."

"How come?"

"Don't you want a career, too? To get a degree and make your own money."

"But he's rich," I said.

"And what if he leaves? How would you take care of yourself — and all these kids?"

"He can't leave," Melissa chimed in. "He's the husband."

I chuckled, but my father's expression was flat.

"D'you hear me, Delia? No more of this stay-at-home-mom stuff."

"Okay, Daddy," I said, feeling like I had learned the secret to life.

Although it wasn't my mother who'd told me this, it reminded me of how independent she was, and I felt more confident about broaching the subject with her. When Melissa offered to make extra ice for possible injuries, I threw one of my slippers at her.

We held off on eating until Mother arrived. At dinner she was quiet but upbeat, even acknowledging my much-improved corned beef with cabbage dish. Melissa rushed through her meal quickly.

"I'm going to bed," she announced with a fake yawn.

"Have a good sleep, honey. Love you."

Even I was surprised that Mother had barely looked up from her plate.

A soft breath of relief escaped Melissa as she brushed by me.

"Good luck," she said quietly before rushing up the steps.

I took a deep breath. "So, I have some good news."

Mother's forehead wrinkled, my idea of "good" news being debatable.

"I got a summer job working for the government … like you."

She squinted at me like she was putting me in focus, then with a wave of a hand, permitting me to go on.

"It's a clerk position in an office." I swallowed. "The property office. Here."

"Hm." She blinked and tugged at her right ear. "So, you'll be working with Mrs. Blanchard. She brought this opportunity to your attention?"

"Uh." I drummed my fingers on the table. "No, I asked around and that's how I found out about it. I went to her and applied. She interviewed me and everything."

"When did this all happen?"

"Today. I would've told you, but you were already gone when I got up." I bit my lip.

"Delia." Mother pushed her seat away from the table and stood with her arms folded.

"It's a good thing to have on my resumé, too. I —"

"I'm proud of you," she said. "It's important to be ambitious and want to earn your own money. You'll learn the value of a dollar and be able to save."

She took both of our empty plates to the sink.

"In a few years you'll be off to university or college. Whichever you choose, I don't care. If you save your earnings every summer, you may be able to graduate without borrowing a single penny. That's the smart way to do it."

We discussed future possibilities, a part-time gig during the school year if I could keep my marks up, and maybe babysitting on weekends for parents in Don Mount who worked nights.

I nodded enthusiastically, noting her use of the words "off to university," wondering if this was consent for me apply to schools out of town. I grinned. I couldn't wait to tell Mario and Richa.

She stood at the sink, sleeves rolled back, silver watch deposited on the counter beside the bobby pins she'd plucked out of a perfectly formed bun. I joined her, and picked up where she left off, drying the dishes and putting them in the cupboards. She let out a deep exhale.

"What a long day."

I rested the dish cloth on the drying mat and wrapped my arms around her tightly. I wanted very badly to tell her it would be okay, but unsure of what worried her, I didn't want to lie. I just wanted her to know she wasn't alone.

•

My mother had a philosophy. Well, she had many, but one in particular: to be content, to be truly happy (because apparently a lot of people were pretending), people had to know their "place." Women, she said, had twice as much work to do because of all the different parts they played at home and in the world at large. The husband is the lead, but the wife is the visionary. Raising a family is a job for two. Not one. Not ever. She had a strong opinion of how things should be, and nobody was going to convince her otherwise.

Within a year of my father's leaving, Neville became his proxy. Even though Mother had chosen him, I couldn't figure out why he was sticking around. He clearly had options, and she knew it, but Neville seemed willing to stick it out. I felt there was something in Mother's grief that he found attractive. He was attentive and present most of the time with her and seemed to enjoy playing the role of husband, but as for fatherhood, he was unprepared. Still, he sat in the seat where my father would've been, night after night, and as I ate, I wondered how it was that I felt closer to my father, who was miles away, than to this man.

Mother wiped her hands on a kitchen towel before taking a seat. She always ate last — it was the proper thing to do, she told us once. You can always tell whether a man or woman made a rule by who it benefitted the most.

Neville wiped his prickly chin with a napkin, leaving white tufts behind in his stubble. He lifted his head and said to us, "Did you hear what happened over at the prison?"

Mother shot him a glaring look. "Don't."

"You mean the riot?" Melissa said.

Neville gave our mother a defiant look. "That's right. A prisoner escaped just this week and they're looking for him around here."

Though Mother preferred us not to mention the Don Jail, Neville was right; it was the worst-kept secret in the neighbourhood. Whenever there was a tragedy, it was all the kids talked about. Melissa would bring it up and Mother would change the topic. When it came on the news, she changed the channel, as if acknowledging its existence would make us victims to some cosmic delinquent destiny. While she drew invisible protective circles around us, it became more difficult to keep the outside world at bay.

"Neville, I determine what my children see, hear, and know. It kills me to have to wake up in this place, not knowing what my children will be exposed to. If you want to have a say — to be a father — then get us the hell out of here."

Neville stared back in shock.

Melissa and I abandoned our plates. I looked back to see him pull his chair closer to hers.

"Meet me halfway," he said. "Just sign the papers."

Mother buried her face into his shoulder and sobbed. It was like this all the time now, her mood flipping like a coin.

Everything was changing and I could do nothing to stop it. I wondered how things had shifted — how I, the one trying to keep everyone together, had ended up without someone to comfort me.

•

I spent an hour putting my outfit together for my first day of work, then ended up in a pair of jeans and a long-sleeved black top.

"You're just giving up," Melissa said. "Stop pretending you don't want him to like you."

"I'm not desperate."

She took me by the shoulders, which was easy for her now that she was taller than me.

"If you haven't noticed, you're the only one of your friends who hasn't had a boyfriend. I'm worried."

"Well, hurry up," I said. "I'd rather be employed than pretty."

By the time we got done, I had only twenty minutes before the start of my shift. I went to the table and scanned the notepad with Mother's notes.

"She didn't make breakfast," Melissa whined.

I pulled out the smallest pot, filled it with water, and set it on the stove. I told her to sit so I could braid her hair while we waited for the water to boil.

"The water's boiling. Put the oats in."

"Can't we just have cereal? Porridge takes forever."

"Do it, or I'll slap you so hard you'll end up in the future."

"Will Dad be there?"

Our laughter, which filled the house, was followed by an affecting silence that left us alone with our thoughts. There were no words. We laughed again.

•

It was a nerve-wracking hike across the courtyard and up the steps to the office. I knocked to let Camille know I was there, even though the door was open just enough for me to get in. The radio was playing, tuned to station AM 640.

"You're early. Mario will be here soon." She waved me over.

Drips of dark liquid splattered out of the mug she held.

"Have some coffee."

"No, thank you," I said.

I took a seat.

"You'll be drinking it by the time summer is over. I need you to handle the Blue House food bank rounds. The residents on this list need to have their food orders delivered every morning." She pointed to a sheet of paper mounted on a nearby bulletin board.

Mario showed up just as Camille was leaving for a meeting. He strode in wearing a collared shirt, khakis, and loafers. He took one of the chairs across the room and brought it over beside mine. My heart raced.

"Hey." He sat angling his legs away from me. "What do you need me to do, boss?"

I relayed Camille's instructions.

Within the first hour, we had a great deal of the filing done and had begun to field the calls coming in on the office line. We had run out of small talk.

"So, what if your mother shows up?"

"Then she'll know the truth."

"Why are you acting so brave all of a sudden?"

"I'm nearly sixteen — not some kid acting out."

Appearing satisfied, he returned to his work. I took to day-dreaming about what kind of man he would become. His neatly cropped hair, which faded down to his neck — his shirt, fitted enough to show the defined curvature in his shoulders and biceps. His broad, regal nose that flared slightly when he was serious. His funny laugh that sounded like a hiccup. Would he become my father, unassuming and loyal until he grew tired of it? Or Neville, whose good qualities were mainly external. They were both young once. I found myself longing to be in Mario's life long enough to find out. I decided right then what I wanted — just one person, not a series of romances to reminisce upon in my later years with the best of my life behind me. Maybe Melissa was right. I could be the one to say something first. How could I know how he'd react?

I thought on Mother's choices. I'd need to write it all out. Think things through. I'd never repeat her mistakes.

Camille was the first adult with whom I'd formed an independent relationship — she was unrelated to me and had no ties with my kin. Yet in our discussions I censored myself. She had a habit of oversharing — and mostly about the lives of others. On the slower days, we all sat talking over carrot cake and eventually — coffee. I learned of her only child, a stepson from a previous marriage whom Mario had met only once. She was happily married again, though, to a Bahamian business owner she'd met on a cruise, paid for with proceeds of her divorce.

"I thought he was from Florida. That's why I even bothered to talk to him. An early retirement in Boca Raton. Can't do Bahamas, though."

"Why not?"

"Too hot. Too small. I bet you think it's odd for two people to be married and live apart." She reached into her drawer and brought out a pack of Du Maurier.

"Not really."

"Right. Maybe not you but other people do. Going to do my rounds. I'll be back." She gathered her lilac dress and left.

Mario got off a call. He rifled through the documents in front of him.

"I just scheduled the sixth maintenance appointment for the week." He reached over and grabbed the pencil sharpener.

"No surprise. This place is a dump. I don't care if it makes me sound hoity-toity." I picked up a sheet. "Guess who's being transferred out? Mr. Kadam, because his ceiling has a hole in it and there's water pouring into his kitchen."

"That's the second transfer this month."

"There's more than that. Look."

I opened a tabbed page in a binder.

"Hm," he said. "This guy isn't even here anymore. He died."

In that moment, dying in Don Mount Court became more frightening than living there.

Later, we confronted Camille about the applications.

"Mr. Kadam is being moved as a priority because of his emphysema, plus it would cost too much to put him up temporarily."

"What about the rest? Tonya Kerry? She's got six kids?" Mario said.

"Those are not transfer forms, and you two are hired to organize, not audit." Camille went over to the cabinet, slid the folders aside, and dropped the papers in. "Neither of you are supposed to have access to anything but maintenance forms. None of this information leaves this office. In fact, go see if they need extra hands at the wading pool."

We stayed put.

"One thing," Mario said. "The engineers are coming tomorrow around six."

"They're coming back? I hope they don't expect me to stay late. I have a full day. Albert is moving."

"Lucky him," I chided.

I stepped past her and went out onto the balcony to see if I could spot what on the earth the engineers were being called in for. If the building was falling apart, we'd be the last to know. In the court, a girl waved from her father's shoulders as her brother sped by on roller skates. I yelled down at him to slow down. The boy braked hard to avoid crashing into a well-dressed woman going by. I bolted into the office.

"My mom's coming."

"That's my cue." Camille grabbed her purse and made a quick exit, turning left at the door so she and Mother would not meet.

Mario and I busied ourselves on opposite ends of the small office. Mother burst in with a "got you" look on her face.

She addressed us from the doorway. "Hello, young man. Where was your boss going in such a hurry?"

"I don't know. I just work here," Mario answered dryly.

She glared in my direction. "And when are you done, five o' clock?"

"Yes, Mommy."

"Come home any later than five minutes past — it'll be me and you." She shut the door.

I doubled over, my stomach in knots.

Breathe, Delia, breathe.

Mario stood up and gave his chair a hard shove. It hit the wall with a crack. I looked up in shock, forgetting the sharp pain in my abdomen.

"I knew it." He pointed at me. "You should've told her I work here, too."

He stood and slammed his hands on the desk. His arms seamed with bulging veins that led to clenched fists.

Know it, Mother had taught me. *Know and measure the rage of a man.*

"Easy for you to say." I was breathing hard.

He turned to face me. "It was only a matter of time before she came up here. Now she'll be more pissed and what is she going to do this time? Break your arm? Punch your teeth out? You don't know."

"I ... I don't think so. She wouldn't ... it's not like that. She can't." I couldn't believe he was blaming me.

"Don't lie. Melissa told me how she hits you and threatens you and reads your diary. She knows you like me."

"Excuse me?" I balked.

"She knows I like you," he said slowly.

He stopped talking, a horrified expression crossing his face. He hadn't meant to say it aloud.

I stood there with my mouth open, thinking at any moment someone could come in and the conversation would end.

"All she does is yell and throw things and, yeah, sometimes she hits me, but I never get hurt. You and Richa are the only kids

I know that don't get licks. It's a very Canadian thing … it's … normal."

He walked over to me and brought his hand to my face, and I felt the wetness of my tears across my cheek. I was crying but hadn't noticed.

"This isn't normal. Johnson isn't normal. I know and I accept it, so I know when and what I can't handle. That's how I deal. That's how I protect myself, 'cause Tia can't do it. My parents can't do it. It's on me. Delia — this is on you. Your mom …" — he glanced at the door — "she's not built like anyone I've ever met, but the way she gets when she's mad. I know that. I recognize that."

He went over to the desk, grabbed some Kleenex out of the box, then handed them to me. For a while I just stood there, thinking about what he said while he picked up some documents that had fallen off the desk. In two hours I'd be walking into a war zone, and already my hands were shaking. Maybe it wouldn't be so bad. Maybe she'd see that Mario was ambitious and dependable, and she would come to understand why we were friends.

"I can run out to the store and get you some Coke and some Hickory Sticks — if you want." Mario sounded remorseful.

"Thanks, but I can't eat anything right now. So … is this why you haven't asked me out?"

He rested his lean body against the desk and scratched his neck. "Well, even if I wanted to, it's too late now. Coach thinks I can at least land a partial scholarship next year. A couple of scouts are interested in me."

"What? Already? So you're leaving after the hard time you've been giving me?"

"Delia, just chill. I'm not sure yet. I'm just saying if I'm only going to be here for a short time … you're special to me and … well, what if it messes up our friendship. I already have Johnson to worry about … and you. I don't even want you to go home right now."

Something inside me fractured. "She's supposed to be my mother — not a fucking dictator. I'm sick of her shit. She ruins everything that makes me happy. And everyone — including you — lets her do it."

A small part of me sensed I was overreacting, but it was the hurting part — over-nourished, and desperate for purging — that won out. I took off with Mario yelling at my back.

Mother met me at the door, her fury palpable and foul. The first word out of her mouth was merciless. I turned to run. Her strong hands clutched my collar, and my shirt ripped. She jerked me around a little.

"You're a liar and a whore. You won't be going back."

"No," I said, my voice sounding like someone else. "I don't want to quit. I didn't do anything wrong."

My mother's eyes widened. I could sense her disbelief sinking in.

I stomped all the way up the steps and waited for her to follow. I'd shove her right down them if she came for me. I was ready.

"Where do you think you're going? I'm talking to you, Delia Ellis," she yelled, but did not follow me.

I went to my room and shut the door. Melissa was already waiting.

"I hate her."

"Don't say that." Melissa tried to straighten my shirt.

"You will, too. Just wait."

"She knew about Mario all along and came home super early to catch you."

She put me to sit on the bed, then patted my face with a damp, warm towel.

"Did she hit you?"

"No," I said. "But she might as well have."

"What about Mario?"

"I wish she would've. He likes me but doesn't want to date me. Oh, did I mention he's leaving?"

"What? He said that?"

My sister seemed more shocked that I was divulging details at all. For a long while I'd stopped telling her anything because she had a big mouth, and her friends at school knew my business.

Mother was already on the phone, yelling. I buried my face into my hands.

"Great. Now she's bringing Dad into this. What the hell is he going to do?"

Melissa said, oddly calm, "I think they call it leverage. Well, just 'cause they're splitting up doesn't give her the right to take it out on you."

She scanned the courtyard casually as if the loss was mine alone.

"It's all a bluff," I said. "She thought he would come back. She thought he would fail and that he would choose us over his own happiness. As if any of that makes any sense."

"I know what'll make you feel better," Melissa said. "I'll be right back."

I nursed my wounds. She returned a while later. I stared at her empty hands and shrugged.

"Just wait by the window. Sit over there."

I looked out. A few seconds later, Mario turned the corner, standing a few metres from the front door in his dress shirt and shorts. I could see him searching for the perfect spot where he would not get caught. My mother would kill him. I caught myself smiling. He made three signs with his hands.

I love you.

I restrained myself. I was supposed to be angry.

Melissa opened the window. "Ask her!"

He cupped his mouth with his hands. "Be my girl."

I scrunched up my face.

"Come on, Delia."

"Fine," I said, then shooed him off.

He blew me a kiss, then, seemingly alarmed by something or someone spotted in the kitchen window, disappeared around the bend.

Chapter 20

Low Tide

August 1995

Dear Diary,

I'm sure now that Neville is cheating. Richa and I saw him at Caribana with the lady from the party. I can't tell Mom because I wasn't even supposed to be there. It's bad enough that I snuck out of church, but it's practically the only place she lets us go alone.

Forget Neville. Mom has enough on her plate. Money is tight. She hasn't been to the hairdresser in weeks and saves the grocery flyers she used to toss out. Can you believe that? She won't even let me help out. Even though Grandma convinced her to let me keep my job, she took all my cheques to "save" them for me. She's so spiteful. Next time, I'll find a cash job. Maybe Richa can teach me how

to braid extensions or I'll tutor her friends (Lord
knows they need it).

I can't wait for the first day of school. Richa,
Nicole, the twins, and I are going to the Eaton Centre
after lunch. All the high schools are supposed to meet
up there. It's going to be so dope.

I am
Delia

Mother left us sliced fried plantains draining on paper towels and,
on a saucer, four slices of hard-dough bread cut thick. Why only one
saucer? Did she want me to give Melissa the saucer? Was that the test?
I read into everything Mother did — looking for clues. Everything
in our house was a trap of some sort. For mice. For critters. For me.
I fed myself a slice while deciphering the instructions she'd left. Two
cheques bookmarked the place where her notes were messily scratched:
*Deliver the rent to Camille and pay the car insurance ($125). Don't
forget the receipt!*

I flipped through the notepad, seeing numerous lists of expenses:
insurance, $125; rent, $750; Zeller's credit card, $250; Leon's, $1,000.
On another page, *Sell the car* (with a single red stroke through it).
Further on, strange names, job titles, and phone numbers.

Spotting the clock, I shoved the cheques into my purse and set
out to Camille's office.

Just as I approached the door, it opened, and three unfamiliar men strutted past me without saying hello. I went in. Camille
looked up and saw me.

"Oh, thank goodness. I thought you were one of the engineers.
If I didn't ever have to talk to one of them again it would be too
soon." Her eyes went to my hands. "Rent?"

I nodded and handed her the cheque. "Sorry it's late. It just slipped her mind."

She examined it.

"Something wrong? Mom's good with her figures. She doesn't make mistakes."

Camille adjusted her glasses. "Last time there was a bit of a misunderstanding with the amount. She thought the subsidy was processed, but this is right."

I eyed her. "I didn't think we qualified for subsidized housing."

"That was before," Camille said.

Before what? What changed?

"Don't worry, I'll find other options if the application stalls. I, for one, believe working folk should get priority."

Though her insult wasn't directed at us, I couldn't help but feel that before long we, too, would land in that bucket of the pitied and undeserving. It had felt that way back in Hadsworth, even when life, by comparison, was very good. I sought Camille's eyes for evidence of hidden judgment as I bid her goodbye and thanked her for promises she would never keep.

•

I was in eleventh grade, and it was Melissa's first year in high school. She attended an arts school farther into the city and loved that she could be home later than me. At the end of the first week, Richa, Mario, and I walked to Don Mount together. Mario was preparing for his final year and Richa, well, she was excited about getting her driver's licence. Her boyfriend, she claimed, had a spare car he was willing to gift her. She had booked her first road test and was studying for it harder than anything I'd ever seen her study in school.

I lagged a short distance behind them, rolling my eyes at Richa's comments. They both seemed different. Richa was growing her hair out, and she had dyed the ends to match her new red Fila sneakers.

Mario wore black from head to toe and was over-accessorized in his headband, cap, watch, and wristband. Every dress-down day, guys from the Catholic school came by to show off their personal style, and as we walked, girls gawked and called out to Mario, prompting Richa to shout unkind things and encourage me to do the same. I thought he looked absolutely ridiculous.

"Richa," Mario said, "calm down. You can't get into any fights."

She nodded at him, recommitting some quiet promise, and for a moment it was like I wasn't even there. I quickened my pace to catch up.

"Did you book your SAT exam?" I asked Mario.

"Yup, and since Johnson is out with his buddies, I can focus on my applications tonight. Whatch'all up to?"

"Braiding Melissa's hair," Richa said.

"What?" He turned to me. "Where's Tyson?"

"Geez, she's not a monster. Richa can come over. I asked."

"She did say 'hi' to me the last time I saw her," Richa was talking to me, but she was still looking back at the girls we'd passed.

"You were with your grandmother. That doesn't count."

I changed the topic. Where Richa was concerned, my mother was off limits.

We were almost home when a police cruiser approached. Just ahead of us it pulled over beside a young man headed our way. Richa pulled us in a different direction.

"Come this way," she said. "They're always around now. I saw some undercover guys acting like workers."

I sighed. "They're engineers. They've been here all summer."

Richa continued to defend her conspiracy theory. We argued for a bit.

"Delia's right," Mario said. "They're gentrifying the area."

I blinked at him. "They're doing what?"

"Wow. A new word for you?" Mario said.

Richa slapped him across the back of his neck.

"Ouch! All right — all right. They're knocking the whole thing down. Even Regent."

"For real?" I said, stopping momentarily to look around at the wide network of buildings.

"Yup. They just haven't told everybody yet." Mario rubbed his neck. "Everybody is being relocated until the new buildings are built."

Richa sucked her teeth. "People live here. They can't do that."

"They can." I thought of my parents' predictions on the future of public housing in the city. "We're borrowing valuable space. It was only a matter of time."

We took the side street and climbed the small hill to the parking lot, where we ran into my mother peering into the open trunk of her car. Mario opted for another route. We came up behind her.

"Perfect timing. There was a sale at Knob Hill Farms, so I stocked up. Everyone's shopping now, before it gets cold."

I noticed her flats. "Did you take the day off?"

"No." Her tone intensified. "Is there anything else you'd like to know?"

I stayed quiet while we unloaded the black baskets. After a few trips, only a leather case remained. I reached for it.

She swatted away my hand. "Leave it. That's mine."

Her gaze held mine until I yielded. Then she waited for me to move off before shutting the trunk, growing evidence of our mutual distrust. I didn't let her scare me off. I joined her in the kitchen to help with dinner. She had the pressure cooker on the stove.

"Pass me the red peas, a green onion, coconut milk, chicken stock, black pepper, seasoning salt, thyme, and rice."

I dashed between the cupboards and fridge, gathering the ingredients and daydreaming about the day I'd be cooking at my own stove. She watched over my shoulder as she directed me, kindly but firmly pointing out my missteps. When it was nearly done, she let me taste it.

"I'll never get it this good on my own."

She smiled, flattered by my self-deprecating compliment.

"Practice and patience. That's all it takes to perfect anything."

We chatted about the new stores she discovered on Spadina Road. I wondered where she found the time. Feeling good, I settled into a chair and made like I wanted to have a longer conversation. As if I had forgotten who my mother was. Midway through a sentence, she cut me off.

"Don't you have homework?"

I grabbed my bag and promptly got to my tasks.

With Richa gone and Melissa upstairs admiring her new braids, Mother was free to speak her mind. I braced for a talk about Richa having a lighter. I'd seen Mother studying her as she burnt the ends of Melissa's hair extensions to seal the braids.

"I have good news," she said. "Starting this week, my work hours will be changing."

"How?"

"I'll be taking on fewer shifts. I can't let you be latchkey kids like these other poor children around here."

I blinked, not knowing what to say.

"If the office calls, ignore it. They'll try to keep track of my whereabouts to see if I'm working anywhere else. They don't have the right to do that."

As she spoke, I got the impression that her revised schedule was involuntary, and though she tried to conjure a celebratory mood, more questions hung in the air, the answers trapped in the cobwebs at the corners of the room.

"It will be good." She gave a final nod.

That's how I knew it was bothering her. My mouth twitched with worry.

"Maybe we can get our rent lowered," I said. "People who work still qualify for subsidized housing and since we're already —"

"I know. I taught you that." She wagged a finger at me. "I haven't sunk that low. I help people." She jabbed at her own chest.

"Yes, Mommy." I lowered my gaze, sensing her embarrassment.

She chastised me a while longer for my brazenness and stupidity. Clearly, Don Mount was rubbing off on me. A poor state of mind is like chalk, she went on — it leaves residue everywhere. I was glad for my sister's timely interruption.

"Um, the pipe in the bathroom is leaking."

"I'll tell Camille," I said.

"No, that woman would do anything to get in here and see what I have."

We barely made it upstairs before she was on the phone ordering Neville over to fix the pipes.

Melissa and I decided to play a game of Scrabble before bed. Half an hour later, the game board remained empty.

"She's getting worse. We have to tell Dad. I mean — Cliff." Melissa switched out her letter blocks.

"Stop calling him that. It's rude. He already sends her money for us. Grandma said it's not a lot but at least he does. Plus, she'll obviously get another job."

I went over Mother's talk in my mind, trying to recall where she mentioned an intent to find a new job. Then I remembered the leather case in the car trunk and the new barrel she was packing.

•

Mother's transition to hybrid working woman started out better than expected. The Monday after she broke the news, I came home to the woodsy smell of smoked herring and a loud chugging from the sewing machine. Melissa met me at the door.

"Did you see?"

I scanned the room. A bouquet of fresh chrysanthemums had replaced the artificial orchids on the table and in the cabinet behind, the crystal shone.

"There's more. You gotta go downstairs."

"Okay, but later. I have a ton of homework."

"For which subject, math or Mario?"

"Oh, shut up."

I put my textbooks out on the table, then checked on Mother. She had set up the sewing machine on a desk next to a floor lamp where my father's table had been. Her new station was surrounded by rolls of various materials. She hit the pedal on the machine, then stopped to rethread the needle.

"How do people who stay home ever get bored? I've never been so busy."

Stay home? I concealed my terror by digging my nails into my palms.

"What are you making?"

"These two are curtains." She pointed to a pile of white lace. "And this is the valance that'll come across the top. I saw it in a magazine."

"For the living room window?" I counted three open barrels.

"Mm-hm," she said.

Was she packing or unpacking? I observed her briefly then said, "I'll get your dinner ready."

"Thanks," she said without looking up, "but I'm not hungry yet."

Open barrels, new curtains, and a Saturday dinner on a Monday. Maybe Mother had finally given up on her ambitions and decided to get comfortable.

Neville's arrival reinforced my idea. I watched as he presented Mother with fresh meat from her favourite butcher. When he laid the brown paper packages on the table, she rushed off to the kitchen with them like someone who was glad to have something to do.

I lamented as we brushed our teeth before bed.

"It's like I'm living in ancient times." I pounded my chest with my fists. "Man bring meat. Woman cook."

Melissa spat toothpaste all over the sink as she laughed. Then, being the more empathetic one, she said, "He did buy groceries without being asked, and he fixed the pipes." She pointed at the hole in the wall.

"I know. He's super awesome now that she's been domesticated."

"Do you want Mom to be with Neville or not? Make up your mind already."

"I have mixed feelings," I said.

"Fair enough." Melissa set the toothbrush in the holder and dried her hands. "That's how I feel about Cliff, who still hasn't sent us a ticket. I bet he's gonna put us off till Christmas."

I didn't bother telling her that he already had pushed our visit to next year. It was only October.

"Delia? Melissa? Come down here," Neville called.

We shrugged at each other before joining Neville, who was in the living room with Mother, shuffling a deck of cards.

"I bet you can't win."

It felt like he was speaking directly to me.

"You're on." Melissa pushed past me.

I hesitated, considering whether his invitation was akin to collusion.

He smirked at me. "You 'fraid?"

Mother sat by his side, caressing his back as he dealt cards onto the table.

I stepped forward to join them, trying to think positively about my new reality, and for a little while it worked. I saw my mother sit on the carpet beside us, something she never did. She played cards hard and smack-talked and boasted. Mother smiled the entire time and so I did, too. Even Melissa, a sore loser, enjoyed herself. I didn't think about what came before or what would come after. We played for two hours. As for Neville, he wasn't bluffing. He won every game.

•

It wasn't planned, but Richa and I skipped last class on the Friday before Thanksgiving weekend so we could catch the basketball tournament. We got there during the third quarter and sat on one of the lower bleachers. When Mario spotted us, he waved. I waved back enthusiastically, wanting people to notice.

Richa snapped her fingers to get my attention. "Hey, I've been trying to call you. Your number changed."

"No, it didn't."

"I have something to tell you."

I figured it was something to do with her boyfriend.

"I'm pregnant."

I froze. I could only think of what my mother would say. *This is why girls should be kept in the house.* Something like that.

"Congrats?" I shrugged. "Now I get why you've been away so much and why Nicole and Jess have been guarding you. Does Mario know?"

She nodded. "He's not happy."

"Because you may be giving birth to the anti-Christ."

"Delia!"

"Just kidding. What did your grandma say?"

"She cried. She says I'm going to be dropout like my mom. It was the worst, Delia." Her eyes teared up.

"Hey." I pulled her close to me. "You can do correspondence and night school. I'll help."

"How? Babies are a big responsibility."

"You're having a baby, not going off to war. Plus," I said, "I'm only helping with your homework. Between Mom, Melissa, and Neville, I'm raising three kids of my own."

Richa pulled away from me and rushed out of the gym. I follow-ed, afraid I'd upset her, and was relieved to find her hunched over a garbage can. I brought over paper towels.

"Yet again, our day ends early because of your drama," I joked.

"Still doesn't beat your mom catching you at the freaky Friday party."

"Problems are clearly subjective. Let's go home."

At once, I was afraid of how different our lives would become. How could she let this happen? Especially with a guy like Naveed? I never let on how I felt. It was unfair for me to project my expectations onto her. While I was disappointed that Richa would be hitched forever to her unfit boyfriend, she was one of the toughest and most loving people I'd ever met. She'd be a great mother. She could do this. Me? Not a chance.

My grandma Liz once said, "Delia, if you don't plan your life, the universe will plan it for you."

It was time for me to plot my own path.

At home, Mother's friend Pearl typed at the computer while Mother placed large pink rollers in her hair. I greeted them and hurried into the kitchen for a snack.

"You can live in the ghetto without having a ghetto mentality," Mother said.

"What do you mean by that?" asked Pearl.

"When I am on the street, no one knows I live in public housing. I am here partly out of choice, partly circumstance."

"That sounds very wise."

Poor Pearl didn't realize Mother was insulting her. For as long as we'd known her, Pearl hadn't married or worked. She lived in the same rundown townhome in south Regent Park. Ironically, Pearl's twin daughters were stellar students who carried Bibles in their knapsacks. We would never be them. Mother should have been asking her for advice.

I made myself a root beer float and considered Richa's news, then remembered her comment about our phone. I dialed our number and got an automated service message that the number had been changed. I slammed the handset down. Why would Mother keep this a secret from us? It was also clear she had kept it from our father as well. I'd have to convince Melissa to get a hold of Neville's new cellphone. It was the only way.

Mother was still lecturing Pearl when Melissa arrived from a late school trip to the museum. On the way to meet her at the door, the pulsing cursor on the computer screen caught my attention. I eyed the monitor. Mother's work history was typed out before me. I squinted at the details of her recent position, with an end date of June 1995. Mother reached out in front of Pearl to hit the power button.

Chapter 21

The Hummingbird

November 1995

On the morning of my birthday, Melissa strolled into my room, singing like she did every year. She dropped a handmade card onto my bed.

"Sorry. You're the first casualty of my allowance reduction."

"Your outfit is a casualty. Where is the rest of it?"

"Everyone wears tights. Plus, I'm going to the breakfast club."

"That's for poor kids," I whispered.

"Exactly." She snickered. "Did you ask Mom about Red Lobster?"

"No, she doesn't have a job. Why would I?" I said. "And I won't beg to go to McDonald's like you did."

"You don't ask, you don't get." She shook her hair and batted her long lashes at me. "Well, at least ask for your money back. Anyway, I'm off to eat pancakes and bacon. See ya later."

"That better be turkey bacon."

She stuck her tongue out at me and left. I heard her strut down the steps, then a loud commotion.

"Where the hell are you going in that? Put some clothes on."

A parade of movement. Melissa sprinted up the stairs and past my room, followed closely by my mother, robe trailing behind her, shouting. I laughed to myself. It was pointless. Melissa would pull on a pair of jeans over her tights and change at school. Since my mother had hijacked my birthday and my father didn't care about me anymore, I skipped my shower, threw on the first clean outfit I could find, and went to school.

Mario met me at the crosswalk.

"What's up, birthday girl?" He guided me away from the crowd and over to the bench. "I have something for you."

"The streetcar is coming," I said.

"We'll catch the next one." He rubbed his hands together. "Your sixteenth birthday is special, so naturally I had to deliver. Especially since I might miss your next one."

He squeezed my hand.

"So this should keep you until we celebrate your next birthday together."

I scanned the street. No sign of Mother.

"Close your eyes."

He took my hand, then placed a package in my palm. I opened my eyes.

I flipped open the tiny lid and studied him. "I don't have any money for bail."

"It's completely legit. I've been saving for a hot minute. Here."

He removed the thin gold necklace and placed it around my neck, before fastening the clasp. From it hung a pendant: a gold, green-eyed hummingbird, with a tiny tail coiled under its belly. It was the most beautiful thing I'd ever seen.

"I know you're not allowed to wear jewellery, which I still think is stupid, but I figured as long as you have it, you won't forget me." He watched me intently.

"Are you sure?" I studied the pendant. "You haven't even gotten accepted yet."

"I'm leaving soon. I feel it in my gut."

I wrapped my arms around him. "I'd kiss you but not here."

"No," he said, looking around. "Definitely not here."

A car went by. I flinched.

"I should get you to school."

"Yes, please."

We got to the stop just as another streetcar pulled up.

Richa and a few other friends waited by my locker, now disguised in pink and silver streamers and glitter. She noticed my new accessory right away. They all cheered and congratulated me like he'd proposed. During class, the office paged me down. I found Mother chatting casually to the receptionist, which made me curious. She wore a black wrap dress and gold accessories, which reminded me of the necklace. I quickly tucked it into my shirt.

"Happy birthday, honey." She kissed me on the cheek. "I came to take you to lunch."

"Lucky girl," the secretary said.

"There's a lovely Japanese restaurant in the financial district."

"Sounds fancy," I said, unable to hide my glee as she signed me out of school.

She rested a hand on the counter, displaying the foreign ring on her wedding finger. I wondered if this display was for me or the people in the front office.

On the way downtown, I watched the business workers making their way between the buildings. Everyone looked like they were on a racetrack, in lanes only they could see. I wondered what each of them did for a living, where they lived, and whether the women had families. I wondered what my mother thought of them — if this was something she aspired to, but I couldn't find the courage to ask anything.

We sat near the fireplace in the second-floor restaurant.

"It's beautiful here." I surveyed the glass walls. "How did you find it?"

"I do a lot of exploring during the day."

The server showed up and took our orders of teriyaki salmon and a sushi bento box.

"I didn't know you liked sushi," she said. "I'm terrified to try it."

I didn't know you were afraid of anything. We agreed she would try some of mine.

I looked up at the mezzanine. "I'd like to work somewhere like this one day."

Mother looked intrigued. "What are you planning to study in college? You only have two years left."

One, actually.

"I really like architecture ... and language."

"You could write for a magazine like the ones your father used to collect." She had a faraway look about her.

The food arrived.

"Here, taste." I offered a small piece of yellowfin with my chopsticks.

She chewed and considered. "Not bad. I would try that again."

Lunch sped by and soon we were back in the car, heading east on Queen Street.

I swallowed. "Mom, I was thinking of babysitting to make some extra money, so I don't have to bother you for an allowance."

"Things aren't that bad. Plus, I've decided to broaden my options. I'm looking for property outside the city. Houses are cheaper." She disarmed me with her unusually upbeat attitude.

But you don't have a job. Are we moving in with Neville?

"Where?" I said. "When?"

We pulled up outside of the front office.

"I'm working on it," she said. "Mommy's got it figured out. Soon you'll be finished school and working, and we'll both be able to carry whatever expenses we have."

She reached over and kissed me on the cheek.

"Right," I said. "Thanks for lunch, Mommy. I really appreciate it."

"Of course." She pressed the button to release my seat belt. "Come straight home after school."

I watched the car pull away, thinking how nice it was to get a glimpse at how normal Mother could be. It was the first time she'd made her intentions for me known. When the car turned the corner onto the main road, I pulled the necklace out of my shirt and rubbed the pendant, considering my own plans.

•

Later, at home, when everyone was asleep, I called Mario from the kitchen phone.

"Hey, you sound sleepy," I said when he picked up.

"I am, but *Tales from the Crypt* is on. Come watch it with me."

I stifled my laughter. "If my mother caught me at your house, she would punch us both in the face."

"True. Did you tell her that you want to go away for school after grade twelve?"

"No. I aim to live past my birthday. I'll wait till Neville's around."

"What about Melissa?"

"I'm waiting for her to piss me off. Seems like the right time to say that sort of thing."

"So, you like the necklace, right? If you don't —"

"Are you crazy? I love it. It's safely tucked away in my underwear drawer."

"Interesting choice."

I could tell he was smiling, which made me giggle. Perhaps too loudly. During a lull of rustling leaves outside came a soft click from the other line.

"I hear bees," I said.

"Love you." He hung up at my signal.

With the soft ticking of the clock at my back, I tiptoed up the steps, feeling my way in the dark, then climbed into bed.

The shadow in my dream floated in front of the dresser. In the mirror, there was no reflection of it, and when it slipped its branch-like fingers into the top drawer, I tried to shoo it away. It got angry and pulled the blanket over me. I couldn't breathe.

At some point in the night, I awoke and, remembering the dream, crept over to the dresser and went into the top drawer for the box. Nearly reassured, I opened it. In the moonlight, the blue velvet interior became a blank, grey swatch. It was empty. I switched on the light and spun around. I went back into the drawer, searching. I tossed around the contents. I lifted my mattress, then set it down. I went for my knapsack. It was gone. I went to Melissa's room and flipped on the switch.

"Where's your knapsack?" I asked her, looking around. "It's not in here and mine is gone. So is my necklace."

She rubbed her eyes and squinted. "Turn the light off!"

The commotion alerted our mother. She sashayed across the hall in a black robe, hands grasping the handles of two knapsacks. From the doorway, she threw them into the room, sending the contents tumbling onto the floor.

"Someone," she said, "keeps calling late at night and listening. Just listening to hear what's happening in this house. I checked your school agendas to see if the numbers matched up to any of your friends' numbers. When I change the number this time, neither of you will get it."

She came closer.

"By the way," she said to me. "Don't use my phone to plot your escape with Mario."

Melissa looked at me.

"I know you don't care about me, but to think you'd abandon your sister for a boy. You are your father's child." She glared, then turned on her heel and left.

"What's she talking about?" Melissa's expression reminded me of her younger self.

I saw myself years into the future, standing in the same room, steeling myself against Mother's anger, absorbing her disappointments, and trying to retain my composure for my sister's sake.

"Hold on. Give me a minute," I told her in the mirror.

My hands shook as I bent to scoop the books into our respective bags.

Chapter 22

Nurture

December 1995

Our parents were on speaking terms again, though during their brief calls, they spoke mostly about money or when "the papers" would be signed. Mother discussed this openly, as she walked about redressing our space with floral wallpaper and sheet sets. She established a new routine: Seek. Acquire. Create. Consume. Repeat. When she perfected her groove, she branched out, leveraging my relationship with Camille to land a volunteer position at the Blue House. By this time, our enthusiasm for her domestic efforts had waned. The roast beef tasted stringy in our teeth; the fried snapper fish a lethal dose of fine bones.

Even though I was angry with him, I still called my father, and he, missing me (though not nearly enough to visit), was pleased. He always had good news, which was nice because I had none to share. I just couldn't hold a grudge like my sister could.

"It's a custom-built house," he said, when I called him. "On just over one acre."

"That's great. I can't wait to see you and, of course, the house. Christmas break starts —"

"I know — but I was thinking March break would be best. The house will close just before then."

I counted the months. "Sure."

"We could even take a road trip to Florida to see your grandmother Liz and your uncles."

The more grandiose the promises, the less I believed them. Words like *hope* and *soon* were a call to action for people like my father who were always in the market for buying time. I kept talking to him, though, because a part of me was still the thirteen-year-old who saw her father as a safety net. Neville, on the other hand, seemed more adept at this double life, bouncing between houses at the bequest of each caller to his phone. Mother watched him take his calls outside, sometimes seeming upset, other days, relieved. One day she stopped watching him at all.

Around the winter holiday, Mario met me inside the double door exit of school, where the smokers hung out. It would be our last visit before the new year. He was spending the break with his mother's family. Johnson was in the hospital. Though he'd been quiet about it, I could see it had been wearing him down.

"Hey." He opened his coat and brought out a slightly bent envelope.

He was wearing the same jersey as the day before. I didn't mention it.

"A card."

"Yeah, with a lot of writing, just the way you like it. Plus, it's from me, and well ..."

I went to open it, but he stopped me.

"For later — don't let your mother find this. In fact — burn it after you read it."

"Then you might as well just tell me."

It took him nearly the whole way home to explain what he had written. When he was finished, we were already in the parking lot, and I was speechless.

"This can work," he said. "If you apply next year, you can get into the same college. We can get student loans and live off campus."

"Let me think about it," I said.

He pulled me close and kissed me firmly on the lips. I kissed him back.

We broke apart when my toes went numb.

"Be ready to talk about it when I get back," he said. "You better be thinking of me the whole time I'm gone."

"Merry Christmas to you, too."

I had a habit of looking down when I walked, to avoid the cold drifts and the wind, which is why I missed Mother staring out her window as I entered the backyard.

Melissa did her best, making small talk to break the tension, but our mother armoured the house with her silence. Then later, as I waited for her to come in and whale on me, she went into the kitchen and began to throw the dishes to the floor.

"After all I've done to raise you right, this is what you want?" she said, "To have a baby, like your friend? Not my child. Not my house!"

Mother's outcry vibrated everything in close range: the china, the windowpanes, my insides. When she was finished shattering our dishes, she came to me.

"He just brought me a card. For Christmas," I said, even though I suspected she had seen us making out.

She looked appalled. "Oh, must be nice to be brought cards and jewellery and live in la-la land. You've been so caught up in romance, my insurance has lapsed. Where's the cheque I gave you to pay it months ago?"

I blinked, then glanced at the front pocket of my knapsack. I'd bought the stamps but ...

She rolled up her sleeves. Melissa, who was sitting behind me, tried to pull me out of range, but Mother ripped me out of her tender clutch. Buttons flew from my shirt.

"Move." She pushed Melissa out of the way.

"Get up," Mother said to me.

I would not have time to compose myself.

•

Neville searched me out that night. When I came to the door, he took one look at me and shook his head. His eyes darted around like he was looking for someone else to take his place. Finally, he offered a single pat on the shoulder.

"Ugh, it's okay," he said. "I'll clean up the mess."

Melissa showed up on cue. She'd been snooping like I'd taught her to. She told him everything I didn't know, like how Mother had asked for my diary that morning.

He rubbed his temple.

"Delia, you know how your mother is. Why take that risk? Just talk to your friends when you're outside. Stop all this writing down yuh business."

I eyed the drawer in which I'd thrown my diary. I'd only brought it home for the holidays. I began to fret.

"Can you stay here tonight, please?" Melissa said to Neville.

He mumbled something about Jesus under his breath and went to find our mother.

The two of them finally emerged from the basement an hour later, talking calmly. Neville promised Mother the cash to cover the insurance. She thanked him and insisted he stay for dinner. Later, when I heard laughter from across the hall, it was only Mother's voice that I heard.

I thought on what Neville had asked me about writing in my journal — why it was important. It would have been so much easier not to have something to hide. I could keep the thoughts in my head. I had tried, but there just wasn't room for it all. All my ideas old and new became jumbled up with feelings, and I couldn't make my way through a thing that needed to be talked out with myself. I needed to write, to see myself for who I truly was at a point in time, and measure against my heart how close I was to who I wanted to be.

•

Near the end of winter break, Richa came by. I knew it was urgent because she hated the cold. She confirmed my mother wasn't home and told me to call her in ten minutes sharp. When I did, she put me on hold, then patched in Mario using the three-way service.

"I'm putting down this phone for fifteen minutes," Richa said.

"Hey, babes," he said. "You all right?"

I took a deep breath, elated at the sound of his voice. "Yeah."

"Honestly, I think the whole thing with Richa is freaking her out. She's scared."

"Well, her patented kick-the-shit-out-of-you birth control method is very effective. I swear she never wanted kids at all. She hates me."

Mario sighed like he was searching for an answer. "Although, she didn't leave her kids with an ill-equipped guardian. Points for that."

"Should you really get credit for doing what you're supposed to?"

Why should I lower the bar for adults? They had the freedom to create fewer problems for themselves.

"How's Johnson?" I said.

"Off and on."

"Now that you have your conditional offers, what next?"

"The family's taking over. I'm trying to get used to it. Funny thing. Yesterday, Johnson told me not to worry — that you'd take care of him. He said he'd met your mom, and that you come from good stock." He laughed. "He had some more things to say about her, but they aren't for your ears."

"I can guess. She's gorgeous and men fall over her — hence her problems. Glad I won't have to be bothered with all that."

Mario ignored my attempt to fish for compliments.

"I told Johnson that you'd only be around for another year or so."

I smiled. It didn't seem so far away.

"Did you tell him why? What did he say?"

"He said that if I had any kind of sense, that I would — you know what, it doesn't matter. He was drunk. I miss you," he whispered.

"You, too."

Richa joined the line and we chatted about her plans for school. After we hung up, I enlisted Melissa's help to find the necklace. I wasn't sure how much time we had before Mother came back, so I used a butter knife to unlock the master bedroom door. Melissa searched the drawers as I carefully lifted, then replaced, the shoe-boxes on the upper shelf of the closet.

"I think I see something," Melissa said.

She lay flat on the ground, waving her hand underneath the box spring, then brought out a white rectangular device. We inspected it. It was a baby monitor.

"A baby gift for Richa?" Melissa said.

I shook my head, horrified. "We need to find the other one."

Melissa claimed she had found more items and retrieved them as I went to search our rooms, where I suspected I'd find the other device. When I returned, Melissa had spread a bounty across the violet sheet: a large manila envelope, Toby, and a teal dress. I placed the two monitors beside them. We stood back, taking it all in.

"I bet she's heard everything," I said.

"But why my room?" Melissa said, sounding hurt. "All we do in there is —"

"Talk."

She cupped a hand over her mouth. "Oh."

I took the envelope and removed the contents, scanning them.

"She still hasn't signed the divorce papers," I said, sliding them back in.

Melissa ran her fingers across Toby's lone beady eye but did not pick up the toy. Instead, she reached for the dress and held it up.

"Whose is this?" she said. "It's not Mom's style."

"Or size," I added, though I knew exactly who it belonged to.

How did it end up at our place? What had Mother done?

It would have been easier for us to process if the necklace had turned up or the envelope held keepsakes, like a lock of hair or baby teeth. Mother was gathering evidence. What for? Against whom? What else had gone missing?

I sat on the bed. A brisk draft pierced through the defective plastic barrier Mother put over the window. Melissa wrapped her arms around her chest.

"So, what are we gonna do with the monitors?"

Switch them. That's what she would do.

"Throw them out." I handed them to her. "And if she asks, you can tell her that I did it."

•

Mother hadn't left the house in days. I couldn't wait any longer to act on my plan. First, I convinced Melissa to accompany me on a walk. It cost me two Skor bars, but it was worth it. I needed her to be in a good mood. After wandering the second court, we explored the backroads to admire the tall, narrow century homes in the tight corridors that led to De Grassi Street. Beautiful wreaths hung from the doors, and Christmas lights reflected off the snow.

I stopped at a house with a steeply pitched roof and tiny irregular windows.

"Dad would like this one," I said.

Melissa nodded. "It has character. Delia, can you believe we've never been allowed to trick-or-treat? We should go next year."

"Okay."

She looked at me. "You mean it?"

I said, "Yeah, we should try new things. All we do is listen to Mom and she can't even figure out her own shit."

Melissa pretended to clutch her pearls.

We got to her old middle school, a single-storey building with bright murals painted across the exterior. On the lawn bordering the drop-off lane was a stunning twelve-foot replica of a totem pole.

"There." I pointed nearby. "By that oak tree."

I brushed the snow away from the trunk with my boots, then unzipped my jacket and brought out the book I'd stuffed inside. I flipped the diary over in my hands, then dropped it to the ground.

"Lighter."

Melissa pressed the switch and lowered it to the edge of the book.

"Hey." I stepped in front of her.

"Move, Delia. You won't do it. I know you."

I stood back and waited as she clicked the switch repeatedly. Soon, a wisp of smoke and a short crackle escaped from my written words. Mother could never have them. My tongue burned. I pushed Melissa and kicked the book over into the ice.

"Seriously?"

"I can't." I went over and picked it up.

"You'll regret it. She'll get to it again. You can't keep it in your locker all the time."

"This is mine. I'm keeping it forever."

"Figures you'd make me walk all the way out here for nothing."

"I wanted to talk."

"About?"

"Mom. I love her, but I don't want to be like her or Dad. I'll keep my word." I took a deep breath. "If I leave for school, I'll find a way to bring you with me."

She stopped walking. "So, you are taking off."

I looked her in the eye. "No. I'm going away to school. Away from her, and it has nothing to do with Mario."

Melissa shoved her hands into her pockets. "Or me?"

"In another year you can join me, but it'll have to be your choice. I can't force you."

Down a back alley, we trudged over fallen branches. They snapped beneath our feet. Melissa went quiet, which made me nervous. She gathered a handful of snow, rounded it into a ball, and threw it at a tree. I began to second-guess myself.

"Are you sure this is what you want, or is this Mario's idea?" she said to me.

I thumbed the wet, crumbling edges of my diary, praying the pages were still intact. I didn't answer, Telling someone else's truth was so much easier than telling your own.

Chapter 23

The First Episode

May 1996

The event my sister and I would come to refer to as the "first episode" was neither a first nor a singular occurrence, but we recounted it as such due to its novelty. In time we'd come to realize we were bearing witness to a pattern of unfamiliar behaviour. For us, Mother's emergent illness was indistinguishable from her nature: a hot-headed, strong-willed Jamaican woman. So what if she was talking to herself and flying off the handle at the simplest of errors? We paid her no mind. We had lives, extracurricular activities, and friends. Mother could take care of herself.

Richa's pregnancy was a hot topic at school, and each of her closest friends professed their loyalty to the unborn child through some sacrifice. Nicole stole three packs of maternity vitamins, and Jess was suspended for telling off a teacher who questioned Richa's maternal fitness. Somehow, without any reliable source of income, they held a baby shower. I had nothing to offer besides emotional support, which is why I was surprised when she asked me to be her child's godmother.

"Me? Why not Jessica or Nicole? They've been competing for months."

"Because I like the way your mother raised you guys. I want her to be smart."

"Thanks, but I'm still not sure what a godparent does."

"You know, be there for her growing up. Buy gifts, come to parties ... don't you have a godmother?"

"No. Why don't you ask a couple?"

"That's what I'm doing. Mario will be the godfather."

I tried not to make a face. "If it would be anyone, it would be him, I guess."

"Delia, is it a yes or no?"

"Yes, yes. I accept."

Richa squealed and threw her arms around me, nearly toppling me over.

"Mario won't be able to turn me down now. By the way, have you seen him this week?"

"For a quick sec. He was on his way to see Johnson in the hospital."

"You going to visit?"

"Uh-uh."

We approached the science lab.

"I hate coming to school like this." She motioned at her belly.

"Just one more month, then the semester's over. Is he picking you up today?"

I hated saying Naveed's name.

"Yeah. Do you want a ride?"

"Nope. I just want to make sure he's doing his job."

"See, that's why you're the godmother."

I watched her go in and waited until she was seated before heading to my next class.

•

A group project kept me late after school. By the time I left, the hallways were practically empty. I turned the corner to the foyer and was surprised to see Richa looking out at the street. I came up behind her.

"Hey."

She turned around, teary-eyed. "Hey."

"Are you ready to go?" I said.

She squinted in confusion.

"You've been waiting for me, right?" I grabbed her hand. "Fairy godmother has an extra bus ticket."

She leaned against me as we walked. "Why do I like him?"

"Beats me. I'm just your friend," I said. "He should treat you better than I do."

"So, what am I supposed to do? Stay single?"

As usual, she was completely missing the point.

"You're bringing a child into the world before you're old enough to vote. Isn't that enough?"

She moved a section of dark curls behind her ear, revealing plump cheeks. It was true what people said about the glowing and whatnot. She looked beautiful.

"Easy for you to say. Mario will whisk you away and you'll live happily ever after."

"Oh please — you and I know that isn't real life. I think he realizes that, too, which is why he's been avoiding me. I left a message telling him I'm dropping by. He better be home."

"What's there to talk about? Just go. You've wanted to leave as soon as you moved here. Guess that was my fault, huh?"

We bickered all the way to Don Mount but were laughing by the time we entered the courtyard. We came to Mario's place.

"Well, good luck." Richa patted me on the shoulder, then set off on her own way.

I stood outside, rehearsing the main points I'd written the night before. I'd start with the missing necklace, then move on to explain how my mom needed help, and transition to my final decision about school. At the sound of the screen door, I looked up, startled.

"Uh, hey, Tia. Is Mario there?"

Tia jarred me. I'd only seen her a handful of times and rarely up close. I could never tell what she was thinking. She had a piercing stare that never broke and spoke only when it suited her, which always made me nervous.

"Not now, Delia." Her voice trembled.

I stepped forward. "Is everything okay?"

Tia's response was a swift close of the door.

I went home, took a minute to regain my composure, then once my embarrassment subsided, called Richa. Tia's presence and Mario's absence was a cause for concern.

The phone rang late. I snatched it up.

"Did you find out anything?"

"Yeah," Richa said, her voice airy and hoarse. "Nana just came back from over there."

"So? Where is he?"

"Johnson died, Delia. Mario got upset and took off."

"Oh my God. When?"

"This morning, but Mario didn't find out until he showed up at the hospital, and then he took off. He's probably close by. I'd ask Tia, but Nana doesn't want me near the dead house because of the baby. It's bad luck."

"I'm going to look for him."

"Don't, Delia. Let him cool off."

I was restless.

I checked to make sure everyone else was still asleep, then slipped into my blue hooded sweater. It was easier for me to think in the night air. Normally, Mario would have come along. I missed him and felt hurt that he hadn't come by or called. Mario hadn't let on how sick Johnson was. Maybe he expected him to make a full recovery. It was the family's fault — they left a child to care for an elderly man. Mario was probably on a basketball court alone, pounding away his guilt.

He must've been lonely. I was.

The scent of wet earth followed me through the walk. Finally, the trees gave way to the vacant road, which I crossed. I went past the bench, walking until I reached the perimeter of the jail grounds. If one were to stumble upon both buildings, one might mistake Don Jail for a courthouse and Don Mount Court for a penitentiary, the complexity of their relationship evident as I stood between them. It was not unlike that between Mother and me; she held me hostage and fed off my vulnerabilities while I remained in her orbit, our genealogy tethering us. Maybe even after she was gone.

Images of Johnson flickered before me as my mind hurried to commit him to memory. Then he was gone, and in his place, I saw my father. Not dead but gone, too. Once bound to his family — now a man free to roam wherever he pleased. Mario, now relieved of his commitment to Johnson, would soon know this feeling, and a small part of me envied him. Men had a great deal of freedom, I realized. At the sound of a faint whistle, I looked up at the jail's barred windows. *Not all men are free*, I reminded myself, gradually feeling less miserable about my own problems.

I returned without being detected and through the narrow opening of her bedroom door I saw Melissa, face to the wall and body so tightly curled she disappeared into the folds of the sheet. I approached her and was surprised when she turned around.

"Delia, are you going to run away and leave me?"

I swallowed and shook my head.

"She said so. She said you plan to run off with Mario. Don't let her take me."

"What are you talking about?"

"All the barrels have addresses written on them."

"Nobody can force us to go anywhere."

Melissa leaned back against the wall with a pensive look.

"Do you think Dad will ever come back?" she said.

"No." The word flew from my mouth without effort.

•

I was late. I ran along the fences beneath the trees to shelter me from the drizzling rain. As I came to the gate, the curtain in the window shifted, and he appeared briefly before moving to the door and opening it. I went into the yard.

"Hey," I said.

When I got to the door, Mario picked me up playfully before setting me down inside on the tawny carpet. A faint scent of cigarettes and a chill made me second-guess removing my jacket. He brushed the dew drops from my hair.

"Why don't you ever bring your umbrella?"

We fawned over each other, not knowing what to say. We'd only been able to exchange cryptic messages through brief three-way calls with Richa. I only knew a few things. It was kidney failure. There was a viewing and a funeral. His sister had leapt into the grave and had to be pulled out.

He brushed his damp shirt. "You're gonna get sick. I'll grab you something to wear."

He was already halfway down the hall, returning soon after with one of his sister's track suits. I changed in the bathroom, then joined him on the couch where he waited with two cans of Coke. His downturned mouth and clenched jaw reminded me of his moods when Johnson was drinking. Same symptoms. Different diagnosis. No point in talking around things.

"Mom stole my necklace. I looked everywhere but no luck."

"Oh," he said and looked away.

"I'll pay you back. She still has my money from the summer job. I'll ask for it."

I touched him on the shoulder. It was met with a shrug.

"Why are you mad at me? It's not my fault."

"I don't care about the necklace. I'm moving, Delia."

"You're going away to school in the fall. I know that."

"No, it's not that. Now that … Johnson isn't here, we can't stay. I'm going to live with my aunt and uncle in Guelph until it's time to start freshman year. If I even bother."

I swallowed hard and reached for his hand. "It doesn't mean you have to give up everything."

After giving it some thought, he added, "I feel stuck. It's like no matter how hard I try, I'm doomed to fail. There's a fucking catastrophe around every corner."

He started to cry.

I shifted closer to him, but when I reached out to touch him, he stood and fled down the hall and up the steps, leaving my empty hand dangling off the cushion. I glanced at the door.

Don't run.

When he calmed down, he returned and took a seat beside me.

"I'm sorry." I rested my hands in my lap. "About your granddad. About everything."

He touched my hair, then he leaned closer, burying his face into my neck. Then he ran his hands over my arms like he was checking for broken bones. Our eyes met, and I sensed traces of something else stirring in him. He kissed me. After a while, he was lost in thought again.

He put a finger to his chin. "Did you know Johnson left home when he was fourteen?"

I shook my head.

"Let me tell you how he did it …"

I listened as Mario recounted stories about Johnson's early years, his voice returning to him as he went on, his laughter more boisterous — as if the very memories were healing him. As he spoke, he stroked my chest where the necklace should have been.

"He's the only person I've ever met that never had to answer to anyone. I want that. We should be like him. I can defer my year and work while you finish your classes, then we can leave together — Delia, why are you looking at me like that?"

I should have written him a letter.

"There's no easy out for me. Things at home are bad. I have to stay for however long it takes. But you don't. Go to school, Mario. Visit your parents if you want but don't let them hold you back. I saw how hard you worked to get that scholarship — they didn't, and if they get a little upset — so what? They'll get over it and be upset over some other thing you do or don't do. Maybe I'll join you in a year or two. Gotta wait my turn, remember?"

It felt good to say it finally, but for a long while he sat quietly, looking at his hands.

I checked my watch. I had to beat my mom home.

"My grandma Liz says that when the road ahead closes, you just have to find another way to get where you're going."

He held my hand. "But how am I going to find another way back to you?"

"Not back — we never go back," I said. "I'll meet you there — wherever you'll be."

I left before the rain let up so Melissa wouldn't be able to see that I'd been crying. She was standing over the freezer, sorting through the bills.

"Is Mom here?"

"Nope, she left this morning all determined to go to the police station to file a report."

"I really don't think the lady from the Blue House is breaking in and stealing linen from the barrels."

She eyeballed my outfit. "Did you go shopping?"

"It's Tia's."

Her hands went to her hips.

"I had to change. It's raining. Look at my hair."

"Phew." She clutched her chest. "Because I saw Richa earlier and she is pure misery. Please don't get pregnant."

I made a face. "Do I look like I have a death wish? Plus, Mario's moving so that's definitely not happening."

Paper went sailing about.

"It's no big deal, we're still friends."

"Friends? I knew it. You didn't put out and now it's over."

I barely managed a laugh.

She came over and wrapped her arms around me. "I'm sorry, Delia."

"Yeah." I looked up at the ceiling and swallowed. "Story of my life."

After we'd sorted through the pile of mail, Melissa took a short walk to Mother's liquor cabinet.

"What are you doing?"

"It's what normal adults do when things go poorly."

She reached in for a bottle of vodka.

"Don't worry. I don't drink, but Curtis's older brother works at a bar and he's always making fancy alcohol for his friends."

"You went to his house?"

My younger sister handed me a glass.

"It's better than here," she said. "Anyway, I always take Tricia when I go, and we stay on the main floor like you taught me. His grandma's there all the time. She likes it when I bring her fruit nut chocolate bars. And Pop Rocks. You ever met an old person who likes Pop Rocks?"

•

The week after, I stopped by Camille's office early one morning. The place was in complete disarray.

"Looks like you need some help around here, and I need a part-time job."

Camille raised her manicured hands to her cheeks. "Is that why you're here? I thought you brought the rent. Anyway, that's a great idea. They promised me an assistant, but I should've known better. How soon can you start?"

"Tomorrow."

"You're a godsend," she said. "Your mother raised some great kids. Good for you stepping in and helping out. She was very brave to step down from her position. Not many people have the guts the stand up to their employers. You should be proud of her, too."

I avoided her gaze. "Yeah, I guess. I heard they may be tearing down the building."

She took a swig of coffee. "It's in the early stages, but I know people high up and its going to pass in council. I advised your mother to file transfer documents early so she gets a nice place. Once they open this up to everyone, all the good units will be gone."

"Did she file for the transfer?"

"Not yet. It's a shame that a woman as intelligent and capable as her must resort to relying on the system." Camille shifted positions so that she faced away from the door. "It should be families like yours that we help in this country. Not these freeloaders popping out one kid after the other. Take your friend Richa, for example — see what I mean?"

I didn't respond. I was in no position to show Camille how greatly she had offended me. I needed her help. However, I would always remember the way her eyes danced as she spoke and the tinge of victory at her mention of providing us with "help." It would never be the same between Camille and me. Never again.

•

I intended to take up the topic of the transfer with Mother that evening, but she came in through the back door and walked past us like a stranger who'd stumbled into our house. She spun around twice in the hallway, then went up to her room muttering curses. Melissa and I looked on curiously. A clatter of closet doors erupted from her bedroom.

Shortly after, Neville marched in, his white shirt stained with an orange liquid, his collar shredded, like the newspaper the rats got into.

"She gone up?" he asked, out of breath.

We nodded.

He went up without taking off his shoes. Soon they began to argue.

Melissa turned to me, pretending to hold a microphone, and spoke into an invisible camera.

"Ladies and gentlemen, we're here on the red carpet with Neville Reid. Neville, tell us what you're wearing?"

She tilted the pretend microphone toward me. I cleared my throat and put on my Neville voice.

"Hi — hello, folks. I'm wearing an original Aretha Ellis tie-dyed shirt …"

More noise and thrashing.

I hurried up the steps in time to see Mother snatch Neville's cellphone out of his hand. When he reached for it, she held it behind her back.

"Don't," she said.

Her voice had taken on a calm, terrifying quality.

She saw me. "Delia. There's an envelope beneath the vase on the table. Take the rent to the office. Bring your sister."

I started down the steps and heard footsteps close behind.

"Where do you think you're going?" Mother said.

"Keep the cellphone, Aretha."

"Why thank you, Neville. She gets the fancy dinner and I get the cellphone."

"You had no right to carry on like that in the people's establishment."

They bickered all the way to the first floor, to the table where Mother backed Neville into a chair. We hastily tied our laces and escaped into the courtyard. Through the kitchen window, I saw Neville sitting erect, his eyes fixated on some terrifying scene.

It was good to be away from them.

Across the court, on the second-floor balcony, Camille leaned over the terrace, tapping a lit cigarette against the rail. I wondered if she heard the arguing when the door was opened.

"What are you two up to?" she called down.

"Keeping a roof over our heads," Melissa said.

Camille laughed herself into a coughing fit.

We joined her to look out at the wall of illuminated windows behind which the lives of others played out. Two children jumped on a bed in a room across the way. That was Jenny's house. And muffled by the howling wind, the clamour of cast iron from the Singhs' residence.

"Why are you still here?" I said to Camille. "Engineers again?"

"Paperwork." She crushed the butt of the cigarette against the rail but kept it in her hand. "I can take the cheque inside. I haven't locked up yet."

I patted my pockets. "Oh no. I'll be right back."

"My sister can be quite forgetful," I heard Melissa say as I left the office to head back home.

I went to knock on the door of our place, but Neville's voice stopped me.

"Every day you pressure me about this. Aretha, I work hard. I spend time with you. I give you whatever you ask for, but ..."

"But what? I'm not fun enough anymore?"

"You're too hung up on the house thing. A house don't make happiness."

"Oh, really. So, I must live in government housing forever while you traipse around with your little girlfriend in your mother's house? That's what you want. Someone with no responsibilities."

An inaudible grumble.

Out of Mother's mouth came a string of curse words, but Neville's deep voice cut through in a rare display of utter frustration.

"Aretha, how could you be mad at me for this? Really. I care for you and love dem girls, but I can't give you everything when I have half of you and the other half is hanging on to Cliff's coattail."

Two kids rolled by on their scooters, making a racket. One stopped and asked if I was locked out. I shook my head and shooed them off. A loud scraping erupted from inside, followed by sounds of a scuffle. Something crashed to the floor.

"Mom?" I tried the door, then pounded it with my fists.

A few seconds passed before the door unlocked and Mother faced me, red-eyed and chest heaving.

"I — I forgot the cheque." I inched inside.

When she handed me the envelope, I caught a glare of the light from something metal she held in her other hand. A meat cleaver. My eyes went to Neville. He stood, hands apart by the table, staring down at his feet at the remnants of what had moments earlier been a perfectly intact cellphone. Without explanation or apology, Mother led me out.

I replayed what I'd heard and seen all the way back to the office. Even my bruises did not convey the new level of violence Mother had resorted to. The cleaver in hand — the one she called the "axe" and used to chop raw meat. That image would never leave me.

In the office, Melissa was regaling Camille with a school tale. I dropped the envelope on the desk and grabbed her.

"Ouch, Delia, stop dragging me."

When Camille was out of earshot, I told her, "We can't go home. Not yet."

Dundas Street was loud. We followed the road over the noise of the highway and the dark, gurgling river that ran along the trail. After crossing at River Street, we cut through the townhomes that led to 605 Whiteside Place — a rust-brown and yellow building that stood out. Melissa and I stopped to count the storeys. As we did, I saw the figure of a woman at a window — waving. I waved back. My sister asked who it was because she didn't see anyone.

I tugged Melissa's hand. "Don't look back. Come on."

The path around the building led to a shop. At the sound of the door chime, the owner glanced wearily at the clock and paused his work to rest on a ropey mop. He saw me.

"Deh-lia! It's so late for you. And so far."

"Mr. Lee, you know this is my favourite place."

He smiled and went behind the counter to wash his hands.

"Fries with gravy, lightly done?"

"Yes, please. Two."

We perched on the stools, watching the basket being lowered into the fryer with a hiss. Two minutes later, the fries were tipped onto fresh newsprint, then scooped into cardboard boxes. Mr. Lee then ladled thick brown gravy into the containers, and slid the boxes across the counter toward us. We immediately stuck our two-pronged wooden forks into each.

"Go home now, okay?" He ushered us to the door.

Behind us, he flipped the "Open" tag in the window to "Closed."

We walked quickly until we reached the bridge where a luxury car dealership stood. Across the way was Don Mount Court — shrouded in shadow. We leaned against the bridge and with tingling fingers ploughed into our meal while admiring the glistening silver sedan displayed on the dealership's second storey. After a while, Melissa turned to me.

"This is the part where the girl wins the guy back, then realizes he doesn't like her anymore," she said. "Think they're done for good?"

"Yep." I shoved a forkful of soggy fries into my mouth.

We ate until we'd scraped the boxes dry. All the while above our heads the brilliant Mercedes symbol rotated, a beguiling beacon.

At home, we found Mother sleeping on the sofa in her day clothes, the broom tossed aside on the nearby carpet. There were no remnants of metal or glass by the dining table. There was no trace of Neville, and he did not return that night. Or the next. Or the next.

Chapter 24

The Last Entry

June 1996

Dear Diary,

Richa named her baby girl Adrienne Delia Velasquez, and she is the sweetest but loudest baby I've ever seen. Richa is in full mommy mode, like God flipped a switch. It makes me wonder what Mom was like before me. Before Dad ... or Neville. Whoever came first. I bet she wanted everything to be perfect. Meanwhile, Richa hasn't showered in two days. She says it's no big deal.

Mom should take notes. She takes everything so hard. Ever since Neville dumped her, she's been rambling on about moving to Jamaica. Sometimes I just wish she'd be gone already. Everyone else leaves.

I am
Delia

•

The morning of Mario's departure, Melissa brought me a pair of jean shorts and a sleeveless, purple button-down shirt she'd outgrown. I slipped on the outfit, then stared at my hair in the mirror. She came up behind me with a brush and a jean scrunchie.

"Let me do it. He'll be here soon. Geez. Couldn't you have gotten up early and made an effort?"

She brushed my wiry hair into a low ponytail. When she left me, I stayed back, turning my head side to side, looking in the mirror. It was Mario's last day in Don Mount. I needed to look like someone who deserved to be remembered. As soon as I spotted him through the window, I ran downstairs to open the door.

"Finally," he joked. "I've been waiting for hours."

I laughed and he reached for my hand to lead me away.

As we chatted, I noted how unchanged he seemed. I imagined that if I were leaving, I'd be immaculately dressed, excited — and impatient to get on with things. Mario strolled alongside me, hands in his pockets as he talked, as we walked down the path that led to every doorstep in the court.

"Richa could use some of that stuff you're getting rid of," I said.

"I asked her and get this — she's superstitious." He gave me a look. "I bet as soon as I leave, she'll call, asking for the TV."

"And I bet Adrienne's dad will be right there, like, yeah, and the VCR, too, in his fake Yankee accent."

"Can't stand that guy." Mario drew a deep breath, then waved at a gentleman watering his patchy yard.

People were outside in droves, all around, the sound of screen doors slamming, high-strung grade-schoolers, and toddlers who tossed themselves to the floor for attention. On occasion, an adult appeared in an entryway to keep an eye on them over at the park.

As we crossed over into the second court, neighbours converged, forming a disjointed queue along the skirt of the pathway. Word had spread that Mario was leaving, and as we went by, they pulled him into lively chit-chats of varying matters: Johnson, basketball, the big move. All were sad to see him go.

"Come by before you leave. I have a little something for you."

"Make us proud!"

We stopped at the basketball court. The sky above was etched with thin clouds that formed a line eastward over the bay-and-gable rooftops across the way. Mario shaded his eyes and followed a plane passing overhead. Soon he would be out there, too, free to be someone else, perhaps even someone else's.

On the court, twin boys frolicked, half-dressed. They were four-foot giants making swooping air balls with the confidence of pro athletes, their gummy grins reminiscent of the hockey players they pretended to be in winter. I sauntered over to where their lime-green jackets were strewn. There was an echoing *thwack* from the ball hitting the ground. When I called them, they approached, both speaking at the same time.

"You coming to watch us, Delia?"

"Is Mario your boyfriend?"

The boys rambled on like bratty tots. I ignored them. Little boys enjoyed hearing themselves and didn't ever listen to what they were being told.

Mario ran his hand across his mouth and gazed into the air, glassy-eyed.

"What's the latest?" I said, wondering what he was thinking. He could be elusive when guarding his feelings.

"I can't believe that after today, it's all over." He gazed above my hair.

"And then ..."

"Off to see my parents, then campus."

"Right." I kicked at a stray cheese curl. "Johnson would be so proud."

"Yeah." He smiled a little. "He's probably giving you all the credit, wherever he is."

One of the twins asked him to join their game of twenty-one.

"He's not dressed for that," I said to them.

Mario unbuckled his belt and dropped his trousers to reveal his favourite shorts underneath. Off went the shirt. He strode onto the court in socks alone, toward the excited six-year-olds. I sat on the cement barrier on the sidelines and laid his clothes across my lap.

Over by the chalk-etched free-throw line, he had one boy on his shoulders, allowing him to take a proper throw at the net. The other begged for his turn. When they grew tired of his assistance, they insisted he play fair. Play on the level. We can take you, they threatened. Mario started off toward the net, passing the ball effortlessly through his parted legs, then launched into a sprint. He leapt, body extended, a flutter of white-tipped brown legs, and his outstretched arms came crashing down onto the rim with both hands.

The twins went mad, clenching their fists and bumping their birdlike chests together. Mario stood under the net, beaming. The entire performance nothing short of spectacular.

I will miss this more than I have ever missed anything.

Eventually, he finished his round of farewells, and we drifted toward his home, our steps slowing as we got closer to the door. We approached the last entryway by Camille's office just as she descended the steps. We stopped when we saw her.

"Mario, I was about to come and get you. Your sister is ready."

She came over and embraced him.

"Don't forget me." Her voice broke.

She turned to me. "Delia, I hope you don't mind me speaking openly in front of your friend here. The paperwork finally came through. Your mother can expect a letter shortly with an appointment date to see the worker."

"Great. Thanks."

She soon left to chat with some tenants. We continued our slow stroll.

"That's good news," I said. "At least with the rent subsidized we won't be homeless."

"If you end up homeless, you know where to find me." He didn't look at me.

Melissa rushed out the door and tackled Mario. "Take me with you."

"I wish I could, Freckles."

She hugged him, then went inside.

Mario and I lingered by the door, waiting out the clock.

"I'll take care of things here," I said. "I'll make sure that no one crazy moves into your old place and that Mr. Cho gets his food from the Blue House. I'll check in on Richa after she moves, and don't worry about having to call or whatever."

He went to speak but I cut him off.

"Maybe write me a letter or something. Then when you get to school, you can call."

It was my way of accepting his departure. Others before him had denied me the opportunity to say goodbye. In my stunted journey into young adulthood, I learned a few key things about love, fear, and faith, and when he kissed me goodbye, I drew much comfort in knowing it wasn't me he was leaving — and that made it all right.

•

Mother's singing greeted me at the door, the sound of it calm and soothing. I wanted her to hold me and let me cry. Maybe I could try it for once. Then I saw her.

"Hey, Mom." I tried not to stare at the purse still strung around her neck and the shoes she hadn't removed.

There was something transitory about her presence.

"Mm-hm." She touched the side of her head as if feeling for a stray strand of hair.

"Did you sign the transfer forms yet?"

"Won't need it."

"Just in case, we should apply before the deadline."

"Foolishness. This is all a part of the plan to chase us out — get the people off the land. I want nothing to do with them."

I'd be forced to forge her signature. Again.

What's the lightest sentence for fraud?

She touched her neck and coughed.

"What's wrong?" I said.

"Something in the air is choking me. Can you smell it?"

I sniffed. "No."

This was her new tactic to ignore me.

"Every day around this time, the smell gets worse."

She remained at the window, gazing out while I made myself a cheese sandwich and observed her from my seat at the table. Soon after, the irritant seemed to return. She snapped the back of her tongue against the roof of her mouth in rapid succession.

"What did you eat today? Maybe you're allergic to something."

"No-no-no." She dismissed me.

I felt silly for trying to help.

"Come here," she whispered.

I went hesitantly. She pulled me into the tight corner and cupped the back of my head with her hand, catching the end of my braid. The chair pressed into my ribs.

"They're listening," she said. "You have to be quiet."

"Who?"

"Shh. Let me tell you."

She leaned toward my ear and whispered all the secrets she did not want them to hear.

•

Autumn set in early, and by the first week of October, the trees were nearly bare. The neighbourhood kids eagerly gathered the fallen leaves into mounds. A small group of them pummelled the piles repeatedly with limbs and whole body before the wind could blow the leaves away. Melissa and I watched from the window while I twisted her hair into two ropey cornrows.

"Did he call?" She asked me this at least once a week.

"No. He's busy with school. That's what he needs to focus on."

I went to wash my hands. While at the sink, I adjusted the crooked painting Mother had hung over the hole in the bathroom wall.

Melissa popped in.

"Delia, did you remember to get money for my volleyball trip?"

"It's already in your purse. This time make it stretch. Buy a beef patty and take a juice box. I'm not dipping into my savings because of your long belly."

"Why do you have to be such a nag?"

I gave her a look.

"Thank you," she said.

I wasn't in the best of moods. I hadn't heard from Mario in weeks, and school felt more like a chore without Richa, who was taking her classes by correspondence. I should've been looking at colleges since it was my senior year. Instead, I was monitoring my sister — and Mother, whose new habits included disappearing for hours at a time and attending church three days a week.

As soon as Melissa went through the front door, I heard Mother sliding open the locks to her bedroom. She came into my room.

"Morning, Mom."

"I need you to call your father."

She had dragged the phone in with her, the cord stretched to the limit.

"Um. Okay — what do you —"

"No, no." She laughed a little. "Don't ask. Just call and when you get him on the phone, pass it to me."

"I'm heading to school."

"Call."

She shoved the phone at me.

With reluctance, I dialed.

"Hello?"

"Hi —" I stared at an empty spot on the wall. "I may have the wrong number."

Mother's eyes stayed fixed on me. A burst of sweat dampened the skin beneath my arms.

"Are you looking for Cliff?" It sounded strange to hear my father's name drip from a stranger's tongue.

"Yes."

Mother snapped her fingers and yanked the handset. She pinned it beneath a bony shoulder and ear.

"Hello?" I heard the woman say repeatedly.

My mother hurried off to her room, gathering the phone cord along the way — making her way back to safety where the curtains were drawn and the family pictures once displayed on her behemoth dresser were shoved into the bottom drawers.

I pondered my father's new life. Who was this woman? Did he love her? Would there be children? I imagined how happy he was to have found her. She was different from my mother, of course — otherwise, what would be the point? This lady was easy to love. I could hear it in her voice — a certain genial quality. Maybe Mother was like this once? When? Why does it change? I felt a deep sadness for Mother and a terrible foreboding of my own future.

Later, Melissa, Richa, and I congregated in the living room, listening to Adrienne coo as she bounced on her mother's lap.

"She just started doing this." Richa gently wiped Adrienne's mouth with the edge of a thin blanket.

Adrienne leaned into the softness of her mother's body, searching.

Richa smiled. "Food?"

Melissa looked at the clock, then over at me. "Mom didn't go far."

Richa set Adrienne in the car seat and began to gather her belongings. Adrienne wailed.

"Sorry, Richa," I said. "It's like living with a terrorist. I just don't know when she's gonna strike."

"It's cool. I'm packing tonight. I booked the truck for Tuesday."

Adrienne's cries mutated into a piercing scream. Melissa plugged her ears. Richa magically produced a pacifier from some hidden location and stuck it in Adrienne's mouth. If she was irritated, she didn't let on. Motherhood seemed to unlock special powers like patience and irrepressible joy, a kind of magic that burned out over time.

"Oh, Mario said to call him tomorrow at six," Richa said on her way out. "You can use my phone."

"Glad he can make time for me."

She gave me a motherly look.

"I'll be there," I said.

•

When I called the next day, Mario picked up on the first ring.

"You were sitting by the phone, weren't you?" I said.

"I had to. My roommate literally lives on the phone. If I didn't threaten to knock him out, I'd be waiting still."

"That's not your style."

"What does he know?" He laughed. "I'm from the 'hood."

I joined in. "So, what's it like?"

"You'd love it," he said. "The library is the size of my old school. The people are chill, and the dorms … they kinda remind me of Don Mount."

"Seriously? Well, at least you have a phone."

"Speaking of which, when are you getting your phone back?"

"No idea. She ran up the long-distance bill again. I'm not paying it this time."

"Do you want me to send you —"

"No," I said. "I'll just call you from Richa's new place."

Mario covered the phone and broke into a sidebar conversation. Then he came back.

"Sorry, practice is like a twenty-minute walk from this building."

Female voices interjected in the background. He was gone again.

"Hey, Delia. Call me when Richa gets her phone hooked up. I'll send — hang on, I'm coming. Sorry, Delia — I gotta go."

"Sure. Talk to you soon," I said.

He had already hung up.

"So?" Richa said.

I shrugged. "It is what it is."

Richa looked at me with an intent to comfort just before her daughter's crying erupted from the bedroom. She darted off.

I left Richa's and went home. I found Melissa in the middle of the living room with her shoes on. The television and VCR were unplugged, the wires piled carelessly around the speaker.

"I just found them like this," she said. "Maybe a power outage?"

"Maybe."

I opened a can of chili, which I reheated, then split into two helpings.

"Is he dating anyone?" Melissa sprinkled chunks of cheese over her stew.

I shook my head. He sounded happier than I'd ever heard him, and to celebrate with him meant supressing my own longing to be elsewhere — at times, just to be with him.

I changed the topic. "What are we going to eat for the rest of the week? I've got thirty bucks."

"What about the food bank? My friend saw canned crab there once. We may get lucky."

"Half that stuff is on the verge of expiry or already there," I said. "Chinatown it is."

"You just don't want to run into Camille."

"No, I don't. I'm embarrassed. We have parents," I said. "We shouldn't have to beg."

She scrunched up her nose, pulling the freckles closer together. "Please call him, Delia."

"Fine."

I called my father from a pay phone. He sounded glad to be asked and agreed to mail us a cheque, which he knew would take weeks to clear.

"I haven't been able to get a hold of your mother." He sounded upset, then adjusted his tone. "Tell her I'm sending tickets for you to visit this Christmas."

"Really?"

"Sheryl and I —"

"Sheryl?" My excitement dampened.

"Yes, the woman you spoke to. Delia, I know you spoke to her, and it's all right. I'm sure your mother orchestrated the whole thing."

He drew a deep breath. "Anyway, as I was saying, Sheryl and I booked tours with a few colleges. I think you'll love them."

"Dad, I would love to, but I can't miss work."

I sensed in his reaction a bit of surprise.

"Well, it's good to have discipline, and I don't want you to lose your job."

"I can visit in a few months. As soon as exams are over."

"Yes, that would work. Delia, are you calling from a pay phone? Did your mother disconnect the phone line again?"

I hesitated.

"It's amazing the lengths she's willing to take to shut me out. Yet she is always intruding on my life. I'm writing the cheque in your name, and I want a full account of how the money is spent. I'll send a little extra for your birthday but it's for you. Your mother is not to get a penny."

I agreed, but promised myself it would be the last time I asked him for anything. Sometimes it's the little things.

•

By Remembrance Day, I'd used up all the pages in my diary, so my infrequent entries were written on loose paper stapled onto its last page. One more entry, then I'd retire the sacred text for good — bury it in a time capsule for ten years. I opened my closet and searched the corner, finding the white shoebox I used to store my cash, snacks, and diary. I stared at the folded bills and package of Pepperettes.

"Melissa?"

My sister came in. "Yeah."

"I never thought I'd be saying this, but please tell me you have my diary."

Her brows went up. "No."

Melissa had warned me for weeks that she suspected Mother had been going through our things again. In a panic, I ransacked my room even though I knew it was useless. I didn't want Melissa to lecture me as she tended to do. I waited that evening for Mother to come upstairs for bed. When she did, I stopped her in the hall.

"Have you seen my diary?"

Silence.

"Mommy?"

"No." She seemed confused. "I don't know what's going on around here. Things go missing. I'm glad it's not just happening to me."

"What do you mean?"

"Someone comes into my room at night and takes my things."

A strong feeling of doubt prevented me from asking who had the ability to break the deadbolts on the inside of the front door.

"Nobody," I said aloud, "nobody broke in. You took my diary. Give it back."

I was inches away from her now, my voice and arms raised.

Mother staggered back. We were both surprised.

I dropped my arms to my side. A curious look settled over her face, and she went to bed without addressing me.

Later that night, Mother came in to see me — something she hadn't done in a while. She sat at the edge of the bed.

I propped myself up on my elbows.

"Delia," she said, looking at the wall behind me, "one day you'll miss my voice ... all my guidance and instruction that you write about like it's punishment. It's love, but you're young and you don't get it yet."

She smiled and scratched at the grey roots that sprouted around the orange strands from her home dye job. I opened my mouth, and she got up and walked out before I could speak. For the first time, I felt ashamed, if not sorry for what I'd written. Yet my guilt was soon quelled with anger. Above all the things she'd taken from me: the necklace, my freedom, my father ... the diary hurt the most.

Chapter 25

The Other Mother

December 1996

Christmas was coming — depending on what side of Don Mount you were on. In the southern court, the sporadic display of lights failed to conjure the ambiance of past years. I trudged through it feeling as foreign as I did my first Christmas there. Still, the scent of burning oak reminded me of winter nights when Mario and I would steal away for a stroll along the back roads. On our side of the complex, bright bulbs flecked the outer screen doors all the way to the top floor, creating the illusion of a decorated birdcage. I stepped into the enclosure, then arrived at our unadorned door, the lone dark entryway in the yard.

I removed my snow-covered boots on the stoop before going inside since Mother had been complaining about the grit on the floor. A familiar hum came from downstairs. I called out for her.

No response.

I discovered her in the basement, hunched beneath the naked

bulb, mumbling and shuffling boxes. I cleared my throat, then knocked on the banister. She turned and eyed me, offering a curt "Good evening" when she confirmed I wasn't a predator.

"Hey, Mom."

She stared through me.

I left her to see about dinner and found the stove and counter bare. In the sink, a single white cup with a bit of tea. Had she even eaten? Homework would have to wait. I opened the fridge and pulled out an uncovered bowl of rice and a rubbery carrot. In a cupboard, a dusty can of lentils, powdered curry, and the last cube of chicken stock. Mother taught me how to make much out of little, but nobody, she said, could make something out of nothing.

At the sound of her trudging upstairs, I prepared her dinner plate. She came up and stood by the window, dressed as if for work and clutching an envelope to her side. Two suitcases sat on the carpet, blocking the television, not that anyone could watch it anymore. Mother had severed the power cord with a knife, similarly, our beloved Nintendo and each component of the sound system she'd bought for Father on various anniversaries.

"Did you go out today?" I said.

"Shh." She signalled with a finger, then moved the sheers aside to peer out.

I approached slowly to see what held her attention this time. Was it the large white van parked for hours in the same spot? Or the man in uniform and sunglasses lingering about the phone box? She was convinced someone was following her. The parking lot was abuzz with its daily players: idle teen boys harassing fellow schoolmates and transit riders rushing to escape the cold, heading home to housework, the second shift.

A glance at her watch. Her frown deepened.

"It's Wednesday," I reminded her, "Melissa has volleyball practice."

I felt I hadn't lied. The volleyball team did practise on Wednesdays, and my sister was a team member, but she was likely elsewhere. She often tried to be anywhere but home.

"I know." Mother narrowed her eyes at me.

I was in her ever-expanding personal space. It was best to tread carefully. As unpredictable as she had become, I could tell something was seriously off by the way she clutched that envelope. The appearance of the suitcases — less alarming. There had been talk about moving again, but that would pass. It always did.

I shifted my gaze to the luggage. "Should I put those in the basement?"

"No, thank you," she replied firmly as if speaking to some baggage handler at the airport. Then asked almost sweetly, "Is dinner ready?"

I nodded at the two plates of curried lentil stew and rice on the table. My sister still hadn't shown up, so we proceeded without her. Mother set the envelope beside the plate, touching it occasionally as she ate.

I briefly met her stare. I had not inherited her owlish brown eyes, which now looked upward to the left.

"So," I said. "I got an eighty-five on my math test."

She spun the gold band around her ring finger while she chewed.

I tried again. "You look nice. Did you get out today?"

"No." There was a trace of a smile, and then it was gone.

I cleared my throat. "Heading out?"

She set down her fork. "Stop. I'd appreciate a meal without the interrogation. I'm the adult here — don't forget." She ended on a sharp, rattling note.

I gripped my fork tightly.

"What's wrong?" She reached across the table and grabbed my right hand. A clump of rice fell off my fork.

"Nothing," I lied again. "Is that the rent?"

She studied the envelope, looked at me, then carefully handed it over.

"Go ahead. Open it."

I held it up and tilted the opening, letting the documents slide out onto the clear plastic tablecloth cover. It was my parents' divorce agreement. I skimmed the pages, holding my breath until I saw Mother's smudged signature. Adjacent to it was Father's; though dated long before, it appeared carefully crafted. I wondered what the difference would be now that the papers were finally signed. It took a moment for me to digest that an important connection had been severed, not just between my father and mother, but between him and us. He had won their war in the most convenient, cost-effective way, by sacrificing Melissa and me.

Mother clapped loudly.

"That's it," she said with a strange grin. "He wants to move on with his life — as if I was stopping him. I wish him the best of luck." She let out a salty chuckle, then choked on whatever emotion she was trying to hide.

I felt the tears well up.

She smirked. "You were always trying to put us together again ... scheming. Plotting in your book. You think I didn't know? Should've minded your own business. You could never let anything go ..." Her voice trailed off.

Earlier on in my teenage years, I believed my parents' dwindling relationship was due to the interference of a third party. Ironically, I thought by inserting myself into their affairs that I could save them. I had arrived at the finish line, finally, and here was the manifestation of my wishful thinking.

This is what it all led to, Delia.

I pushed the papers away, intending to escape before her mood shifted to anger. For some reason, my distress was a trigger.

"Delia, don't cr—"

I had already begun to cry.

I fled the kitchen table. Left the house. Hopped on the first streetcar that went east, and before I knew it, I was headed for Richa's. She had moved to a high-rise twenty minutes away. When I got there, she answered the door and took one look at me.

"I'm calling Mario," she said.

I protested but she went ahead. When he answered, my stomach tightened.

"Hey, Mario," I said.

"Delia, where've you been?"

He was so excited. A friend had a job lined up for him, but maybe he'd visit at Easter. "Yes, that's great," I said repeatedly, only interjecting with more questions so there would be no time for any to be posed to me.

My feelings volleyed between envy and inspiration. Yet, I needed his positivity to arm myself before facing Mother again. Even before the divorce was finalized, it had been an especially terrible week. She was barely sleeping and spent nights roaming the house. After my conversation with Mario, his energy buzzed around me like static. I went into the bedroom and found Richa and Adrienne napping soundly. The sight of tiny Adrienne, her hands resting, caressing her mother's face while they slept, and the protective curve of Richa's body around the child gave me peace. I kissed them both lightly on their foreheads, then used the spare key to lock the door before leaving for Chinatown.

Most stalls were already empty, and the rest had fruits and vegetables bagged and ticketed at a discount for quick sale. I picked through the lesser bruised of the lot and purchased a dozen fruits. I carried the McIntosh apples to Richa's grandmother, leaving the Bartlett pears for Mother. As I approached our stoop, I noticed a track of fresh footprints leading away from the front door. Melissa had left. A seed of anxiety spawned. Things were better when she was home. I hesitated by the door, took a deep breath, then went in.

I stepped into the unlit corridor and felt a gush of relief. Mother was out. I could avoid any talk about the divorce for one more day. This was my last thought as I met a barrier of flesh. Before I could speak, I was picked up and braced against the wall. I dropped the remaining bag, my screams muddled by the sound of pears hitting the floor.

I struggled against the intruder, my hands jutting out before me, clawing at the hidden face. They released me and I felt frantically for the light switch and found it. I flicked it on.

The person looked at me.

"Who are you?" she said, a hand to her face.

"Mommy, it's me — Delia."

She drew back, examining me. "No. You look like my daughter. But that's not her voice."

"B-but — it's me."

Mother blinked. She moved a hand to her mouth. A long welt remained on her cheek.

"No. My daughter wouldn't do this to me. I know who you are. I'll call the police."

I fled up the steps, keeping Mother in sight as she looked on like a frightened bird. I slipped and fell onto the landing. This appeared to startle her. Without a word, she started down the hall and descended to the basement. I brought out the phone from Mother's room and set it beside me at the top of the steps, wanting to escape but knowing I couldn't let Melissa stumble into this alone. I waited there, eyes burning, until late evening when Melissa came through the door. I rushed to pull her up the steps.

"Shh." I pointed at the basement.

Her eyes darted from the basement door to the top of the steps.

"Hurry," I whispered.

She nodded, gripped my hand tightly, and didn't let go, even while we lay down on the twin bed in my room. It took a while for either of us to fall asleep, but eventually we did, our bodies lulled into the familiar comfort of our beds and the chug of the sewing machine below us. I wanted to believe that our mother was still our protector. Yet, a separate part of me, the part I could not name, remained on watch. It jerked me awake at dawn. Melissa opened her eyes just then.

"Did you hear it, too?" she asked.

I listened. There was movement about the house — beneath us.

A rush of cool air swept in. Then the floor shuddered as the front door shut. I moved to the foot of the bed and clawed at the curtain, seeing flat grey sky and fog. Where was she going? I stepped on the floor, which was littered with books from the shelf we'd secured against the door. I moved the shelf as quickly as I could, then raced down the steps and went out in my bare feet.

"Mom!" My voice echoed into the court.

I jogged on a bit, but the fog had swallowed her. I turned back and rushed inside to probe for clues: both sets of car keys hung from the rack. Upstairs, everything seemed in place except the unlocked safe open on the bed and beside it, a scattered pile of paperwork. Her passport was missing from the remaining documents, but she'd left her bank card and account book. A glare in the mirror caught my attention. Atop her jewellery box, two golden rings.

•

The first person I called was Neville. It turned out to be a good move. He came over that very afternoon. He seemed certain that our mother was all right and that she'd been trying to get in touch. Well, sort of. Someone, he said, had called repeatedly from a private number.

"Do you think she's in Jamaica?" I asked.

"Maybe." He seemed to know something I did not. "She had some old-time friends from back home and school."

"Pearl?"

"No, not Pearl. I talked to her."

"You think she's staying with them?"

"Could be. But I don't understand how she could just pick up, go, and leave all her furniture and the barrels and ..."

"Us."

"Yes ... I'm not saying I agree with how she went about it, but she was always preparing for you to take over. You could see it. I just didn't know it would be so soon."

"I don't think she planned this, Neville. I think we should report her missing."

"No, no, no. I don't think getting the police involved is a good idea."

"What if something happened to her? She was so upset. She'd been ... she hasn't been good."

"Let's wait. Don't do anything yet. We must think 'bout this carefully."

"How am I supposed to pay the bills? We're already behind on rent."

"Hm. I see now. Does your grandmother know yet?"

I shook my head. "She's my next call. I guess she'll know how to help."

Neville perked up. "I will call your grandmother. You leave that to me."

"Are you sure?"

He nodded confidently, deep in thought. Then he removed his hat and set it between us and clasped his hands. He told me his plan.

Neville would arrange for us to sublet space in Pearl's house until we finished out the school year. When I told him we couldn't afford it, he sucked his teeth.

"You must think I'm really worthless. I'll take care of it."

"Thanks, Neville," I said, surprised by his common-sense solution and kindness. "Okay, then what?"

"Well." He thumbed at his beard. "Come summer, you can go to your father. He can't turn you away now. Or ... you can both come live with me. If you want. It's up to you."

It's up to me. I smiled to myself.

"I'll think about it."

I was already sure of what I wanted to do, but it felt good to have options. Options are important.

•

When we finally called Grandma Liz, it was from a pay phone near the library. A car drove by, sending a wave of water crashing onto the sidewalk.

"Neville told me everything," she said. "Why did you take so long to call me?"

There followed an inquisition of sorts, and soon Uncle Bryan was called into the conversation, and Uncle Brent and his wife were patched in by three-way. From their matter-of-fact banter, I gathered they spoke of my mother often.

"Sorry, Grandma, what'd you say?"

"Honey, why didn't you borrow a friend's phone? You're on the street like a pauper."

Melissa and I kept to ourselves as much as possible and had kept our situation secret from most of our friends.

"Richa and Mario don't live here anymore," I said.

"Oh, Lord, you did tell me they moved. I am getting old, don't mind me. Listen, I'd go find her myself, but my pressure has been acting up and your aunt has me at the doctor's office every other day. Did you call your father?"

"No."

"Delia!"

"I'm done with him. I told him she was acting strange. He completely ignored me. He has his dream house and his girlfriend and whatever."

"All right — all right, take it easy."

"I knew something was wrong with her."

"Well, she's always had her moods, I told you that. She just puts so much stress on herself and she's so stubborn. Delia, I don't know what happened to … my child."

"Grandma? Don't cry … please. I'm sure she's okay. Neville said someone crank-called him. He's sure it was her."

"Oh?" Her voice steadied. "Well, that sounds like her, yes. I have to run, but we'll sort this out soon-soon-soon. Delia, you can't tell anybody. People at school cannot know. We can't file a report. They'll put you in foster care."

"I know, Grandma. Don't worry, we're on break until the new year."

I considered filing a report with the police station anyway, then imagined officers descending upon our home and how Melissa and I would be hauled off to live with strangers. Then there was the inevitable outcome; one day Mother would return. I felt conflicted at the prospect of her turning up at the front door. It would not be business as usual. It hadn't been that way for a very long time.

•

On Christmas Day, Melissa and I continued our family tradition. We rose early to clean, hung plastic wreaths on the doors, volunteered at the food bank, then played Mother's favourite Christmas reggae cassette while cooking supper. Melissa steamed cabbage to serve with the stuffed roast beef and garlic mashed potatoes. As we worked, I found myself singing holiday carols in sharp soprano notes the way Mother did. Around five o'clock, we settled around the candlelit table, which was meticulously set with Mother's fine tableware. I wore an emerald velvet dress she had custom made for the middle school graduation I never attended. Melissa opted for the dress Mother wore to Neville's party. At a glance, Melissa reminded me of Mother — the strong arms, broad shoulders, and eyes that never asked for permission.

Melissa caught me staring.

"What's wrong?" She formed a wine-coloured pout.

"Nothing." I smiled. "Let's eat."

I poured myself a glass of grape juice but when I offered some to Melissa, she covered the top of her glass with a hand and pointed toward the bottle of Manischewitz in the liquor cabinet.

"I'm having wine."

If I denied her, she would surely tell me off, say that I was only three years older and that at fourteen she was old enough to marry — with parental permission. I was constantly being reminded of what little authority I had. From my seat I could see the pile of "final notice" letters from the insurance and cable companies.

I sighed. "Fine. Might as well get me a glass."

Chapter 26

The Wanderers

January 1997

The 1997 calendar hung crooked on the refrigerator door. I scratched a large red X on the second Monday in January, the date of Mother's annual case worker appointment. Barring her miraculous reappearance, her absence would freeze her welfare payments and our subsidized rent would skyrocket. I could only estimate the final numbers, but the equation certainly would add up to a shitshow beyond my means to repair. Sure enough, in late March, while I was mending a rip in my jean jacket, a notice of eviction shot through the mail slot like a dart and skated down the hall, coming to rest where the plastic runner started. I abandoned my task and went to call Grandma Liz from the pay phone by the corner store.

"Already? Lord, have mercy," she said. "Your uncles and I discussed your coming here, but it would be easier if your father applied for your citizenship. I'm trying to get a hold of him — and before you object, I know what I'm doing." Her voice was faint over the noisy road.

"Yes, Grandma. Thanks."

"Does Neville check in?" she said.

"When he can."

"Good. Glad to see he came to be of some use. He'll bring you money tomorrow, but don't use it to pay the rent. We have a plan."

"Okay."

She spoke and I listened.

After hanging up, I deposited another quarter and dialed Richa's number. Naveed answered and cheerily referred to me as her "little friend" before handing over the phone.

"Hey," she said, quietly. "How come you didn't show last week? Mario called."

"I picked up an extra shift. I can't be at his beck and call."

"It's cool — he's not mad. We talked for, like, five minutes. He's working at the campus bookstore. I told him you were busy, too. Camille still hassling you about the rent?"

"Not anymore. We're out."

"Aw, man. Girl, I wish I had space for you to stay."

"It's okay. We're staying with my mom's friend. Neville's helping out. Yeah, you heard me."

"Mario is going to faint when he hears that. Come see me when you're settled in. Tell your sister I said hi. Love ya."

"I will. You, too."

●

We spent the next week packing. Nothing our parents taught us could have prepared us for this. We needed to be out by the end of the month and could only take a fraction of our belongings. The night before the move, I stood in the ransacked master bedroom surrounded by Mother's things; my diary was nowhere to be found. I couldn't believe my mother was so cruel to take it with her. Melissa finally convinced me to turn in for the night.

On moving day, Neville and Jude arrived early with hot chocolate, two dollies, and a few large plastic containers. As they shuffled our overstuffed bins out to the van, Melissa and I scrambled to collect our overlooked, undervalued belongings: Mom's CDs, her perfume, and a sixty-four-pack of Crayola crayons we hadn't touched in years. Our knapsacks and purses stretched at the seams with novels and Nintendo game cartridges. Melissa paced the house resembling an open jewellery box with Mother's crown jewels strung over her body.

I pressed my face into my hands, overwhelmed.

"Have you seen Toby?" Melissa called downstairs.

I was at the door, shoes on, writing a list of contents on one of the bins. "No. Melissa, I told you to pack all your stuff last night. Did you check the closet?"

She pivoted at the top of the steps and stomped across the upstairs hall. "It's not here."

Neville wheeled a dolly in. "Last call. I gotta make my shift — come on."

"We're not going anywhere until I find Toby," Melissa shouted.

I saw a shift in Neville's stance. He stood the dolly up and wiped his mouth.

"Melissa?"

She came down to meet him, arms folded. "Yes?"

His mouth fell open. He paused for a moment as if changing gears.

"This is not easy on anyone," he said, "but we have to leave some things behind. Delia, too."

"It's probably in one of the boxes," I added.

Melissa blinked her lashes rapidly. She sniffed and wiped her eyes with a sleeve full of rattling bangles.

Neville shot me a concerned look. I nodded back.

It's fine. Everything is fine.

Neville had already sold the car to a mechanic after I forged Mother's signature on the ownership, so there was one less item to get rid of. We piled into the van.

"Jude and I will try to grab some more things later." Neville spoke to us in the rear-view mirror. "I'll keep them at my place."

Melissa, still crying, sat tightly in the cold corner seat as we made our way to south Regent Park.

I touched her arm. "Don't worry, it'll be a five-minute ride, then it'll be over."

She closed her eyes.

Pearl's eldest daughter, Gloria, opened the door. Her turtle-neck stretched up her long neck, skirt down to her ankles. She was the mean one. For a minute I thought she wouldn't let us in, but her mother showed up and we followed her into the earthy, low-ceilinged basement. The room was accessible through a set of steps off the front foyer. Here, lit by a drawstring light, an amassment of items had been shoved aside in preparation for our arrival. Neville placed our bed in the centre of the open area, atop a square floor mat fashioned from a large section of carpet.

After we were all moved in, Neville lingered, playing with his keys.

"Thanks for doing all this," I said.

He eyed the ceiling. "I'll bring a smoke detector tomorrow and check in every week. I won't leave you here long, I promise."

He turned to Melissa, who was already in bed. "Make sure you go to school and don't give your sister any problems. She's in charge."

I gave him a hug.

After Neville and Jude left, Pearl reviewed the house rules: Curfew, Bible study on Fridays. Keep the Sabbath. No boys. She didn't drive, so we were to arrange our schedules accordingly.

"And there's a lock on the inside," Pearl said. "I told Neville to keep his money. You're free to stay as long as you need."

I looked around. To complain would have been foolish.

"Thank you, Miss Pearl," I said. "I'll find a way to pay you."

"No, no. I knew your mother from when she was a little girl. Our families go back a long time. If it wasn't for her, I wouldn't even have come to this country. Us island folk, we take care of people no matter what little we have. Today, it's your problems … tomorrow, it's mine. So it go."

I thanked her again, but this time it was for her words. I missed my mother's tokens of wisdom and was so grateful for what she had shared because those words had kept my sister and I safe and together.

•

On mornings, the windowless room gave up no secrets until I reached over to the lamp on the ground. I'd trace the smooth bulb and twist, letting in a dull light that stressed the closeness of the corners in the room. Then we'd wait for our appointed shower time, eat the porridge Pearl cooked, then get dressed and go about our days, pressing forward with the habitual behaviours of the living. While Melissa immersed herself in her studies, my interest in my own waned, and despite my commitments I seemed to have an infinite amount of time to think about where Mother may have gone and what she was doing. I tried not to mention her. Once, Melissa said her name and I began ruminating on the ordeals of the past, and the trauma replayed in my mind, skipping like a record. I couldn't move on from it for a long time.

I had been thinking about my diary and the necklace, so when Melissa suggested we go back to look for Toby, I agreed. We waited for Pearl and the girls to leave for their Pathfinder Club meeting before heading out, and as we came to the bridge and saw the building beyond, our steps quickened. When we got to the back gate I stopped.

"Aren't you coming, Delia?" Melissa asked, lifting the latch.

I didn't answer and she didn't question me. She went on into the yard and up to the door. I watched her fumble with the lock and felt a little relief. I looked over my shoulder and told her to hurry up.

She came out and walked past me. "I'm gonna try the front."

"Come on, we're not supposed to be here," I said.

I followed behind, barely able to keep up with her. She was going so fast, and I couldn't understand how easy it was for her when I felt like I was going to pass out. I wasn't even sure what I was afraid of, but every step past the parking lot frightened me. I wanted to leave. Melissa approached the front door, fists clenched. I could see her trying the keys in the lock. I came up behind her.

"They changed the locks. Forget it."

Melissa jiggled the knob.

"Mel." I patted her shoulder lightly. "Let it go. I know it meant a lot to you, but he was falling apart. Seriously, we'll get another one."

She turned around, her eyes welled up with tears and her nose and cheeks red. I pulled her into a hug. She stooped so she could weep into my shoulder and hearing her, I let my tears fall freely to the sound of her sobs.

We bought lunch at the Kentucky Fried Chicken spot near Gerrard Avenue, then brought it to the bench across from the complex, where we sat to eat. Don Mount's demolition was another impending loss. It was the last place we'd watched Mother put on her favourite earrings and admire herself in the mirror. It was the last place I'd heard the whirring sewing machine where she sat to create her future. Why did she stop?

"Mom is going to be livid when she finds out we gave up the place."

"You're right," I said. "Especially when she finds out we're back to living in a basement — and Pearl's at that."

"She'll have to get a job after all."

"That's for sure. I can't afford a two-bedroom all on my own."

"Two?" Melissa said. "I still want my own room and all-new furniture. White and shiny."

"Okay," I said. "A three-bedroom."

"When?"

"Maybe summer."

It was the perfect shift in thought that we needed to distract us from all that could not be solved, fantasizing about tomorrow's possible problems, because those weren't real.

It was still cold in May, and the damp seeped through the springs of our mattress. We were getting sick all the time, so Neville bought two heated blankets and brought them by one Sunday. I met him at the door with a comforter around my shoulders.

"Don't get too close," I said, as he came up the walk. "I still have a cold."

Neville kept his pace and came right up to the door.

"A strong man like me ain't afraid of no little cold. You ever see me sick?"

I thought about it. "No, actually, I haven't."

He chuckled like he had presented me with the world's greatest mystery. I let him in and rolled my eyes when he wasn't looking. I was about to close the door when I noticed movement in the vehicle parked outside. Neville had gone down to see Melissa and so I stayed by the door a little longer. There was a woman in the front seat. She was looking right at me. It had been a long while since I'd laid eyes on her — the woman from the party. I pulled back out of sight and gently closed the door.

Downstairs, Melissa was wrapped up in one of the new blankets and chatting with Neville between coughs. The whole basement smelled of eucalyptus, Limacol lotion, and cough syrup. I stood by the dresser and studied Neville. Was he a better boyfriend to the woman in the car than he was to Mother? He certainly had been more of a father since she'd left.

"So, I have some news," he said.

"Great," said Melissa. "When are you breaking us out of this hellhole?"

Neville howled with laughter. "You must be psychic."

"What do you mean?" I asked.

He addressed me. "Expect to hear from your father soon. He's started on your immigration papers." He smiled shallowly. "I know you girls will be happy about that."

"Grandma told you?" Melissa asked.

"No," Neville said. "I spoke to him."

It was strange hearing the news from Neville, though if he was upset by the talk they'd had, he didn't show it. Melissa took to jumping on the bed, raising her arms above her head to prevent it from smashing into the ceiling.

"Melissa, knock it off. So that's it?" I said to him. "It's all in his hands now?"

Neville took his gloves from his pocket and started to pull them over his hands. "Only what you give him to carry, Delia. Nothing more."

Long after he was gone, I sat and thought on what Neville had said.

•

My father called a few days later with instructions and from then on, when we weren't packing, we huddled in bed reading and nursing our shared cold. Mostly, we waited.

Then on the agreed-upon date and time, Gloria called us up. While ascending the basement steps, I could see his black boots shuffling on the front mat. He closed the door and I laid eyes on him for the first time in three years.

"My God," he said.

"Hi, Dad." I wrapped my arms around him, unable to help myself.

Any anger I'd anticipated did not manifest. It felt good to be around someone who knew and loved me. I did not want to experience another loss.

But it's all temporary. *Everything.*

Chapter 27

2004

March 2004

The office was north of the city, above a Persian rug store. Dr. Alethea Rankin, a petite, dark-haired woman in her late thirties, greeted me with a smile.

I'd been seeing Alethea weekly during my short-term leave from work. My manager had referred me to her after my consecutive days off, which were a deviation from my typical ten-hour workday. Desperate, I confessed that my mother was missing. I didn't tell her it had been seven years or that I had started experiencing night terrors. I left out the part where I woke up on my seventeenth-floor balcony, hands gripping the rails.

She suggested that I take a leave of absence for my mental health and assured me that my job, unlike my health, would always be there.

It was bitterly cold, and the hour trip by public transit was gruelling. Alethea was nice enough and always willing to go at my pace, but she could not ask questions she did not know to ask. She could not validate my truths. I fumbled my way through conversations about my current state of mind and coping mechanisms. I spoke about work. A few bad dates from years before. I spoke of my loneliness and trouble sleeping. She recommended medication. I filled the prescriptions and shoved the pill bottles to the far reaches of the kitchen cupboard shelves. So went the course of my treatment.

It was my twelfth appointment. I didn't plan on telling her about the meltdown I had after stumbling across an article about the upcoming Don Mount demolition in the newspaper. This was the session where I planned to tell her that I was done — that therapy had reaped the results I'd hoped for. That I was fixed. I didn't think this at all. I just wanted to get out of it without hurting Alethea's feelings.

Then she opened our session by asking, "What was your mother like?"

I was stumped.

I thought of Mother, the jovial songbird who sang along with the broadcast of the Mississippi Children's Choir on Sunday mornings. The soapy scent of her handwashed blouses and the softness beneath when she held me. I remembered feeling loved and valued. Then I thought of the strength of those arms when she was angry, the animosity in her voice. I turned to Alethea and asked, "Which one?"

Chapter 28

Seeking the Lost

August 2004

If Mother were around, she would've asked:

Delia, why did you go back?

I would have said, "Because I remain tethered to the past. Because your departure seven years ago occurred without a proper transition, leaving me stuck in coping mode long after the incident. Because I'm lonely and tired of living on the fringes, and this diary is all I have left of who I was."

Father would be pleased with himself if he knew. He had warned me, and my father is a man who likes to be right.

After Pearl's, Melissa and I settled in a two-bedroom apartment our father rented for us. He covered the costs in full, and when the school year was over, he showed up with a pair of empty suitcases. Once we'd gotten caught up on school and his job, he set several hundred-dollar bills on the coffee table and said, "First thing on Monday, go to Velma's travel agency and buy two tickets to Atlanta. She's expecting you."

It may have been his confidence or some defiance Mother had passed on to me, but once he said the word *expecting* I decided not to go.

He warned me that if I chose to stay, I'd end up like my mother — lost. Had he smiled when he said it? My last memory of his face was not of his true likeness but that of the image on his colourful Georgia driver's licence: a square-jawed man, bald, with a jutting Adam's apple and deep-set eyes that gave him a menacing disposition. His portrait, unfamiliar, like someone who might be my father's half-brother.

I felt proud of myself for turning him down, for being the one who said no to an invitation I'd been waiting a lifetime for. However, I hadn't accounted for Melissa's feelings, and on that very Monday, I returned to the office after lunch to find Melissa waiting at reception. I had landed a temporary administrative assistant role and was furious that she dropped in unannounced. That's when she told me she was leaving with our father. She didn't even wait until we were in a private spot. She said it right in the open for everyone to hear. Even though I didn't regret my decision, things took a turn for me after that. Returning to Don Mount, to my home, was an important step in a long journey of one-way streets. People I loved always seemed to leave and no one came back the way I wanted them to. I thought maybe I could.

•

I stepped through the house with reverence, stopping in the dining room to let in an influx of memories: dinner with my father present, a half-eaten Scotch bonnet pepper the only item remaining in his bowl.

"I smell sweet potato pudding," he had said, smiling at me.

I had gone into the kitchen and slit my finger open while cutting his slice. My father made a joke about blood pudding. I grinned and discovered that happiness could dampen pain. I wanted to grin forever. I could hear Mother singing to Elvis Presley's *You'll Never Walk Alone* album, my sister's raucous laughter, and the repeated *pang* of a basketball slamming against concrete.

Upstairs, sunlight poured into the debris-filled hall, its mellow hue reminiscent of mornings past. Next to her room, the bathroom, its door ajar.

I went in.

I imagined Mother in robe and curlers, waltzing out of her room, slippers scraping against the laminate as she entered the adjacent room. I could hear her unhitching the painting from the wall beside the tub and the flutter and thud of my diary as it fell into the cavity. Then my eyes went to the drywall littered all over the ground. Why did she hide my diary there? What else did she hide? I set the diary on the ledge of the tub and began to search.

Later, I stood in front of the door to Mother's room, covered in dust but feeling calmer. Clearer.

As I turned the handle, I noted how much my slender fingers resembled hers. Uncanny the comparison, or "same-same way," as my grandma Liz would have said, because she liked to double up her words instead of learning new ones. I walked in. Like the rest of the house, it was bare. I reached up and swept my hand along the closet shelf. A leaf of paper floated down and a dead insect fell from it, landing belly up on the floor. It had perished across my mother's field of verbal landmines: licence plate numbers, car models, and endless lists. Words, in copious amounts. Never at a loss for them, she used them to wield power both hostilely and amicably. They belonged to her — words. It was why she had taken my diary.

When I had my fill of nostalgia, I went out the door by the courtyard and sat on the metal ledge that bordered the yard. Then I opened the book and ran my fingers across the loops and lines of depressed ink. I flipped one page. Then another, an extensive entry written in the summer of '96. The name *Mario* written on every line. I read through the entry. Then seven more.

Why are you still here?

The voice in my head was not Mother's. It was mine. I stood, turned away from my childhood home, and marched across the court to Camille's office. This time, I'd say goodbye.

I entered the office quietly, startling Camille.

"Hi," I said. "I'm leaving now — oh, sorry."

She was not alone. A thin, broad-shouldered man, whose uniform was covered in white dust, sat in the chair facing her.

"I can wait until —" I started to say.

Camille's gaze went from the man to me, and her face broke into a grin so wide her lips disappeared. The man looked over his shoulder. He shoved a piece of pudding in his mouth.

"You still got it, short stuff."

My pulse quickened. "Mario?"

Before I could speak again, he jumped out of his seat and threw his arms around me. I clung to him. He picked me up and spun me around so fast we became the only ones in the room.

•

Mario and I talked as we strolled down Queen Street, re-enacting our surprised expressions and gushing over how Camille's meddling finally came in handy. He'd returned to Toronto soon after completing his engineering degree but only recently had reached out to Camille, hoping she could provide a contact number for me. Richa was out of town and everyone else was gone. Two months after that, I left a message with Camille about the diary and she called Mario.

"When she told me why you were coming, I insisted that she let me get it for you."

"So, you aren't working there?"

"No. I borrowed some gear, that's all."

I held the diary up so he could see. "You have no idea how much this means to me."

"I remember. Even Johnson used to mention you and your little book." His gaze softened.

I nodded, now understanding the deep sorrow that comes with loss.

"Now you owe me something. I know how much you hate that." He shot me a mischievous look.

It gave me thoughts that I had to shake away.

Is he even better looking than I remembered, or am I just desperate?

"I'll treat you to lunch," I offered.

"I guess that'll do."

When we entered the restaurant, the elderly couple behind the counter greeted us by name, though they barely looked up from the fryer.

"Two fish cake and fries?" the woman asked.

"Yes, please," we both answered.

"And two Cokes," Mario added.

We grabbed our drinks and sauntered over to our usual seats by the back wall, the red seat still worn and ripped. I collapsed onto it feeling like I'd just run a marathon.

"They look exactly the same." I gestured at the owners.

"Did you expect them to look older?" Mario said. "There was nothing for them to transform into but a pair of standing corpses."

This made me laugh harder and louder than I intended to. I stopped myself when I nearly burst into tears.

Mario passed his hand over his head. He sported a low fade haircut that needed refreshing and a short beard.

"I have so many questions for you. I hope you don't have any plans for the rest of the day."

I was so nervous I could only shake my head.

We dug into our meal and agreed that it still held up as the best fish and chips in all of Toronto. I couldn't remember the last time

I'd gone out to eat and silently chided myself for not returning sooner.

"Do you live downtown?" he asked.

"Yeah. I'm not too far away. You?"

"I'm just up at Danforth and Broadview."

"That's really close." I put my drink down. "Why do you keep looking at me like that?"

"I can't help it," he said. "It's been way too long."

I felt a flutter in my chest.

"This day has turned out much different from what I expected," I admitted. "Until hours ago, I felt like everyone I've known and the places where I spent my life were vanishing. I'm tired of starting over. It's hard for me to meet new people."

He nodded in agreement. "I get that. You always took a while to warm up, so I figured you'd keep to yourself. Truth is, aside from the people at work and my family, it's been a little lonely. Not too many folks left around here. No one I'd talk to."

He exhaled loudly. "Anyway, tell me about you and Melissa. No one's heard from you or seen you in years. I thought … I don't know. Maybe something happened. Maybe something with your mom."

"Melissa's in Georgia. She's good." I bit my lip. "Mom. Well, that's a long story I'd rather not get into."

"Is she okay?"

I looked him in the eye. "I ask myself that question every day. Truth is, I have no idea. It's been a long time since anyone has heard from her. She's nowhere to be found."

"Oh, okay." He acknowledged my news with a nod, and I felt understood.

I reached for my drink and accidentally nudged the can. Mario slid the diary aside, catching the Coke just before it fell. My shoulders arched back, and our eyes met.

"Here," he said quickly and handed me the book. "Saved. Again."

I dropped my shoulders. "Thanks."

"How'd it end up in the wall?"

"It was her," I said. "I thought she took it with her, but Neville finally confessed that she'd told him not to patch the wall because she planned on hiding the diary there. He was afraid I'd blame him so he kept it from me."

Mario responded with a raised brow. It may have been a question or a polite show of surprise, but neither of us said anything more about it.

The entrance door chime rang, and a set of patrons came in: a teenage boy and girl. I let my glance linger on them for a while. Mario changed the topic to Richa and her foray into the trades. A bit more chit-chat and we came to the hard part.

"You haven't kept in touch with Richa either. Why, Delia? And why'd you ghost me?"

"That's not fair. I check in with her every couple of months, but I'm really bad at returning calls. And before you ask, I told her not to give out my number. It wasn't anything against you personally. I had a lot going on. It was hard to talk to anyone. Do you remember the last time we spoke?"

He frowned. "Yeah. You decided to take that job instead of going to college, which I thought was a cop-out. We had a disagreement about my social life. You refused to visit. Then you cut me off."

My gaze fell. I felt myself locking up. Shutting down.

"I figured you didn't want to see me," he said, "and I couldn't call you, and I couldn't just keep calling Richa and have to deal with Naveed." A forced chuckle. "So when you stopped trying to get a hold of me, I didn't really get it. What happened?"

"Life," I said. "Life happened, and you were off living your dream and forgetting. That's how I felt. I stayed because I thought I had to. No regrets about that, but staying here didn't help me remember all of the important things. I still had to go searching anyway."

He drummed the table with his thumbs.

"I didn't forget anything. At first it was nice to be somewhere new, but the novelty wears off. I struggled. School was hard. Playing was hard. Pretty much everyone I loved was here. Why do you think I came back?"

I noticed he stopped drumming. His crestfallen expression conveyed a heartbreak that went beyond what I knew of him. What else had happened in his life? Where had he been?

When I took his hands in mine, they felt calloused and warm. He seemed surprised.

"I'm really proud of you," I said. "For going. And for coming back. You did good. By the way, I still have that job and I've been studying part-time."

He perked up. "No shit. I shouldn't be surprised that you found a way to make it work. What's that thing your grandma used to say?"

"Find another way to get where you're going. That's what she used to say." I smiled.

He nodded. "I was sorry to hear she passed. She was so cool. I used to wish Johnson would smarten up so he could catch a woman like her."

"What? But then we'd be family."

"I know. It was stupid. Not sure I would have cared, though."

We laughed uncontrollably, and the heaviness within me lifted. The day was good again.

"So, are you heading in the right direction?" Mario asked.

I was taken aback. My therapist had asked me the very same question just weeks before.

"I think so. Apparently, sometimes you have to go back in case you forgot something or to remember the right things."

"Hm." He eyed the diary.

"It's like a compass for me," I said.

"Is there anything in there about me?"

I leaned back in my seat. What did I have to lose? "Pick a year."

●

Two hours later, we made our way to the bench in the old parkette where we used to hang out. We talked about the Don Jail: the ghosts, the hangings, and the bodies beneath the parking lot. I told him I still didn't believe it was haunted.

"My dad confirmed it when he came out. I asked him. It's true." He really wanted me to believe him, which made me laugh more.

We talked about Adrienne, our goddaughter whom neither of us had seen in years. We were terrible godparents, but we had warned Richa — we had. We sat, reminiscing, letting several streetcars go by.

"Okay, I have to get going now, really," I said finally. "Oh, wait."

I had remembered the minute I laid eyes on him but wanted to wait for the right moment. I reached into my back pocket and brought out a tiny clear bag.

He took it from me and removed a thin gold necklace. "Where the hell did you find it? I ripped the whole place apart looking for this thing."

"It was in the toilet tank."

The look on his face was sheer joy. I couldn't help but to reflect it. I hoped he saw me in that moment.

"I'm gonna get it cleaned," he said. "Then I'll bring it to you."

"Good. I can't wait to wear it." I couldn't stop smiling.

"Delia, this is the best day I've had in a long time. I'm never going to lose you again."

It was strange to hear it. I had never thought of myself as someone who needed to be found. Someone others would want to find.

"How do you plan to accomplish that?" I asked him.

He opened his arms — an invitation.

•

I barely got my shoes off at home before I called my sister. She picked up after the first ring.

"I've literally been sitting by the phone, so you better make this good."

"First. I have to tell you that I'm coming to see you."

"Don't kid with me."

"I stopped at the Greyhound station and bought a ticket. Melissa, stop screaming."

"Okay."

"And — are you sitting down?"

"I am. You found Toby?"

"No. Better." I took a deep breath. "I saw Mario."

My sister yelled with delight, then began to sob. I waited until she calmed down.

"Delia," she said, voice trembling. "He came back for you."

My sister saw the world through rose-tinted glasses. She must've bought the last pair.

"Yeah," was all I could say.

We spoke a bit more about my day, and Dad, and I promised her I'd call him soon.

"Delia, remember that time …" Melissa started.

We reminisced on our early years "at the apartment" and "in the basement" and then living in Don Mount — which was the only place we called home.

After speaking to my sister, I made one last call, to Neville. He'd left several messages.

"Delia, I been calling all day. You gave me a real scare," he said. "Did you find it?"

"I'm fine. Yeah, it was there just like you said, but I couldn't find Melissa's bear — the one my dad gave to her. Do you remember seeing it during the move?"

He paused. "Maybe. Why?"

"She still asks for it. Did you take it or get rid of it?"

I had been waiting for this opportunity.

"You think I would do that?"

"Yes, because she loved it and she loved him."

Neville grunted and groaned like his words got stuck in his throat. Like he was unsure if it was my voice or his conscience he was hearing.

"No, I don't know what happened to that. Only the book," he said. "Delia, you really think that's the kind of person I am?"

"I do. I'm not judging you. I just need to know."

"Have you ever said anything to Melissa?"

"I'm trying not to be that kind of person, but it's been difficult keeping it to myself."

"I don't want to cause any more damage."

"I'm not sure if it's the right thing to do, but I understand."

He cleared his throat nervously.

"Okay, well anyway, um, listen, I'm getting married. It's a small thing at City Hall. You know how I feel about church, but I'm inviting you guys to come."

"Well, that's great. I'll be there, but Melissa is another story. She'll expect a plane ticket. Your daughter — like you — prefers to travel comfortably."

Epilogue

September 2004

Ribbons of daylight cut through the grove of trees below. I'm on the balcony with a cup of coffee, looking away from the void, seventeen storeys deep. Every day I spend more time out here. It helps with the fear. And it's almost gone now. Almost. I hear a flutter of wings; a bird takes flight, flapping desperately to catch up with its soaring flock. It makes me smile, and I feel compelled to write.

The diary is kept beside the pictures of my mother that sit on the cherry-wood armoire in my bedroom. I've read the whole thing twice and found four yellowed blank pages, which I've marked with tabs. I flip to one and pull the blue ballpoint pen from the book's metal spine.

Dear Diary,

Long before I came to be, there was a girl who became a woman. This woman became my mother, and
her smile was the rarest in all my world. Only I didn't
realize how uncommon it was until I was older, its
value ever increasing with its diminishing frequency.
Eventually I could discern it from similar features
she displayed that mimicked its likeness but never its
warmth. Without it I'm not sure I'd be able to recognize her — the way she was.

In the first photograph she is a little girl named
Aretha Palmer. The yard in which she stands looks
still and monochrome, but in reality, here, where she
stands under the giant almond tree in her parents'
front yard, it would have been a motley scene, full of
life. Copper ants would have been funnelling up the
trunk, in and out of shadows cast by lime-armoured
almonds dangling like turtle shells from the tangled
branches. I notice for the first time a cluster of airy
orbs that hover above her head and something resembling the wings of a hummingbird that curtains
the left corner of the lens. She seems dismissive, her
expression austere as if the photographer has rudely
interrupted her search for some missing thing or person. You won't see the smile here, because this child
is my mother back when they called her "Rita." Rita
is dressed in black from head to toe in the searing
Jamaican sun. It is the day of her father's funeral.

The resemblance between us is striking, though
she looks nothing like the mother I remember —
another tragedy of youth. Yet Aretha, Rita, and my

mother are one and the same despite the sickle scars of time.

There is a picture of a much taller Rita standing against a fence of shrubs with luggage clutched tightly to her sides. Her younger brothers, the twins, Brent and Bryan, stand on either side of her rounded hips with an arm on each of her shoulders. They are "going abroad," as they say, to live with their mother who had left some years ago in search of a better life. They are the envy of their neighbours, and by the time they arrive at the airport, many of their belongings have been picked over, shared, or taken without permission. No matter, they say. They will find new friends and new things in the new country. Everything is waiting for them there.

Rita's face is a soft, sable complexion framed with heavy brows and bright, piercing eyes that seek hope. The fine dark hairs that fall low on her brow salute her Indian roots, but her African locks claim dominance. Cavernous dimples sink deep into her cheeks. Her lips, pulled apart from each other, reveal a gap between her front teeth. I haven't yet figured out if what I'm looking at is a smile.

In the sepia portrait, she is older. Her face has become an enigma, with each feature more pronounced, pointing in on itself and claiming loudly, "Here is my mother, the daughter of an Indo-Trinidadian merchant. Don't forget my father! He was a man of transport like his father, and our bloodline is marked with genes from every stop along the Jamaican railway line. This is his jawbone — here." Rita has returned to the island of rolling emerald hills, pregnant plants, and hummingbirds. Why is she here? Where are her brothers? I look closely in the shadow cast by her hat. She is frowning. Her grandmother has died.

In another picture, there is no shrubbery, just a grey flatness. Aretha, in a simple but elegant white dress, breaks the monotony. It is her wedding day. Her mouth is spread crosswise like melting butter, but she is not smiling. I look closer. The frown formed under the hat years ago has ascended slowly over time, dodging her dimples, edging the contours of her chiselled jaw, climbing the precipice of her cheekbones, and diving into the abyss of her eyes. She is accompanied by a trim man dressed in a fine russet suit, the likes of an ornament adorning his person. He holds her in place with both hands and a flinty smile that warns, "Don't run." He is looking into the lens, she, at something off to the left. It's a damaged image, wrought by heat. I wonder who took this photograph of my parents.

Here, in this last photograph, she is a woman. She is no longer called Rita, nor is she Aretha Palmer. She is officially Aretha Ellis, validated and legitimized. Her body lies gracefully across the length of a mustard settee, her bulbous belly covered in a soft periwinkle frock. The neckline cuts squarely across her collarbones, disappearing into the depths of the chair arm where she is resting her head. Her hair is loosed and wild with bangs curled just above her curious, sculpted brows. She is my mother, an excellent caretaker (that is what people loved most about her), and I am the little girl standing next to the couch looking over at her. The tilt of my head is fixed as is my smile. I am saying "Cheese!" She did not tell me to say it but does not object, so I'd like to think this meant she approved of my initiative. Look at me; my perfectly smoothed plaits are purposefully unadorned, and my kilt falls appropriately below my knees. I am a trophy — the personification of her perfection.

And there it is, almost hidden behind the light — her smile, astute and brilliant. Even in a picture it provides sustenance like that of the sun on a cold winter day. And yet I am implored to ask, Why? Why was she smiling? Was it that I pleased her? Was it her pregnancy? Or perhaps my father was still "making her happy," because this is what people asked her all the time: "Is he making you happy?" And telling him: "You better make her happy," and as a child I began to wonder just what had to be done to make happiness last? And why would something so fleeting as a smile be the defining index of this feeling?

She became so different from this woman captured here. This mother was the one before I learned to tie my shoelaces. Before the man in the suit went away and long before I became aware that Aretha was not just my mother or my father's wife but someone else, too. This is what haunts me. The question of who I am. Who I was. Who I will become.

This version of us is my favourite. She is radiant and I am absolutely darling. I think she had "it" that day — the "happy." I think I did, too. I knew her then.

Often, especially on my bad days, I'm tempted to place each photo into the restored underside drawers of the old cabinet, but I stop myself. Sometimes, concealing sows seeds of calamity. So I keep them where I can be reminded of my mother's courage and the brevity of life.

And you, Diary, are kept there, too, to remind me of the time I dared to look back — and saw myself, a crumbling pillar of salt. And I embraced her, and listened to her, and knew myself again. Then I could go on.

I am, always and forever,
Delia

There is a knock at my apartment door. I dab frankincense oil onto my wrists, then adjust my necklace in the mirror before making my way to answer the door. As I get nearer, I pause to quiet the thoughts seeping in, before finally reaching out to turn the cold metal handle. Only then do I open the door to him. And let the world back in.

THE END

Acknowledgements

During the evolution of this story, I've received a great deal of support and encouragement that has led to its publication. There aren't enough pages to thank all the people who've inspired and guided me in some way. I've whittled it down to the most focused list I can. To my editor, Shannon Whibbs, you are an absolute gift. Thank you for your attention to detail and for your ability to intuitively guide me to what I want to say in better ways than I ever could.

To the staff at Dundurn Press, associate publisher Kathryn Lane, and freelance copy editor Robyn So, thank you for shepherding this story into the world and making this such a positive experience. I am incredibly grateful for the mentorship and workshops facilitated through the Diaspora Dialogues program and to its team members Zalika Reid-Benta, Helen Walsh, and mentor Alissa York. To the gracious Shyam Selvadurai, whose mentorship through the Humber Creative Writing Program was a critical part of my journey, these organizations and their staff continue to provide me with guidance and community. Also, to Sandra Otto, whose early feedback was a pivotal turning point for this work, thank you.

I will be forever grateful to my early readers, Alexis, Andre, Melissa, Ashley, Dalia, Marsha, Carlisha, and Anayah; to my mother-in-law for being my cheerleader; to my parents for surrounding me with books; especially to Mother, for her gift of literacy and love for the written word.

I owe a debt of gratitude to Dr. Michelle Walker, who read almost every iteration of this story and insisted it be a romance novel. I miss you, dear friend. My love for you extends beyond place and time.

Lastly, I thank my husband, whose love shines so brightly it allows me to explore difficult moments of the human experience and still see so much beauty.

About the Author

Denise Da Costa is an author and visual artist. Born in Toronto, she spent her early years in Jamaica. She is a graduate of York University and Seneca College School of Communication Arts, and is an alumna of the Humber Creative Writing program. She's lived in various cities across the Greater Toronto Area and Niagara region and travels whenever time allows. Her work explores the complications of love and the impact of class, gender, and race on identity. She is currently working on her next novel.